BLAN

BLANKET BOY'S MOON

BY

PETER LANHAM

BASED ON AN
ORIGINAL STORY BY

A. S. MOPELI-PAULUS

CHIEFTAIN
OF BASUTOLAND

AFRICASOUTH PAPERBACKS
CAPE TOWN : JOHANNESBURG
DAVID PHILIP

AFRICASOUTH PAPERBACKS

This series includes important works of southern African literature that are at present available only in hardback or are out of print or n̲ readily accessible or 'banned'; there is also provision for new writing. The books chosen will be not only those whose worth has become ac knowledged, but also interesting and significant works that need resc̲ from neglect. Among the titles contracted are a number of books recently 'unbanned', after having been sent by the publisher for revie̲ Also included in *Africasouth Paperbacks* are books from Africa south of-the-Sahara, i.e. west, central and east African works not before av̲ able in southern Africa in paperback, but of particular interest or ne̲ for study purposes. The first titles available in this landmark series ar̲

TRANSVAAL EPISODE by Harry Bloom
KAROO MORNING by Guy Butler
CALTROP'S DESIRE by Stephen Gray
THE WILL TO DIE by Can Themba
PETALS OF BLOOD by Ngugi wa Thiong'o
CHOCOLATES FOR MY WIFE by Todd Matshikiza
SPONONO by Alan Paton & Krishna Shah
FREEDOM FOR MY PEOPLE by Z. K. Matthews
SECOND-CLASS TAXI by Sylvester Stein
MARGARET HARDING by Perceval Gibbon
THE GREAT KAROO by John Howland Beaumont
A STATE OF FEAR by Menán du Plessis
ELEGY FOR A REVOLUTIONARY by C. J. Driver
AKE by Wole Soyinka
BLANKET BOY'S MOON by Peter Lanham & A. S. Mopeli-Paulus

First published 1953 by William Collins Ltd, London
Published 1984 in Africasouth Paperbacks by David Philip, Publisher (Pty) Ltd, 217 Werdmuller Centre, Claremont, Cape, South Africa
ISBN 0 86486 016 1
© Peter Lanham & A. S. Mopeli-Paulus

Printed by Creda Press (Pty) Ltd, Solan Road, Cape Town, South Afr̲

TO MY WIFE
AGNES CATHERINE
*without whose constructive criticism
and co-operation this book could not
have been written*

PETER LANHAM

"To know how the Putu was spoiled, must one have been present at its cooking. . . ."

BASUTO PROVERB

CONTENTS

Introduction — page 9

PHASE ONE—FIRST QUARTER
I Johannesburg—The Arrest — 13
II Valley of Contentment — 16
III Third Degree at Number Four — 26
IV Kaffir Mail — 29
V Courtyard *PITSO* — 35
VI City of Gold — 38
VII Koto—Friend of the Heart — 60
VIII Monare the Merchant — 62
IX The Trial — 69
X Retribution — 76

PHASE TWO—FULL MOON
I Mountain School — 87
II Ritual Murder — 97
III The Victim — 101
IV The Fugitive — 110
V Father and Son — 122
VI Dagga — 131
VII Regeneration — 139

CONTENTS

PHASE THREE—LAST QUARTER
  I City of Sugar   149
  II Black Fire   161
  III The Gratitude of the Amasuleiman   176

PHASE FOUR—CRESCENT
  I The Friend of Ghulam   page 187
  II The Radiant Stranger   193
  III "One More River"   204
  IV Jordan Crossing   221
  V The Promised Land   227

PHASE FIVE—NEW MOON
  I At the Rua Salazar   237
  II The Mills of God   244
  III False Dawn   260
  IV Judgment Day   281
  V The Unknown Mercy of God   300

Glossary   319

INTRODUCTION

It is not generally considered necessary for a novel to have an introduction. But in this case, where the points of view of different sections of the African Community are concerned, a word of explanation is required and we feel that what must be told geographically and historically about the country of Basutoland should be set down by a member of one of its Ruling Houses.

Basutoland or Lesotho (as we call it) is one of the three British Protectorates in Southern Africa. It is completely surrounded by the territory of the Union of South Africa, and its area is 11,760 square miles, and its present population 553,827. The capital is Maseru, where the British Resident Commissioner has his Headquarters. The country is ruled by a Paramount Chieftainess, under whom serve powerful Chiefs—heads of Tribes—and minor sub-Chiefs—heads of Clans.

The country is mountainous, and the Basutos are fine horsemen; the traditional wear of the men is the colourful blanket. The inhabitants are mostly small farmers, who grow maize, and breed Basuto ponies and cattle; some authorities have stated that the country is overstocked with cattle, to the detriment of both cattle and soil. But as the Basuto still pays for his wife in cows, he can be persuaded with difficulty to breed for quality rather than for quantity. Like most Africans, the Basuto judges the wealth and standing of his fellow-man by the number of his cattle.

The country is rich in untapped mineral wealth, and there is reported to be much diamondiferous ground.

INTRODUCTION

The beginnings of the Basuto Race are lost in the troublous days of the Zulu Kings; but it is believed that the Great Chief Moshoeshoe, my ancestor, formed the nation from the remnants of the tribes broken up and disrupted by the Black Napoleon, Chaka.

To the North of Basutoland lies the Witzieshoek Reserve, in which live those other Basuto tribesmen whose territory was lost to them as the result of one of the many wars the Dutch waged against them in the 19th Century. The African's most urgent need is for more land—and this is true of all the Protectorates and Reserves—this lack was the primary cause of the troubles which started in 1950 at Witzieshoek. With the praiseworthy motive of improving the quality of the livestock and the soil, the Union Government imposed a limit on the number of head of cattle allowed in the Reserve. What the authorities did not take into consideration were the facts that firstly the Basuto looks upon the herds as you look upon your banking account, and secondly that the population of the Reserve is steadily increasing; the number of head of cattle was limited to 10,000, whereas the number of inhabitants is 16,000!

Sub-standard cattle, or cattle in excess of the allowed number are culled, or branded, and have to be sold outside the Reserve, or slaughtered for food.

The views expressed in this book on questions of colour and segregation are substantially those held by the majority of my people; the descriptions of the treatment accorded to the Black people by the White people are not exaggerated.

A. S. MOPELI-PAULUS
Witzieshoek, 1952

Phase One

FIRST QUARTER

" No one can foretell how the Rooster will crow whilst it is yet in the Egg...."
                                        BASUTO PROVERB

Chapter One

JOHANNESBURG—THE ARREST

MONARE LIVED.

At this exact moment of his living, the sun was slowly sinking behind the mine-dumps that guard the western approaches of the City of Gold; that unofficial, uncrowned capital of the Union of South Africa, Johannesburg; most evil and vicious city in the world, where black man is forced to work for white man, yet where few of the white men care how the black men live or die.

On this high plateau of Southern Africa, it would be dark before half an hour had passed.

Monare sat in a motor-bus which made its riotous way along the tarred highway which leads into the City of Gold from the west.

At the corner of Diagonal and Bree Streets, where halt these omnibuses which groan into town from the West Rand, stood a detective of the white man race, who, sufficiently hidden from the view of those that passed by, examined carefully the faces of all travellers.

With the care and cunning of a jackal, did the white man detective await his quarry, and in the fullness of time was his patience rewarded; the passenger whose arrival he hoped for, at length stepped down from an omnibus, and walked eastwards towards the City Hall.

Monare the Mosotho walked along the street briskly, humming to himself a song of the Basotho people; he had no cares, for the day's trading had been successful, and his money-belt was well filled. Monare—a comely young man in his middle twenties of strong build and graceful carriage—was an African merchant. He made his living by buying from the Indian wholesalers in Market Street, cloth from which he fashioned trousers of extreme elegance which found high favour with the African workers on the Mines.

But Monare was not permitted to arrive in the tram-thronged, brilliantly-lit, canyon-like, skyscraper-bound centre of the City; for just as he was about to emerge into the open space in front of the Library, the hunter pounced.

In the far-famed City of Gold, the seizing of the person of an African is a matter of small moment—there are so many crimes against the Law of the white man of which he might be guilty (from failure to carry a Pass to indulgence in Liquor)—that a policeman has no difficulty in framing a charge.

When the white man's hand fell on his shoulder, Monare swung round to see who it was who had thus stopped his progress. When his eyes fell on the detective's face, extreme fear bludgeoned his heart, for he recognised the face of "Van," who had once before tried to have him imprisoned.

The detective spoke. "Well, you black bastard, I've caught you at last! . . . Come, open that bundle!"

"*Baas*, it is but the cloth for the making of trousers."

"Open it, kaffir! I'll guarantee it's stolen property. Come on, quick!"

The unfortunate black man hastened to do Van's bidding. As the detective's eyes fell on the contents of the bundle—several pairs of trousers, and part of a bale of cloth—he grunted with satisfaction, and spoke these terrifying words: "As I thought, you bloody nigger—stolen goods! A long spell in Number Four for this!"

Without further argument he handcuffed Monare's wrist to his own, and forced the unwilling Mosotho—with many a kick and a blow—to retrace his steps southward to the Charge Office at Marshall Square.

2

The next morning Monare was taken before the Magistrate and remanded for a week. He was then removed to the ill-famed

JOHANNESBURG—THE ARREST

Number Four Fort on Hospital Hill, the jail known as the "small hell." Men who have served sentences there say it is the worst of all jails. Monare found it to be the home of the lost, the forgotten, and the God-forsaken.

The prisoners were secured two in each cell, and Monare's companion, an old jail-bird, did not worry much about his present predicament. He said: "My friend, what have you done?"

"They say I stole goods."

"They say you stole goods—what goods?"

"I make trousers. Usually I buy cloth from the Indian merchants in Market Street; but this time I bought suit-lengths from a fellow who offered them to me at a good price."

"Have you no receipt for the money you paid?"

"I did not ask for any—the fellow was in a great hurry."

"Yes—this is Johannesburg!"

"Have you been to jail before?"

"Yes, many times—but you are worrying, why are you worrying?"

"I am worrying about my wife Ma-Libe and my son Libe."

"Where is your home?"

"In Basutoland."

"Ah, Lesotho is far. . . . I am from the North . . . tell me about the land of the Blanket, Lesotho—I have never been there."

And Monare lost for the time being, his fears as he spoke of his youth in his far-off homeland.

Chapter Two

VALLEY OF CONTENTMENT

THE MOSOTHO, MONARE, was born in a little village situated directly beneath the foothills of the Maluti Mountains in Basutoland. Overlooking this small village of Lomontsa is the high peak of Libeleteng, whose other face gazes eternally at Montaux-Sources.

Lomontsa is almost encircled by two streams of glassy-clear water, and is sunk like a jewel in its rugged setting. The soil—sandy loam—is fertile, with a rich production of maize crops, pastures suitable for livestock; and the villagers take pride in their small farming.

High above the village, flocks of sheep and goats graze slowly and peacefully on the green hills and kloofs; and steadily following them, to protect the weak and the young, come the hardy herd-boys. Proud in their wearing of the *stertreim*—sign of manhood—these young boys, clad in their tribal clothes of well-trimmed, round-cut goatskins, play about on the grassy banks of the stream and in the crystal waters. But their eyes are keenly on their flocks, to see that they do not crop from the preserved lands which will be used for grazing later in the year, when the grass is short.

There is no loneliness in those clustered hills which seem always damp with mist; late in the afternoons rain rarely fails to bless the soil.

From these hills, year in year out, young men travel the road of enchantment which leads to the City of Gold, there to work on the mines. Nine months is the shortest period of contract, and the men of the valley take it in turns to accept these contracts—while

VALLEY OF CONTENTMENT

one team is away, the other team stays at home. Great is the responsibility of these stay-at-homes, for theirs is the job of ploughing the lands and keeping them free from weeds.

At such *letsoma* times, Kaffir beer is brewed and small livestock killed to provide drink and food for the working-parties; tribal songs—such as the *Mokorotlo*, or Chant of Praise—are sung, and every man and woman in the village has to attend.

The simple people of Lomontsa enjoy their lives—and why not? Have they not the annual circumcision ceremonies to look forward to? Have they not their many wives to help them with the work? for these Basotho are still polygamists, and the wealthier men can afford from six to ten wives each; and it is not unusual to count the Chief's wives from one to twenty!

The Chief is highly respected by his subjects, who call him, *Morena*; during tribal meetings or *Pitso*, the Chief is the last to speak—only when every member of the *Pitso* has given his opinion, does the Chief sum up. After the Chief's speech, the tribesmen shout out " *Pula! Khotso! Morena!* "—Rain! Peace! Chief! The Chief then instructs his Headman or *letona* to have meat and kaffir Beer brought to the *khotla* or place of gathering.

Always at such a *Pitso* is there a large number of horses, for the Basotho people take much pride in riding well-fed, well-groomed horses, and an equal pleasure in donning clean and colourful clothes for the occasion—most popular among the Basotho people is the bright-striped blanket.

Into this community was the Mosotho, Monare, born. His eyes opened in a wattle-and-daub hut—windowless, but with a pointed thatched roof. If at times he wakened to cry for his mother, doubtless she was in the *mokhore*—the kitchen hut which stood near by. Soon he must have realised that all life in the hut revolved around the comings and goings of that big man, his father.

As he grew into small boyhood, he followed this man into the family fields, into the family stables; he watched him—and in later days, helped him to—milk the cows.

Then one day, when he was about to enter the mountain circumcision school, the big man departed and appeared no more. Though

Monare knew it not, his father had gone to fight for the Great White King, and was drowned when the immortal transport *Mendi* sank beneath the waves in the English Channel.

Thus it followed that now it was Monare who was waited on hand and foot; Monare who received the choicest piece of meat from the pot; Monare who was wept over when he left for his six months' stay in the mountains; Monare who was greeted with joy on his return as a man.

Now Monare lived in his father's shoes, and took to himself a wife.

This woman was carefully chosen for him by his mother, and she proved to be a fine worker in the home and in the fields. A new hut was built, and the freshly-married couple started their true life together.

And Monare was happy.

When Monare became a man he was not rich, with many herds of sheep and cattle; he owned but one span of oxen, a few milking cows, and a horse. He was a moderate beer drinker, but he did not believe in spending his nights going from one beer-party to another, as did most of the men and women of the village. His wife, Florinah, was a very religious woman, and went to church each Sunday, and fulfilled all her religion's requirements.

Monare's behaviour won him the confidence of his Chief, who at length appointed him to be his second Headman or *letona*. His duties were to take full charge of the Chief's household, and to issue mealies and Kaffircorn to the Chief's many wives.

2

When some years had passed, a man-child was born to Florinah and Monare; although this circumstance was a great blessing, yet it brought about a change in the good behaviour of Monare. Now he had to wait for his home-brewed beer sometimes, the door would not always be opened to him at his first knock; and his wife, Florinah—now known as Ma-Libe, Mother of Libe, the son—would sometimes be absent on mysterious business when she should have been at home to attend to his comfort.

Ma-Libe's happy home life was shattered by this change in Monare, who would too often now arrive at his home drunk, and beat on the door, and accuse his wife of flirting with other men when she went to draw water at the well. The accusation which most hurt the heart of the poor Ma-Libe, was the wicked suggestion that she indulged in sin with the African Christian Priest of her church, the Moruti Lefa.

During this sad time, Monare also came near to destroying his old Mother's fondest hopes, for he spoke of travelling away into strange lands and seeking a second rich wife, who must be the daughter of wealthy parents.

His mother chided him thus:

"Is your head an empty cooking-pot? . . . Are you to listen to foolish people. I would not advise you to marry a *moqekoa*—youngest wife—for wealth! Only men rich in cattle can afford many wives. You know very well you have no cattle to pay *bohali*—dowry—for a rich wife the father might demand twenty-five head of cattle!"

Monare walked alongside the reed barrier leading to his stable. He had come from this angry meeting with his mother. He was murmuring to himself and swearing as he walked, and pointing his finger at the Minister's house.

He returned to his home only in the early hours of the next day, in the faint light of dawn. To his surprise, a lamp was lit within his house, and at the door, peering anxiously into the dim haze, was his mother.

"Your son is sick."

From within came a pain-filled moaning.

"Where is Ma-Libe?"

"She is gone to call the Moruti—the Priest."

Monare, who had drunk much kaffir beer that night, suddenly, to his great surprise, found himself sober. His son—the son of his beloved wife, Ma-Libe—ill? So ill that the help of the Moruti had been sought?

Into these thoughts broke the running feet of his wife, closely followed by those of the Moruti. All through what remained of that night, and all the next day did the four Basotho labour—the child was on fire, its skin was like a stone in the midday sun; its breathing was like an old man's.

Monare looked—and felt himself to be—an old man. To himself he prayed silently:

"O God of my Moruti. I have sinned. I have done much evil. Let but the fire leave my small son's body, and I will walk no more late at nights, and I will cherish my wife Ma-Libe as she deserves!"

God of the Moruti made no immediate answer to this prayer; the heart of Monare was to bleed still more; it was near midnight again before the sweat started to pour down the small Mosotho boy's face. At length his eyes opened, and he smiled.

A sigh of relief rose in the thick air of the hut; Moruti sat down and said to Monare's mother:

"Make tea, please, Mother."

Monare dared to breathe again.

By the morning, all was well. Libe was cool, and in a deep sleep. Soon the others, too, stretched and yawned. God of the Moruti had, apparently, kept awake!

That night, Monare made his peace with his wife, Florinah.

3

One Sunday morning, Monare asked his wife Ma-Libe to take him to the Moruti, because he had some business to settle with him. This was a great surprise to his wife, and she did not utter one word in reply—it was not that she was unhappy, but that she could not believe he was at last going to the church.

On the way to the church, the minister's small girl-child met them, and asked them to come to the house, as her father had not yet left for the church. The Moruti greeted them warmly at the door of his house, and calling his wife, asked her to bring some tea.

There was yet time for conversation before the church bell should ring, so the Moruti said:

"I am ready to have a little talk with you, Monare."

Monare did not hesitate; he at once plunged his hand into the pot, boiling though it was.

"It has long been my desire to come to you; I have a difficulty

VALLEY OF CONTENTMENT

in my house; I quarrel all the time with my wife. I know you are next to God, and have power to help me."

The kind-hearted Moruti smiled.

"What do you think is the cause of your fighting, Monare?"

"That I cannot say, Moruti——"

"You have come to me for help, will you not honour me with the truth?"

"Moruti, I think so—but ... well, yes."

"Monare, when you drink the home-brewed kaffir beer prepared by the hands of Florinah here, do you then quarrel?"

"No, Moruti."

"Then it is when you roam about in the darkness of the night, and step from one beer-drink to another, that you return to the mother of your son and see her with inflamed eyes, and make false accusations against her with your incensed heart?"

"Yes, Moruti, I suppose so."

"Monare, the drink made by the old widows and others who gain their living from this trade is not pure and wholesome like the home-brewed kaffir beer; in order that they may supply less for more money, they add certain liquors to their brew which quickly make men drunk and senseless."

"Yes, Moruti."

"This I have seen amongst the white men—when they make a drinking-party in their homes, even although the men may get merry and laugh loudly and get up to strange pranks, yet may their wives and daughters be present without taking harm, even enjoying the same liquors—in moderation—and joining in the singing and jokes and games. Now, Monare, by their very presence do these womenfolk of the house restrain the men from the more outrageous actions in which you have indulged."

"I hear you, Moruti."

"Listen further, Monare—the white man also has another sort of drinking place——apart from the shop from which he can buy his white man's beer and brandy to take to his home—there are places called Bars in which he can sit or stand and drink for as long as he has the money to pay for what he orders ... and it is usually after spending time in such places that the white man becomes angry and turns towards violence ... many white men spend their nights going from Bar to Bar, much as you go in the darkness from one beer brewer to the next!"

"Moruti—since the days of the Great Moshoeshoe has God given the Basotho people kaffir beer as their food!"

"Yes, Monare, before the Basotho people started to visit the City of Gold to work on the Mines, everyone in Lesotho drank the wholesome, home-brewed kaffir beer."

"Why then, O Moruti, do the old women and others who brew beer for sale, add these other liquors you spoke of, to their pots?"

"That, Monare, is a long story ... the white man is inclined to judge others by himself; fearing that the Basotho mine boys might become drunk with too much beer-drinking—as do many of their own people—he refused to allow the brewing of home-made kaffir beer in the Compounds and Locations of the City of Gold. As you rightly said, the real beer of Lesotho is a food, and the Basotho people desire it. When—in Johannesburg—they could neither brew nor buy this beer, certain cunning Africans decided that they could, with profit to themselves, brew beer by stealth; to strengthen this brew they craftily added such *sehlare*—medicine—of the white man as methylated spirits ... thus would one calabash or tin of beer supply four or five times as many customers. This evil drink quickly takes effect on those who consume it, and makes them lose their senses, so that if weak, they are the more easily robbed by the brewers, and if strong, their thoughts more easily turned to deeds of violence."

"Moruti, I hear and understand."

"Is there aught else, Monare?"

"Moruti, why should the brewers here in Lesotho make such a drink?"

"Because, Monare, few there are of the Basotho race, who having attained men's years, have not visited either the City of Gold or the City of Sugar, and there tasted this drink, and formed the habit of partaking of it. . . . Wherever there is a demand, whether for good or for evil, my son, there, sooner or later, will appear the supply. . . . It is the white man himself who has given the African his taste for strong liquor—had the free brewing of home-made

Kaffir beer been permitted, the African people would have remained content with this."

"Father Moruti, I freely promise that I will go no more at night from beer-drink to beer-drink."

At these astounding words, Ma-Libe wept tears of joy, but uttered no word of reproach for past injuries.

The Moruti Lefa now called his wife and asked her to conduct Florinah to the church, as he had words to say to Monare, not meet for the ears of women. And when the women had withdrawn, the Moruti spoke thus:

"There remains this matter of a second wife—were you not baptised a Christian, Monare?"

"Yes, Moruti, I was baptised during childhood at the French Mission, by a Moruti who bore your name."

"Monare, this was the Moruti who baptised you.... I was away from the Mission for ten years, but was recalled a few years ago ... therefore I have some right to ask you to listen to my words."

Monare scratched his head.

"*Ka Thesele!*" he said in wonderment.

"Polygamy," said the Moruti, "is a tradition of the Bosotho people."

"The Chief has many wives," ventured Monare.

Said the Moruti, sternly:

"In the days of the Great Moshoeshoe certain of the Basotho people ate human flesh—are we then to do the same?"

"But the Chief lives *now*—to-day!"

"The Chief is not a Christian ... you, Monare, are a Christian—and if you are to remain one, you must put out of your mind for ever any thought of a second wife. It is not an easy thing to do, my son—but maybe it will help you if I tell you my own story ... it will be easier for you than it was for me."

"For *you*, Moruti?"

"Yes, Monare—*your* father was a Christian, but my father was a polygamist, and had seven wives!"

"*Fe!* ... Moruti ..."

"I had to conquer my desires, Monare ... but believe me, in the end I was happier for it. Strange things may happen where one man weds many wives. I was the son of my father's first wife, and when I attained manhood my father married his seventh wife, who was a young and beautiful girl. . . . I was young and lusty then, and I fell in love with my father's youngest wife, and thus brought dishonour on the house . . . but I have atoned for my sins . . . to-day I am very happy—my wife and I grow old together. . . . Now I shall never be an old man craving for young girls, and, perhaps, being unable to satisfy them ! . . . These are strange words, perhaps, from the lips of a Moruti, but I wish you to know that others have trod the same path, and conquered their desires. . . ."

There was silence for a while; then Moruti said:

"Moreover—for good or for ill—Lesotho is now joined to the civilisation of the West, and as the years pass, doubtless in some ways we shall live more and more like the white man, and amongst them there is no place for polygamy. . . . You will see, Monare, that where the children are the fruit of the loins of one man, and of the womb of one woman, there is less jealousy and more loyalty, and the family stands against the world as one."

The Moruti now knelt in prayer and asked Monare to join him.

Monare felt a different man when he left the house of Moruti Lefa; he had changed his concepts about drinking-dens, war-dances, and going about in the darkness of the night. He gained the villagers' respect and was loved by all.

His mother learned about this sudden change in Monare's habits, and decided to pay him a visit.

Said Monare:

"I owe you an apology because I declined from my good upbringing, and followed the wrong way."

His mother, being overjoyed, replied thus:

"God is a kind Father to us all; He does all He can for those who ask His help sincerely."

"I have abandoned my desire to marry a second wife," declared Monare, to his mother's further great happiness.

She said:

"I have always told you that our choice of Florinah as a wife for you was a wise one—she comes from a good home. Her mother, too, has a great respect for her husband. I still say, son, that you were lucky to marry such a good woman—she is not like some women who order their husbands to draw water from the well!"

Monare replied:

"Mother—it is now that I begin to believe you—you made a good choice. . . . O I love Ma-Libe, my wife! I hope God shall continue to bless our marriage!"

Chapter Three

THIRD DEGREE AT NUMBER FOUR

At this point in his story Monare's emotion was so deep that he saw only with the eyes of his heart—the eyes of his head were closed to reality; then suddenly he realised that he was in Number Four.

Monare returned from his day-dreaming with the tears pouring from his eyes. His sympathetic cell-mate asked:

" Are you going to write to your wife ? "

" No, I am afraid my wife will kill herself to learn that I am in jail ! "

" Jail ? Jail is nothing ! It is just like home—a home for the poor; you get your food in time, you get clothing, you don't pay rent, and you have no need for money, for there is nothing to spend it on ! "

Monare sighed. . . .

" Well, my friend, I don't know about that—life is not easy for me. I was making money fast, and was sending most of it home to my wife for the purchase of cattle. . . . But what is your case ? "

" My case is worse than yours—I killed a man ! "

" You say you killed a man ! "

" I say it to you—but not to them ! If you tell too much of the truth you may go to jail, for the white man Magistrate will not say, I pardon you because you told the Court the whole truth. Oh, no ! Sometimes a lie helps a lot. Last time I told a lie and was discharged."

" Do you mean that if I tell the Magistrate a lie, I shall come out all right ? "

THIRD DEGREE AT NUMBER FOUR

" Oh, no! Don't be a child, man! I don't mean that! What I mean is, that if they won't believe the truth, then you must tell them a lie—now do you understand?"

" Yes, I think so . . . although *eeee*! . . ."

" If you think telling a lie would not help you, then tell the truth—always tell the truth if you can, for the truth helps more than a lie. . . . But always be careful how you put it to the Court. . . ."

Later in the morning, Van and another detective came to the jail to question Monare; and he was taken to an office to confront them. Monare was led into a small, bare room; as he hesitated at the door, he found himself roughly pushed from behind so that he fell through the doorway on to the floor of the room.

Coming to his knees, dazed, he thought:

" Perhaps my cell-mate was wrong; maybe I have already been judged, and this is the punishment!"

He had no time to think more, for a loud, rough voice shouted:

" Get up quickly, or it will be the worse for you!"

Monare's frightened eyes now met the gaze of the two detectives, dressed in plain clothes; one he recognised as the white man, Van, who had arrested him and taken him, with blows, to Marshall Square. The white man's fierce look made Monare afraid—he thought now of all his cell-mate had told him of Number Four!

" Gently, my baases," he whispered through quivering lips.

" Tula! You black bastard!"

Replied one of the white men, and continued:

" Here is the story of your guilt written on this paper; we know that you cannot write. Admit now that you took the cloth knowing it to be stolen, and we will place the mark of your thumb on the paper as signature, and leave you in peace."

Monare was terrified, yet found courage to reply:

" How can I agree to what is false? By the God of my Moruti, I swear that I am innocent! How could I know that the cloth was stolen?"

To such a plea, there could be but one reply—and Monare got it; one of the detectives seized him and shook him until his teeth rattled in his head; unseen blows descended on his back and stomach, and he cried aloud in pain.

"Now, you lying bastard—will you admit your guilt?"

With what little spirit he had left, Monare murmured:

"I am innocent . . . yet shall the white man's Magistrate learn how you have treated me . . . this is against the law."

Now did Monare feel the impact of a boot against his buttocks; the white man laughed loudly.

"We know that you bloody bastards won't pull your trousers down, and show the Magistrate your bare arse. . . . Come on, give us your thumb."

Now did Monare feel that he was doomed, and, summoning his remaining strength, he let out a loud call for help.

Quickly was a rough hand clapped upon his mouth; yet must the white man have worried, for one of them said:

"We leave you now, but if one word of what has happened passes your lips—to-morrow, when we return, worse will befall."

With parting kicks, they left the room, and locked the door behind them.

As Monare lay groaning, warders came and removed him to the hospital of Number Four. They said to the orderly:

"There has been fighting in the yard—patch him up."

The medicines bit into the bruised flesh of Monare with teeth of fire; he groaned in agony; then was he bandaged and taken back to his cell.

At length entered his cell-mate, and said with sympathy:

"They talked to you with their fists."

Monare stammered: "Their hands talked to me, yes—but I made no reply!"

Monare lay there in violent fear, until his cell-mate sat beside him and soothed him with kind words and cunning caresses which quietened the nerves around his wounds and stimulated others, thus helping him after a while to forget his pain.

Then said his companion to Monare:

"What made you leave Lesotho, and come to the City of Gold?"

And in the telling of the tale, the pain—except when he moved —seemed in truth to be deadened in the poor beaten body of Monare.

Chapter Four

KAFFIR MAIL

Now did Monare recount to his cell-mate how his affairs had prospered after his discussion with the Moruti Lefa: how he was promoted to the office of Headman to the Chief, assuming full charge over all matters during the Chief's absences.

As team after team of young men returned from their sojourn in the City of Gold, Monare became fired by their stories told round the fire of money to be made, of sights to be seen, and of the many strange races of the white man who lived in the city built around the mine dumps.

Often did he speak to his Chief on these matters, and ask to be relieved of his duties, so that he, too, might make this wonderful journey and return with boxes full of dresses for his wife, and ornaments for her adornment, and colourful blankets for his own wearing. Two years passed before the Chief would hear his petition without grumbling, but at last one evening, he gave his consent for Monare to accept a contract on the Mines.

When the Moruti Lefa heard that Monare was about to depart from the village, he sent for him and said:

"I hope you will continue to go to church in the City of Gold, as you have lately done here. God shall be with you and bless your work.... Here is a letter which will prove that you are a member of the Church."

He then prayed and shook Monare by the hand and bade him farewell.

Ma-Libe killed two fowls for her husband's sustenance on the journey, and kneaded dough for his bread. Monare's clothes were washed and patched, and at last the morning of his departure arrived.

Having bidden sad farewell to his wife and son, Monare set off through the hills to the Quoaqoa Store where stood the red bus—known to the Besotho as *Khubelu*—which would carry him to Afrikaskop Station. Monare mounted the bus with a sore heart, for now he was to travel far away from his peaceful valley, and encounter the mighty magic of the white man of which he had heard so much. As the bus went through the Pass, he gave his small, distant village a last fond look, and murmured to himself:

"My beloved country, I have left you behind, but I shall come back to your soil, to enjoy you with my own people. . . ."

Monare found many friends riding in the bus, and took pains to ask those of them that had made the journey before if—on the train—he would be likely to meet any *tsotsis*. One traveller spoke thus in reply:

"I have heard about *tsotsis*—the rascals! When mine boys leave their compounds on Sundays, the *tsotsis* await them outside the gate, and ask for matches. But their real plan is to rob the mine boys of what they possess, whilst their hands are busy searching in their clothes for the matches—you will find plenty of *tsotsis* on the train—they walk up and down the carriages looking for trouble."

"Are they then so strong and muscular?" demanded Monare fearfully.

"No, my relative, they are not all robust; many are little, skinny fellows—but how they can run! You should see them hopping over fences—no man can catch them when they are being chased. They wear *tsotsi* trousers, sixteen inches round the bottoms, that is how you will recognise them."

"But how do they become *tsotsis*?"

"They like not to work, as we do—rather would they rob and fight and drink. Who can say how a man becomes a *tsotsi*? Perhaps because the man is lazy, or takes to the smoking of *matekoane*—dagga—or because some enemy has paid a witch doctor to bury a sheep-horn filled with black magic in the corner of his kraal."

Monare decided to look well about him on the train for Africans wearing trousers with narrow bottoms.

2

Much was there on Afrikaskop Station to attract the interested eyes of Monare—the very rails on which the trains ran were objects of wonder to the Mosotho, who had never before journeyed outside the confines of his quiet valley.

When the " Kaffir Mail " arrived, Monare would have chosen to enter the most comfortable of the coaches, had he not been restrained brutally by a station foreman, who pulled him back from the door and cursed him.

" Get to the front of the train, you bloody kaffir. You Basutos think you're as good as white men."

Thus quickly and painfully did Monare get his first lesson in South African customs; other knowledge was to be acquired with blows and bruises as he came to have more to do with the white man —but this first lesson left its unfading mark. Never before had man laid hands on him except in friendship or enmity—this roughness—instead of courtesy—displayed to a stranger, distressed Monare greatly, for he was a simple man.

After some time, Monare, together with his fellow-travellers, was herded into some bare coaches with wooden seats at the front of the train near the engine. Had he been asked, Monare would have given as his opinion that these coaches were already over-filled, but somehow with the assistance of pushing and shouting from the ticket examiner, all the African passengers were confined in the third-class carriages.

At about six o'clock that evening, as the train slowly drew into the platform at Bethlehem, Monare noticed, standing by the bookstall, a young African well dressed in a *tsotsi* suit, wearing a wide-brimmed American hat and an American tie of vivid colours. Turning to a fellow-passenger, he asked:

" Do you see that boy? Is he not such a *tsotsi* as we were discussing?"

" You can never say until they speak with you; they are not born only in Johannesburg—they come from all parts of Africa; don't forget that a man may wear *tsotsi* trousers without having evil in his heart—it is not the trousers which make the *tsotsis*, but the men in them."

The mind of Monare was filled with doubts about these *tsotsis*, not because he was weak in his body—for indeed he was a strong man—but because when a Mosotho leaves his beloved Lesotho for the first time to travel in the Union, it is, for him, what it would be for a white man suddenly by black magic to be flown to the moon. At the break of dawn the " Kaffir Mail " slowly rumbled across the long iron bridge which joins the Free State to the Transvaal, and entered the station of Vereeniging, where the station officials shouted along the coaches : " All change here."

The platform was quickly flooded with passengers getting off the train, and feelings of sadness invaded the heart of Monare, for his companions were going to Benoni via Germiston, and he must continue his journey to the City of Gold, alone. In comradeship he offered his train friends part of his provisions, for he still had one fowl left. Greetings were exchanged, and Monare was hustled into the Johannesburg train, which was about to leave.

3

About five o'clock as Monare travelled alone in a third-class compartment, he noticed in the dim light of the early morning, a well-dressed man standing in the corridor of the second-class coach next to his. This man—who was wearing his collar back to front, and was therefore an African priest, saw Monare's face peering at him, and at length walked down the corridor into his compartment. Monare stood up, and said :

" I greet you, Moruti."

" I greet you also, man from home. You look unhappy—why ? "

" I am worried because I am a total stranger. How far is it now to Johannesburg ? "

" It is near now. But where are you going when you reach Park station ? "

" Moruti, I go to the Compound of the W.N.L.A.—the Witwatersrand Native Labour Association compound."

"Ah, you go to Msilikazi," said the Moruti, giving the compound its Zulu name.

"Is the Moruti staying in Johannesburg?"

"Yes, I stay at Orlando township—that big location we are now approaching." And the Moruti pointed through the window.

Monare showed amazement.

"*Ee!* Never in my life have I seen such a place—it must be bigger than Johannesburg. Do white people stay there?"

"No. Orlando is for coloured people and Africans only."

"Does not this train stop at Orlando?"

"No, this is an express. We have electric trains running up and down between Johannesburg and Orlando—they are called *mafofonyane*, you will see one just now."

As he spoke, a *mafofonyane* passed at high speed, and poor Monare tried to get under the seat. As the roar died away, Monare's head came up and he gasped:

"*Ka Thesele!* That is a miracle. I have never seen anything travel so fast before."

The train passed slowly through Mayfair, then through the carriage sidings and goods yard at Braamfontein, and finally ran into Johannesburg's main station. The Moruti went back to his coach, and Monare's face began to take on a sorrowful expression. The Moruti shouted from his carriage:

"Man of the Chief, get off the train, we are at Park Station."

"Yes, Father, I thank you."

Monare followed the Moruti through the complicated subways and stairways out of the station and into Eloff Street.

"Monare—this big street will lead you straight to Msilikazi. You must not be afraid to ask your way."

"Yes, Moruti, I thank you. It was God's wish that I met you..."

Monare hesitated as if he had something more to say. Moruti could see that he was troubled.

"Can I help you with anything, Monare?"

Monare took from his pocket the letter which had been given him by the Moruti Lefa, and handed it to his new friend.

"Oh! So you are a member of the Church. This is more than good. You must come out to see me at Orlando on Sunday."

"I would like to, but as a stranger, I shall lose my way."

The Moruti rubbed his fingers against his lips for a while, then spoke.

"Here is my address on this paper. When you get off the train at Orlando Station show the paper to any taxi-driver, and he will bring you to my home."

Now the Moruti put his hand into his pocket again and withdrew five shillings, and gave it to Monare.

"This five shillings you will use for coming to Orlando."

"I thank you very much, Moruṭi. May God bless you always."

They parted quietly and peacefully; and Monare walked up Eloff Street as he had been instructed, finding it very difficult to pass through the traffic.

Chapter Five

COURTYARD *PITSO*

As Monare told of his journey from Lesotho to the City of Gold, his cell-mate listened with interest to his observations, but as Monare finished, he laughed, and said:

"Little have I had to do with Morutis! ... Yes, I have listened to their praising of the white men's God. They say that before Him all men are as equal. Yet not only do they forbid me to enter their churches, but they will not allow me to sit next to them in the trains or buses or bioscopes. Man, talk to me rather of beer drinks and women, or even—if your fancy lies that way—of handsome boys."

A flush of shame mounted within Monare's heart, for, in truth, he had found much comfort in the ministrations of his companion's hands. And in his eagerness to relate his story he had not rebuffed those hands when they strayed. Yet these thoughts ran through his mind, and he gave voice to them.

"Although we Basotho are polygamists, we do not strike up chance affairs with women—at least only those who hold not their pride dear, who lack self-respect and love for their families and race."

His cell-mate replied:

"Yet in the shanty towns and locations of this City of Gold, are there many prostitutes to be found. And the sickness of women is widely suffered from."

"Yes, it is hard for the African to remain chaste and continent. Is there not talk even among the white men of the shortage of houses ? How much harder then, must it be for the African with a wife to find shelter in this city ! "

His cell-mate pointed at Monare.

"When you first came, the mines provided you with food and shelter."

"True, friend, but such privileges are not for my family. Furthermore, when I first arrived, I was young with downy cheeks, and in the first week I had advances made to me by the older men, who had been denied the comfort of their wives for so long. And what about our brothers who take up the work of cleaners and messengers—is there roof provided for their families ? "

"No, my companion—what you say is truth—best off are those African men or women who work as house-servants ; for sometimes the white Baas will allow a man's wife to live with him in the quarters, in exchange for her labour in the washing of clothes. And if the woman is employed in the house, sometimes is her husband permitted to sleep with her, should he agree to cut the white man's grass and wash his car."

The two men lay silent for a while.

Monare then said, somewhat diffidently :

"Yes, boys, or the friendship of the hand—these are what many of us Africans are reduced to. Yet the truth is that this friendship of boys leads one to a lonely path at the end. There is little chance of living in such a manner in the homeland."

His cell-mate laughed again.

"Women, boys—I have tried them all. . . . But this companionship of boys is against the white man's law. Should you see your Orlando Moruti again ask him how the white men can condemn us for a crime which they themselves have forced on us by separating us from our families. What that other Moruti—the Moruti Lefa in your village—said about the brewing of beer is also true. How can the white man hold us guilty of drunkenness when he will not permit the brewing of home-made kaffir beer ? "

Food was brought, and when they had eaten, Monare's cellmate spoke again.

"The mixtures I have drunk in the locations of this City of Gold ! It is a wonder that my stomach has not rebelled. . . . But tell me, you who consort with Baruti, how came you to this pass ? I should rather have thought to see you following behind the white men who beat the big drum and wear the red caps. Or armed with a white pole, followed by women with white and red crosses on their dresses. How came you to be mixed up in this frolicsome business of the selling of trousers ? . . . Perhaps you like the measuring and the fitting ? . . . Are you that sort ? "

Monare felt again the blush of shame; yet he realised that his cell-mate was but trying to move his mind from too much dwelling on his present sorrow, and was seeking to arouse him with wicked raillery. So with good grace, he went on with his tale from the time he parted with the Orlando Moruti in Eloff Street.

Chapter Six

CITY OF GOLD

But before many words were spoken, the order came for the prisoners to be exercised; and it was in the yard of Number Four, under the remote skies of the highveld, that the two Africans talked of the strange ways of the white man.

It was not only Monare's eyes that worked overtime as he plodded up Eloff Street—his nose also found full-time occupation. Not only did he notice the already familiar fumes of petrol and oil, but a whole *impi* of unidentified odours attacked his nostrils. He did not know yet that the white man reckoned that the black man stank, but passing quietly through the crowds of white men and white women busy with their shopping, he speedily became aware that the fair-skinned people carried with them a scent, which to him, was faintly unpleasant.

Monare spent two hours on his passage of the Main Street of the City of Gold; he stopped for long minutes to watch the trams and trolley-buses and the motor-buses. The contents of the windows of the shops amazed him beyond the power of words. Even could I write, he mused, how could I tell Ma-Libe of the wonders that I have this day seen.

One sight there was which turned the taste of all his pleasure sour in his mouth—as he stood at the corner of Commissioner Street a lorry passed by slowly, carrying on its open platform at the back an iron cage filled with Africans.

Monare turned to an African policeman who stood on the corner, and asked:

"Is there war? And are these prisoners being taken across the Great Sea to prostrate themselves before the Great White King?"

The policeman spat and laughed coarsely.

"You're just from the homeland? They're prisoners all right, serving their sentences in one of the farm gaols. Some farmer on the other side of the city desires their services, and is willing to pay the government good money in exchange. And so—they are being taken from the prison to the farm."

"*Ee!* But home-boys have told me that the wild animals are kept in just such a cage in the Johannesburg Zoo!"

The policeman smiled sourly.

"Once you're in jail there's no difference."

Monare plucked up courage to demand of the policeman where the Compound of Msilikazi might be. The reply was given that Monare should proceed along Eloff Street until he came to a high wall built of red bricks—there he should ask again. After some time Monare found the red-brick wall, and upon inquiring his way had pointed out to him the gate of Msilikazi on the opposite corner of the street. Showing a letter which his Chief had written to the compound manager, Monare was conducted by the policeman at the gate to the office of the *Makulu Baas*.

Now was the heart of Monare lightened, for the *Makulu Baas* turned out to be the sort of white man who spoke his language, Sesotho, and who had travelled in his homeland, Lesotho. For a while white man and black man spoke of crops and weather and other such important things, until gradually Monare came to feel at ease. *Makulu Baas* then told Monare that he would appear before the Medical Officer the next morning, and that if found fit, would be enrolled in the Police of the Compound, and would not be sent to labour in the bowels of the earth. This, said *Makulu Baas*, was a great honour, as only such Africans as brought strong letters from their chiefs were recruited as policemen, for the post carried with it many privileges such as extra pay, regular hours, and a free uniform.

Cutting short Monare's heartfelt thanks, *Makulu Baas* now called an *Induna*, and requested him to take Monare to the barrack in which lived another policeman, Ntoane, who also came from Lesotho.

Ntoane looked up as the *Induna* brought Monare into his room, and seeing the blanket around Monare's shoulders, said:

"Welcome, home-boy. What work are you to do?"

"Greetings, O my relative! *Makulu Baas* tell me that if I pass the doctor, I am to be a police-boy."

"Home-boy, you are really very lucky; your roots are working; your witch-doctor must be a good one."

"I do not think that roots are the cause of it; my luck is due to the prayers of my Moruti at home."

"Are you a member of the Church?"

"Yes, and I have here the address of a Moruti at Orlando, whom I met on the train. He wants me to visit him on Sunday. Will you accompany me?"

Ntoane grinned.

"What shall we get to drink at a Moruti's house—only that tea of theirs, which I do not enjoy. That's no food for men like you and me—we need something stronger! But still, when Sunday comes, we shall see."

"Have you ever been to Orlando, home-boy?"

"Nearly every Sunday, my relative—either there or to Sophiatown, where I have an excellent brewer. But remember, if you become a police-boy, you must never come back to Msilikazi drunk—the *Makulu Baas* doesn't like it. But before Sunday I'll tell you plenty about the locations, and about the *tsotsis*."

Monare pulled out his stick from his blanket.

"With this stick I can knock holes in the heads of these *tsotsis* of yours."

Ntoane smiled again.

"Do you always wear the blanket? Don't you wear clothes when you go out visiting—a suit?"

"Oh, no! Not me! I'm no rock-rabbit without a tail. I wear my blanket and look like a proper Mosotho!"

"Listen, home-boy—I left off wearing the blanket when I came here to work. The police are always after you when you wear a blanket—demanding to see your pass; they wonder what you might be carrying beneath that blanket—if not a stick, then stolen goods or white man's brandy."

Monare realised that he had much to learn; and after passing the medical examination the next day, he spent his leisure hours asking the friendly Ntoane all sorts of questions about passes and the prices of suits and the names of brewers of home-brewed kaffir beer, until Ntoane's ears grew tired.

2

At last Sunday arrived, and the weather was beautiful; the winds had ceased from blowing and the sand from the mine dumps had stopped flying through the air; it was altogether an admirable day. From the door of his room, nothing could Monare see except the red-brick wall of the compound, and rising above it the tall buildings of the city and the blue sky beyond.

Monare walked out through the gate of Msilikazi. Here am I, he said to himself, in the midst of the famed City of Gold, one of the richest towns in the world. He was suddenly seized with the desire to climb to the top of a mine dump, and from the heights, look out upon the city. It was a strenuous climb, but eventually he reached the top, leaving behind him his footsteps to be covered by the rolling sand. He arrived, panting on the summit of the dump; a feeling of importance seemed to possess him; he felt carefree and content.

Slowly from behind one of the mine dumps the beautiful golden sun came peeping and rolling to shine over the misty city. How beautiful that city looked! From the shining multi-coloured roofs lit up by the sun's rays, emerged the tall sky-poking fingers of the skyscrapers tickling the fleecy clouds.

Towards the outskirts of the city the buildings thinned out, giving way to trees and flowers and beautiful dwelling houses. As the sun spread its rays over the now golden-tinted buildings, the trams and buses and motor cars started to move through the streets. From somewhere in the distance came the chiming of a tolling church bell, which awoke Monare from his dreaming with a start—he suddenly remembered that this day he was to visit Orlando.

When he had scrambled down the crumbling slope of the mine dump, Monare found the faithful Ntoane awaiting him with bowls of *mahleu* or sour porridge. In honour of his home-boy, Ntoane to-day also wore the blanket of tradition; and having refreshed themselves, the two Basotho passed through the gate of Msilikazi on their way to Park Station.

In his excitement, Monare lost sight of his home-boy, Ntoane. When he reached the corner of de Villiers Street and Eloff Street, he felt an air of relief come over him, for on the other side of the road stood Ntoane.

Without looking to left or right, the simple Monare made a dash across the street—little did he know that he was crossing against the traffic signal. A traffic inspector called savagely after him:

"Hey, you! Get back where you came from."

The shouting but caused further confusion in Monare's mind, and made him run faster still.

"Look out, you are running into a car."

With screeching tyres, a crossing car was brought to a standstill with Monare clinging to its front mudguard. It was with tears in his eyes that he pleaded for freedom after the traffic police had arrested him.

"*Baas!* I am a new one here. I know nothing about these lights of yours, *Baas*. It is the first time in my life that I have seen such things."

Eventually the police let him go, after giving him a stern warning. And Monare and Ntoane walked into the entrance of Park Station.

An air of friendliness seemed to possess the station crowd, and there were hundreds of people passing up and down to the subways. These were the days before the imposition of segregation at the railway stations, and as Monare and Ntoane descended the steps and made their way past the fish pond, they passed through groups of white men and white women who stood with happy children watching the fountains play. *Mafofonyane* were pulling into the station and pulling out again, and never had Monare seen such crowds of people, well dressed and happy. He cried to Ntoane:

"Ntoane! Ntoane! Where are all these people going to?

Look at the beautiful girls. They are dressed like white women!"

"Home-boy—you have seen nothing yet. Wait until we get to Orlando."

The two Basotho got their tickets and made their way to Platform Number Four, and as they waited in the crowd, the loud-speakers gave Monare a fright as they blared:

"Orlando train on Number Four. Orlando train on Number Four. First stop Croesus. First stop Croesus."

They boarded the train, the siren sounded, and the *mafofonyane* shot away in its usual speedy manner. But alas! Although African labour is the life-blood of the Reef, the trains that run along the Rand offer no welcome or comfort to any black man. Added now to the injury of segregation—or apartheid—on the trains, came the insult of the abusive remarks of the uncouth ticket examiners, who respect not age, nor sex, nor dignity, as they demand with curses and sometimes blows, the tickets of those who have paid to travel in the cattle-truck-like coaches.

Monare was interested in the people who travelled, and asked his home-boy, Ntoane, many questions.

When the train stopped at Croesus, he said:

"Where are they all going?"

"Some are going to the Coronation Hospital, and some to the Newclare Location, known as Seteketekeng."

Monare sat up.

"Even I've heard of that. Why, people are killed like flies there at week-ends."

"Yes, Monare, half the people there are blanketed Basotho; some come from Matsieng, some from Leribe, and some from Quoaqoa."

"Is it a location especially for the Basotho?"

"Not especially, but I think our people like it for they can brew beer there, and drink themselves out."

"*Ee!* Home-boy—it must be a small Lesotho. You should take me there one day. I might meet one of our women who lives there—MaKalebe. I can remember her telling me of one big fight which took place at Seteketekeng between Molapos and Matsieng people. She said that men, women and children were running like animals, and the streets looked as though they had been painted with blood."

At this point Monare's bloodthirsty thoughts were diverted at the sight of some Basotho girls who got into the train, and he nudged Ntoane.

"Those women over there speak Sesotho—yet they look like white women. . . . You don't mean to tell me, home-boy, that girls like that can do the exact same work as our women at home. *Ka Thesele!* I don't believe it. They couldn't even go to clear the lands of weeds, nor grind mealies."

But now *mafofonyane* drew up at Orlando Station and soon Monare and Ntoane were crossing the bridge towards the taxi-rank.

3

At the rank, they were met by a shouting man.

"Taxi! Taxi! Come inside."

He opened the car doors and Ntoane and Monare and several others got in. The taxi started off quickly, and as he drove, the taximan said:

"Who's first, please? Please give me your house numbers."

Monare gave the driver the Moruti's paper, and soon the car arrived at the designated address, and the friends dismounted and paid the driver.

On the veranda of the house stood the Moruti with a worried face, which melted into a wide smile as he saw the clanking vehicle drive off. With hospitable gestures he met them at the gate, and drew them into his dining-room.

"Well, gentlemen—have you come? I am so pleased, Monare, that you and your friend are paying me a visit to-day. Of course Sunday is a busy day for a minister, but we shall find time for talk. Are you still alive?"

"We are very well, Moruti, and this is my home-boy, Ntoane."

"So you two are home-boys. What beautiful blankets you are wearing."

"Do you like blankets, too, Moruti?"

"Yes! And I can wear one if I like."

"I don't believe it, Moruti. Don't tell me that you are a Mosotho?"

"Yes, I am Mosotho, too. I was born in the Witjieshoek Reserve in the Free State, and wore a blanket when I was still herding my father's cattle. . . . But you must meet my wife and daughter—Mary."

"Yes, Father."

"Come in with your mother, and meet these two gentlemen."

Outside the door Mary whispered to her mother:

"Two blanketed men."

In the room, the Moruti introduced Monare and Ntoane, who acknowledged the introduction in true Basotho style.

"We greet you, our Mother, it is our pleasure to know you. I, Monare, met my friend the Moruti along my journey from home."

Greetings over, the two women retired to the kitchen, and Mary brought them tea.

The Moruti then said:

"I must go now to the church to get ready for the service. Are you, Monare, and you, Ntoane, coming?"

"Moruti, to our shame we must say that we did not wear our suits to-day, and we cannot enter the church with these blankets—next time, if we may?"

Church bells sounded through the morning air and Moruti said:

"I must go now for a while; but I hope you will drink more tea; on this occasion my wife and daughter will stay and keep you company until I return. There is much that I would desire to say to you."

And the Moruti swept away into the clangour of the bells.

In the parsonage, the four Basotho talked busily about the home country; but Monare found time to sum up with his eyes the beauties of the Moruti's daughter, Mary. He found his ancient longings for a second wife rising in his blood. What he looked on gave pleasure to his eyes—the small, firm breasts which thrust themselves against the dress; the shapely legs, not wholly concealed; the full lips, the white teeth, the red tip of her tongue. Her eyes, when they met Monare's, were innocent, yet unknowingly promising.

"I think this Moruti has found new member of his Church."
Thus laughed Monare to himself.

His feelings, however, were not permitted to disclose themselves to his friend Ntoane, nor to the wife of the Moruti—but who shall say whether Mary, the lovely Mosotho maid, knew what was in Monare's mind?

4

And so passed the time until church was done; and the Moruti returned somewhat sweating from his labours.... Now was the time for more tea to be brewed; and the wife and daughter of the Moruti, having seen that the teapot was filled again, withdrew to the kitchen to prepare something to fill the belching stomachs of the menfolk.

Moruti asked:

"How now—man of the Chief. What do you think of this City of Gold?"

Monare replied:

"*Ka Thesele!* I did not know that there were so many tribes of the white man."

"Your eyes are not blind, home-boy. So soon in this wicked city, and yet you know that the white men are not all of the same kraal."

"I have seen, Moruti, that most of the police and the men who work on the railway, and on the trams, seem to be of the Afrikaner nation; most of these—not all—speak to us Africans with a rough and surly tongue. And their eyes tell mine, that should I show anger, they would willingly put the matter to the test of force."

Ntoane chuckled.

"*Ee!* My relative, I have lived here long. Yet have you placed the bean in its right pod!"

Moruti added:

"There is some reason for hate; in the days of the Zulu King Chaka, many Afrikaners were eaten up by his *impis*. These people, too, have never forgotten the treachery of Dingaan, who killed without warning Piet Retief and his unarmed warriors.... That

CITY OF GOLD

Dingaan might have had good reason to fear and distrust them, is not a portion of their feeling. But since I have left home, I have read and talked much with others about these things. There is more than milk in a coconut—there is the flesh itself."

Monare looked puzzled; then the Moruti smiled, and continued:

"When the white man first came to this country, he did not bring women with him. Many turned to the African woman for comfort, and—in finding comfort—also found sons. You have only to look at some of these white men, to see the hand of Africa in their faces, and in their hair. Even among their Great Ones, have such signs been noted and spoken of."

"Is this then a cause for hatred?"

"Men like not to be reminded of their sins, nor yet the sins of their fathers. This, too, will you learn, Monare, that of all the white men's tribes, some Afrikaners are close to us both in their poverty, and in their love of land. They like not trades nor business; few of them are craftsmen, nor are many of them storekeepers. Their customs, too, are strange. When one dies who owns land, the eldest son does not enter into possession—nay, that land is divided into as many portions as there are sons."

Monare quickly picked out the meaning.

"Then rich landowner's great-grandson would hardly have ground enough to build a kitchen."

The Moruti laughed.

"Ntoane, you are right—Monare's mind needs no sharpening. In ancient times, Monare, when as the generations were born the land grew too small for each son to tend a farm, these people travelled northwards and took possession of new lands. But to-day that is no longer possible. Many white men have had born in their minds the thought that the African, too, must have land on which to dwell, to plough and to till, and to keep his cattle."

Monare, justifying his reputation, added:

"Another reason for hatred!"

They paused a while, and drinking tea, pondered on the Moruti's words.

Monare put down his cup, and said:

"There is yet another tribe among the white men; they strike hard bargains with us, yet do their eyes disclose some measure of sympathy and understanding, as if they too had felt the whip of persecution. Of all the white men, these alone never resort to violence in their dealings with us. I refer to the hook-nosed people."

The Moruti said:

"Yes, the Jewish people have suffered much. Violence does not appeal to them, but they have the courage born of hardship and poverty. Strange people, they give what they have so hardly earned to help their relatives or friends. Yet do they desire money and the power it brings."

Ntoane held up his hand.

"It is because of this desire perhaps, that the Jewish people treat us with some justice—they judge a man not by his colour, but by the quality of the work he will do in exchange for his wages."

After a pause, Ntoane continued: "Yet all these people—and I count among them the Indians, whom the white men hate, and the British—live in some comfort in houses with their wives and children. This happiness given by God even to the animals and beasts of the fields, is denied to most of us Africans."

The three Basotho thought a while on this great sorrow.

Then Moruti gave his opinion.

"The white man it is who desires the African to work on the mines, in the factories, and in his very home. Yet even in the white man's house but rarely is the *kia* or *ntlo* built for the use of married African servants. Few of us can afford to build our own houses in a city such as this. Where would we obtain such wealth as is required? Where would we obtain ground? Yes, the white man has built locations for the Africans, but for every husband and father who finds a roof under which to shelter his family, there are a hundred at least, working in the city, for whom there is no such accommodation."

Ntoane interrupted this to say:

"Some white men say that the Chiefs should build houses for the Africans."

But the Moruti disputed this.

"Even Chiefs are not so rich in lands and cattle, as to build so many homes.

CITY OF GOLD

Monare thought a while.

"Why do not the white men who own the mines and the factories build such houses?"

"That is the true answer to this trouble, but white men do not want to use their gains for such purposes. In this I think they wrong themselves, for I have seen hundreds of Africans come to the city, and learn the work of mining, and of this and that. After the passing of some time, the man's heart yearns after his wife and children, and he takes train to his home. Now the white man has to teach the same work to a new African; and even should his first worker return to his employ, he will have forgotten much after his sojourn in the homeland. The money that the white man spends on teaching new workers . . ."

Monare cannot restrain himself:

"Could be better spent on building family houses."

Ntoane and the Moruti exchanged glances of approval at Monare's sharp ideas.

Moruti said:

"I do not know if these problems will be settled in our lifetime. Many of the white men look upon us as of less account than their dogs and horses; they fear us, and they fear us because in their hearts they know that we do not receive justice. They know that one day justice will be demanded—and that is the day they dread."

Ntoane warned:

"Monare, you will find many who are brave and kind among the white men; all flowers do not give off the same scent. Down by the City of Sugar—in Natal—there will you find the best understanding between the white man and the black man, for in that land, the white man learns the Zulu language, and knowing it, has some knowledge of and sympathy with the African people."

The Moruti then added these words:

"But at no place in this land, except perhaps in Basutoland, Bechuanaland, and Swaziland, does the African feel that he lives in his own home-country. I—as Moruti—cannot give consent to the drinking of kaffir beer. Yet I think that the proper home-brew does less harm to man than the strong liquors made in the locations and backyards of the City of Gold. And why is such poison made?"

Ntoane had the right answer to this.

"Because the African is not allowed to drink when and where he will, as is the white man. He cannot drink at home, save at danger of arrest. At the beer-halls set up by the City Council, he cannot drink as much as he likes, nor the beer he likes, nor when he likes."

The Moruti held up his hand.

"If you should stay here more than one year, Monare, you will also find that the taxes you will have to pay to the white man's government in poll-tax and hut tax, will come to as much as that paid by white men who earn more than £300 in one year. Now what African can earn such wealth?"

Ntoane smiled.

"None. Unless he be secret beer-brewer, or *semokolara*—a seller of dagga!"

It was well that the women now called them to eat, for Monare's brain was burning with all the new facts and opinions that were being forced into his head. During the meal, they were silent—they had better things to do than to talk: there was the excellent food cooked by Mary and her mother.

There was no opportunity for further talk after the meal, for Mary had to teach at the Sunday school, and the Moruti had to think over the topic for his evening sermon.

So, at length, the time came for good-byes.

5

As the Basotho stood on the veranda of the parsonage, suddenly an uproar started farther down the street; police whistles blew, and there was the sound of loud shouting. Monare and the Moruti rushed to the gate to see what was happening. As they walked on to the pavement, a woman ran across the street with a tin of kaffir beer in her arms. As she ran, she cried:

"Police! Police! The pick-up van's coming."

Even as she shouted the warning, the police arrived in their closed van with a squealing of brakes. A policeman jumped out and seized the shouting woman.

"*Tixo! Tixo!*" she cried, in her language of Xosa, but a squad of policemen—black and white—fell on her and threw her inside the idling van. Without making further inquiries they seized a few innocent but grumbling bystanders, and dealt with them in the same manner.

Monare could not believe his eyes. Surely the innocent were not to suffer with the guilty? Pushing off the restraining hands of the Moruti and Ntoane, he ran up to the policeman who appeared to be in charge, and said:

"My *Baas*, you cannot take these innocent people to jail. What have they done—they were not drinking? They were only sad to see a woman treated so roughly."

The policeman glared at Monare, then without warning struck him a blow on his head, shouting:

"You bloody insolent bastard—you'll go along too for that."

And before Ntoane or the Moruti could reach the pick-up van, it had rushed off towards the police station.

At the parsonage there was much crying and upset among the womenfolk; but the Moruti soothed them, saying:

"I know where he's been taken—to Klip River Police Station. I am acquainted with the sergeant in charge; he is a good man, and later Ntoane and I will walk down and speak with him."

Later, when Ntoane and the Moruti entered the Klip River Police Station, the sergeant looked up. When he recognised the Moruti, a friendly smile broke on his face, and he said:

"Good evening, Reverend. Some of your flock in trouble?"

The Moruti looked pleased at his jocular yet not unfriendly reception.

"Yes, Sergeant, sir. One Monare, a mine-boy, friend of Ntoane here, was watching when your van picked up a woman who had been brewing beer. When the *Baas* in charge arrested some people who were looking on, this foolish Monare, who has only just come here from Basutoland, went to intervene."

The sergeant smiled, but it was rather a forced smile.

"That's probably Van again. Poor old Van just can't stand cheek from natives."

The Moruti spoke.

"Sergeant, Monare didn't mean to be cheeky; he felt that your Mr. Van was arresting innocent people."

The sergeant pressed a bell-push and, after a short interval, the policeman who had arrested Monare walked in.

"Have you got a Basuto boy called Monare booked?"

"Yes."

"What charge?"

"Resisting arrest."

An almost imperceptible look passed between the sergeant and the Moruti. The sergeant commanded:

"Release Monare, Van."

"But he's a bloody insolent kaffir."

"Release him, Van—I'll take the responsibility."

A few minutes later a woebegone Monare appeared in the Charge office, helped on his way by a shove from Van, who muttered as he kicked him:

"I'll get you yet, you black bastard."

The Moruti thanked the sergeant, and the three Basotho left the police station.

"I won't ask you what happened inside," said the Moruti. "It's better for me not to know, or I'll lose what influence I have with the sergeant—but I'd keep clear of the policeman they call Van, if I were you."

Ntoane and Monare refused offers of further refreshment at the Moruti's house, and decided to return to Msilikazi, promising, however, to come to Orlando again.

In the train, Monare related how he had been belaboured by the policeman, until he had decided to keep his mouth shut and not answer Van's taunts.

Ntoane smiled grimly.

"You've learned a lot to-day," he said.

6

Such was the manner of Monare's introduction to the City of Gold; yet were not many more days to pass before the occasion of his first encounter with the dreaded *tsotsis*.

When pay day arrived, everyone was happy in the Msilikazi compound. On the Saturday which followed, Ntoane and Monare decided to go shopping; Monare had decided to spend a large portion of his first month's wages on a magnificent present for his wife—a fine " Victorian " blanket. After much examination of goods, and words of advice from Ntoane, this blanket was at length bought. As the two home-boys strolled down the street, they were stopped by two well-dressed Africans.

" Where are you people from ? "

Ntoane and Monare stood dumb.

" I am talking to you, man. Can't you speak ? "

Ntoane queried :

" Who are you to ask such questions ? "

One of the strangers said :

" Take out your passes."

" We have not got our passes with us—we left them in the compound, we are mine police at Msilikazi."

" You may be mine police in the compound, but not outside."

Monare's mind was clouded with thoughts of *tsotsis*, but it seemed that he was wrong, for the other stranger spoke :

" No passes ? Then we arrest you. Come along with us. See that other one doesn't escape, he looks like a *skelim*. Take his parcel from him, then he won't try to run away ! "

The strangers escorted Ntoane and Monare through the streets of Johannesburg towards Malay Camp, and finally halted in a large backyard.

" Bring the handcuffs, Joe," said one stranger to the other. " We'll handcuff them together."

" Yes, Bill, that would be a sound idea."

So Monare and Ntoane were left handcuffed to each other in the backyard of a strange house. The parcel containing the expensive blanket intended for Ma-Libe, was removed by the strangers with a muttered remark that they'd be back in a minute. Ntoane was told to hand over his wages, which he had not yet spent, and was given a receipt for the amount—and for Monare's blanket, by one of the strangers.

The two well-dressed Africans then disappeared round the

corner of the house, leaving Ntoane and Monare not quite sure whether they were already in jail, or still had to be taken to their cells.

After a while a man dressed in overalls entered the yard, but took no notice of them.

Monare shouted:

"Hey, you! Please come to our help."

The man came towards them.

"What are you two doing here? Are you drunk?"

Then, catching sight of the handcuffs, he added:

"Oh, escaped prisoners."

Ntoane spoke.

"Not escaped prisoners—prisoners, yes, but wrongfully arrested by two plain-clothes African detectives."

"But if they were detectives—how could they leave you in this yard?"

"They took my blanket and his money, and gave us receipts, and asked us to wait a minute."

The man in overalls grinned.

"*Tsotsis!*" he said.

Monare and Ntoane groaned to think of their vanished possession.

"Undo us," they cried.

The man in the overalls promised to go away and bring a genuine policeman. When the European constable arrived he was not amused.

"Now what is all this? *Kom julle daar nit?* How did you get here like this?"

Monare answered:

"We were arrested, my *Baas*."

"By whom, and why—you damned Kaffirs?"

"By two African detectives, *Baas*, or may be they were *tsotsis*."

"Why, what did you do?"

"Nothing, *Baas*; true, nothing, *Baas*."

"Better come along to Marshall Square with me."

The white man constable helped the two friends on with a few kicks and insults.

"*Gou, gou!* Kaffirs!"

CITY OF GOLD

Arrived in front of the sergeant at Marshall Square they told their tale, during which a broad grin appeared on the sergeant's face.

"*Tsotsis* again, I'm certain," he said, and ordered the constable to ring Msilikazi to establish that Ntoane and Monare were, in truth, employed there. When this business had been completed to his satisfaction, he ordered the handcuffs to be unlocked.

Set free, the two home-boys returned to Msilikazi with very sore hearts and empty pockets.

7

Monare was quite broken-hearted about his loss; he said to Ntoane:

"I must make some money quickly."

"Money? What for?"

"To replace the blanket . . . and also to take Mary to the bioscope."

Ntoane laughed loudly.

"Do you think Mary would ever go to the bioscope with you?"

Monare swung his blanket over his shoulder and paced the floor.

"Why—don't you think I'm a handsome fellow?"

"Not that! Not that! . . . Home-boy, Mary speaks English—the Moruti is going to send her to college. Anyway, where would you get the money for the cattle for a second marriage? And aren't you a Christian?"

In spite of his promises to the Moruti and to his wife Ma-Libe, Monare could not subdue this instinct for polygamy so deeply rooted in the Basotho race. Forced to live a celibate life on the mines, Monare's thoughts did not turn in the direction of the prostitutes in the locations, but rather to contracting another marriage. But thoughts of Mary were to be driven right out of his mind for a long time by an unexpected encounter with an old friend.

It so happened that a few weeks later, the anniversary of the sinking of the troopship *Mendi* was to be celebrated; the loss of this vessel off the English coast with six hundred black men on board has never been forgotten. When the day dawned, the Bantu Sports Ground was filled with Africans from all parts of the Reef.

At last there was cheering, and some white men and Africans mounted the dais.

The loudspeakers blared:

"Here is the Chief Native Commissioner, who was in France when the *Mendi* was sunk. He is a sympathiser with the sufferings of the African people, and has their welfare at heart."

After the uproar had lessened, a Moruti who was the secretary of the Mendi Memorial Fund, spoke to the men about the sinking of the ship, and how the fund had helped the widows and orphans throughout the long years. Monare thought as he listened of his forgotten father, who was one of the *Mendi* heroes.

As Monare sat thus, and watched the crowds, suddenly he felt a hard blow on the back, and—looking up—saw a face he remembered, yet for the moment, knew not.

In front of him stood a smart Mosotho, dressed in a white man's suit of fashionable cut. The man held gloves in his hand and a stick; a smart hat with a feather sat on his head.

Memory awoke.

"Koto!"

"Monare!"

These two had been boyhood friends in far-off Lesotho; close friends such as there are in boys of all nations—a David-and-Jonathan pair. The love between them had endured until the time of Monare's marriage—then, slowly they had drifted apart. But they looked at each other with joy and happiness at the reunion—both far from home, their intimacy could be renewed.

Monare said:

"Heart's friend, what are you doing here?"

"I am a businessman, my relative."

Monare now made Koto known to Ntoane, and for a time the three home-boys sat and exchanged news about the home country. Koto had never married, he said.

"Too busy making money," he added, with a laugh.

Monare sat deep in thought; his mind was on his forgotten father, who had left home when he was very young. Monare asked himself the question: "Why don't they remember the sinking of the *Mendi* at home?" He knew that many men from Lomontsa

CITY OF GOLD

had died when the ship sank, and there must be more from other parts of Lesotho.

As the sad story was unfolded by the various speakers on the dais, Monare was inspired to cry out in public words of praise of the *Mendi* heroes. This is a custom of the Basotho people; they are given to the praising of great men and historic events; they wait until moved by the spirit, and then rise from the ground and speak.

As a speaker finished his words of remembrance from the dais, and there came a short pause, Monare rose from the ground and, seeing him rise, most of the gathering turned to watch, for Monare's family was well known as a family of " praisers." His grandfather had been a praiser of the Great Chief Moshoeshoe, and had praised him after the Battle of Tlapaneng—the Battle of the Flat Stone—where the Basotho had been victorious over the Baralong. So, in the footsteps of his ancestors, Monare followed, and cried out to the gathering:

"I praise not my chief, nor my father, nor this gathering, but I give praise to the men who died when the *Mendi* sank beneath the waves." And here are some of the words he spoke, taken from that *lithoko* which has since become famous in the land:

> " *Men get your lifebelts ready!*
> *We sons of the Black Mother,*
> *Now are to die!*
> *Down in the sea's dark stomach,*
> *The Grave of the Africans,*
> *Black men of Africa*
> *Deep lies our doom!*
> *Men die like men!*
> *So saith the Wagon Captain.*
>
> *No Last Post was blown,*
> *No signal was given,*
> *No scriptures were read,*
> *No horn was sounded!*
> *Down " Mendi " descended.*

*She stirred the Blue Waters
And the Waves of her Passing
Cried on the Rocks
Of the English Shore!*

*' Mendi! '—where are you gone?
Cattle! Rain! Peace to the son of Thesele! "*

Dead quiet was the gathering as Monare finished—then the ground shook with the stamping of feet, and the air exploded with noise. Cheers, clapping of hands, and shouting. The Chief Native Commissioner called:

"Come, come to the microphone."

But Monare was spent; the flood of his inspiration had left him weak; so the Commissioner said:

"I stand here to thank all you present to-day. Africans are gifted in the praising of their Chiefs—they have the talent. I am glad to hear this man here saying such heart-breaking words on the sinking of the *Mendi*. He has given you a truly graphic picture. According to the African expression, we shall say, ' Monare, you are a hero—a son of a hero is a hero himself. May there be rain. And may there be peace. Cattle to all Chiefs.' "

From the far end of the ground a voice was heard raised—it was a middle-aged man wearing a blanket who rose, and chanted:

*" Likhomo helele banna
Hona keapa re tsoang
Helele banna kea tsaba! "*

This was the War Song, the *Mokorotlo*.

The singer was joined in his singing by many voices; a man could be seen dashing up and down the ground raising his stick and blanket in the air—a real Basotho war song. The Basotho women raised their beautiful soprano voices to strengthen the men as they started to dance. The crowd was now out of hand, moved beyond control by Monare's stirring words of praise, but not in a dangerous mood, merely emotional.

After the war song and the war dance, the crowd slowly dispersed.

During the weeks that followed, Monare did not see again his heart's friend Koto, after parting with him on the Bantu Sports Ground. Koto had promised to visit him at Msilikazi, but so far had not kept his word. But Koto was much in the thoughts of Monare, who wondered what sort of businessman Koto was, to be able to afford to dress so fashionably and well. He imagined himself calling on the Orlando Moruti's daughter Mary, clad in such a suit.

But such dreams made him somewhat hot and uncomfortable, and he reserved them for the darkness of the night.

Nor did Monare's police duties permit him to visit Orlando again for the present.

Chapter Seven

KOTO—FRIEND OF THE HEART

As Monare concluded this further telling of his story, his mind being on Koto, the wonder came to him that Koto had not yet appeared at Number Four to learn what had happened; for amongst the African people, should one's expected companion be late, or not arrive, inquiries are directed to the nearest charge office. The most usual cause of any delay is arrest.

Monare's cell-mate laughed long and heartily at his adventures with the *tsotsis*, but he felt that Monare was still mixed up with Baruti and Native Commissioners and other high officials, and he could not see yet how Monare had come to that walk of life in which he now found himself, where his companions were not of the standing of Baruti, or even of mine policemen—but were jailors, thieves and detectives.

It was now about three o'clock in the afternoon, and Monare was about to continue with the story of his adventures, when there was a commotion at the gate, and his cell-mate said: "Visiting time. Go, see if your dear friend Koto is not by the gate."

And so it happened to turn out—there, waiting for him, was his friend Koto.

As Koto saw Monare limping towards the gate with his face all bandaged, he looked worried.

"*Ee*, Monare! Did you fall under a tramcar on your way to jail?"

Monare whispered:

"I cannot tell you now, do not speak of what you see."

Koto gave him a knowing glance in reply, and went on to say:

KOTO—FRIEND OF THE HEART

"I came rushing to see you—I did not even know you were at Number Four. I have been to all the charge offices in Johannesburg. But don't worry, I am getting you a lawyer, and will pay your bail-money."

Monare said plaintively:

"When will that be, heart's friend? Please home-boy, make it soon.

Koto replied:

"The lawyer is applying for your bail at nine o'clock to-morrow morning. Then he and I shall come here to Number Four with your release. Do not worry, home-boy."

"Your visit has lifted my spirit, Koto."

"Here are cakes, oranges, bananas, for you."

Koto's face paled as he recognised the work of the white men's boots, but the Zulu guard said that the time was up. Koto left, and Monare returned to his cell companion, much cheered, though in great pain. The two Basotho now shared the good things which Koto had brought. After a while Monare said:

"I have never seen so bitter a life as the life in Number Four Fort; in these few days I have learned much. I should have spent more time praying, I should have visited the Moruti's church. I should have thought more of Ma-Libe, wife of the cattle of my father. . . . These huge walls dug into the hill, have oppressed my spirit. Think of the thousands upon thousands of people who have been imprisoned here—men of all ages and all African communities, charged with all sorts of crimes—robbery, murder, rape, sodomy. A cursed place where the Devil alone rules—a small hell indeed. . . . I shall pray to my God, the God of my father and my Moruti, that the bail may be paid to-morrow. Maybe I have given too much love to my friend Koto, and not enough to God."

At this Monare's shameless cell-mate pricked up his ears, hoping to hear bawdy talk to his taste, and said:

"Come, friend—you have not yet told me how you came to be a maker of trousers."

And through the long night which Monare hoped would be his last in Number Four Fort, he went on recounting his story to his companion.

Chapter Eight

MONARE THE MERCHANT

WITH MANY A PAUSE FOR QUESTION and answer, Monare related his adventures in the City of Gold right down to the day on which his contract period at Msilikazi expired, by which time he was getting a wage of £5 per month. *Makulu Baas* had taken a liking to the Mosotho, and asked him to extend his contract. Although Monare had now saved some money, the loss of the parcel still rankled, and after some thought, he agreed to serve another nine months. No doubt Ntoane's influence told here, for Ntoane had not been home for four years. There was also the matter of Mary.

It was at this interview that Monare learned something of the white man's point of view, for *Makulu Baas* questioned him and asked for his impression of the City of Gold.

When Monare had finished telling of his experiences since his arrival, *Makulu Baas* spoke.

"You have been unfortunate in the white men you have met, Monare—they are not all thus. You must be told that some white men are greatly influenced by their priests, who interpret the Bible to give themselves authority to say, 'The children of Ham shall for ever be hewers of wood and drawers of water'—in this attitude of the Dutch Church does much of the brutality and indifference have its birth. You must remember again, Monare, that all Africans are not like you—steady, hard-working, and honest. Many are criminals, and again many—though honest—are as little children, who put out their hands to grasp things whose use they do not understand, and which may cause them harm. Remember, Monare, that had the white man not come to your country, many of the things which the more childish among you so ardently desire—such as motor cars, bioscopes, good smart clothes, beautiful houses—would also never have come to your notice. . . . Yes, I know what you are going to say—that to desire good clothes, comfortable houses, and so on, is not childish. I agree with you if you admit that such things must be earned and paid for. Unfortunately, not every African is sufficiently intelligent or educated yet to receive the training which would enable him to earn enough money to satisfy his desires. But the time will come—the time will come. . . . To the shame of the white man I must admit that everything which could be done is not being done, and here I can blame my own people as much as the Dutch, for apart from segregation—which has always been practised to some degree—you Africans are not much worse off under the Nationalist Government than you were in United Party days. But don't judge us all too harshly, Monare."

These words of the *Makulu Baas*—repeated to Ntoane and others—made the compound an even happier place to live in, for the Africans felt that their Baas really was one who wished them well and sympathised with them in their troubles.

2

Some time after Monare had renewed his contract, *Makulu Baas* arranged a big War Dance Competition in the compound at Msilikazi, at which all the Reef mines would be represented. On the great day Monare met a lot of men from the homeland, who were working at different mines on the Witwatersrand. Like Monare, who had forgotten his vows to the Moruti, many of them had fallen victim to the spell of the City of Gold, and had no desire to return home. At this function, Monare met again his old friend Koto.

" Koto ! "

" Monare ! "

" Koto, what are you doing now ? "

" The same as you, Monare. I am still looking for a lot of money."

" Yes, you are a businessman, but what is your business ? "

"Do you like my suit, Monare?"

"It is a very beautiful suit, which shows that you already have a lot of money. You look like a white man."

"I have many more like this in my suitcase and in my room. Would there be any chance of my selling such things in Msilikazi?"

"So you are a seller of trousers, heart's friend—there is the source of your prosperity?"

"Yes."

"What do you charge for a pair?"

"Three pounds ten shillings."

Monare thought of the Orlando Moruti's daughter, and what a figure he would cut in these fashionable trousers, and soon he was telling Koto all about her.

Koto now revealed that he had come to the war dance to ask Monare to join him in his business. First, only as a traveller to visit the mines on one side of the City of Gold, to sell to the mine-boys trousers which would be made by Koto, and by Monare, when he should learn the method—at home. Koto said that his trousers were becoming famous, and that he was hard put to it to fulfil all the orders he was getting.

The three Basotho talked late into the night, and eventually Monare agreed that as soon as his contract should expire, he would join Koto in his business.

Ntoane—not anxious to lose the companionship of Monare, to whom he had become greatly attached—advised his friend not to leave the compound, where at least he was safe from the attentions of the police; for he said, no sooner did an African start in business on his own, than trouble started to seek him out.

However, Monare was not to be dissuaded, and when his time ended, he said good-bye to *Makulu Baas*, telling him with shame in his heart the lie that he was returning to Lesotho. Ntoane he promised to visit sometimes on Sundays when *Makulu Baas* would normally be absent.

The quarters to which Koto took Monare in Sophiatown were quite luxurious, and Koto's manner of life was in keeping with his home. He disappeared for a short while, then returned flourishing a bottle.

"I hope I was not too long. To-night we drink white man's brandy."

Koto poured a small glass for Monare, then filling his own, spilled a few drops—with intent—on the floor.

"For the gods," he said.

"Why do you do that? We don't do that with kaffir beer."

"The old people of Lesotho used to do it. My grandfather told me about it. But drink up. Here's to the new partnership."

"*Ka Thesele!*" cried Monare, spluttering. "I certainly learn in this city."

3

The next morning Koto took Monare round to the wholesalers in Market Street.

"I am introducing you to these people," he said, "so that one day you may come by yourself."

The still-innocent Monare said:

"But what about *tsotsis*? Will they not rob me as they did before?"

"You have been robbed?"

Monare told Koto how he had been relieved of his blanket, and how Ntoane had lost his wages.

Koto laughed loudly and long.

"Fancy that old fox Ntoane being caught."

And he laughed again.

"Last year I was nearly robbed by *tsotsis*," said Koto. "One stopped me, and said, 'Your money or your life.' But I drew my revolver, and you should have seen him run."

"How did you know they were *tsotsis*?"

"I have been in Johannesburg a long time, and you get to know who's who and what's what."

"But what would have happened if you'd had to fire your revolver, and had killed the *tsotsi*?"

"Nothing . . . nothing. . . . They are nothing themselves—it's just like shooting a dog."

"Could I sometime get a gun?"

"I have another one. Would you like to carry it? But be careful, for if you are arrested, and the gun is found on you, you are taken to Number Four."

The following morning Koto fitted Monare with a suit. Monare went to the big mirror and tried it on and looked at himself. Koto was delighted with Monare's antics; he had a generous heart and liked to make others happy. Furthermore, he loved Monare more than a brother. He was unconsciously jealous of Ma-Libe and Libe and even of old Ntoane, for he did not know how far Monare's friendship with him had gone. He was delighted at finding Monare again, for he felt lonely, and looked forward to getting on the old footing of intimacy with him again.

Monare proved an apt pupil. His pleasing personality made him a good salesman, and in the evenings, under Koto's expert teaching, he soon became proficient at cutting and sewing and pressing. He wrote to Ma-Libe at times, and sent her most of his earnings, which were steadily increasing; but his activities in other directions would not have met with his Moruti's approval, for he had taken up drinking again—although not to excess—and he was getting a taste for the white man's drinks. These were not easy to get, and cost at least four times their retail price. Through this, Monare came into contact with another sort of white man—the illicit liquor-seller. These white men were mostly down on their luck, men who could find no work, and who went into the risky business of selling liquor to Africans in order to provide food and shelter for their families. Of course, amongst them, were men attracted by the large profits to be made, and such men could pay for police protection, whereas the smaller dealers were often arrested and fined.

In spite of his delight in his new clothes Monare did not visit Orlando, for he and Koto renewed the games of their youth to their mutual satisfaction.

When, one Sunday, Monare visited Msilikazi to see Ntoane, that worthy man did not at first recognise him. The flattered Monare had brought as a gift a pair of the trousers he had made and, when the trousers had been tried on and admired and the giver thanked, Ntoane asked:

"Do you write to Ma-Libe?"

Monare laughed.

"Yes, and she wants to leave Monontsa and come to live here."

Ntoane frowned.

"Don't be foolish, home-boy, and allow that. You know what is happening to the Basotho women who came from Lesotho to stay and live in the City of Gold. . . . Some of them have left their husbands for other men, who can—they say—make more money, and so on. . . . Look at those women at Newclare, Seteketekeng, and some of the other locations. This is the game played in Johannesburg—you go to work on the mine, you leave your wife in the location; when you come back at the week-end, you find she is gone with another man. There are a lot of men whose occupation it is to roam through the locations and mark down the houses of the men who have gone to work, and later rape their women and steal their goods. . . . No, Monare, you leave Ma-Libe at home, and continue to send her clothes, blankets and money to buy cattle."

This advice was so welcome to Monare's own inclinations, that he said nothing.

Monare was taken up entirely now with town life. He found that his good looks and pleasing manners made him many friends; at the week-ends he went to football matches and dances and parties. He thought but seldom of his little village of Lomontsa, of his wife Ma-Libe and his son Libe. He did not even think of his beautiful country, Lesotho, of the Great Chief Moshoeshoe, the king of the marvellous Theba-Bosin—Mountain of the Night—and of his race's proud history.

No, Monare's heart was stolen by the happiness he had found in the Golden City. Little did he know that one day a great trouble was to overtake him.

Before many months had passed, Monare entered into a full partnership with Koto, and their affairs prospered greatly. Had he listened to his heart-friend Koto's advice—that handsome Mosotho who was almost his other self—he would have avoided the period of terror which he had to endure. He should have bought only from the Indian merchants—but he knew better—poor Monare.

There was about the city at this time a gang of scalliwags and thieves, who would slit a man's throat as soon as offer him snuff! They did no work by day, but at night—in stolen cars would they visit the men's outfitting shops, and in a lightning raid, smash the windows and abscond with the materials and suits. Twice in one month did they break into and rob a shop which stood at the corner of Bree Street and Smal Street. These men were super-*tsotsis*, who concerned themselves with big things only. The innocent Monare met members of the gang at a party, and they realised at once that here was an ideal person to whom they could sell some of their stolen goods.

The night when the white man, Van, arrested him, was the night of the day on which the foolish Monare had purchased from these rogues, a fine suit-length at a most reasonable price.

Chapter Nine

THE TRIAL

IN THE MORNING Koto and the lawyer appeared at the gate of Number Four Fort with an order for the release of Monare on bail. Monare bade farewell to his cell-mate, giving him all the cigarettes and snuff that Koto had on his person.

The lawyer took Koto and Monare to his office, and Monare related to the lawyer the whole truth, including the story of his beating at Number Four.

The lawyer said at once:

"Quickly come to a doctor friend of mine; he will examine your scars and take you to the District Surgeon. Not only shall those two detectives find themselves inside Number Four, but we shall sue them for much gold and many cattle."

But Monare could not agree to the idea of taking down his trousers and exposing his scarred and livid thighs and bottom to the gaze of a stranger. Doubtless, before the tale was told, policemen, lawyers, magistrates and the public in a crowded court would also peer at his private parts. Nothing that the lawyer could say would make Monare change his mind. Although the lawyer was a kind and honest Jewish man, he scented further profit from the making of a case for damages. For this no one could blame him, for his charges to the unfortunate Monare were moderate enough.

Then Koto pointed out:

"In our business it would be foolish to incur the extra enmity of the white detectives. If not these two, then others of their friends would soon arrange for us to enter Number Four on some false yet serious charge, and I doubt in such circumstances whether we should come out alive."

So was it left.

Koto said:

"My home-boy, man has to go through all sorts of experiences in this world before he can call himself truly a man."

"Yes, Koto—and I cannot blame you for what has happened—it was all my own fault."

"Don't be like a woman, Monare. Here is something to cool you off."

And he took from his pocket a half-jack of white man's brandy.

2

The day of the trial came.

Evidence was given as to the ownership of the suit-length; thus was it proved that the cloth was stolen. The detective "Van" gave his story of the arrest of Monare with the stolen cloth in his possession.

Then was it the turn of Monare to be questioned.

When the Prosecutor had noted his name and birthplace, his lawyer started to examine him.

"You say you are a Mosotho. Where is your blanket?"

"Sir, I usually wear a blanket, but in honour of the worshipful magistrate here, to-day I wore a suit."

The magistrate smiled behind his hand at the ingenuous reply of Monare.

The lawyer went on:

"How did you get yourself into this mess?"

"I did not know, sir, that I had no right to buy from Africans."

"Where did you think that they obtained the goods, Monare?"

"Well, sir, I could not say. I know that many Africans keep shops at Orlando."

"You thought the goods came out of one of these shops?"

"Yes, sir."

The lawyer addressed the magistrate:

"Your Worship, this man since his arrival from Basutoland has

THE TRIAL

been working on the mines; he is not a Johannesburg African. Even the suit he is wearing is not really his own, it was lent him by a friend."

The magistrate appeared to agree.

"Yes, I can see that. He appears to be quite an honest man. Who was with you, Monare, when you bought the suit-length?"

"Your Worship, I was walking alone to the station, dressed in my blanket. The men asked me if I wanted to buy a suit-length cheap, and as I was soon going home to Lesotho, and wanted a present for the Chief, I bought it."

Well had Monare learned the lessons taught him by his cell-mate at Number Four.

"Did you not know that the cloth was stolen?"

"No, Your Honour. I didn't even think about it."

"Have you been in jail before?"

"*Eee!* My *Baas*! You see my home-boy Ntoane and I were once handcuffed together and left in a yard."

There was loud laughter in Court.

"Left in a yard?" said the magistrate. "Why?"

"You see, sir, two *tsotsis* pretended to be African detectives and arrested us and handcuffed us, and stole all we had, giving us receipts, and then left us!"

Those in Court again laughed loudly, then up stood a sergeant, and said:

"Your Worship, I remember them being brought into Marshall Square Charge Office."

Thus did the cunning Monare establish a reputation for himself as a simple countryman.

The lawyer said:

"You can see, Your Worship, that the man is ignorant of the whole issue and, on such grounds, although ignorance of the law is no excuse, I ask for Monare's discharge."

The magistrate nodded his head slowly.

"I think you are a deserving case. You are found Not Guilty." You may go."

Monare was the happiest man in the City of Gold. He said to

himself: "God of my wife, of the cattle of my father. God of my Moruti. God that I had forgotten. He sets me free from jail."

But as the freed Monare left the Court in company with Koto and the lawyer, the two white detectives who had questioned him with their *sjamboks* looked at him with hot, angry eyes, as if to fix his face in their memories.

3

Koto now suggested:

"Let us go to the Mayibuye Restaurant to eat. We shall get good food there, and we can celebrate your release. Come."

On the way the two Basotho encountered Monare's old home-boy, Ntoane, and they invited him to join them. Ntoane enjoyed the good food very much, and during the meal told them that he was no longer a police-boy, but a messenger; he carried *Makulu Baas's* messages all over the Reef. In the course of his travels he had met many home-boys, working on the different mines.

Koto remarked:

"I wonder when our people are going to leave the mines? All the time underground until one day the roof falls in and you die like a rat in a tunnel."

Monare did not tell Ntoane of his recent life in Number Four, for Koto and he had planned between them to ask Ntoane to leave Msilikazi and join their business, which was now too much for the two of them. After some discussion, Ntoane agreed that he would not renew his contract at Msilikazi, but would join Koto and Monare. He was partly influenced by the thick wad of notes which Koto took care should not escape his notice.

It was arranged that Ntoane would spend the evening at Koto's house in Sophiatown to arrange the final details, and learn something of the business of buying cloth and cutting out and selling.

Not long after Ntoane's departure from the house that night, Koto suggested a drink of the white man's brandy to celebrate what he thought of as a day worthy of praise, in that his dearest friend had been restored to him, and a new partner had been secured whose

THE TRIAL

wide knowledge of the Reef must have excellent results for the business.

While Koto was pouring the drinks, Monare got from under his mattress his revolver, which fortunately he had not been carrying when he was arrested.

Koto said:

"I begin to think it is a mistake to carry a gun; it is so easy for the police to stop and search an African. A policeman need give no reason at all for his actions."

Before taking his drink, Monare thought on what his friend had said. Then, handing the revolver to Koto, he stated his agreement:

"But where shall we keep them?"

"I shall hide them under the floor. I have often kept much gold under this loose plank on which my steel trunk lies, see."

And Koto removed his trunk and lifted the plank, and taking his own revolver, he placed the two guns in the hiding place. He then replaced the loose plank and moved back his trunk to cover it.

Most of Monare's money had been sent to Ma-Libe for the purchase of cattle; he was now quite a rich man, for an African. His arrest moved him to speak to Koto on the possibility of future trouble. And it was arranged that should any of the three of them be arrested again, the two still at liberty would pay out any monies required to be disbursed on behalf of the imprisoned one, would pay bail or fines, and provide sufficient funds for his defence.

The two Basotho now got down to the serious business of lowering the level of the brandy in the bottle. They grew somewhat heated and noisy in their friendly arguments, discussions, and recollections of the homeland, so that when there came a banging on the door, neither of them paid much attention, other than to direct a stream of abuse at the intruder—doubtless, it was one of the neighbours who was working a day-shift, and who wanted his sleep. Well, they had often been disturbed by the people next door, so what?

But the knocking and banging did not stop; rather did the attack on the door increase in strength, and soon the panels gave way, and the room was opened.

Standing in the door frame were the two detectives who had beaten up Monare.

Van spoke.

" I told you I'd catch you, you black bastard ! "

Turning to his companion, he growled :

" Collect that brandy bottle and the glasses."

Now should the two Basotho have thanked their roots that the revolvers had been safely hidden. Indeed, Koto was in the frame of mind to do so, for he knew that he would probably get off with a fine, maybe a big one, but still a fine—for he had no criminal record. And after all, money was plentiful.

Monare had no such knowledge, however. He thought that imprisonment was the inevitable result of arrest. He remembered, too, the two beatings he had had at the hands of Van. His rage suddenly boiled over, and he launched himself at the white man, and started to belabour him with his fists.

Fortunately for Koto, who was about to jump to his friend's assistance, the two detectives had not come alone. Immediately the room was full of policemen, and Monare was quickly handcuffed, but not before he had left his mark on Van's face. The police now secured Koto, and taking the two Basotho and the evidence they piled into the pick-up van and raced back to Marshall Square.

As Monare was thrown into a cell, Van put his head in, and said :

" You won't escape this time, you bloody bastard ! That's why I shan't beat you up to-night. But when you've been sentenced to-morrow, look out. I've relatives and friends in most of the jails."

In the morning the two Basotho were dealt with quickly and with justice.

They were taken before the magistrate, both charged with being in illegal possession of the white man's brandy, and Monare in addition, was charged with resisting arrest.

Koto was fined twenty-five pounds and released upon the payment of his fine later in the day, but Monare was—in addition to the imposition of a similar fine—sentenced to six months' hard labour.

That night Monare found himself temporarily back at Number Four. Strangely enough, his cell companion was the same

THE TRIAL

African, awaiting trial for murder, with whom he had been lodged before.

His cell-mate, who had been lying down daydreaming, sat up and grinned.

"Well, if it's not the Baruti's friend," he said. "You're certainly making up for lost time. What have you been doing this time? Pinching candles from the church?"

But this unknown African, in spite of his wicked humour, had a heart filled with sympathy, and during the hours of darkness he comforted Monare, and taught him much that it was necessary for him to know about life in a jail, for Monare was no longer awaiting trial—he was a convicted criminal.

Now, could Monare see that although he had been guilty of no disgraceful act, although he had received in this same Number Four a painful beating up when he was wrongfully accused, yet he was guilty of one thing, and that was that he had forsworn himself—he had broken his solemn oath to his Moruti Lefa.

That was why the Hand of God lay heavily on him.

Chapter Ten

RETRIBUTION

MONARE'S LOT WAS NOT HAPPY; in spite of what his cell-mate had said about free food, free clothes, and no worry, imprisonment was a heartbreaking thing to any freedom-loving Mosotho. Perhaps in the cases of the unemployed and the starving, could such arguments be put forward, but he was a man of wealth, and a proud one.

He was soon made to realise that there were few crimes more vicious in the eyes of the white men, than that of striking one of their fellows. Many tales had been told Monare about the treatment he might receive in jail; particularly did he dread the Water Torture, of which he had heard talk in the streets. It was said that in a police station in a small town near the City of Sugar, a white man had forced into the mouth of a black man prisoner the nozzle of a hose-pipe, and had then turned the tap on to its fullest pressure.

Monare thought:

"This must be torture indeed. If that African did not die from his pain and terror, he must doubtless have suffered agonies since, for the God of all Baruti did not intend us to live like fishes."

But Monare's roots were potent, and no such horror was he called upon to endure. Some of his cell-mate's advice came to Monare's mind, and he determined that no matter what violence were done to him, he would not retaliate in word or deed, or even look. He desired most ardently to earn what remission of his sentence he could, for good behaviour.

This ambition was a difficult one for Monare to bring successfully to fruition, for he was a marked man in the jail to which he was transferred. Some of the warders openly mocked him and provoked

RETRIBUTION

him, in the hopes that some gesture of revolt would give them the chance to strike him. . . . Of striking there was plenty in that jail. Some of the warders secreted *sjamboks* on their persons when prisoners were taken outside the jail to work, and with these they beat the defenceless prisoners for little or no reason. They were always careful to ask first:

"Will you accept my punishment with the *sjambok*, or shall I have you taken before the head jailer?"

What reply could poor uneducated Africans make to such a question? If taken before the head jailer, their state would be far worse, for he would be bound to accept the word of his warders, and would impose not only strokes from the *sjambok*, but bread-and-water, and solitary confinement.

Yet in this jail did Monare discover that there were white men of good heart. Such men, when they had made certain that Monare intended his behaviour to be of the best, would guard him—when they could—from the vicious teasing of their fellows. Some said to him:

"You're not such a bad kaffir!"

And others advised him thus:

"When you get out—remember, to hit a white man is the African's blackest crime."

Monare was adequately clothed and fed, and the exercise and the impossibility of obtaining beer or other strong liquors, caused his health to improve considerably. Snuff and cigarettes were smuggled into the jail; some of the more vicious type of warder taking an active and profitable part in this trade.

Monare's eyes were opened to much that was wicked and sordid, for there were all sorts of men in the prison. Monare had heard of, and indeed, to some extent known that friendship of men which is born of a great love, much as marriage springs from a great love of woman, but what he saw here filled him with disgust and with dismay. Older vicious prisoners took the younger, innocent ones to their own uses, and here there was no thought of affection or love—bestial lust dictated their actions. Such men, he felt, could not blame prison for their depravity, for they would obviously behave with the same wickedness outside its walls.

But even such a time of anguish must end, and the day came when Monare found himself a free man.

2

Monare's first thought was for his heart's friend Koto, but when he arrived at the Sophiatown house he found Koto gone. Ntoane was overjoyed to see him, and said that Koto had gone back to Lesotho for a spell, and that he, Ntoane, had been looking after the business. According to results, the trouser business had flourished, and there was plenty of money available for Monare's use.

For a few weeks Monare once more sold his trousers around the Reef compounds, and at night, sat with Ntoane and sewed and pressed.

But he was restless; he could not forget his vile experiences in jail. He thought of his home and the wife and child he had not seen for so long. He thought of the Moruti Lefa, and the oath he had made.

During this time, Monare touched not the liquor of the white man, and even took but sparingly of the home-brewed kaffir beer which Ntoane provided.

One Sunday, saying nothing to Ntoane, he felt impelled to visit the Orlando Moruti, and place his troubled thoughts before him.

He was received in friendliness and with warmth by the Moruti, who called out:

"Come, Mary and Mother, and see who is here!"

When greetings had been exchanged, and the women had retired to make tea, Monare recounted to the Moruti such of his adventures as he deemed fit for him to hear. That is to say, he spoke only of his earlier arrest, and said nothing about his brandy drinking.

"Why should these white men hate me so much?" he asked. "In my heart I know that they were aware of my innocence."

The Moruti frowned.

"These men are paid but little by the Government. Many of them have large families. In my youth I can remember the policemen on horses. *Ka Thesele!* But those were men."

Monare wondered.

RETRITBUTION

"Is not the position of policeman one of great honour? Is he not a protector of the poor and weak, and an enemy of the wicked?"

"So should it be, man of the Chief! And so it was in years gone by. Still are most of the white policemen men of truth, and guardians of the weak."

"But what of these others, Father Moruti?"

Said the Moruti:

"The white man's government has made too many laws—laws for taxing the African; laws forbidding him to do this or that."

"But these detectives——"

"Patience, Monare, I come to the kernel after shelling the nut. Because of these laws, much of the policeman's time is taken up with asking for passes and tax receipts, and in looking for drums of kaffir beer."

They were silent a while; then Moruti continued:

"These men who ill treated you would doubtless have done the same even had they not been of the police—provided they wanted something that you were not willing to give."

Even the puzzled Monare could see the truth of this, but . . .

"How then, my Father, do such men join the ranks of the police?"

"I told you, Monare, that the pay is poor; therefore, poor men of two kinds become policemen."

"Such as?"

"Those who are just and upright, and who by study, and through the long years, hope to rise to serve near the Chiefs."

"And the other kind?"

"Those the white man calls 'poor whites'; used only to the land—land they possess no longer. Brain they have, but not much more than the beasts of the field. Strength often they own, and with it a desire to use it to hurt others."

Monare nodded his head.

"Of this tribe were the two detectives."

Monare wrestled further with his thoughts.

"Why does the Great King beyond the water not put an end to this cruelty?"

"If he knew, Monare, doubtless he would. Even the white man magistrate who judged you would put those two white detectives behind the bars at Number Four—without delay and without remorse—if he could be shown what they had done to you."

Monare thirsted for knowledge.

"Tell me more about these poor whites, Moruti."

"I think there are many in this country who desire to be *Makulu Baases*, and only few who wish to serve."

"And these poor whites?"

"Are not able enough to be masters, nor willing to be servants. If left alone, they would sink back to mingle with the Africans from whom some of them sprang. The white man's government has too much pride to allow this—they think that white men of other lands will laugh to see their white-skinned tribesmen mixing with people with black skins."

"How then, do they prevent this, Moruti?"

"The government allows these people to do such work as does not require too much thought—making roads and railways, helping to load and unload railway trucks and ships. They let them work in the prisons, and some, as you know, work in the police."

"But if they are so poor, why have they no sympathy with us?"

"Do you not remember the tale of the tortoise who, by accident, rode for a while on the elephant's back, and none dared ever again to call him tortoise? Give such people a little power, and they are harsh and rough."

Now tea was served, and for a while the women were included in the talk, which was general. But when Mary and her mother had again withdrawn to the kitchen, the Moruti continued:

"The *pitso* of the white man has a difficult task. In order to support these useless servants, many extra taxes must be gathered."

Monare suggested:

"To collect the taxes, more policemen are required."

The Moruti nodded and smiled.

"More policemen, still more taxes required with which to pay them."

RETRIBUTION

Monare laughed.

"No, stop, Moruti, please. I am no college boy."

The Moruti chuckled, then said:

"These men that made the *sjambok* talk to you—they have not the cleverness nor cunning to catch a real criminal. Therefore, whosoever falls into their hands on suspicion they must try to turn into a criminal in truth. For by convictions only shall their promotion come."

"And if no prisoners are sentenced?"

Moruti laughed.

"Then there are those who will rise in the *pitso* of the white man, and say: 'Why must we pay so many policemen if there is no crime?' And then many heads will fall."

Now it was Monare's turn to laugh, but the Moruti said warningly:

"But, Monare, remember—it has been asked, why should dogs sniff one another, unless it be that they are all of different smells? And so with the white man. Let not your bitter experience put you against the whole tribe, for amongst them are many who are both good and kind."

And in such manner did Monare learn from the Moruti the reasons for the many acts of cruelty and injustice which daily occurred in the City of Gold.

In another direction he was not so successful. In spite of his reformation, Monare could not subdue the strong instincts of his race, and whenever Mary entered the room, his eyes strove to pierce her clothes to that forbidden territory which lay beneath. He felt the rising of the old desire for her.

But late that evening, the conversation took a different turn, for the Moruti asked:

"Where is that letter you showed me that day at Park Station?"

Monare had to admit in a shamefaced way that he had lost it.

"And which churches have you been attending in Johannesburg?"

"I have been too busy with my work to attend church, Moruti."

"You have changed a lot, Monare."

"It must be Johannesburg, Moruti."

"That may be, but remember, the city changes men for ill, as well as for good."

"Yes, Moruti."

"Have you got a wife?"

"Me, Moruti?"

"Yes, you, my friend."

Monare hesitated, then said:

"The Basotho are born polygamists, Moruti."

"Do you mean to tell me that you are one?"

"Not me, Moruti. But my grandfather was."

"Don't forget, Monare, we are Christians."

"Yes, but I must do what my grandfather did. What was good for him must be good for me."

"Be that as it may. But you have not yet answered my question."

"What question, Moruti?"

"Are you married?"

"Yes, Moruti."

"How many wives?"

"Only one, Moruti."

"If what your grandfather did was good—why only one?"

"I am still going on, Moruti."

"Do you realise that with more than one wife you will be refused Church membership?"

"Yes, Moruti."

"I think it better that you do not visit my home again until you have made up your mind about polygamy. I do not wish my only daughter's mind clouded by un-Christian-like thoughts. God be with you until we meet again—and may you see the Light!"

Monare's heart was very sore, for he felt he would not get the chance to see the Moruti's beautiful daughter again, but he answered, cheerfully enough:

"Remain in peace, Moruti!"

3

Suddenly Monare decided to go home to Lesotho. It was not only that he was bereft of the friendship of Koto, and denied the companionship of Mary, it was a real strong desire to see what was happening in the homeland.

He told Ntoane of his decision, and asked him to look after the business until he or Koto returned, and to send to him at Lomontsa, his due share of the profits. Now Monare went into the streets of the city to visit the finest shops to buy gifts for his wife, Ma-Libe, his son Libe, and his chief—gifts of a quality that his position as a man of wealth demanded.

It was on Sunday evening that Monare left Park Station. He was now a well-known man, both as a " praiser " and as a merchant, and there were many friends to see him off. Ntoane was there with parting presents of fruit and sweets, and a few parcels which he wished delivered in Lesotho.

At length farewells were done, and the train drew out of the station.

Monare's thoughts wandered over the years of his life in the City of Gold. If there is a Time for Remembering, there is also a Time for Action. To live in the Past, is not to live in the Present, and he who is dead in the Present might as well be buried. If the Stew is too salty, the salt cannot be removed, and all one's tears are not sufficient to lessen the tang. Either must the Pot be emptied, and a new mess prepared, or must fresh meat and broth and herbs be added to the Stew, until the taste which offended is forgotten as the lips water anew. Thus mused Monare the Mosotho as he sped towards Lesotho in the Kaffir Mail. This part of his life was ended—well, bury it.

Phase Two

FULL MOON

"It were better to have lived in Lesotho a hundred years ago, or to live a hundred years hence, than to live in these in-between times. . . ."

THE MORUTI LEFA OF LOMONTSA

"God I fear plenty! . . . Look what is happening with the Children of Moshoeshoe!"

AN OLD WOMAN OF SOPHIATOWN

Chapter One

MOUNTAIN SCHOOL

Monare the Mosotho arrived in his native village of Lomontsa during the hours of darkness, for the Basotho people are a superstitious race, and Monare did not want anyone to set eyes on him before he entered his house.

The Basotho people use the services of a witch doctor to an extent even greater than that to which a white man calls in a doctor; for they believe that the witch doctor holds power over the forces of Nature, and that when anybody is struck by a thunderbolt, or burned by the lightning, such injury is caused by bewitchment.

Through bewitchment brought about by a witch doctor, women can be rendered barren, girls can fail to find husbands, men can be made to fail in their manhood, and crops can fail to grow or be destroyed.

For winter protection, the Basotho cut their flesh with a blade and rub into the wound a magic black powder supplied by the witch doctor, mixed with the fat of a black sheep, specially slaughtered for the purpose.

This cutting of the flesh and the rubbing-in of magic powder can be likened to the pricks that the white doctors give in the arms of the healthy to protect them against the throat sicknesses, or the pox. What the white man calls " acts of God," the Mosotho knows to be bewitchment.

Monare was thinking back many years to a morning when he was going into the stable, and found a short sheep-horn stuffed with black medicine, half-buried at the door. When he took this horn to his medicine man, he was warned that he was being bewitched, and that if he were not very careful, his life would be loosed from him.

It was therefore to avoid the gaze of any possible enemies, that Monare arrived home at cockcrow.

He received a warm welcome from his wife Florinah, who cried, when she opened the door:

"Oh my husband! The Father of Libe! You have come! I am so happy! . . . Libe! . . . Libe! . . . wake up! Your father is here. Will you have some home-brewed beer, or will you eat first? I am so happy!"

After eating and resting, Monare's first duty was to greet his Chief; custom prohibited him from speaking to any of his fellow-villagers until he had performed this act of courtesy.

When he found the Chief in the *khotla*, Monare raised his hat, and said:

"*Helele!* The son of *Thesele!* Cattle the son of Moshoeshoe! We are yours, the son of *Thesele!* May the Chief live long for us."

The Chief shook Monare warmly by the hand and greeted him thus:

"I am more than happy to see you back home, Monare. You left a gap in tribal affairs which I have never been able to fill. You look quite healthy, and I hear you have prospered."

"Yes, my Chief, I have, but I am glad to be back, and at your service."

It is the tradition and custom of the Basotho people that even the educated man must wear the blanket in the early morning, and the Chief showed his good manners by conforming to this convention.

It is also a custom for Basotho returning to the kraal, to bring their Chief a present from the outer world—therefore, did Monare say, on withdrawing:

"My Chief, I ask permission to bring an offering later in the day."

2

Monare's son Libe was now approaching manhood, and it was time for him to attend the mountain school of circumcision, for which a new class was now assembling from all parts of the district. Monare ordered Libe to go on this six months' training for manhood, but by so doing antagonised not only his wife, but the Moruti Lefa.

The Moruti called on Monare.

"Those who met, meet again. Is it not a great pleasure that we meet alive?"

"You are right, Moruti. It is the wish of the Almighty who rides the clouds above us. The lands do not look bad this year—it seems a year of plenty."

"Yes, Monare, you are quite right, it is not the year of starvation. This year we shall not have to go out and buy mealies from the white men in the Free State. God is great and bountiful."

But the coming of other visitors to Monare's house prevented the Moruti from making his attack on the circumcision rites. The majority of the people of Lomontsa were Christians, and did not allow their sons to be circumcised; but Monare was one who believed in the old customs. Although he intended to have his fine son Libe educated, he thought it best for him first to undergo the rites of circumcision.

An important saying with Monare was:

"If a man does away with his traditional way of living, and throws away his good customs, he had better first make certain that he has something of value to replace them."

He did not consider the six months which Libe must spend at the Mountain School a waste of time; he could catch up with his studies on his return. Of course, the boys returned from their initiation puffed up with self-importance—but this soon wore off. After all, the time had to come for every boy to accept responsibility and become a man.

At last one day the Moruti found Monare alone.

"Peace, Monare!"

PHASE TWO—FULL MOON

" Peace, Moruti ! "

" You know that—as a Christian—your son should not be circumcised ? "

" I know, but I hold to the old customs. My father was circumcised, my grandfather was circumcised, and I am circumcised."

" Christians should not be circumcised."

" Tell me why not, O Moruti Lefa."

" Monare, think back on your own circumcisional rites."

" Father, I was taught to be strong, to fight, to work, to be a man."

" What else were you taught, Monare ? "

" What else, Moruti ? "

" Do not blush the blush of shame—it is your Moruti you are speaking to. I repeat, Monare, what else were you taught ? "

" I was taught how to take a woman, Moruti."

" Nature and love, Monare, should teach Christians such things. It should not be for the hand of man to caress the manhood of another to make it flower. That is why Christians should not attend the Mountain School."

" But my father, and my grandfather——"

" And your son Libe—what of him ? Does not the thought of a stranger's hands wandering over your son's slim body cause you shame ? "

" But, Moruti, they are the hands of the lawfully-appointed Teacher."

" Teacher or not, Monare, he is but human like yourself, and has the same weaknesses. This is a great sin for a Christian."

Monare's thoughts were troubled ; he recalled his own months at the circumcisional school ; he felt again the first touch of another's hands on him. He said to himself :

" But this had no lasting effect on me. I have proved myself a man, I am a husband and a father. . . . Yes, I have given way to mad desires when I was young, and later in the City of Gold. But what was the harm ? Better that surely than the greedy, perhaps unclean and sick body of the prostitute ? . . . My Libe is surely the same—a man, strong, well built, male. It can soon be put to the proof when he returns, by getting him to talk on marriage."

Thus thought Monare on the things that trouble all men—some more, some less.

Monare worried a little over his decision, but did not alter it, and Libe went to the Mountain School. Monare felt that it was too late to scoop up spilled porridge. He went to his cattle kraals and looked with interest at his cows and other stock, saying to himself:

"If I married another wife, all these beautiful cattle of mine would be finished, and then what? If my son wants to get married, I can afford *Bohali*—the dowry—I think I have done a good thing."

Monare felt that he had been both wrong and foolish to stay away from Lesotho for so long. He was rich, and could afford to come home frequently, and thus—as he thought, and as many others have done before him—enjoy the best of two worlds.

3

Libe came back from Circumcision, and a great feast was arranged for all those who had passed through the school. Cattle were slaughtered, and plenty of beer was brewed. When the boys appeared in the *khotla*, they wore red blankets heavily smeared with red clay. Each boy was called upon to recite a " praise "; and before he recited, had to give out to those assembled, his new circumcisional name. Libe's new name was Leaba.

Libe's recitation was eagerly awaited, for he came of a family renowned for its " praising." It was received with acclamation, and his proud father publicly announced that Libe could now get married, and that he would personally see to it that he married the daughter of a hero.

The newly circumcised boys are now regarded as men—they are free to walk about and make love to the girls if they should so desire, or to marry. Out on the veld with the cattle, they teach circumcisional songs to the young herd-boys, thus preparing them for their initiation; these songs are secret, and may not be repeated at home, for they deal with sexual matters.

During the days following the feasting, Libe rose early in the morning and led the cattle from the kraal for their early-morning grazing; by tradition, this act signified to his father that Libe now wanted to get married.

When Monare observed what his son was doing he was overjoyed, and called to his wife:

"Ma-Libe! Ma-Libe!"

"The Father-of-Libe!"

"Appear here!"

When Florinah came running from the house, Monare said:

"I want you to see the cattle."

"Cattle?"

Florinah looked puzzled.

"Libe has taken them away to graze. Has he not perhaps whispered to you something about which girl he wants to wed?"

"No, Father-of-Libe—he has always been a quiet child."

When Libe returned, Monare asked:

"Tell me, Libe my son, have you yet had a girl? Or is there one you wish to wed?"

Libe trembled and said falteringly:

"My Father, I have not yet had a girl, nor met one I desire."

"We are willing for you to marry—when you have decided, let us know the name of the parents."

"I thank you, my Father. May I take a horse and go to the feast at Molumong?"

Monare gave his consent, and on the appointed day quite a crowd of young men set off on horseback for the feast.

4

The Great Feast of Molumong was given in honour of the young women who had also just finished their circumcisional rites. The girls do not go into the mountains like the boys; their school is held in a secluded house in the village itself. *Lebello*—circumcision—is one of the most important of Basotho tribal customs. Girls from the age of twelve upwards are circumcised, also women who, for some reason, were not circumcised as children. The Basotho mock at uncircumcised girls over the age of twelve—they are said to have grown a "tail," which "surrounds the mountain." Such women would not be favoured as wives by orthodox Basotho.

The *Mophato* or circumcisional school, is run by the old women of the tribe, part of whose work it is to protect the school by supernatural means under the supervision of a *ngaka*, or witch doctor. It is believed that anyone attempting to overlook the rites or learn the secrets of the school, will be struck dead by enchantment.

The first night of the school is known as the *Marallo*, the secret night. This night is spent outside the village in the *dongas*, where ritual dances are taught, and new code-names are given to the girls—so that they can afterwards challenge the claim of any woman who states that she is circumcised.

At *Marallo*, too, the *Khokhobisa-tsoene*, or "Hiding-of-the-monkey" is encompassed. The girls are cut with a blade in their outer sexual organs, and a flap of flesh is drawn down to cover that mischievous "monkey" which can be the source of much pleasure to uncircumcised girls. The performance of this rite tends to encourage chastity among the women, for a circumcised girl can know little of the joys and passions of physical love. During this ceremony when the blood flows from the wounded flesh, black magic medicine is rubbed in as a protection against bewitchment.

It can perhaps be said that the circumcision of women not only denies the girl great pleasure and joy in the sexual act, but must in consequence lessen the happiness and exaltation of the man, and thus shut out any upliftment of the spirit—lying with a woman then, becomes a selfish, rather than a mutual pleasure. Here in the very homeland, in this circumcision of women, lie the seeds of the physical love of man for man, which is brought to flower by the living conditions imposed on African mine workers by the white man.

In Lesotho, uncircumcised men are also mocked with cries of *Mohatla!*—"Tail!"

The course ends with a parade of the naked graduates in front of the villagers, and a young man wishing to become engaged, places a string of polished beads around the neck of his chosen girl.

PHASE TWO—FULL MOON

Then comes the Feast, for which each girl's father gives a beast for slaughter.

Libe and his friends rode over the hills to the Great Feast of Momulong. They arrived soon after the naked women started their dance across the kraal. Libe went close, to pick out a beautiful girl for his bride.

Libe's friends knew of his intentions, so they betrayed no surprise at his actions. At last Libe shouted:

"This is the girl I choose." And he placed the ceremonial beads around the neck of a lovely *setsoejane*.

Later a woman accosted Libe:

"Are you the young man who has engaged himself to Makopoi?"

Libe found it difficult to answer this direct question, but at last managed to stammer out his answer and his father's name.

The woman said:

"If you are the son of Monare of Lomontsa, I know your father and mother well. They are very good people and I judge you by them."

Libe was shy in discussing these matters with the old woman, until he discovered that she was Makopoi's grandmother. It was only when he got home that he found out that he had engaged himself to a member of the royal family.

Said his mother:

"Libe, my son, what are you doing with a Chief's daughter?"

"Mother, I did not know—is my father going to be angry?"

"Child, I do not think so—but he will have to pay at least thirty cattle for a Chief's daughter."

Monare, however, offered no objections; he agreed with his son's choice of Makopoi, daughter of a Chief. He was worried lest she should be unable to do the work of the house, but Ma-Libe reassured him on this point, as she was a friend of the mother of Makopoi. According to Basotho custom, Monare got up early the next morning, took his stick and, in accordance with tribal convention, advised his own Chief of Libe's engagement. A cow also had to be sent to the other Chief, Makopoi's father, to seal the agreement.

MOUNTAIN SCHOOL

5

Libe now decided to go to work on the mines, to earn money to buy clothes and blankets and ornaments for his future bride. Although Monare was a rich man, he did not seek to dissuade Libe from his purpose, for he knew that a young man must learn to be independent.

He did, however, give his son certain advice.

"Libe, my son, I am your father. I am not trying to restrain you from the pleasures of youth; you are a young man and the blood runs strongly within you. You must remember that you are engaged to a Chief's daughter. Now, I have been in Johannesburg for many years, and I want you to beware of going to locations; there you will find not only the *tsotsis*, the wicked rascals, but you will find bad women who will cast lustful and covetous eyes on the freshness of your youth. Do not be tempted, for many of these women have the sickness which can destroy your manhood, and prevent you from fathering a child. As you know, it is the dearest wish of your mother and myself that Makopoi should be blessed with a child of your loins. Beware, too my son, of the lustful approaches of older men, which may seem to you but as the fondlings of an elder brother. For the white man has condemned those Africans who go to dwell in the City of Gold, to live in a world without women. I would say that there is not one African woman to a thousand African men and, of these, few are clean and wholesome. In such conditions, strange sins are born, and many men who would otherwise know them not, practise them. No doubt, at times, desire will torment your body. Rather the friendship of the hand than the dangers I have warned you against. If you desire to leave the compound, go to football matches. When you have made friends, you will be able to drink home-made kaffir beer, but beware of the drinks sold in the locations—that way lies madness. The time of idleness in the Golden City is bad for the Basotho. The white men have their drinking and their bioscopes and their motor cars, but for the Basotho there is no amusement such as they are used to here at home. Even the drink they cannot partake of, except in holes and corners, for fear of arrest by the police. And that is why the Basotho drink so much on Sundays. Stolen pleasures are ever dearest to the heart of man. If the Basotho were allowed to brew their beer openly, the number of prisoners on Monday mornings in Number Four Fort would grow less and less. I will give you the address of my great friends, Ntoane and Koto."

Thus Monare to his son Libe.

Monare did not intend to return to the City of Gold at present. He possessed many cattle, and sheep which he could shear at the end of the year, and sell the wool which would bring him in plenty of money. The cattle he owned were now beyond eighty, and his wife had also bought several span of oxen. He could make good use of his lands, and even plough in shares for the people who possessed no oxen.

A lot of things he could do as the Chief's keyman. And now—since his son's engagement to Makopoi—he was looked upon as the Chief's relative, for his Chief was cousin to Makopoi's father.

Monare asked his wife Florinah to take a blade and make a few cuts on Libe's body, and apply the horn medicine which would bring him luck at work, and keep him safe from bewitchment.

Chapter Two

RITUAL MURDER

LIBE WAS FORTUNATE enough to obtain a good job on the mines on the Reef. Through the recommendations of Monare's friend Ntoane, he was able to get work at Nourse Mines, and before long became a *baas-boy* underground.

Monare was well pleased with his son's progress, and directed his wife Florinah to let Libe know that the wedding had been arranged for June, and that he was about to send to the Chief, Makopoi's father, the *bohali* arranged, namely, thirty head of cattle, ten goats, and a horse.

In spite of his wealth, Monare was an illiterate man.

Monare was now about to face the most tragic and worrying time of his whole life. One cool day the Chief summoned the headmen and notables of the tribe together for *Pitso* in the *khotla*. The previous night it had rained in torrents, and the streams were flooded, and the rivers outran their banks. This delayed the opening of the meeting, and men could be seen riding their horses up and down the muddy banks of the *vlei*, trying to choose the safest place to cross.

A man was heard shouting:

" All men to the Chief at *khotla* ! "

Women carrying water-pots were shaken by the echoes of this shout; some even put down their pots and wondered what had happened. The whole village was in a state of unrest, because the summoning of the immediate *pitso* was not whispered among the men, as it usually was, but was shouted from the roof tops. Even those close to the Chief, knew nothing of the purpose of this meeting.

When the *khotla* was filled with the men entitled to be present, the Chief opened the *pitso* by telling those assembled that his eldest son was to be given some land to establish a new village. It was the custom that the eldest son of the family should be allotted a specially selected site for the forming of a new community. Some few men would go with him to act as a council. He would be given about fifty oxen, about forty milking cows, and a hundred goats and sheep to slaughter. Many young men got ready to follow the new Chief, Addis Ababa—New Leaf—to the new village. Then prominent members of the tribe were asked to remain behind in the *khotla* after the *pitso* had closed, as the Chief had something to say to them.

At the appropriate time the Chief's *Letona* arose, and said:

" You know that a new village is to be established. It is an important thing, this sending out of a Chief's son. You elders of the tribe should know just how important. According to our ancient custom, the witch doctors have decided that a medicine horn must be prepared to ward off bewitchment, and ensure prosperity and success to the new community. This medicine horn will require as one of its magic ingredients the blood and flesh of a man of the Bafokeng clan."

Thus spoke the *Letona* of the Chief.

The gathering was dead quiet for a time, for nobody dared to say a word until it was demanded of them by the *Letona*. Their hearts turned sad within them, and their eyes filled with tears. They bowed their heads, and here and there could a man be seen scratching the earth with his toe, or with a stick, or stroking his bald head. To many of them this Ritual Murder spoken of was not a new thing, but it was, none the less, a terrifying prospect. To the younger men it was something outside their understanding. They could not credit that such orders should come from the mouth of their respected, educated Chief.

The *Letona* spoke again:

" It was said by the Chief that this should be regarded as a matter of great importance, and should be treated very confidentially. If

RITUAL MURDER

any one of you should be the cause of leakage in this matter, rest assured that such a man shall be severely punished."

Now, men were to be seen rising from their seats, walking about aimlessly and sitting down again. Pipes were lit, teeth were dug into blankets, snuff was partaken of and tobacco chewed. But they were given no chance to get back to their homes to think matters over. Like soldiers they had received their orders, and their part was to obey. Amongst those assembled in the *khotla* were two members of the Bafokeng clan; one of these rose in his place, and said:

"It has thundered."

The *Letona* only replied:

"The Chief wishes to see you again in a few days."

A brief respite was gained, but at the next meeting of the *pitso*, it was decided that the victim should be chosen from an outside district. Although this decision eased some of the sore hearts, it did not remove the feeling of cruel guilt from the hearts of those members of the *pitso* who were ordered to perform this inhuman act. Such men would fight willingly enough armed with spear, assegai, stick, stone, or gun, provided that the men they fought against were equally well armed, but to draw innocent blood . . .

Who was to blame? This they discussed among themselves as they rode home along the *vleis*, *krantzes*, and *kloofs*.

Who was to blame? In spite of the number of Christians in Lesotho, the influence of the dreaded witch doctors stood behind the word of the chiefs. Such an order could not be disobeyed, save at the risk of the wrath of the *ngaka* being directed against the disobedient one. Therefore, must this cruel order to mutilate and murder an innocent man be put into effect.

2

Monare was put in charge of the hunting party.

This was not woman's business and could not be discussed with Florinah; if it were not woman's business, still less was it the concern of the Church, and the Moruti's advice could therefore not be obtained.

Monare's own instincts were against participation in this crime, but his superstitious fear of the witch doctors silenced his protests. That refusal to obey would jeopardise his position with his Chief did not weigh so heavily with Monare, as the fact that such rebellion would bring down on his family the vengeance of the witch doctors.

Therefore, he collected his men and set out for the west.

The *impi* was given ample funds for the purchase of kaffir beer, so that wherever they might find people drinking, they might—from chance words spoken in liquor—find traces of a suitable man from the designated clan.

The second evening they met a woman carrying water from a well; they asked her where they could buy some beer. The woman pointed out a hut in the nearby village, and went with them to this house, hoping that there might be some drink left over from yesterday's brewing.

Here Monare bought drinks for himself and his men. He warned his *impi* to be careful, but to engage the villagers in conversation, so that they should find out whether or not a member of the Bafokeng clan were present.

After some hours of drinking, darkness fell. Monare was thinking of sleeping in the village, when one of his men came to him, and whispered:

"That drunken man over there—he is of the Bafokeng clan, and—see, he is now leaving for his home."

"Let us follow him," said Monare, and one by one he ordered his followers to leave the hut very quietly. The *impi* caught up with the chosen victim on the banks of a stream not far from the village. There he sat in a drunken daze on the grassy bank, unsuspecting of the dreadful fate which stalked him.

Chapter Three

THE VICTIM

HORROR INDEED WALKED through the darkness of Lesotho that night, and none was to escape the searing touch of its garment.

The drunken member of the Bafokeng clan thought—in his innocence—that he was free and happy and homeward-bound—for rarely does Death give warning of its approach; like the *tsotsis*, it advances with stealth. The night was the night of the full moon, yet was the air heavy with darkness, for the moon was hidden behind the clouds.

The *impi* dismounted and left its horses in the care of one of the men. Monare advanced towards the recumbent figure, and said:

"How far are you going, man of the Chief?"

"I am to Kolo."

Monare felt as if a witch doctor had struck him down with a bolt of lightning, for the voice was the voice of Koto.

This was the moment of Destiny, towards which Monare's life had been marching. As it is said a drowning man's past life flashes before his eyes, so now in the mind of Monare, instincts waged rapid war, scenes, visions, memories of Chiefs and Baruti jostled each other confusedly in his thoughts.

This instant in Time, shorter than the momentary hovering in the flight of a dragon-fly, was fraught with grave consequence; and with its passing, free choice was lost to the will of Monare, and the labouring seconds carried him on to a point of no return.

What happened can be told.

Had Monare's roots at this hour been stronger, doubtless would his wits have counselled him to withdraw quickly with his men, whilst their wills were still subservient to his. Certainly would he have remounted his *impi* and ridden far in the opposite direction without giving them an opportunity to disobey and ask questions. Such chance could have come later.

The consequences of such high-handed action might have been —even—fatal for Monare, but the whole course of his life would have run in a different channel.

In the event, Monare stood there long enough—dazed by the terrible choice confronting him—to give time for his followers to gather around, their blood-lust mounting in their veins.

Yet, when it was too late, Monare did his poor best.

He made an impassioned appeal to his men:

" Men, this man must we leave unharmed. He is my heart's friend, my blood-brother, my benefactor. In the City of Gold did he save me from the jail. All my present prosperity do I owe to this man, Koto ! "

In the meantime the slowly-sobering ears of Koto recognised the tones of Monare's voice, and called his name.

Now spoke the voice of one, Phafa :

" The Chief's orders must be carried out."

Monare cried in a desperate voice :

" Plenty other victims can we find in other places at another time."

Again Phafa was the spokesman.

" But this man is a suitable sacrifice. We cannot now speak as men with hearts and feelings. We can only speak with the voice of the Chief. Are we not, in this matter, his slaves ? . . . Come, let us put an end to it. The man is drunk, and will know nothing. Where shall we find another such victim—not sickly, not skinny ? And here, too, are no witnesses."

There was for a moment dead silence, even the night scurryings of the animals, and the shu-shu of the wind seemed to wait, poised.

Again Phafa spoke, for the third time :

" Monare, if you disobey the Chief's orders, you yourself will be killed."

Such indeed were the thoughts, which—flashing through

THE VICTIM

Monare's mind—had robbed him of his initiative. Dread of losing his new-found intimacy with the Chief, fear for the consequences to his family of disobedience, stark, primitive terror of the vengeance of the witch doctors. Blame not Monare too much. Can he be scorned for thinking first of those dependent on him? Yet should his instinct have been—as he was to realise with dreadful pain thereafter—to do the right which lay closest to his hand, and leave the consequences to the God who watched from the night sky.

Yet was there more to this crisis than even Monare knew—the man called Phafa—(accursed be his name!)—was jealous of Monare's influence with the Chief, and with unexpected insight, of a sudden knew quite clearly that his suit would prosper only if Koto were killed.

Can the feelings of the innocent Koto be imagined? There he lay, his senses returning to him with every gasping breath, listening to the loved and remembered voice of his heart's friend pleading against his murder.

Now Phafa, seizing the opportune moment, and relying on the blood-lust of the *impi* for support, struck Koto the first vile blow.

Good men of warm heart were there amongst that *impi*, but their judgment was clouded by the fumes of liquor, and their humanity oppressed by superstitious fears.

With warlike shouts then, did they run to Phafa's side, and started to belabour the defenceless Koto.

Monare, too, wasted no more breath, but ranged himself by Koto's side and tried to defend him. But how can two—one of whom is unarmed and dazed—fight against six filled with the lust of killing?

Soon was Monare struck down and held. As he lay on the ground, impotent and despairing, he heard Phafa shout the terrible words:

"Do not kill this Koto too quickly. First must we cut out a piece of his lower lip. Then must we cut off his right ear. Then must we pluck out his right eye. And all this, while yet he lives. Else will the medicine for the horn be useless, and the *ngaka* will bewitch us instead.... Hold close the calabash to his wounds, and waste not one drop of his blood."

The groans of the tortured Koto caused Monare unutterable anguish, and he strove with all his strength to loosen himself, calling on God in a mighty voice. But in vain. Now was to follow the most wicked and heart-searing villainy of all that night's work. As the mutilated Koto struggled for breath, Phafa spoke for the last time:

"Let the blood-guilt be shared," he shouted. "Let not Monare later claim that he had no hand in this."

And with the aid of the others, he raised the fallen Monare, and holding him close, he placed his hunting-knife in Monare's hand, and forced him—with all his maddened strength—to plunge the knife deep into Koto's breast.

Koto gurgled, and gasped:

"You have killed me. . . . But you . . . kill yourselves . . . through this flesh and blood of mine . . . shall you remain unlucky and accursed all your lives. . . ."

These were the terrible words which Monare heard, but Koto, his heart's friend, was dead—his breath had left him.

2

Two of the *impi* now restrained Monare while the remainder hurriedly buried the shattered, mutilated body of Koto.

When all was done, Phafa seated himself on the ground beside Monare, and spoke thus:

"Monare, let it be peace between us to this extent. We could now kill you and bury you, and none but the ants and moles would know where your dead body lay. Yet would such a course affect my plans adversely; the Chief would require of us explanations; even if we told him the truth, that Koto was your friend, and that we had to kill you to fill the medicine horn, still is his temper so uncertain and his regard for you so sure, that our own breath might be loosed from our bodies. Rather shall you still appear in the Chief's sight as our leader, and make your report to him of the success of our mission, and hand over to the witch doctors the magic for their horn. If you will agree to this, and will swear a solemn oath not

THE VICTIM

to take revenge on any one of us, but to leave Lesotho within the week, my purpose will be served, and I shall be content."

Monare lay, his heart eaten away with the corroding anguish of remorse; he could not face life in Lomontsa, where the everyday sight of his companions would but remind him of the horrors of this night. He needed no persuading to leave Lesotho—he wished to place as many miles as possible between himself and the scene of the tragedy.

Therefore said he:

"I agree."

And was straightway released from his bondage.

The *impi* rode back to Lomontsa where Monare reported to his Chief, and heard with breaking heart the compliments which were paid him on the success of his undertaking.

The pitiful relics of his dead friend Koto he refused to handle, shrinking from them in horror and dismay. And it fell to the lot of Phafa to receive the thanks of the witch doctors.

The stricken Monare returned to his house and slept the deep sleep of shock and exhaustion.

Ma-Libe got up the next morning, early, as was her custom, and prepared her husband some food. But Monare would not eat, he simply said:

"Leave me, I am sick."

Libe's mother cried out:

"O Ra-Libe! I fear you are sick indeed. Never have I seen your face like this. Shall I send for the Moruti?"

Monare managed to murmur:

"My heart is very sore. Perhaps Moruti would be able to do something. I let it be done."

"What did you allow to be done, Ra-Libe?"

But Monare knew that he had no right to discuss the Chief's secret business with anyone, least of all with a woman, although that woman might be his beloved wife, Florinah.

Ma-Libe ran all the way to the Moruti's house.

When she knocked, the door opened, and there stood the Moruti Lefa and his wife.

Ma-Libe covered her face with a corner of her blanket and cried bitterly. The Moruti and his wife tried to comfort her; they led her inside the Parsonage, they sat her down, they brought her tea. At last the weeping stopped, and Ma-Libe said brokenly:

"Father Moruti, it is Monare."

"What is wrong with Monare?"

"He is sick, and yet not sick. There is something terrible on his mind and he will not tell me. I fear that he is bewitched."

"My child, you are a Christian. What is this talk of bewitchment?"

The Moruti had heard rumours of what had happened at the *pitso* in the *khotla*, but had been powerless to take any action. His mind now jumped to the conclusion that Monare's sickness was due to the Ritual Murder, but he had no idea of how terrible was the position in which Monare was placed.

Saying no more to Ma-Libe than:

"Go in peace, my child, I will come," he went inside to dress. When he arrived at Monare's house he stated:

"Monare, I have come to see you because your wife tells me you are worried. Is there anything that I can help you with, my son?"

Monare lay quiet for a while with his face turned to the wall.

"You may pray for me, Moruti," he said.

The Moruti smiled.

"I am glad to hear that, Monare, for prayer is the key to all the doors of trouble."

And so they prayed together.

Then the Moruti said:

"Monare, tell me what the trouble is."

Monare's eyes filled with tears; his hands groped for the Moruti's. Through his sobs he said:

"I let them do it."

"You let who do what?"

Monare remained silent. At length he said:

"Ma-Libe, my wife, wife of the cattle of my father, I wish to talk alone with the Moruti Lefa."

Ma-Libe said nothing, but walked across to the mud kitchen and closed the door.

3

Monare then spoke again:

"I now speak to you as man to man. I have been involved in a cruel Ritual Murder. I have no wish or desire to kill anyone or hurt anyone, but it was by the Chief's orders. Moruti, the man..."

Here Monare was shaken by bitter sobs for a time.

"Moruti," he continued when he had regained control of himself; "Moruti, the man we carved up was my heart's friend, Koto." And he related to the Moruti the whole terrible tale.

"If only I had acted as soon as I recognised his voice," mourned Monare, "I could have perhaps led the *impi* away after other game, but the flesh is weak, Moruti, and in that short space of time while I thought of what might happen to Ma-Libe and my son, the knives were out and searching for blood."

"Did you do nothing to try to save him, Monare?"

"Yes, when it was too late I fought by his side, until I was overpowered. And then, in front of my eyes, and while Koto still lived, they mutilated him."

Monare wept again. It was painful to watch him and to hear him.

"Koto," he muttered. "Koto, who saved me from jail—the friend of my boyhood, the companion of my manhood. O Koto, my friend! My friend!"

Monare told the Moruti brokenly of the last wicked atrocity which Phafa had committed, how he had guided Monare's arm to strike the final blow into the yet-living body of Koto.

The Moruti's face was set and sad. He thought to himself: "How terrible it is to be born a Mosotho. To have the white man's religion, and yet to have the customs of the land as they had been before the coming of the missionaries. It would have been better to have lived in Lesotho a hundred years ago, or to have been born a hundred years hence. To live in these in-between times is difficult. God give me strength."

He smiled sadly at Monare.

"What is done, my son, is done. We must look to the future."

They sat a while, and at last the Moruti saw clearly what he must say.

"Monare, it was bad that the murdered man was your heart's friend, Koto. But tell me truly, would your heart be as sore, had the victim been a stranger?"

"My Moruti, I understand that it is against the law to commit murder, but Ritual Murder is an old custom of Lesotho, and what the Chief orders, we must obey."

"Monare, you have not answered my question."

Monare sat silent for a long while, and then spoke thus:

"No, Moruti, my heart would not have been so sore——"

"So, Monare, you are guilty of murder, even though at the last, you tried to save Koto. Yes, you are guilty equally with Phafa and the others. Monare, according to the law of the white man, he who assists in even the planning of a murder, is guilty with him who strikes the fatal blow. As you left Lomontsa with the intent to murder some person at that time unknown, the fact that you then risked your life in Koto's defence does not absolve you. And if ever this crime is discovered, you will hang with the others. Doubtless your late repentance will count with God, but not with man."

The Moruti now remained quiet, his eyes covered by his hands, as if praying—and, indeed, he might have been.

At the end of a time he took Monare's hands in his own, and said softly:

"You know in your heart, Monare, that you will be punished. You will accept it and rejoice in it. Either the remains of Koto will be discovered, and a hue and cry will be raised by the white man to discover the murderers, or if nothing arouses suspicion, still will your remorseful heart condemn you, and you will take no more joy in this lovely homeland, in your family, or in your lands. Yes, Monare, remorse is a terrible thing to live with. Poor Monare! And poor, poor Ma-Libe!"

He looked with compassion on the bowed head of Monare, then continued:

"It is better to say nothing to Ma-Libe. We must hope for her sake that poor Koto's grave is never found. And you, Monare, will

THE VICTIM

have to live with your memories. We can but pray that one day a way of atonement may show itself."

The Moruti prayed a while, and then blessed Monare and departed to his own place.

No longer was Monare interested in anything; even the approaching marriage of his son Libe failed to arouse him, for if Koto's remains were found, he, Monare, would not be alive to attend the wedding.

The vivid picture of his friend Koto's last moments was always present in his mind.

One night, without saying a word to his Chief, or to his Moruti, or to his beloved wife Ma-Libe, he packed a bag, and took train to the City of Gold. There he hoped not to be reminded of his crime, there, should the police search for him, he could escape. There would he bring less disgrace on his beloved wife Florinah.

Chapter Four

THE FUGITIVE

MANY WERE THE INFLUENCES which worked in Monare's mind, and which between them brought about his flight from Lesotho to the City of Gold. Chief amongst them was the horror and remorse which he felt at the murder of his friend Koto. He, too, perceived dimly that which the Moruti had put plainly—that the Basotho people were forced to live in two worlds—the tribal world —ruled by the witch doctors, the Chiefs, and by custom; and the white men's world government by the white man's law. He saw that in the world of the white man—no matter how much beer of any sort he had inbibed—no decision such as had confronted him on the night of Koto's murder, could possibly have been set in his path. He admitted to himself, too, that the beer that he and the members of his impi had drunk at the village, had slowed down his reactions, and increased the desire of his companions for the letting of blood.

Monare felt that to remain in Lomontsa would be to place himself in the position where he would be tempted to take revenge on Phafa. He felt that his roots had been against him since the beginning of the enterprise, and he preferred to disappear for a while lest the mutilated corpse of Koto be discovered. Far away he could at least endeavour to keep disgrace from his family—and he could still provide for them.

Arrived in the City of Gold, Monare visited none of his old haunts; he did not even seek out his son, or his old home-boy, Ntoane. Strangely enough, for reasons which he himself could not discern, he went straight to the house of the Orlando Moruti—possibly because great tragedies and keen emotions often stimulate the nerves of sex.

The Moruti was sitting on his veranda when Monare arrived.

"Ah, my friend Monare, the polygamist! Where do you come from?"

Monare, who was dressed in his best suit, replied:

"From Lesotho."

The Moruti rose from his chair.

"A happy reunion, Monare. That is, if you are cured of your polygamous ideas?"

"Yes, Father Moruti."

"Come in, Monare, we will drink tea. Tell me the news of the home country."

And, as of old, the womenfolk were called in and tea was served, and news exchanged.

After a while, the Moruti said:

"Monare, my wife and I have to go to the funeral of a church member who died two days ago. But you stay until our return, and Mary will give you some more tea."

Monare, in spite of his dazed feelings, experienced an arising of his old desire for the beautiful Mary, and thought to himself, what a golden opportunity for furthering his ends.

When they were alone, Monare tried to persuade Mary to keep company with him, but Mary shied off this question—she remembered Monare's last visit, and the conversation she had overheard between Monare and her father, in the course of which the Mosotho had unwillingly admitted that he was married.

She put him to the test.

"I like you well enough, Monare. But tell me, are you not married?"

"No," lied Monare calmly, "I am not married."

Monare, his heart full of bitterness and remorse and longing for his home and his loved ones, himself did not understand why he lied, why he desired to see more of this well-educated girl with whom he could really have so little in common. He was, in reality, seeking a way of escape from his thoughts; what he was really attracted to was the girl's body; her well-shaped legs promised further delights which he wanted to sample. He imagined himself lying with her, and knew that he would be the first. He felt on fire and swollen—it was all he could do to keep his hands from touching her. He imagined her shy and innocent reactions to his experienced fondlings, and thought of how she might behave when he had succeeded in arousing her. While these lustful ideas occupied his mind, there was no room for remorse or regret.

Mary was too polite to give offence to a guest of her father's, so she did not question the truth of Monare's statement. She simply said:

"Now that my education is finished, I am going to teach in a school at Springs Location, so that I do not think we shall see much of each other, Brother Monare."

Monare's mind thrilled to the prospect of a Mary away from her parents' influence, and he determined to have her. There and then he started to plan the details, and other thoughts were banished. He said to her:

"It is unlikely that I shall be seeing you again, Mary, but should I by chance visit Springs, where will you be staying?"

"I have a cousin at Springs, who is employed on a mine, and I shall stay with him and his wife."

Casually, Monare probed for this cousin's name, and unthinkingly, Mary gave it to him.

Monare then took his leave, asking Mary to pay his respects to her father and her mother.

2

Monare rented a room in a courtyard in Sophiatown, but still did not visit his son or his home-boy. He did, however, ask a casual acquaintance to write a short letter for him to his wife, telling her not to worry.

Monare took up again his work as a merchant; not that he really needed the money, but this trade gave him an excuse to visit Springs and keep his eye on the location against the day when Mary would take up residence there.

THE FUGITIVE

In Johannesburg he studied the white man, and wondered at the ignorance and prejudice that many of them showed in their treatment of Africans. Blows and abuse were given to servants and messengers for very trivial offences. He had already learned to avoid the police like the plague, for he knew how ready they were to use their truncheons, and to open their conversations with Africans with a blow rather than with a kind word.

In the main streets of the city, which he sometimes frequented in his search for cloth, he often found himself pushed off the pavements with the remark, " Bloody Kaffir ! " thrown at him. He found that buses and trams did not always stop when hailed by Africans, and he often saw African women trying to dismount from trams which restarted before they were safely on the ground ; usually these happenings were added to by some shouted insults from the conductor. He wondered how people who were supposed to be Christians like his Moruti, could behave in such a manner, and often wished that he could talk matters over with the Moruti Lefa.

At such times his thoughts of home seemed to thrust into his heart like a knife ; he would choke with longing for a sight of his wife Florinah, and would think with sorrow of his cattle and his crops. During all this time he did not again ask anyone to write a letter for him to his home in Lomontsa, and he had no tidings from his village. Knowing that Libe was employed at Nourse Mines, he avoided that neighbourhood as if it had been bewitched.

He had no word, either, of the Moruti's daughter, Mary. Often in his lonely room he was oppressed by longings and desires which were centred on this lovely girl. In the early hours, bereft of sleep, his thoughts, unable to absorb any more remorse, longing, or regret, would turn, in escape, to the shapely body of Mary, and in imagination, his hands explored her breasts and thighs, and more daring, found a thrilling response when they wandered into forbidden places.

His one regular visiting place was a house at Seteketekeng, where, with due consideration for the police, he drank home-brewed kaffir beer, and ate meat and stiff porridge. He did not usually visit this house on Sundays, which day is often chosen by the white man's police for raids. It was here that he met with the delights and dangers of dagga, which were to lead him still farther away from his home village of Lomontsa, and from the wife-of-the-cattle-of-his-father, Ma-Libe.

3

Libe, working underground at Nourse Mines as a *baas-boy*, was frightened when he received a letter from the Moruti Lefa asking him to look for his father, Monare, in the City of Gold. Moruti Lefa believed in leaving well alone—he knew the reasons for Monare's disappearance, but the heartbroken cries of Ma-Libe, now bereft of both husband and son, prevailed upon his generous heart. He therefore wrote to Libe, giving no facts, other than that Monare was somewhere on the Reef.

For many weeks Libe devoted his spare time to searching for his father without success. One day he heard that his father had once stayed in Sophiatown, so one Sunday, accompanied by a friend from the mine, he visited the address which had been suggested to him.

Arrived in the yard of the house, the two youths met an old woman who told them that Monare had left the house about a year before. She wailed:

"God, I fear plenty!" And was silent for a time, pulling her face into an expression of sadness.

Libe could not bear this, so he asked:

"Grandmother, what do you fear? Do you fear us? We are but your children."

The old woman replied:

"I fear not you, my son's children. I fear this killing of people in Lesotho for the medicine horn. Look what is happening to the children of Moshoeshoe. Oh, the end of the Black People! Oh, the end of the Black Kingdom! We go to Lesotho, or we stay in *Gaudeng*—Johannesburg—and we are killed by the *tsotsis*, or beaten by the police. Now where shall we go?"

The old woman burst into tears.

When her sobbing had ended, Libe asked:

THE FUGITIVE

"Old woman, whom did these Chiefs kill in Lesotho? Was it my father?"

The old woman wailed again:

"No, my children, but one man who stayed in this house with Monare was killed, one Koto. He was killed for the medicine horn."

The old woman went on weeping.

Said Libe's friend:

"Come, let us go."

"But where is my father?"

"The heart of the old woman is too painful for her to speak."

"Let us wait until her grief has passed."

While they waited a man came into the yard who knew both Monare and Koto very well.

"I greet you, young men."

"We greet you, our Father."

"You look like Monare."

"I am his son."

"I saw him yesterday at Seteketekeng. What is this that I hear about Koto being murdered in Lesotho?"

Libe asked:

"But who is Koto?"

The newcomer told the two youths that Koto had been a friend and partner of Libe's father, but Libe knew nothing of *liretlo*—ritual murder. Bidding farewell to the old woman and the man from Seteketekeng, Libe and his friend left the courtyard and proceeded to Seteketekeng. But the wary Monare was not in his usual haunt, because of the police raids. The very careful and close-mouthed keeper of the place, refused Libe all telling of Monare's address. He said that he would inform Monare of his son's visit, should he see him again. Although he quite believed that Libe was in fact the son of Monare—for there was a great resemblance in their looks—the brewer kept his clients' custom by telling no one of their private business, and by keeping his own counsel about all that he saw and heard.

No success attended the searching of Libe for his father. For one reason, the purveyor of kaffir beer liked to retain his customers, and had wasted no time in letting Monare know that inquiries had been made about his whereabouts. He did venture to remark that the fine young home-boy who had asked for Monare seemed to be a member of his house, for he bore a strong facial likeness. When he noticed that his suggestion brought a sour look to his customer's eyes, he said no more.

4

For some weeks after this incident, Monare did not visit his brewer at Seteketekeng, for he had other crops to tend—he had at last found out that Mary was now teaching in the school at Springs Location, and he was busy preparing the soil for what he hoped would be a good harvest. He took great pains in making the acquaintance of Mary's cousin, in whose house she was staying, a Mosotho called Phakoe. Monare was careful not to ripen this friendship at the house of Mary's cousin; he had cunningly arranged that he should meet Phakoe at his place of work, a big factory, where he had obtained the job of *Induna* or head-boy, when he had decided to leave the mines to better his position.

Monare's first call on Phakoe was paid in the lunch-hour, and Monare was careful to take with him the most beautiful of his goods, the smartest trousers of the most elegant cut and fashion. Monare opened the talking thus:

"Man of the Chief! Permission to enter is sought. I am Monare of Lomontsa."

Phakoe, who was a well-dispositioned man, replied:

"Enter and be seated, Monare of Lomontsa! What is the news of the homeland? Are the crops good? How are the cattle feeding? . . . Rest, man. I can see you are not asking me for work."

Phakoe gazed with admiration at Monare's smart suit and hat and shoes, and at the leather bag which he carried. Monare looked around him with interest, for after so many years in the City of Gold, he was now able to judge at a glance the position and cattle of any man he visited.

"What is the home-boy's name?"

"I am Phakoe of Maseru. And I welcome you as a home-boy."

"You have an office just like a white man's. *Ee!* You are

undoubtedly a man of wealth, a big *Induna*. I am glad to see you, Phakoe."

Thus flattered Monare.

After due time had been given to the traditional courtesies and to talk of the home country, Phakoe was led by curiosity to ask Monare what was in the smart leather case which was lodged by his chair.

With well-concealed eagerness, Monare opened the case to display many beautiful pairs of trousers, some very nice shoes, and some fine ties.

" I am just a poor merchant, home-boy. Many Basotho buy my goods, and as you can see, they are made of the finest cloth, and cut in the latest fashion."

Phakoe's eyes brightened. One tie in the case was of a brighter plumage than any he had yet seen, and his gaze was fastened to a pair of shining white-and-brown shoes.

" *Ee !* Man of the Chief ! The goods you sell are of the first-class quality. Does it take much money to buy such things ? "

Monare smiled in his throat.

" *Induna*, you joke with me. Doubtless such clothes are common in your house ; a man of your standing must have many such."

Then, bending over, he removed the tie and the shoes from the case—the tie with the pungent colours, and the shoes with the two tones.

Holding out the articles towards Phakoe, he said :

" Take these, Phakoe, with my good will, for always when I do business in a compound or in a factory where the *Induna* is a man of taste and fashion, such as you are, I ask such *Induna* to sample my goods at no cost to himself, so that he may be certain that his workers are not being cheated. Take these things—and if it be your will, give them to your servant."

Phakoe was quite unable to withstand this flattery, and his eyes shone with pure joy as they rested on the tie and shoes in Monare's hands. It was not long before Phakoe was admiring these articles on his own neck and feet.

" Man ! " he cried. " It will be hard to tell which is the *Makulu Buus*, now."

The cunning Monare did in truth sell many pairs of trousers at Phakoe's factory, but such was not his real intent. Every week or ten days he called at Phakoe's little office, and by means of flattery and small gifts, was soon on the most intimate of terms with Mary's cousin.

Said Phakoe one day, much pleased at the gift of a small but smart tie-clip:

"Man, you must visit my house this Sunday. We will drink tea with the women, and then we will visit a man I know in Springs, who brews a fine kaffir beer."

Hiding the glint of triumph in his eyes, Monare agreed.

5

And so it was, that dressed in his smartest suit, Monare made his way the following Sunday afternoon to Phakoe's house, where his friend greeted him at the gate.

"Come in, home-boy, and make yourself comfortable."

He called to his wife and cousin, and as they entered, introduced the newcomer.

"This is Mr. Monare, my dear. Here is my wife, and behind her my cousin Mary from Orlando, who teaches in the school here."

"Good afternoon, Mother and Sister," replied Monare in true home-boy style, and then continued:

"Why, Phakoe, my relative, this is indeed a day for praises. I know the father of Mary, the Moruti at Orlando, and I have met Miss Mary before, too."

And Monare looked at Mary with considerable impudence. Mary was changed from when he had last seen her—had Monare only known it—for she was lonely, and missed the busyness of her previous life as a Moruti's daughter, and the visits she had been in the habit of making with her parents, to the City of Gold.

She was happy with her cousin and his wife, but rather bored, and she had not forgotten the fine figure of Monare. She was of the age for marriage, but had not yet been asked for, although she would have been mocked in Lesotho with cries of "Tail! Tail! Tail long enough to go round the mountain!"—for she was uncircumcised and ignorant of sexual rites and exercises—she had her feelings stirred by Monare's hot looks.

Monare politely asked for news of the Moruti her father, and sipped his tea in an elegant manner. But when Mary encountered his gaze, she retired to the kitchen in some confusion, making as her excuse, the remark that more water had to be boiled. Mary was certainly a beautiful Mosotho girl; she could not help knowing that she attracted the ardent Mosotho man. How could the most pure of girls fail to feel a response to so much male admiration?

Monare had been a good pupil at the Mountain School, and he was able to read other signs than weather signs. He crossed his legs as his reactions became too prominent, and thought to himself:

"What does it matter if Phakoe carries me off to the brewer's? I have made a start with Mary, and when I start I shall surely finish."

And so it turned out to be, for shortly after, Phakoe suggested that he and Monare should go out for a little beer.

When Mary retired to bed that night she sat for a while with strange hot feelings, but when she realised where her imagination was carrying her, she flushed with shame, and her heart was filled with remorse. She knelt down to pray, and after a time achieved calmness. She remembered that Monare was undoubtedly a married man, though she knew that in the home country it was lawful for a Mosotho to have as many wives as he could afford or desire. But, she mused, I am a Christian and a college graduate, and my father, the Moruti would hang his head in shame were I to become Monare's second wife. She decided that by cunning inquiry she would discover when Monare was expected at the house again, and that she would make sure that on this occasion, she would not be present.

This praiseworthy decision did not prevent Mary's rest from being disturbed by dreams of a kind she had never before experienced.

6

In the meantime the news of the killing of Koto by *liretlo*—ritual murder—was spreading among the Basotho of the City of Gold. As Moruti Lefa had foreseen, it was the mutilation of Koto's body which had told the truth to the police of Lesotho, when the grave of the murdered man had been uncovered by wild beasts, and discovered by a young herd-boy.

But it was not easy for the Great Detectives to bring home the murder to the *kraals* of the guilty men. Where witch doctors wield powerful influence, such cuttings of the living flesh could have been ordered for more purposes than one. Nevertheless, it had not escaped the notice of these Great Trackers, that at the same season as the commission of the Ritual Murder, the son of the Chief of Lomontsa had founded a new village, for which, tradition demanded the provision of a medicine horn. But to suspect and to prove, were two very different things, and at this particular time there was no evidence to indicate that the discovery of Koto's body would bring trouble on the heads of the Great Ones of Lesotho. Besides, many Basotho were policemen in the service of the Great King across the waters, and many of these, although loyal to their commanders, were of the elder generation. If circumcised, then they held belief in the ancient customs, and would not, of their own will, place their necks, or the necks of home-boys, in the Noose of the *ngaka*. It was wiser to keep clear of *ngaka's* business.

Libe, too, had heard murmurings about this Ritual Murder, but his heart was not over-troubled, for it held no suspicion that this talk might have aught to do with his father—nor, for that matter, had any man, as yet.

The boy was growing in understanding and in wisdom, and now, on his Sunday journeyings, when he made inquiries about his father, he no longer asked, " Have you seen Monare, my father ? " But rather said, " Have you any knowledge of Monare the merchant, who is my uncle's cousin ? "

Finally, he dropped the name of Monare from his questions, and spent his time tracking down all makers and sellers of trousers.

It was thus that Libe met Phakoe. When Monare no longer went to Seteketekeng to drink beer, Libe started to widen the circle of his searchings. One Sunday, at Springs, he heard of the wonderful goods which were brought round there and sold by a Mosotho merchant. After many innocent-seeming questions, Libe realised that the description of this Mosotho merchant tallied with that of his father, Monare. He then learned that this merchant always made a point of calling at the office of the factory *Induna*, Phakoe. Libe then asked his *Makulu Baas* for a day's unpaid leave, and learned by discreet questions the location of Phakoe's residence. In the course of these inquiries, Libe learned that the Mosotho merchant usually visited the house of Phakoe each Sunday.

Libe thereupon made up his mind.

" I, Libe, will also be present at the house of Phakoe this coming Sunday."

Chapter Five

FATHER AND SON

DURING THESE MONTHS, Monare had been improving upon his friendship with Phakoe and his wife, and had been lucky enough to see Mary almost every Sunday. Monare still held to the story that he was unmarried, and Phakoe saw no reason therefore to frown on his visits. Neither had it occurred to Phakoe to advise the Moruti at Orlando about Monare's visits to his house—it had certainly not struck Mary with any force that she was deceiving her worthy parent.

But a public holiday was fast approaching which spelt doom to Monare's plans. The Moruti at Orlando had written to Phakoe privately to acquaint him with the fact that Mary's hand had been asked for in marriage by a very respectable member of his congregation. He proposed bringing his wife to Springs Location on this imminent holiday, to discuss the matter with his daughter. This secret, which Phakoe had wisely kept from the ears of the womenfolk, had become known to Monare through the compulsion of kaffir beer.

Monare's plans had received a severe jolt, for he knew that Mary's marriage, or even engagement, would put a sudden end to his lustful dreams. Time was low in the gourd. He must act.

So far, Monare had acted with propriety towards Mary, but one Sunday evening, he had been prevailed upon to accompany the family to church, where a lantern lecture was to be given by the missionary Moruti, after the service.

On the way home in the dusk, Monare and Mary had become

separated from the others, and as they strolled across the veld towards Phakoe's house, Mary's ankle turned on a stone, and she uttered a cry of pain.

"I must sit, Brother Monare, my ankle is hurt."

"Mary, I am skilled in the treatment of sprains, let me massage the ankle for you, and it will recover its strength."

Mary was too much in pain to examine the guile in Monare's words; she sat down and lay back against a grassy bank. Monare carefully removed her shoe, and without protest from her, pulled down her stocking, and gently began to rub the tender spot. For a while Mary was too stricken with pain to notice, but as the wave of agony ebbed, she noted that Monare's hands seemed to have reached higher than her ankle, and were, in fact, caressing her knees. She noted, too, that the sensation of pain had given way to a feeling of quite a different kind.

Before Mary could—by word or action—stop Monare, his hands had slipped up under her dress and were smoothing her thighs. Mary, being uncircumcised, and therefore ignorant of sexual matters, had no knowledge of the methods employed by the male to rouse the female, and for several moments she lay relaxed, for the sensation was truly soothing.

When, however, by accident or design, one of Monare's fingers slipped up between the elastic of her bloomers and her leg, she experienced a thrill so delicious that she immediately knew it to be sinful. Her father, the Moruti, had taught her to distrust anything which pleased the senses too much, like bioscopes, dancing, over-eating, and over-drinking, and " tail-wearer " though she might be, Mary was not without sense—she felt herself floating down the river, and with a broken cry, sat up and seized Monare's hand.

"Brother, would you bring shame on a Moruti's daughter? Know you not that passing people will say, 'There lies a *tsotsi* and his woman.'"

Had she struggled, Monare might have put the matter to an issue, but as it chanced, as Mary spoke, voices and footsteps were heard nearby. All he said was:

"Forgive me, Mary. I was overcome by your beauty."

As they rose from the grass, Monare asked Mary if her ankle

was better. Mary found that it could now bear her weight, though still tender. Slowly, with thoughts that were like a field of corn with the wind rustling through it, they made their way home. In their concern over the sprained ankle, Phakoe and his wife did not notice that the faces of Mary and Monare were troubled.

Mary's night was filled with wonder about Monare; she realised that she loved his body, but she also knew that although a successful merchant, Monare was entirely uneducated. What influenced her most was the fact that he was married; yet, she admitted, that should Monare ask her, she might—in this mood—even consent to become his second wife, in spite of her father's horror. But something inside her told her that she was destined to no lasting happiness with Monare. This did not prevent Mary from experiencing again dreams of a wanton nature.

Monare, too, suffered from his frustrated lust, and a fire burned in his loins the long night through.

2

So the fateful Sunday approached, the day on which Libe had determined to visit the house of Phakoe. Who was to tell Libe that which was to befall that day? Who was to warn Mary of the shame that was to be hers? The Sunday was fine, the day was warm, but not hot.

What were Libe's feelings, as he approached the house of Phakoe? Who can tell, except the birds of the air? For he told none of his home-boys of his plans and, as he drank only the genuine home-brewed kaffir beer—when he could obtain it— he had no drinking companions to share his secrets. He must have hoped that he would at last find his long-lost father, and be able to write good news to his mother in the far-off village of Lomontsa.

Monare's thoughts were quite clear within him; he had but one object, and that was to fulfil his desire with Mary. His thoughts were hot, they were vivid like a bioscope picture—he did not yet know how, he only knew that to-day should the deed be done.

Mary's thoughts did not lie all in the one furrow; she was

FATHER AND SON

happy to see Monare again, but she had fixed in her mind the decision that she would allow no more fondlings, however innocent. She did not intend to remain alone with Monare, if she could avoid it.

After Monare's arrival in the early afternoon, the four Basotho sat for a time and talked; then Mary and Phakoe's wife prepared tea. As they were drinking the tea and eating the sweet cakes that had been baked, came one knocking on the door and shouting the name of Phakoe. This bearer of ill-news brought the message that Phakoe's wife's mother had been taken ill, and that man and wife must hurry to the hospital.

What a hurry and a scurry there was. What a putting on of hats and coats. What a mouthful of instructions to Mary. What a dash. What a *pisto*.

What chokes one man, feeds another, and so Monare found himself alone with Mary, and before Mary had time to think " Is it Sunday or is it Monday ? " she was clasped in Monare's arms, and his mouth and hands were all over her body.

Although Mary's flesh responded to Monare's ardour, she determined to protect her virginity as best she could, and she resisted silently, for she was a well-brought-up girl, who valued her self-respect. Even when she felt Monare's hands pulling at her clothes, she kept her voice quiet. Monare had by now unclasped his belt, and with his fashionable trousers draped about his feet, was on the point of committing the shameful act of forcing Mary against her pleas.

Suddenly, as if struck by *ngaka's* lightning, all Monare's fire was turned to ice—changed in a moment of time, changed by two words, spoken in a frightened voice.

The words were, " Father, father ! "

And the voice was Libe's.

For while the silent lustful attack had closed the ears of Mary and Monare to all but their own hurried breathing, Libe, who had been keeping a watch on Phakoe's house, and seen Phakoe and his wife leave, had decided that now was his chance to enter, and speak to his father, whom he had seen arrive earlier. In his innocence he thought that the other woman—Mary—would have retired to the kitchen, leaving his father sitting in solitary splendour in the living-room.

Oh, the shame! Oh, the disgrace! That a son should see a respected and beloved father engaged thus. To the most pure, things are known which are not spoken of. Could Libe's shocked eyes ever forget this sight? Could Monare's eyes ever boldly meet his son's gaze again?

And what of Mary? To be found thus, partly unclothed by the son of the very man who was trying to seduce her. Indeed, her instincts had been right. No happiness with Monare. . . . Hastily pulling her creased and crumpled clothes into position, Mary ran from the room with downcast eyes.

Monare's eyes, too, remained fixed on the ground as he covered his manhood and belted his trousers.

He said no word to Mary, made no attempt to see her, but gave his son one gruff word:

" Come! "

And he walked savagely away towards the station.

3

As Libe followed his father, he felt that there was some bewitchment behind all these happenings; behind his father's flight from Lomontsa, behind his long silence, and behind the soul-breaking sight he had just witnessed. But when Libe, still respectfully, tried to ask his father what all these things amounted to, Monare remained silent, other than to repeat, in a rough voice:

" Come! "

For this was the biggest disaster which could overtake Monare. At the station he boarded a *mafofonyane*, followed by Libe, and sat in the crowded compartment, as the train sped past the mine dumps and through the plantations towards Park Station.

But behind this blanket of silence, his thoughts were busy. It was, surely, a shameful thing to be exposed before a loved one; it was heartbreaking to be shown up in a disguise other than that in which one wished to face the world—it was plain agony. He had

FATHER AND SON

been seen, by the son of his wife Ma-Libe, in the act of taking another woman. The private place of his heart and emotion was exploded and shattered. He wished with a terrible yearning that he had never been so much the Chief's right-hand man, or that he had stayed with Ntoane for ever in the City of Gold, instead of returning to Lesotho; then would he have been absent when the Chief established the new village for his eldest son.... As the train swayed in and out of Benoni, Germiston, George Goch, Jeppe, so the bioscope of his life staggered and flickered before his eyes, in time with the frenzied lurching of the *mafofonyane*.

He thought of his drinking days at Lomontsa, and wished, bitterly, that he had never become a sober man, for had he remained a drunkard, never would the Chief have chosen him for high place in his counsels. He thought of his home-boy, Ntoane, and wished for his friendly presence. He mourned for the murdered Koto, whose blood lay heavy on his soul.

Yet in his present mood, he still lusted after Mary; now more than ever, for he felt he had lost his son's respect, and thirsted to dissipate his strength in mad abandon. There was nothing left to live for.

Arrived at Park Station, still followed by Libe, he went to his room at Sophiatown, drew Libe in behind him, and locked the door. From a hiding place, he pulled out a bottle of white man's brandy, unknowingly saved for such an hour.

" Drink, Libe ! For this once forget all I told you before you came to this accursed city."

Libe silently obeyed him, and passed back the bottle.

Monare drained a great draught, coughed deeply, and said :

" Libe, my son, I am now an outcast from country, village, house and family."

" My Father, please speak not so bitterly. My love, and that of my mother, you have always, no matter what may come to pass. Rather tell me, Father, why you have hidden away from us like a rat in a hole. Why you have deprived my mother of a husband, and me of a father, for so long ? Have people bewitched thee, O my Father ? "

Monare sat for a while in silence, then spoke.

"Libe, my shame is upon me; I hardly dare to speak."

After a time, Libe said:

"O my Father! Did you perhaps know one, Koto?"

Monare's face turned the colour of white man's bread; his eyes stood out from his cheeks; little balls of sweat ran from his hair down his face; his breathing got painful to listen to.

He gasped out:

"What know you, my son, of this Koto?"

"O my Father, nothing, save that he was your friend, so they say, and that he was foully done to death in Lesotho."

"Who says these things?"

"It is common talk in the streets around the house you used to dwell in, my Father."

Monare fell back in his chair, his head held between his hands.

"Has his body then been discovered?"

"There is much coming and going of policemen in Lesotho; they seek to find the criminals; there is talk of medicine horns and bewitchment."

Monare started to sob, hurting his son's ears by his weeping.

"O Koto! My friend! My friend!"

After a while, Libe softly said:

"Do not sorrow beyond bearing, O my Father! Koto shall surely be avenged. The police shall surely handcuff those that slew Koto. Have comfort, my Father. . . ."

Monare could no longer restrain his grief; as the Moruti Lefa had said, his punishment would always sit beside him. His weary brain could not mouth the words he wished to say to Libe. Not only had his son taken him in an act of shame—as between father and son—but would shortly be shrinking from him as a man who had murdered his friend.

He spoke within himself.

"O God! In man's justice is there but one punishment for each crime? Why do you punish me over and over again? I am barred for ever from the clustered hills of Lesotho. Never again shall I see the face of my beloved wife, Florinah. . . . I have lost the respect of my son, Libe. He comforts me, yes—but with promises of vengeance upon the murderers of Koto. I, his father, am the one

FATHER AND SON

upon whom he calls down doom. Better that I should return to Lomontsa, and surrender myself to the police."

Thus mourned Monare within his heart as the painful silence endured. While Libe, the instrument of the punishment of God, sat there with his arms around Monare, comforting him—him whom he would afterwards curse.

4

Libe had to return to his duties at Nourse Mines the next morning, but before going he awoke his father Monare, and embraced him.

"O my Father, let not this happening at Springs weigh too heavily on your heart. I am your son, all my life I have watched and respected your actions, and strived to follow in the same path. At home, are you not the Chief's most trusted adviser? What happened yesterday is a man-matter, not for discussion amongst women. Do not fear that I should dare to mock you, my Father, for the advice you gave me before I left home. Do you think I would say to the father I love, 'He who would teach me to carve, cannot hold a knife?' I feel, O my Father, that something you have not disclosed hides behind your actions. Will you not tell me—your son Libe—so that I may share it with you? It is said, is it not, that 'It is easier to cut the cloth with two blades of the scissors, than with one?' As for the woman, let us forget her—'while one thread holds, who can say that the button is off?' There was no wedding of the flesh."

Monare sat in shamed silence.

"Libe, had you not come——"

"O my Father, who knows where the assegai would fall, had it been thrown? Suffer not alone, my Father!"

Libe whispered and looked down while he spoke.

"I am no innocent boy. I do not know that even the voice of my beloved father could have stayed me, had I seen such a beautiful virgin outspread before me—I, too, am lusty. O my Father, please hear me, and know that you have my love and respect."

Monare's heart filled with joy at the thought of his son's love and understanding, and he embraced him warmly. Yet, he felt, scarcely could Libe's love survive the knowledge that his father had killed Koto. Libe knew little of *liretlo*, he was not of the *pitso*, he knew nothing of the ancient loyalties to Chief and Custom. Monare believed that it could not be long before the police of Lesotho would discover that it was an impi from Lomontsa that had committed the Ritual Murder, and then his—Monare's—name could no longer remain hidden.

After such expression of his son's love, he felt that it would kill him to see that respect turn to loathing. He thought to himself:

"I must again disappear. I will not be able to bear the look on the face of Libe when it shall be turned against me."

Aloud he announced:

"I thank you, my son Libe, for your love; make tea or coffee, and return to your work. When we meet again I shall make you aware of all that has happened."

After drinking together, father and son parted, Libe's heart being much lighter; he looked forward to his next meeting with Monare, when he should hear the truth, and be able to help his father in whatever the trouble should turn out to be.

But before noonday, Monare had disappeared without trace. When Libe again came to the house in Sophiatown, he found the room empty. He asked those within the courtyard, but none could tell him where his father Monare had gone. For weeks he searched, even questioning Phakoe, claiming to be one of Monare's customers, but to no avail. Libe went about his duties at the mine with a heart made heavy by sadness. He did not ever quite give up hope. He wrote cheering letters to his mother and to the Moruti, stating that Monare had been ill, and that when recovered, he would write himself or come home.

Chapter Six

DAGGA

AT HIS KAFFIR BEER BREWER'S HOUSE at Seteketekeng Monare, in his despair, learned the uses and charms of dagga. The owner of this place could see that Monare had been bludgeoned by Fate, for he was both surly and sad. Thinking the matter over, he came to the conclusion that there might be some profit for him in the Mosotho's misfortune. He said to himself:

"Why should I not make a profit out of this man by making known to him the delights of *matekoane*—dagga? Truly, I am not myself a *semokolara*—a drug pedlar—but my brother-in-law is, and surely he will pay me well if I introduce to him a new client, and one, moreover, whose belt is well filled with money?"

Thus mused the brewer, and as the result of his musings, he took Monare one evening to a house in the location at Benoni, where dwelt the *semokolara*, his brother-in-law. There Monare first smoked dagga—although he had heard of it often, for it is grown in Lesotho, too, where it is highly esteemed as a medicinal herb, and especially as a cure for sickness in the stomachs of horses. He found that dagga gave him a means of escape from his thoughts, and he came to an arrangement with the *semokolara* to lodge and eat with him, and there for a time he stayed.

Matekoane is a weed resembling the khaki weed; its growth is forbidden in the Union of South Africa, because of the terrible results of smoking it. There is, however, a huge trade carried on in South Africa in the growing, smuggling and peddling of dagga. So much is grown in defiance of the law, that the white man uses aeroplanes to fly over lands in which he suspects it has been planted, in order to identify it from above. The white man does not usually smoke it, but many white men are making fortunes from smuggling it from place to place, hidden in grain bags slung beneath their motor cars. A moderate price paid for a grain bag filled with *matekoane* is a hundred pounds. It has a strange, pungent, unforgettable smell, and it is by this odour that its smugglers, smokers and pedlars are usually found out. The white men's magistrates award huge fines, and even jail to those caught in this traffic, but the profit is so enormous that those punished always return for more.

It may be smoked in two ways; in the country a hole is dug in the ground, and made wet; coal and dagga are then placed in the hole, which is closed up, except for an opening of a size to take a reed. When the dagga is smouldering, the smoke is drawn through the cane. It can also be mixed with ordinary tobacco and smoked in a pipe, the blending tending to reduce its characteristic smell, and thus also lessen the chances of discovery.

Monare smoked *matekoane* for some time; he found that whilst under its influence, his past misdeeds and crimes lost their power to frighten him—he felt strong and confident.

As the days passed, he soon found that the smoking of *matekoane* also increased his sexual desires. His nights were troubled by lustful dreams, and his days disturbed with lustful thoughts. He found, too, that his fancies increasingly strayed in the direction of handsome youths. He was not ignorant entirely of this side of life—no African who had lived on the mines could be—he had himself passed through phases in his friendship with Koto, in which great affection and loneliness had led to very minor adventures in homosexuality. But this new craving which possessed him was not founded on love, friendship, or a solitary life—it was merely an appetite directed at any good-looking youth who had a graceful figure and a compliant, wanton disposition. But these things, which most men know, but which even the rude speak not about, were, Monare knew, against the white man's law, and, according to the Moruti Lefa, were frowned on by God.

Monare—who had not forgotten his period of imprisonment—therefore held his new-found desires well reined.

DAGGA

2

While Monare smoked, Libe mourned, but did not abandon his search for his father. At last he summoned up courage enough to visit Phakoe's house at Springs, where he hoped to meet Mary, and, risking her displeasure, make inquiries from her about his father. For had not Monare shown great determination in his pursuit of this girl ? And might he not still be fired with the same ambition ? Libe, himself a man, thought it to be quite possible.

Libe bided his time. One Sunday he saw Phakoe and his wife go out dressed for visiting, leaving Mary behind watching their departure from the veranda. He knocked on the door, and Mary appeared. Lowering his eyes, and speaking in a humble voice, he said :

"Miss Mary, do not receive me with hate. It is true that this son, Libe, and his father, Monare, have been the cause to you of much sorrow and shame. But I pray to God, Miss Mary, that you will listen to my sad story, and, should you be able to forgive me, help me."

Libe stood—handsome and contrite—with his head bowed.

Mary was filled with shame at the thought of what this young man's eyes had seen ; she wished that the ground would open up before her, so that she could be hidden from his gaze. But as a Moruti's daughter she had learned how graceful was an act of forgiveness, and how necessary for the soul's salvation. And how handsome was this young man, so near to her own age ; she felt her heart warm towards him in her sorrow, and she said :

"Enter in peace, Libe. Forgiveness is here for you, and for your father, Monare ! "

Thus Libe entered the home of Mary for the second time.

Mary bade Libe be seated, and prepared some tea and cut bread-and-butter. Libe now told Mary all that she had so often wanted to know—of Monare's standing in the village at home, of the trust reposed in him by the Chief ; of his cattle, horses, and fields. He told Mary of his dear mother, and of the Moruti Lefa ; he told of Monare's disappearance from Lomontsa, of his own long and fruitless search; of his love for his father; of what had been said in the house at Sophiatown in the early hours of the morning following his discovery of Monare in Mary's house. He told Mary of Ntoane and Koto, of the Ritual Murder, and of his growing suspicions that Monare must in some way be implicated.

These two young people spoke under some natural constraint; neither of them could forget the happenings at their earlier meeting. Libe was honest enough to feel bitterly ashamed, as—even whilst telling his sad tale to Mary—before his memory flashed a picture of the beautiful girl as he had seen her lying with disarrayed clothing on the bed. But such stirrings he suppressed.

Mary felt she must help Libe, and between them the young people talked over everything, and decided what Phakoe and his wife should be told on their return. It was arranged that the truth should be told about everything, excepting Monare's desire for Mary, which fact had remained hidden from Mary's cousin and his wife.

The simple and kind-hearted couple, on hearing Libe's sad tale, were full of sympathy and eager to help. It thus befell that they invited Libe to spend his Sundays with them, in the hope (they thought) that Monare would one day return to his old friends.

3

Meanwhile Monare continued to smoke *matekoane*. Poor Monare! *Letona* of the Chief! Husband of Florinah! Father of Libe! There he lay, dreaming his wicked dreams, consorting with such handsome boys as would play his wanton game without danger —poor, poor Monare! Monare, once one of the best husbands and fathers; Monare, one of the best reciters of " praises." . . . Curses on Monare! Curses on the white man who had lured the young men from Lesotho to endure such shame. Curses on Chiefs and Baruti alike. Who passed different laws for the same people.

Ah, Monare! Doom on Monare! Doom on Lesotho! Doom on the Basotho people!

One day, in a mad mood, Monare wished once more to look upon Mary, to see if she could still arouse the desire within him.

By *mafofonyane* he travelled from Benoni to Springs; like a jackal he crept towards the location. Was this the smart Monare? Where was his suit, his hat, his tie? Where were his shoes? Could this be Monare, wrapped in a blanket, who slunk along the streets hiding from the eyes of those who might know him?

Arrived near Phakoe's house, Monare hid, and watched the place with maddened eyes.

All day he watched, not too near. He saw Phakoe and his wife. Once he thought he saw Mary, and his heart beat more quickly. Noon passed.

At last Phakoe and his wife left the house. Monare shuddered in recollection. Then, suddenly, a man walked up to the door. What was this? Monare's mind cleared enough for him to remember the talk of Mary's betrothal—perhaps this was the suitor, or even the husband. Such thoughts dulled the riot in Monare's blood; desire left him; he decided to return to Benoni and his graceful youths. But as he started to leave his hiding-place, the man about to enter Mary's house turned. . . . What! Could God be so cruel? . . . Monare saw that the man was his son Libe.

Poor Monare! Maddened with too much *matekoane*. Poor crazed Monare. He muttered to himself:

"O God of my Moruti! Is there then no mercy? Have I led my son by the same path as that which I followed? Is Ma-Libe to lose a son, as well as a husband? Is the honour of my house to fall again?"

So cried Monare in his heart, in a moment when he was suddenly sane. Then his desires rose again to full heat; he thought of the last time when all three of them were in that house together; he thought of how nearly had his object been attained. In mad jealousy he now determined to kill them both, and then to put an end to his own life. Thus would he finish the line and destroy the seed of his accursed house.

Quietly Monare crept on his terrible way, made mad by desire and horror and remorse.

4

Inside the house, Mary spoke to the sad-eyed Libe.

"No news, Brother. Have you none?"

"No, Sister. No news."

These two had become good friends; so far Monare had stood between them. Libe had been true to Makopoi, and Mary to her husband-to-be, chosen for her by the Moruti. The very common interest they shared had drawn them together; it was perhaps sad that they should so often be left alone on Sunday afternoons. But as good friends may be, they were affectionate towards each other, and no one thought them wrong.

But this fateful day, their moons happened to fill the same place in the heavens; and when Libe, innocently enough, happened to place his arm round Mary's shoulder, and let his other hand fall on her knee—he was thinking of other things. Without conscious desire he started absent-mindedly to stroke her leg. Then, the fat was in the fire. The sugar was in the water.

Libe heard Mary cry a little cry, gasp a little gasp, then, like *ngaka*'s lightning, they were in each other's arms. And this time Mary offered no defence, for there had been no attack. It was the impersonal fire of youth which was trying to fuse them.

Was the story again to be told? Must the work started by Monare, be finished by Libe? Was honour to fall?

Again a belt unclasped, and trousers fell. Again naked flesh sought to mingle. But a broken whisper turned their fire to snow on the Maluti Mountains.

"Libe! My son!"

A figure fell across the doorway into the room.

"Mary!" it breathed.

5

When Monare had seen his son enter the house, desire and rage fled for a while, chased out of his blood by horror, which quickly blew up like the white man's balloon within him, and exploded into his broken, whispered words. The man, Monare—as he lay there—looked as if his spirit had been loosed from within him.

"Father," said Libe, as if the saying of the word were strangling him.

"Monare," gasped Mary, and burst into fast, quick sobbing.

The belt was reclasped, the naked flesh hidden. Libe walked slowly to the fallen man as if every step were on sharp knives. A strange smell offended his nostrils.

"*Matekoane!*" He shuddered.

Quickly now, he ran to Mary.

"*Matekoane!*" he repeated.

Mary was stunned to silence.

Libe said:

"We must get him from here, he needs attention. Besides, Phakoe will return."

But Mary had learned something about nursing at her Training College.

"For now, milk and rest," she said.

"But Phakoe?"

"What they need to be told, shall be told to them—after all, they are his friends, and will wish to help him."

"But when he awakes?"

"You must be with him, and stop his mouth when first it opens in reproach, rage, or madness."

Between them they carried Monare to Phakoe's bed. Mary forced milk down the stricken man's throat, then she said:

"When he has awoken, and we have talked a while with Phakoe, you will call the taxi from the next street; take him with you, look after him, try to find out his trouble and share it. As for you and me, we have reached the crossroads where one path stretches to the rising sun, and the other pathway goes on for ever towards the setting sun. On one road will you and your father Monare travel, and on the other road shall I travel. Our moment of madness I forgive you for, and do you forgive me, too—for it was not entirely your fault, nor was it entirely mine. I still have regard for you as a brother, dear Libe, and I say my farewell now, which I cannot do when the others come."

And so saying, Mary kissed Libe on the brow, and left the room.

When Phakoe and his wife returned, Monare was still asleep, yet was his breathing quieter; it was decided that he could be removed to Libe's home. Therefore, was the taxi now called, and the farewells made, the promises were recorded that Libe would bring Monare—when recovered—on a visit; and regrets were expressed that Monare should have fallen victim to *matekoane*. Trouble was disclaimed, friendship was upheld, and so the time of parting arrived.

Phakoe and his wife were unsuspecting of the dramatic and moving incidents which had chosen their humble dwelling to play themselves out—they believed what they were told, they were simple people and good. Only part of the truth was withheld from them, and who could blame Mary for that?

Libe and Phakoe placed Monare in the back seat of the taxi, the doors slammed, the starter whirred, the hooter sounded, the gears clashed, and the car moved.

The cross-roads of the rising and the setting sun had been reached.

Chapter Seven

REGENERATION

IN THE TAXI-CAB, Monare revived somewhat. He groaned and opened his eyes. By the light of the street lamps as they flashed past, he saw and recognised, the face of Libe.

Libe said:

"O my Father!"

"Where am I? And what has happened?"

"Speak not now, my Father, but rest. But first tell me, where is thy house?"

"Take me not back to the house of the *semokolara*. To-morrow I shall claim from him my goods. To-night, direct the driver to that same yard in Sophiatown, where I had a room the last time we met. The old grandmother there will surely find me a room."

And so it befell; the old woman still had the same room vacant. The taxi was paid off, and father and son entered the room. Libe persuaded his father to lie on the string bed whilst he went in search of milk. Returning to the room, he found Monare sleeping uneasily. He stirred, and waking, sat up.

"Libe, my son, what has happened?"

"O my Father!"

"I am remembering now."

Libe smiled wearily.

"We are indeed now wearing the same *stertreim*! As my voice prevented you from taking Mary, so did your voice save me from the same action."

"O God of my Moruti, I thank Thee."

"There need be no more talk of shame between you and me, my Father. We are like two *mafofonyane* on the same line. Where one goes, so must the other also."

"Libe, my son, I thank my God that I was spared from carrying out my intention, which was to kill you both."

"That was the *matekoane*, Father."

"Yes, Libe, to my shame, it was. But I must warn you, I have been smoking this drug for some time. I am all right at the moment, but only God can tell you what I shall be like in the morning without my pipe of *matekoane*."

"How can I help you, Father?"

"My son, I have it in mind that you should take a few days' leave from your mine; to-morrow you can come with me to the house of the *semokolara*, and we can collect my goods. If you came not with me, it strikes my heart that I might be tempted to remain there. Then, Libe, I want you to fetch here my old home-boy, Ntoane."

"Yes, my Father."

"When we three are together, I will tell you all that has transpired since I left the City of Gold to return home for your circumcision. Having talked, we can take counsel. It also seems to be that I shall need the services of some *ngaka*—or perhaps even a white witch doctor—to help me abstain from the taking of *matekoane*."

"To-morrow, O my Father."

"If I ask for *matekoane*, it must not be given to me."

"You shall be obeyed, Father."

"There are shameful things that *matekoane* causes a smoker to do, my son. Perhaps you had better not sleep here."

"There can be no shame between you and me, my Father. We are now brothers as well as father and son. However it can be that I may serve you, have no shame in asking."

And so they slept; but Monare awoke to be the prey of remorse; his hand shook, his cheeks were sunken, his breath was uneven. He pleaded with Libe to get him some *matekoane*; he became cunning, he invented errands for Libe to perform, so that he, Monare, could make his escape and go back to the house of the *semokolara*.

But Libe was steadfast; he would run no more risks of losing his father. Together, having broken bread and drunk coffee, they set out in the *mafofonyane* for the house of the *semokolara* at Benoni.

2

By chance the *semokolara* was absent on business at Seteketekeng when Monare and Libe arrived at his house in the Benoni Location, but loafing about was one of Monare's handsome boys. Seeing the well-built and good-looking Libe, he sneered to Monare: "So the fruit is always sweeter in the next orchard."

Libe speedily acquainted the youth with his relationship to Monare, and proceeded to collect his father's belongings. Whilst he was doing this, the handsome boy strolled over to Monare, and rubbed between his fingers some *matekoane*. Monare, who was almost senseless with desire for the drug, asked for a pipe.

Libe ran across the room, and pushed aside the hand of the youth. He said:

"I shall see to it, Father, that you speedily get the medicine of the white man, which will destroy this craving."

The handsome boy, smiling wantonly, made rude suggestive gestures.

"And what about this craving?" he demanded.

But when Libe moved threateningly towards him, the youth retreated, and said in a defeated voice:

"What about the money owing to the *semokolara*?"

Libe looked towards his father.

Monare took out his purse.

"Here is the rent which is owing. I owe him naught else."

To the false laughter of the good-looking boy, Libe gathered up his father's goods, and taking him by the arm, led him away towards the station.

When they arrived back in Sophiatown, Libe left his father to rest in his bed, and went in search of Ntoane. He arranged with the old woman that a man friend of hers should keep watch on Monare, in case, when he awoke, he should strive to escape and go back to

Benoni. He also feared lest anyone from the *semokolara*'s establishment should have traced their movements, and arrive during his absence to try to tempt his father to return.

Libe also had to visit his mine, to obtain from his *Makulu Baas*, a few days' leave of absence.

Late that night, bearing food and drink and medicine, which he had obtained from the white witch doctor at his mine, came Libe, and with him wondering at such of the tale as Libe had seen fit to tell him, walked Ntoane, Monare's old home-boy and friend.

The old woman heard the two men enter; she came out of her room to tell them that all was well. Monare had woken, had raved and cursed, had fought with her friend who had been posted as sentry, but in the end had collapsed again, and had at last fallen asleep.

When Monare awoke, his craving was almost driven out by his great joy at finding seated on his bed, his old friend, Ntoane. Libe quickly made him swallow some of the white man's *sehlare*, and indeed, it appeared to give Monare some relief. Food and drink were then prepared and served, and the two old friends and Libe settled down to talk.

3

Monare started to tell his story in a quiet voice. Libe, by this time, had some idea that his father's distress was in some way caused by the murder of Koto, but even he could not have imagined the terrible predicament in which Monare had found himself, and which now—in the course of the story—was disclosed to the listening Basotho.

But far from turning from his father in loathing, as Monare had dreaded, when Libe had heard the whole tale, he put his arms around his father, and with great affection said:

"O my Father! Would that I had borne this load in your stead! How could the Great Spirit have placed you so?"

"Yet will the white man blame you," said Ntoane. "But the blanketed Basotho would always understand and forgive," he continued, "for who can disobey the orders of the Chief? What the

Chief decides must be for the good of the tribe. I, too, understand, Monare. Why, had I been the Chief's *Letona*, and you the victim, how could my hand have been stayed."

Libe, with tears running down his cheeks, now cried:

"O my Father! Why could you not have told me this before? How much less would our suffering have been."

They were silent a while.

Libe then continued:

"Maybe through that suffering understanding was born, my Father. We certainly shared some strange experiences."

And he smiled crookedly.

At length Ntoane spoke again.

"It is good that we have met, home-boy, for I have just had a letter from Lesotho, that the great trackers and detectives think that they have at last pinned the murder to the kraal of the Chief of Lomontsa. An old woman who was present when you were all drinking beer before you found Koto, overheard one of your *impi* speak the name of Lomontsa."

"O God of my Moruti! What shall I do?"

"Rest in peace a while yet, old home-boy; they do not as yet suspect that you were in charge of the *impi*, no names have been mentioned abroad so far. Only from the old woman's words have they caught in their minds the thought that the Ritual Murder sprang from the need for a medicine horn for the new village established by your Chief's son. Of course, sooner or later they will know who was in that *impi*. Sooner or later will they start to come after you with handcuffs, my home-boy. But the sun has not yet cast a shadow of that length. First you must rest, and eat this *sehlare* which Libe has obtained for you. But we must also find another lodging—too many people knew Monare here."

After much talk, the two friends and Libe thought that a room on the West Rand should be found for Monare, for most of his business as a maker and seller of trousers had been limited to the East Rand. They also discussed where Monare should make for, when he had recovered completely from the effects of the *matekoane*. Monare implored Libe to ask his *Makulu Baas* for a few weeks' holiday, and added that his, Monare's purse, was still sufficiently well filled to keep Libe and himself, and to pay for the clothes for Libe's wedding, and for presents for the bride.

It was also thought that it would now be right for Libe to write to his mother, and to the Moruti Lefa, to let them know that Monare had in truth been found, that he had been ill, but that he was recovering. But the doubt came into their minds that perhaps the police of Lesotho might open the letter and read it.

Ntoane said:

"I will write to my nephew at home, and ask him to bear a verbal message to the Moruti and Monare's wife."

"But may not all letters to Monontsa be examined?"

"I will write in such words that even the greatest and most cunning of the detectives shall understand naught."

And so matters were arranged and left.

4

Gradually Monare once more began to feel himself a man amongst men, although the remorse for his past misdeeds would never leave his heart. He found that the love and sympathy of his son Libe and the white man's medicine, between them were restoring him to strength and sanity. There would be many times when the craving for *matekoane* would press heavily on him; his strange desires would not altogether abandon him as yet, but he would in the end, recover.

The following Sunday, travelling by *mafofonyane* the three Basotho visited Roodepoort, where lived a friend of Ntoane. In the course of discussion during the day, it was arranged that Monare should take up his residence with Ntoane's friend without delay, and Libe, therefore, took train back to Johannesburg to collect his own and his father's belongings.

That evening, seated in comfort in the new quarters, the talk turned to Monare's movements when he should be fully recovered.

Said Ntoane, at length:

"Many Basotho are working in the City of Sugar; they are working on the ships in Durban docks. There they make much overtime, and they are well looked after and regarded by the white man."

Monare, thinking of the sinking of the *Mendi*, asked:

"Is there not great danger there, that the waters may rise and overwhelm them?"

Ntoane chuckled.

"For one who gave such excellent praise on *Mendi* memorial day, you ask strange questions, Monare."

Monare quoted:

"One may praise God without knowing His secrets."

Ntoane had a friend who was employed by a large stevedoring firm at Maydon Wharf in Durban, and he promised to write to him, and ask him to secure a job for Monare. These men, said Ntoane, had good barracks and food, and generally were well treated.

As the weeks passed, Monare slowly outgrew his craving for *matekoane*—this *sehlare* of the white man was good, he decided. His desires were slower in their changing, and he often felt ashamed, for it was not possible for two men to live as close to each other as did Monare and Libe, without the secrets of the one being known to the other. Libe was the finest son a man could wish for, was Monare's thought. Sometimes, during the earlier days of his getting better time, Monare would lie awake, restless, tormented by his imagination. Although he encouraged Libe to go out and about on the Reef, and to keep on visiting his *Makulu Baas*, and generally to keep ears and eyes open for gossip and visitors from Lesotho, on such nights Libe always refused to stir from his father's side.

Libe did not wish his father to feel lonely, nor shamed by his desires. Therefore, by friendly talk and the recounting of his experiences underground—where Monare had never been—Libe sought to draw his father's thoughts away from lustful dreamings.

And so Monare grew back to complete manhood.

5

The time was fast approaching for Libe's wedding. Monare's heart was very sore that he would not be able to be present at this ceremony, but it would have been foolish for him to place himself in jeopardy.

Soon, too, a letter arrived from Ntoane's friend in the City of Sugar, telling that a post had been found for Monare, and that he should come as soon as possible.

One night in May, therefore, the three Basotho met for the last time on Park Station—Libe to hurry back to Lesotho to get married to his beloved Makopoi, Monare to take train to the City of Sugar, and Ntoane to bid them both farewell.

Monare was full of loving—but of necessity, secret—messages for the wife-of-the-cattle-of-his-father, Florinah, and for the Moruti Lefa. Ntoane on his part promised to look after Libe when he should return to the mines after getting married; he further promised to keep the ears of Monare filled with news of his son in Johannesburg, and of events in Lesotho.

Had these three known where and when it was their fate to meet again, tears could scarcely have been withheld, but mercifully was all knowledge of the future denied to them.

A time came to an end. Hands were shaken, embraces were made, tears were shed, whistles were blown, doors were slammed, flags were waved, engines puffed, steam screamed, wheels turned—and hearts broke.

And so the trains ran away from the City of Gold, and left it glittering in the darkness.

Phase Three

LAST QUARTER

"Blood has but one colour, and Spirit, none!..."

MONARE OF LOMONTSA

Chapter One

CITY OF SUGAR

WHEN MONARE STOOD DOWN from the Kaffir Mail—as the night train which runs between the City of Gold and the City of Sugar is called—he said to himself:

"I have never been in Durban before, but a true man is never lost."

And, turning to a porter, he asked:

"Porter, could you show me the way to Maydon Wharf?"

"I would advise you to take a rickshaw from outside the station, which will carry you through all the way to Maydon Wharf."

Thanking the porter, Monare walked out into Soldiers' Way. Before he could look back at the dirty makeshift station, so different from the magnificence of Pretoria and Johannesburg, a rickshaw boy dashed up, crying:

"*Uyapi, baba?*"

Monare had learned some Zulu on the mines, and answered:

"*Ngiyahamba eMaydon Wharf.*"

He jumped in the rickshaw and held his small suitcase tightly in his hand, as the rickshaw boy—after the fashion of such—jumped madly in the air, blowing his little horn, the bells on his headdress tinkling. As the rickshaw threaded its way through the mass of cars, bicycles, lorries, buses and trolley buses in Gardiner Street, Monare looked around him with interest. His way lay down Gardiner Street to the Victoria Embankment, and there Monare got his first sight of the sea, and the docks, and the ships.

"*Ee! . . .*"

Monare was astounded, and said:

"I have seen such things in a bioscope, but never thought that I would see the real Great Waters themselves."

The rickshaw puller laughed.

"Wait until you see the Point, *Baba*."

After travelling for a time along a road which was crossed by scores of railway lines, the rickshaw turned seawards towards Maydon Wharf, and at last arrived at the compound of the stevedoring firm. The rickshaw stopped, and the puller said:

"Here is compound, *Baba*." And held out his hand for the fare.

After paying the rickshaw-boy, Monare got down into the road and walked across to the compound gate where stood a fat policeman of the stevedoring company. Monare greeted him in Zulu:

"*Baba!*"

"Yes, we see one another."

"Are you alive?"

"I am alive. Are you also?"

"Yes, I am alive, *Baba*."

Monare strolled to the shade of the compound wall, saying:

"*Baba*, your country is hot."

"Yes, it is hot to-day. Where, then, do you come from?"

"I come from Lesotho, but now, from the City of Gold—*Gaudeng*."

A cool breeze from the sea was felt.

The fat policeman looked interested.

"Is your name Monare of Lomontsa?"

"Yes."

"Your home-boy asked me to watch for you. Are you here to work?"

"Yes."

"Come inside, you may sit down. I will call one of your home-boys."

Monare entered.

"Sit down. Do you drink *mahleu*?"

"Yes, I drink *mahleu*."

While they drank someone was dispatched to call the friend of Ntoane, who was now to become the friend of Monare.

The next thing Monare saw was the figure of a blanketed

Mosotho coming towards him. In Sesotho he greeted the new-comer:

"*Oa hae!*"

And back came the reply:

"*Oa heso!*"

Then the man with the blanket said:

"I am Mkize, friend to Ntoane."

"I am Monare, friend to Ntoane."

Mkize took Monare to the room to which he had been posted, and the two home-boys sat down to chat. Mkize told Monare that he would have to see the *Makulu Baas* the next day, but that as he, Mkise was not working to-day, would Monare like to go out with him to see the City of Sugar?

Monare was happy to agree, and the two friends set off together, Monare asking many questions, to which Mkize made reply:

"Yes, do we work on Sundays, when there is cargo to be put in or taken out of the ships. . . . No, we do not work after noon on Saturdays. . . . Yes, the work is hard, but we get well paid."

"How long is it since you were in Lesotho, Mkize?"

"Ten years, Monare."

"Ten years!"

"Yes, why go home? I have enough money, and there are plenty of young girls about."

They were silent a while.

"You don't say it, my relative."

"This is Durban, Monare."

Monare was anxious to look at that great mass of water, the sea. The bay seemed not unlike lakes he had seen on the Rand, but where was this *Mendi*-destroying sea?

"You shall see plenty of it, home-boy. You work in ships that sit in the sea."

Mkize took Monare through Grey Street to the African and Indian markets, and great was Monare's amazement at all that was shown. He was struck by the large numbers of the Indians, and Mkize told him how many years ago their ancestors had been brought across the Black Water by the white man to labour in the sugar plantations, and that now there were so many of them in

Durban, that the white man was getting worried about the future.

"They have beautiful women," said Mkize, rolling his eyes lustfully; "but they keep them behind the iron curtain. But this does not prevent the Indians from desiring our girls."

At last Monare's delighted eyes beheld the sea—the sea that had swallowed *Mendi*. He was entranced at the breaking of the waves, and at the sight of the boats out at sea, rising and falling. Monare and Mkize walked along the Lower Marine Parade, past the paddling ponds and the swimming baths and the Kenilworth, and the amusement park. As they approached the miniature railway, Monare's eyes fell on white men and white women bathing in the sea.

"*Molimo! Molimo!* What a sin! Naked men and naked women bathing together!"

"Softly, softly, home-boy; it is not so great a sin as you think. Wait a while. Farther on we shall see Africans doing the same thing, and then I will explain everything to you."

Monare was excited by the small engine and carriages which carried children and nursemaids along the beach, but Mkize led him on to the Battery, where Monare saw many Africans—both men and women—bathing in the waters of the sea.

Mkize now pointed out to Monare, that as the people emerged from the water, it was obvious that they were not naked, but clothed in short, coloured garments.

"This, my relative, is the costume for bathing. Yet might as well some of them be naked, especially the white women."

Mkize chuckled, and Monare looking round could scarce believe his eyes. There came some beautiful white girls clad in the briefest of shorts, and with but a narrow band of cloth covering their breasts; the delicious points of their bodies were seductively outlined.

"*Ee!* Do not their husbands or fathers beat them, home-boy?"

Mkize laughed.

"You will soon learn that that is what the white people call fashion, and those girls who fail to display their bodies in this manner are unlikely to find husbands."

"*Ka Thesele!* I can see that the City of Sugar has much to teach me."

2

And so from time to time as on Saturday afternoons he visited different parts of the beautiful city, and the hills and valleys and beaches around it, Monare's knowledge of Durban increased.

But the next day, Monare started work.

He found himself in the same gang—headed by an *Induna*—as his home-boy, Mkize. At seven every morning after washing and eating, the Basotho would climb on to big lorries and trailers, and be carried to the wharfside, next to the big ships—sometimes at the Point, where the big cranes were, and sometimes at Maydon Wharf. At twelve noon there would be just over an hour's break for rest and food, and the Basotho would be sped back to their compound in the lorries and trailers. Work stopped for the day soon after half-past four, unless they had work to perform on a ship at night. On such days they would start work again at five, and continue until nine o'clock. For this extra work, and for Sunday work, the Basotho were paid overtime. Monare soon found his purse filling again.

Monare liked the work; especially did he like loading sugar at Maydon Wharf, where in between whiles he could bask in the sunshine, and scoop up spilled sugar from burst bags, and eat it. He liked best to work on the wharf itself, hauling the trucks required along the rails to the ship's side, and then loading into trays or slings the bags or pockets of sugar. It was hard work hauling and pushing these heavily-laden trucks along the lines, but Monare was a renowned "praiser," and he was soon chosen by *Induna* to lead the working songs as his companions hauled the trucks.

The singing of these working songs made certain that each Mosotho exerted his full strength at the same moment in time, and thus the truck was induced to overcome its tiredness.

Monare sang, and his companions joined in.

> "*Hula . . . hula . . . tiisa . . . toosa . . . tiea!*
> *Utloa . . . kemoo . . . hee . . . ea . . . tla . . . tiea!*
> *Ea . . . tla . . . he-ea-tla . . . tiisa!*

And so the men sang and the trucks groaned and the rails screeched, and the sugar was swung aboard.

Monare also preferred Maydon Wharf to the Point because among the white men at the former place were many of the English race, who were always ready with a smile or a joke—or even on occasion, a cigarette—for the willing worker. At the Point he found more Afrikaners, who mostly swore at the workers and cursed them. Worst amongst these latter were the bearded men who called themselves *voortrekkers*.

Monare studied now the customs and habits of the white men, and became acquainted with the justice of many of their laws. This was the first time he had come into daily contact with the Afrikaner and the Englishman. He thought of his tribal laws, and it seemed to him, that no matter how severe the white man might be in his dealings with the black man, no *Makulu Baas* among the white men could command one of his servants to kill another, but the Chief's work is too often to punish or to kill.

And his heart grew sick and cold within him, as he thought of what had happened to him through his Chief. He did not remain sad for too long, however, for a plan was being born in his mind. He had discovered that there were white men of good will in Durban who provided houses for their trusted African workers, so that they could bring their wives and families from the homeland to live with them in peace and happiness. He resolved to become one of those trusted men.

In his mind he thought:

" Libe and Makopoi can look after my cattle and tend my lands, and Ma-Libe can one day join me here."

And the darkness lifted somewhat.

The white man's Christmas came and went, and seeing the scenes of joy and feasting, and the many happy families in the streets, Monare's heart again grew heavy with memories of his homeland. At this time he heard through Ntoane that Libe's marriage had taken place, as planned, in June, and that Libe had now returned to the Reef to work for another spell on the gold mines. Monare was tempted to spend some of his cash on buying a ticket on the train to the City of Gold, but Ntoane had warned him in his letter

CITY OF SUGAR

against this very thing, as the great detectives were now hot on his track.

3

Towards the end of December, before the coming of the great heat, Monare was bathing one evening in the sea by the Battery on the North Beach, when a wave threw him against another African who had just entered the water. Turning to speak his words of regret, Monare saw, to his great joy, that the other man was a home-boy, one Joala, from Lejoeng village, near Lomontsa.

Through his mouthful of sea water, Monare spluttered:

"Do I see you alive?"

"Monare! Yes, I am alive. Are you alive?"

"Yes, home-boy. What are you doing in this City of Sugar?"

"Come and drink lemonade, my relative, and we will talk."

The two Basotho bought bottles of lemonade, and lay down together on the warm sand.

After some gurgling, and some appreciative belching, Joala said:

"I am servant to a white man on the Berea, Monare. What is your work?"

Monare replied by telling his friend some of his adventures, and explained to him that he was now working loading the ships. As always, Monare was thirsty for knowledge, and he wished to learn more intimate details of how the white man lived. He asked Joala, therefore:

"What pay do you get, Joala?"

"Six pounds a month."

Monare thought to himself that this was but snuff or beer money. Why, his first month at Msilikazi all those years ago, he had drawn four pounds ten shillings. He continued:

"Is the work hard, my relative?"

Joala made his smile crooked.

"I would much prefer to work on the docks like you, Monare, but I was knocked down by a white man's car shortly after arriving here, and my back is still weak."

"Did not the white man pay for the injury he had caused?"

Joala's looks blackened, and he frowned.

"The white man's car did not stop."

"Each car has a number. Did you not report to the police?"

"My friend who was with me, saw the number of the car, and the frightened face of the white man looking back at us through the window. But I was out without a pass, and for this crime alone I would have been thrown into jail by the police. And it seemed likely that thereafter, the other matter would have been forgotten or, at least, would they have called me a liar."

"But your back, Joala?"

"It did not hurt me much at the time, but it has caused a lot of pain since."

"*Ee!* This business of passes annoys me greatly. A stranger would think that we Africans were the people from beyond the Great Waters, since we have to carry passes at all times. Yet did not this land belong to our fathers before the coming of the white man."

It was now Joala's turn to laugh.

"*Ka Thesele!* I heard my *Baas* say that the *pitso* in Cape Town has ruled that all the white men and white women are now to be forced to carry passes too."

"Cattle of the Chief! That will I never believe."

And Monare laughed long and lustily.

"I know not the truth of the matter, but thus spoke my white man *Baas*."

"When the wind rises, then shall we see which way it blows. But tell me more about working in a white man's house."

"Well, my relative, I leave my bed when the fowls begin to speak, to light the fires for the white man's bath, and for the baths of the white man's wife and children. I also have to light the fire under the cooking stove."

"Does not the white man then have electricity in his house?"

"Yes, brother. He has machines worked by this electricity for cooking, and for keeping the raw food cool and fresh, and for polishing the floors. He has the electric talking-box and the telephone. But the woman of the house uses the coal stove to make soup upon, and on that too do we servants have to prepare our own food."

CITY OF SUGAR

"Are there many servants in the house, home-boy?"

"There is but one other—a Zulu girl; she washes clothes and irons them, and makes the white man's bed and those of his children; she lays the table for their food."

"What next do you do, brother?"

"While the water is heating I wash white man's car; I then polish the verandas. I put on the white man's porridge to cook. I put water on the stove to boil and take the white man's family tea to their bedsides."

"And your own food?"

"There is little time—yet, sometimes I can take what tea they leave in the pot. But more often must their breakfast be prepared and cooked, for the children have to go to school."

"But the woman of the house—where is she at this time?"

"She rises late, and takes a bath. Mostly I take her breakfast to her in her bedroom."

"And when the man has gone to work, and the children to school?"

"Then may the Zulu girl and myself eat the porridge we have prepared, eat some white man's bread, and drink the tea which remains. Then there are floors to be swept, dishes to be washed, vegetables and meat to be got ready for the white man's lunch."

"*Ka Thesele!* But you work hard, home-boy."

"*Ee!* And then most days in the afternoon is there cutting of grass and pulling of weeds in the garden. But soon comes the time to prepare the food for the evening meal; it must be cooked and served; the dishes must be washed. By eight o'clock in the evening, sometimes all is done."

"And what food is given you at midday, and at night?"

"At midday, bread, jam and tea. At night, sometimes meat which was not required by white people, or more porridge."

"You are working very hard, my relative."

Monare frowned with thought.

"Five in the morning until eight at night—that is fifteen hours. You must be paid much overtime."

"Overtime! There is no such thing as overtime for those who

work in the houses of the white men. . . . Yes, I am allowed Sunday afternoon—after the dishes have been washed—away from my work."

" *Ee !* There is work I would not like. Is the food they eat good ? "

" Sometimes, yes. But from what I hear the white man's wife saying to her husband sometimes, I understand that white man has not really enough money to own a motor car and a big house. The wife is always buying clothes in the big shops in West Street, but in the house she is untidy, and wears dresses that are old and torn. Sometimes I think the white man is going to beat her. He swears big oaths, and cries : ' You and your bloody friends will land me in jail.' "

" Why, home-boy, is he then a *tsotsi* ? "

" No, Monare, I think it is but a manner of speaking. This swearing comes most often at the month end when the postman brings many bills. Often at night the white man and his wife put on fine clothes and have friends to eat with them, and drink much of the white man's liquor. Then, the next morning, when there are maybe no bacon and eggs for the white man's breakfast, then will he shout and swear : ' Why did I leave Redhill ? I was happier with my bloody push-bike and my garden. What's the good of all this bloody show ? This big house ? This huge motor car ? Are your damned friends going to pay the bills ? ' "

" And what does white man's wife say to this ? "

" She always makes the same reply, but the meaning of the words escapes me."

" What are the words ? "

" The words are ' Think of your position. What would the Smiths say if we lived at Redhill, and you went to work on a push-bike ? ' What this position is, that she speaks of, I know not, but her reply makes the white man even angrier."

" What does he do ? "

"Slams down his cup and shouts, 'Bugger my bloody position.' "

" *Ee !* Why does he not beat her ? "

" These people seem afraid of their wives."

" They should live in Lesotho for a while ! "

CITY OF SUGAR

And the two Basotho lay on the beach and laughed loudly and long at the strange behaviour of the white people.

4

At the compound on Maydon Wharf, there came to be some talk about the Indians; the government had taken away from them many privileges. They were no longer allowed to buy white man's liquor in the bottle stores. Some influence that had been promised them in the Provincial *Pitso* of Natal, was now denied to them. Many of these Indians were wealthy and well educated, and owned motor cars, wives, cattle and houses.

Mkize and Monare were of one mind about the Indians. They thought:

"This country of ours—which of the people living in it take all the honey from the comb? The white man. And what is left, the scrapings. Even that comes not to us, the Africans, but goes to the brown man, the Indian, whose ancestors, like those of the white men, came from across the Great Waters."

During this time, white bread, which, during and since the war, had been denied to all the people of the land, no matter what their colour, was again put on sale. Tea, soap and sugar, too, were at this time hard to buy in the shops at this period. When Basotho or Zulu went in search of these things to the shops of the Indians, too often were they told:

"Buy ten shillings worth of goods, then will we supply you with white bread or tea or sugar or soap."

This conditional selling was against the law of the white man, but who in the land will listen to the voice of the black man? Especially as at that time, one or two of the great detectives were making much money from the Indians, by taking from them bribes, and by staying their hands from conducting them to the magistrates when they offended against his law.

The Indians, on their part, when deprived of their privileges, spoke and wrote at great length, and made much noise in the ears of the people, but they did nothing to attempt to gain the sympathy of their black brethren, the Basotho and the Zulu.

Monare and his friends noticed, too, that both English and Afrikaner feared the ever-increasing numbers of the Indians, but when some wise man rose amidst them and said:

" Trade not with these that ye fear—thus shall their wealth and numbers decrease . . . ."

The Afrikaners publicly cried:

" Hear ! Hear ! "

But in secret and by stealth did they still visit the shops of the Indians, for often would these brown men allow them to take away goods without payment, trusting that they would return at the month end, and settle the account.

The white man also seemed to wish to withhold advancement from the African peoples, desiring to keep them as labourers until such time as they could be banished from even such menial work, and forced to live in Basutoland, Bechuanaland and Swaziland, or in one of the Reserves. Monare heard too, that the Afrikaners had cast covetous eyes on his own beloved homeland, Lesotho, and wished to bring it within the boundaries of the Union of South Africa.

But the Basotho put their trust in England, and vowed:

" This shall never come to pass."

Such were the thoughts in the minds of the people of the great City of Sugar, in the early days of the year 1949.

Chapter Two

BLACK FIRE

Working down at Maydon Wharf, Monare did not see many Indians, but one day, busy loading sugar on the ship *Umgeni*, he noticed that some of the men cleaning the decks and hauling on the ropes that supported the vessel's derricks, appeared to be of an Indian tribe. When opportunity came, he asked his friend Mkize if indeed these seamen were Indians.

Mkize looked up from his game of *morabaraba* and answered him thus:

"The white man calls these Indians, lascars. They seem to be different in temper and disposition from the shopkeepers you saw in Grey Street, and widely removed in looks from that other Indian tribe which the white man calls 'Sammies,' and whose members sell fruit and vegetables to the white women."

As Mkize finished speaking, a tall, fair-skinned Indian dressed in a long black coat and trousers—the coat buttoning right up to his neck—and wearing on his head a high, round, black fur cap, passed the truck of sugar which Monare and his friend were busy loading into slings.

Said Monare:

"*Ee!* Home-boy, is this man of yet another Indian tribe?"

His mind swept back to his days as a merchant in the City of Gold. He admired the cut and fashion of the stranger's clothes, and wondered what sort of a price he could have asked the mine boys for such a suit.

Mkize's voice shattered his thoughts.

"That, old home-boy, is an Indian Moruti—a Moulvie, they call him."

"Is this tribe of the Christian faith, my brother?"

"There are some among the Indians of the Christian faith, Monare, but not of this tribe. These lascars are what the Zulu people call *amaSuleiman*—Mohammedans. And this man with the beard is their Moruti, or Moulvie; his name is Abdul Wahid. Whenever a ship tarries here with *amaSuleiman* men aboard, the Moulvie comes to talk and pray with them."

Monare looked at the face of this Moruti and found its expression kind, yet stern. The Moruti, or Moulvie wore a black moustache, and his beard was neatly trimmed.

Some days later, another ship with the same funnel markings tied up at Maydon Wharf, and Monare's gang was busy loading sugar into its holds from the trucks. Monare was resting for a moment whilst the bags in the truck were loosened, when he looked up to see the *iSuleimau* Moulvie passing between the ship's side and the truck. At that moment the ship's winches were hauling up from the wharf, a sling containing fifteen bags of sugar, each weighing two hundred pounds. As the Moulvie passed, Monare saw one bag of sugar start to slip from the sling.

As the bag fell towards the high-capped head of the Moulvie, cries and shouts rose above the rattling of the winch. The Moulvie looked from side to side, puzzled.

Now Monare acted with speed of *mafofonyane*. Like a hawk he darted to the Moulvie and pulled him away from under the bag of death. A yard away from their panting bodies the bag of sugar hit the wharf and exploded into a white cloud.

When the Moulvie had recovered his breath, he thanked his God, Allah, in many heartfelt words, for his salvation and then, turning to Monare, said in Zulu (for he spoke no other African tongue):

"May the blessings of Allah fall upon thee, Brother African! Had you not acted thus, would my life have been loosed from within me. My name is Abdul Wahid, I am Moulvie at a mosque near Cato Manor. If at any time I can be of service to thee, my house and all it contains, are yours. What is thy name, brother?"

"I am Monare, O Moruti. Your words are generous, but this act of mine calls for no reward. No matter who stands beneath the falling bags must be removed. Speak of it no more."

But the *iSuleiman* Moulvie did not forget the face or name of Monare, and whensoever his ministrations brought him to Maydon Wharf, he never failed to inquire from the *Induna* as to Monare's whereabouts. Having found Monare, he would convey to him such gifts as Monare's pride permitted him to accept—such things as mealies, tobacco, fruit in season, and bottles of the white man's lemonade to quench his thirst.

From this good man—for such he soon proved himself to be—Monare and Mkize learned much about the brown-skinned people from India.

For, like Monare himself, the Moulvie came from without the Union, though living within it. He was a Pathan, one of a tribe which lived on the North-West Frontier of India, in the part which is now called Pakistan. The Moulvie made the Basotho's sides quake with laughter with his merry tales of how his tribesmen would descend on the camps of the white men, and steal the very rifles from those on guard.

From this Moulvie, Monare learned much about the peoples of India and their religions; he marvelled greatly when the Moulvie told him that in colour the people varied from black in the extreme south to white in the far north.

2

About this time the South African Police started to treat with some roughness and severity both the brown-skinned people and the black-skinned people. In the newspapers there appeared reports of prisoners being beaten to secure confessions.

Black, brown and white started to look in each other's faces in a strange manner. The sympathy which had existed between the African Congress and the Indian Congress melted away, and was no more. The respect, too, which black and brown had shown to white, began to dissolve.

A fire was laid, a draught was created, and sure enough, the match was forthcoming.

The match was a middle-aged Indian, an instrument doubtless of the Great God of all Baruti. Whom shall it now benefit to make public that name? And the box upon which this match was struck was a Zulu *umfaan*, an innocent young boy.

Spark was set to kindling at 6 p.m. on the afternoon of Thursday the 13th January 1949. The Zulu *umfaan* waited innocently for his brother to finish work; he stood outside a shop at the corner of Victoria Street and Brook Street, where the hundreds of Indian buses await their black and brown passengers in the City of Sugar.

Poor Zulu boy! How could he know that from the blow which was to fell him, hundreds of his people were to die?

As he stood waiting, a hand came against his back with force, and pushed him with the strength of ten so that he flew forward through the air, and crashed through the glass window of the shop. He turned his bleeding head, and saw his assailant walking away with a sneer upon his face.

No *ngaka* of any race has yet been able to smell out the true facts relating to this assault; although the Indian later claimed that he struck the blow to avenge his son, upon whom the *umfaan* had laid rough hands.

But think not that the blow had passed unseen. Bright eyes had watched what happened; Zulus and Basotho were walking towards the bus ranks to take passage to their homes at Cato Manor, Second River and Cavendish.

The cry arose:

"*AmaKula! AmaKula!*"

Feet rushed, and arms were raised.

The cry became stronger and angrier.

"*Bulala amaKula!*" (Kill the Indians!) "*Bulala amaKula!*"

At first the Indians fought as men, but, then, becoming afraid, hid in their shops behind locked doors. The Zulus, thinking of their past searches for white bread, tea, soap and sugar, remembering their women raped by Indians of the *tsotsi* class, seeing their young brother struck down before their very eyes—grew mad.

Shop doors were broken, windows were smashed, goods were removed, buildings were burned, Indians were killed.

Basotho going home from work, saw the fighting, and said:

"We cannot let our Zulu brethren die."

Soon the Indian road known as Grey Street became a street of glass, bordered by fire.

The African people now chased the Indians from the markets, which lay nearby; they overturned the hated Indian buses, and set them afire.

From the whole Indian quarter of the City of Sugar, arose a wailing and a crying, as men died, and women were raped. Passing by stealth behind the looting Zulus, came white men of the baser sort, picking up shirts and food and jewels, as these things were thrown from the wrecked shops by the angry Africans.

Said one Zulu to another:

"Let us now go to Clairwood, to Jacobs, to Wentworth. There, too, is the wealth of *amaKula*."

Answered others:

"And to Second River, to Cato Manor, and to Cavendish."

Yet others cried lustily:

"Too long have *amaKula* kept their beautiful women behind their curtains of iron. Let us seize them and rape them, as have the Indian rascals raped ours."

With maddened shouts they went upon their way, using the very buses of the Indians to help them in their aims.

Thus did the night of terror and of doom descend upon the Indians. Their homes burned, and their lost children wandered crying in the bush. Their young girls called upon their gods to save them from the lust of the Zulus. But it was more than lust, it was a mad blind revenge. Some women were raped in turn by each of twenty Zulus, whilst the bound and powerless husband was forced to watch in death-like anguish.

That night were the snorting fire engines summoned over one hundred times—but in vain.

Yet love and kindness departed not altogether from hearts beating beneath black skins. At Second River, a Mosotho woman hid ten Indian children beneath her blankets and, moreover, fed and clothed them, whilst outside the blood was flowing red in the gutters.

3

And what of the white men's police? They came, and with them soldiers to the number of five hundred, with shielded cars mounting guns. But what could they do against the wrath of the Zulu people? Yet was the rage of the white man mounting, too, and some—when faced by quiet Zulu men, who had taken no part in the fight, but desired only protection—drove the long knives at the end of their rifles into the innocent black bodies.

And it is said, that some, charging upon the fighting crowds, urged on the Zulus hotly, with violent oaths.

" Go on! Now is your chance to kill the bloody coolies."

When all the story was told to the outer, waiting world, many asked why the white man's government did not send more regiments, more police, and more guns—and send those quickly. If, indeed, it were wished that the bloodshed should end. But of this matter, even the cleverest witch doctor could not distinguish the truth.

Near Monare's compound, on Maydon Wharf, a customs officer was arrested and accused of drawing a knife from his belt, which he handed to a Zulu with the injunction and encouragement, or so was it alleged:

" Go, then, and kill the coolies."

Who, indeed, shall now draw the truth from those events? Who shall know what purposes, what private vengeances were served, what living flesh cut for the medicine horn, what vile deeds were done?

Died during that time, one hundred and five, and were injured, over one thousand.

The Zulu king, Cyprian Bhekuzulu, spoke from his royal kraal—Kwandhlamahlahla—soothing words to his people, but they heeded not.

On the third morning, over four hundred lay in jail, arrested by the white men's police.

4

No work was done for three days by the Zulu and Basotho people—they were too busy robbing and avenging. No work was done for many days by the Indians—they were too busy dying.

At Monare's compound on Maydon Wharf, there, too, no work was done, and the ships sat in the water in idleness. Monare's blood-lust was also stirred and, when companions came from the city, acquainting those yet at the compound with what was happening, Monare rushed with Mkize towards the town.

But suddenly, the thought transfixed him, like an assegai in his heart: "O God of my Moruti! What madness is this? What Chief has commanded me to go out and do murder?"

He fell behind his companion, and got separated from him in the crowd of angry Africans.

"Have I not enough to answer for?" he thought. "In this fight, who shall say who is right, and who is wrong? Am I a Zulu, that I should murder *amaKula*? Yes, should *amaKula* attack me or my brethren, then must I be at hand to help. But otherwise will I watch. I shall not stain my hands again in blood."

In such words did Monare of Lomontsa declare his decision. He could not, however, by any means restrain his curiosity. And so he followed the angry mob, taking every care to screen himself from attack by Indian or white man.

The City of Sugar slopes up from the Great Waters that border it, to green, wooded hills. That night was the city surrounded by a ring of flame. Most of all, did the Indian streets within the town suffer, and the Indian suburbs such as Clairwood, Sydenham, Cato Manor, Cavendish and Second River. Thousands were the houses destroyed, and hundreds the buses and motor cars set afire. Rich Indians were seen scurrying from their homes, loading into the big motor cars their jewels and silks, and piling on top of their goods and chattels, such womenfolk and children as they possessed.

The Zulus thought of their days of glory under their kings Chaka and Dingaan. As the blood flowed at Chaka's *kraal*, on the Hill of Slaughter, so would it flow this night.

Brave and kind white men, riding in their motor cars, gave room to terrified Indians, and bore them to safety. Other white men drove into places of great danger and carried wounded and blood-soaked men and women—black and brown—on to the spotless cushions of their motor cars.

Who shall say that this skin is brown, or that that skin is black—when blood is red?

Monare walked down the street of glass, which, a few short hours before, had been Grey Street. From the shattered shop windows Africans were taking food and clothing, and dancing in the light of the burning houses, in hate-maddened patterns.

From windows above the shops came shrill cries for help, as Indian women and children felt the scorching breath of fire draw near, and yet nearer. Some jumped, with piercing shrieks, to plop on the glass-spiked roadway like overripe tomatoes.

Death! Death to the innocent as well as to the guilty. Where the colour of the skin is the enemy's badge, who shall inquire name and address before killing?

Monare thought:

"Yes, if ever we Africans should rise against the white man, to try to gain some of the gold and sugar, and jewels, and wheat and cattle which come from the earth of this our country, and in which we now have no share, who shall, on that Day of Reckoning, ask a white man what tongue he speaks, and whether he has befriended us, or used us ill. On that day, as on this, the foe shall be distinguished only by the colour of his skin. The white skin shall mark its owner down for death."

Monare was saddened by his thoughts, for many were the white men who had treated him kindly. He thought of his own wife, and of how good and loyal she was, and of how hard she worked.

"Many such good wives and mothers having white skins will die on such a day. Not because they deserve death, but because their skins are white. Thus shall the iniquity of some men, of the white man's government, be paid for even by the young and innocent."

And Monare wept deep within his heart, and murmured:

"Why will not the white man try to understand the black man?

We Africans desire but the same things as they do—a house to live in with the loved ones, water, light, freedom to move at will across the fair face of the land; ground to till, or work to do. The right to think and say aloud, without fear, that which we think."

The hours passed, and the Mosotho's eyes grew gloomy with the sights they had witnessed. Here and there was he able to help others—some of his own race, some of the Zulus, and even some of the hated *amaKula*.

Afterwards Monare would shudder at what he had seen—Indian children, even babies—snatched from their mothers' arms, and flung into the flames of the burning homes.

At this mad *pitso* in the *Khotla* of Fire, Hate was the Chief, and mercy was shown to none.

5

Late that first night of the riots, Monare was running behind a band of some twenty Zulus in the neighbourhood of Cato Manor. His home-boy, Mkize, he had not seen again.

The Zulus, with savagely stamping feet, were chanting their war cry, adding for good measure, the never-to-be-forgotten:

"*Bulala amaKula! Bulala amaKula!*"

They approached a house, ringed by burning dwellings, yet itself, so far, not aflame. On the stoep cowered a group of women and young children, hiding behind boxes and bedding-rolls.

Monare rubbed his eyes.

"What crazy man stands there, armed with but a stick, facing the fighting Zulus? Foolish man! In less than minutes shall his spirit leave him—and to what purpose? For naught shall stay the Zulus from raping his women, from stealing his goods, and from burning his house."

Thus mused Monare. Yet was there admiration in his heart for this courageous Indian. He thought:

"In such a manner would I, too, stand, should Ma-Libe and our home be threatened."

As the murdering band got closer, Monare saw, to his horror, that the courageous Indian was the Moruti, the *iSuleiman*

Moulvie, whom he had saved from the falling bag of sugar at Maydon Wharf; standing slightly behind Abdul Wahid was a fair-skinned Indian boy of about fifteen years—obviously the Moulvie's son.

Monare muttered:

"Must I again stand by and see a friend killed?"

For he was just in his heart, and knew that to the blood-maddened Zulus, this was not murder, but a war of revenge.

The words of the Moruti Lefa came to Monare's mind:

"You can only pray that one day a way of atonement may show itself."

Atonement? Would this be atonement, or would it be treachery, disloyalty? No! This was no treachery. His, Monare's help, could but put off the inevitable end for a while—perhaps give the women and younger children some chance of escape. As for him, Monare, he would doubtless die with Abdul Wahid and his son.

So be it.

And Monare—consigning his wife and son to the hands of the Moruti Lefa's god—began to run with great strides through the ranks of the Zulus, shouting as he ran.

When Abdul Wahid saw the tall figure of Monare dash towards him from amongst the terrible ranks of the Zulus, he thought:

"Where a chance existed, now there is none."

He did not recognise Monare, and deemed him to be but one more savage than his fellows. The Moulvie raised his stick to beat off the attack, and spoke words of encouragement to his young son, standing so fair and beloved by his side.

Monare shouted:

"Strike not. I am Monare, the Mosotho, come to your aid."

"Welcome as never before, Brother Monare," cried the Moulvie, now recognising him in the sudden light from a flare-up of the fire.

The Zulu *impi* stopped in a bunch of amazement.

Their leader spoke harshly:

"Ho! Dog of a Mosotho! Whyfor have you turned towards the enemy? Can you afford him protection? Can he share his wealth or women with you, when both you and he, in a short space of time, shall be dead?"

The other Zulus laughed.

"Ho, ho, ho!"

Monare, thinking that reason might still be served, cried out in loud tones:

"This man is a Moruti amongst the *amaSuleiman*. He is a good man, and friend to both Zulu and Basotho. Let us spare him and his family and his possessions."

The leader of the *impi* sneered.

"You must be a servant of some white man Moruti, Mosotho dog. Are we children, that you preach to us thus? Strike him down now, where he stands, and yours shall be the choice of the fairest of his women."

But when he saw that Monare made no answer, the Zulu leader signalled to his *impi*, and they charged towards the house, crying:

"*Bulala amaKula! Bulala amaKula!*"

The children cried and the women screamed, and hard blows were struck. Mingled with the war songs of the Zulus, could be heard Abdul Wahid's voice, shouting in frenzied tones:

"Allah O Akbar! Death to the Unbelievers!"

Sometimes there came a snatch of the Basotho war song, the *Mokorotlo*, howled into the night by the atoning Monare.

Who was to prevail?

Now did Abdul Wahid's brave young son fight with one hand; his one arm was broken. Monare's face and shoulders were running with blood. Abdul Wahid was staggering under the Zulus' strong blows.

In his heart, Monare prayed to the God of his Moruti:

"O God of my Moruti, if it must be that we die, let it be so. But allow these innocent women and children to be saved."

Abdul Wahid was now fighting from his knees; the air was noisy with the thudding blows and pain-filled groans. The women wept as they felt rape approach, and death draw nigh. The children moaned in terror.

Monare found time to think, as he listened to the noise, and saw with his blood-filled eyes the dancing sticks and lurching bodies of the Zulus, in the light of the burning houses:

"Now I know what the Moruti's hell must be like, and I no longer fear to go there."

Yet was God pleased to answer the prayer of the unselfish, for sirens were heard, the searing flight of shot was sensed, and the shouts of white men shattered the ears. Quickly there came a shielded car spouting bullets, and a pick-up van spilling policemen and soldiers.

Those of the Zulus who could still use their legs, turned and fled. The helpless ones lay groaning on the ground.

Before Abdul Wahid could say a word, the leading policeman struck Monare over the head with his truncheon.

"You did well to catch the leader of the bloody bastards," he said to the Moulvie. Before worse could befall Monare, Abdul Wahid quickly explained the truth. Much did he praise Monare's brave action. He told the policemen that this was the second time that he owed his deliverance to the strong arms of Monare. Now was there a commotion in that house, for cries of relief and gladness were as loud as those of woe.

Soon, in response to a message from the leader of the police, a doctor arrived from the road, and speedily were the wounds of the men tended, and their broken and bruised bodies bandaged.

Monare regained his senses when the doctor poured down his throat a tumbler of the white man's brandy. But this attention was refused by the Moulvie and his son. Presently a lorry arrived, and Abdul Wahid and his son, and the womenfolk and the younger children, and Monare were all lifted on. Then were the goods of the Moulvie piled on to the remaining space, to be taken to a place of safety.

The womenfolk of the *amaSuleiman* clung to the legs of Monare in gratitude, and had to be removed forcibly by the police. The kind policeman said that if he liked, Monare could—before going to his compound—accompany the people he had saved to their refugee camp.

To Monare's amusement, the refugee camp turned out to be the white man's church in West street. He was somewhat affected by the truncheon blow, and by the white man's brandy, which is doubtless why he sniggered:

BLACK FIRE

"How did they know you were a *Moruti*?"

Promising to visit the Moulvie in his new temporary quarters, Monare now accepted the offer of the police to drive him back to Maydon Wharf. The police sergeant warned him to report at the police station in Smith Street on the morning of the third day, so that he could tell of the events of the night.

6

Early on the third morning after the events at Cato Manor, Monare woke to find white men standing by his bed.

"*Mushla* boy!" said one.

"Good show!" threw another.

Makulu Baas was also standing there. In Sesotho he spoke:

"I am very proud of you, Monare. You performed a very brave deed."

Monare felt a little bit embarrassed; he said:

"The *amaSuleiman* was my friend."

The *Makulu Baas* replied:

"These white men want to take your picture so that it may be put in all the newspapers, and thus shall all Lesotho know what a brave son she has. Also the mayor of this city desires you to wait upon him at the town hall, for the City Council has decided to reward your bravery with a gift."

All these words fell very smoothly on the ears of Monare, yet in them he sensed some hidden danger, which, as yet, he could not pin down with his assegai. As he thought over this, he replied:

"The white man's police have ordered me to report at the charge office in Smith Street this morning."

The *Makulu Baas* replied:

"That has been the subject of arrangement. First, we shall take the photographs, then shall we visit the city hall, and finally, shall it be time for you to go to the police station."

Monare looked round for his home-boy, Mkize, but could not see him.

Makulu Baas continued:

"This day you shall receive pay, but do no work."

Nevertheless, the strange feeling of discomfort in the stomach of Monare, remained. Somewhere hidden in these fair words, lurked danger.

The white men and the *Makulu Baas* remained in the motor cars outside whilst Monare ate porridge and drank *mahleu*. He was still stiff and sore and bandaged. In spite of the uneasy feeling and unknown fear, he felt grateful that he had been shown the path of atonement.

He thought:

" Even if the great detectives track me down, and I should hang, still do I feel that I have won the forgiveness of the God of my Moruti, and shall not dwell in his hell too long. My friend Koto, I let them kill, but in this affair at least nine lives which might have been loosed, are still tight within their bodies."

When Monare had eaten, many pictures were taken outside the compound on the wharf—some of Monare by himself, and some with the *Makulu Baas*. Monare had wished to don his smart clothes, but the white men wished him to wear his blanket, and so it was.

The white men placed the *Makulu Baas* with Monare in one of the motor cars, and off they drove to the city hall. Monare noticed that many of the white men's shops were still closed, that few Africans appeared on the streets, and no Indians.

Arrived at the city hall, they climbed many steps until they came to a room with carved chairs, which bore on its walls the pictures of many past mayors of the City of Sugar. Here assembled the Mayor and the councillors.

Addressing Monare through the *Makulu Baas*, the Mayor said:

" O Monare, worthy son of *Thesele*, what you did that night of terror, shall be remembered as long as this city stands. I am told that on great occasions, the men of the Basotho race recall brave deeds from the past, and praise them. To me it is certain that always on such occasions will the name of Monare be included. This fight between the Africans and the Indians, still continues; we can only hope that it will soon end. We do not yet know how it started; maybe the truth of that shall never emerge from the mists, but whoever was to blame, there will be bitterness and hatred as a result. Such deeds of bravery as yours, O Monare, will, when recalled,

BLACK FIRE

soften the fierce revengeful feelings, and help to bring about the birth of understanding between the races which dwell in this city. As a mark of our gratitude and esteem, we the councillors, ask that you will accept this gift."

The Mayor gestured to Monare to approach.

" Here is a gold wrist-watch with your name and deed inscribed. And here, O Monare, is a purse of money for your use."

So saying, the Mayor sat down, there was a roar of cheering and the clapping of the hands, lights flashed as the photographers took their pictures, and the tears of pride and joy rolled down Monare's cheeks.

Monare replied modestly and briefly:

" *Morena*, I thank you. The Moulvie was my friend."

Chapter Three

THE GRATITUDE OF THE *AMASULEIMAN*

WHEN THE GATHERING DISPERSED, the *Makulu Baas* led Monare to the car to return to Maydon Wharf; but Monare asked if he could not visit the church nearby in West Street, that he might see his friend the Moulvie.

The *Makulu Baas* was pleased to agree, and the white man and the black man entered the church, which was filled with Indian refugees. These unfortunate people were being tended by kind-hearted white men and white women in the uniforms of the Red Cross and St. John's. No African was to be seen, and as Monare walked in, a deep-throated growl of hate and fear arose from the refugees. This was instantly hushed as Abdul Wahid, who was standing near the door, cried in a piercing voice:

"Peace, brothers. This is the African who saved the lives of my family at risk of his own."

The ominous growl gave way to a murmur of wonder, as the Moulvie told of the fighting on the stoep of his house. To these poor people, it was a promise and a comfort in their time of trouble, to know that there were yet among the African people those who cherished kindness within their hearts. The recounting of the Moulvie's story cheered even those who had lost all—including their loved ones—to face the dark future with more hope.

Monare spoke a while with Abdul Wahid and his son, and then emerged. Somehow the rumour had spread that the African hero of the riots was within the church, and a great crowd of all races had assembled in West Street. As Monare got into the car with the *Makulu Baas*, the people started to cheer.

At last, proudly clasping his gold watch and his purse of money, Monare arrived back at Maydon Wharf. When the *Makulu Baas* asked if he were happy, Monare replied:

"Oh, yes, my *Baas*. Very happy. I wish only that my wife and son could have been here this day."

"Waste no time on regrets, Monare. Your photo and a story of this presentation will be in all the newspapers—even in far Lesotho."

Suddenly a bombshell of light exploded in that dark corner of Monare's mind, where dwelt that gnawing worry—in which the sense of danger had lingered.

"Photos? Name in the papers?"

Monare's thoughts and fears surged like the waves of the Great Waters.

"What is in the papers, will also be seen by the great detectives of Lesotho. Now will they track me down? . . . O God of my Moruti! I do not want to die!"

But aloud, Monare only said:

"Thank you, my *Baas*, for your kindness. I will rest a while, and then go to the police station."

And the *Makulu Baas* replied:

"So be it."

The *Makulu Baas* departed, and Monare tried to rest.

2

Monare awakened at noon, refreshed.

His mind again busied itself with the thoughts which had filled it when sleep fell on his eyes. He rose and fetched a mirror, and studied his face closely.

"This face shall appear only in to-morrow's paper, or at the very earliest, in those on sale in the streets to-night. There are many more than one Monares; and who—looking at this face in the mirror, which shall be the face of the photographs—shall say that it is the face of Monare of Lomontsa? The police saw me the other night and said naught. Let me rather get this business of reporting to the police in Smith Street, over now—before the danger of the photographs smoulders into flame."

Monare then cleansed himself, and still retaining the blanket, set off for the Smith Street Police Station.

His instinct in this case proved itself to be right; for little time was wasted in questioning. The police had other, more urgent matters, to consider and act upon. Mainly they wished to know where Monare might be found should he be required; they also desired to know whether Monare could pick out again the faces of those Zulu people who had attacked the house of Abdul Wahid. Having sucked the kernels of knowledge from Monare, as one with strong teeth deals with a mealie, the great detective dismissed Monare with the Zulu words: "*Hamba kahle!*"

When Monare returned to the compound, he found that many of his home-boys had failed to return from the excitement. Others, he was told, had been thrown into jail—and amongst these latter, to his sorrow, was his friend Mkize. Taking his purse, Monare set off again with the aim of securing Mkize's release. But as he reached the corner of Grey Street and West Street, the afternoon papers were being sold, and he heard one *umfaan* newsvendor call to another:

"The poster says, 'No bail for Riot Prisoners!'"

For the end of the fighting was not yet. The troubles were to continue until well into the month of March, though the flames were such as come from a dying fire.

On the sixteenth, a band of four hundred Africans of all tribes, armed with sticks and knives, parleyed with the white men for terms of surrender, for the blood-lust had left them somewhat. Their leader asked that the Native Commissioner should meet them and hear their words. The leader spoke thus to the Native Commissioner:

"You can ride a horse with a sore back, and he will go; you can press him further and he will still go; but if you continue to flog him too much, he will buck. And that is the position with us— the Indians have exploited us in business; they have ousted us from our livings—some of us even from our houses and our lands. As a result of this we have suffered great financial losses, and our wives and children have had to eat the bread of humiliation. The Indians have overcharged us in their shops; they have made us buy goods that we did not want; they have corrupted our daughters.

"This, then, is why we fought."

Suitable terms were arranged for the laying down of arms, and the leader of these four hundred Africans was promised that those who had not killed, would be forgiven their other crimes. And so it was, and in after days it came about in truth, that the African people did take over many houses, shops, and motor buses that in the days before the riots, had belonged to the Indians. For many weeks all Africans refused to travel in the buses of the Indians, with the result that at long last was the white man forced to give the Africans licences to run their own buses.

Some days passed, and Mkize came before the magistrate, but nothing could be proved against him, other than that he had been carrying a stick. He was therefore fined five pounds, which fine Monare paid.

Mkize's friendship continued to warm Monare's heart, but he found that all his home-boys were not of one mind.

By the time that seven days had gone, everyone in the compound had learned of Monare's action on the night of terror, and had seen with their own eyes, the gift which the city councillors had bestowed on him.

Some said:

"*Ee!* Home-boy, it is a matter for praise."

Others said:

"You are no longer one of us—you are an *iSuleiman*!"

Many were secretly jealous of the results of Monare's bravery, though they themselves would have had neither the boldness nor the strength to have acted as Monare did—these said slyly:

"Take us to these beautiful *amaSuleiman* women of yours, home-boy."

Also, were there those who considered Monare to be a traitor to his race, and these ignored him, except to spit at him in passing, the bitter words:

"*iKula!*"

3

Monare's heart now became sad within him; his work no longer pleased him. When he sang his songs at the hauling of the trucks, those who were against him—and they were many—joined not in the chanting, but laboured in sullen silence.

At this time Monare wrote—by the hand of Mkize—a letter to Ntoane in the City of Gold, telling him of all that had happened, and asking him to let Libe and Ma-Libe know of the honours he had received at the hands of the white men, so that they might rejoice and be proud of him. Especially Monare asked that the Moruti Lefa be told that Monare had found the path of atonement, and had chosen to take it.

When Ntoane's reply arrived, Monare was overjoyed to learn that Libe's wife, Makopoi, was in due course to become a mother. His pleasure was cooled somewhat by Ntoane's news that the great detectives were now strong on the track. Ntoane's advice to Monare was that he should speedily remove himself from the City of Sugar.

Monare wept.

"By saving Abdul Wahid, I have earned the good will of the white man. With continued hard work I should have been able to ask for one of the houses which the white man is building for Africans with families. But by this same deed, I have earned the enmity of most of the Basotho. O God of my Moruti! When shall the Gourd of Punishment be emptied. When shall I again see my wife, Ma-Libe, my son Libe, and his son. Shall I ever see that grandson? Where now shall my feet wander?"

Some days later, the *iSuleiman* Moulvie came down to Maydon Wharf, and making a chance to speak privately, Monare asked that he might be permitted to visit him at his home at Cato Manor, to which the Moulvie had now returned.

The *iSuleiman* replied:

"Brother Monare, that house and all it contains are yours. You do not need to seek permission to visit it. My son, Ghulam Hussain is always speaking of you. His arm is now completely recovered. Come then, this Saturday afternoon."

GRATITUDE OF THE *AMASULEIMAN*

Avoiding for once his tried friend and home-boy, Mkize, whose heart was set on a visit to their brewer of home-style kaffir beer, Monare took bus to the Moulvie's house.

Monare was warmly received by the Moulvie, and also by Ghulam Hussain, his son, to whom Monare was something of a hero.

Now was it in Monare's mind to tell to the Moulvie the story of his life, and ask him for the benefit of his advice at this critical time which had arrived.

"Which God do you worship, O Moulvie?"

"There is no God but Allah, and Mohammed is His Prophet."

"This Mohammed you speak of—is he like the Jesus of my Moruti?"

"Yes, Monare. We, too, have a great regard for Jesus, whom we call Isa. There is but little difference, Monare, at the bottom, between what your Moruti preaches in his church, and what is written in the Holy Quran."

"Does your Great One, Mohammed, stand between sinners and their god, as does this Jesus, as recounted by my Moruti?"

"No one stands between God and man. No man can escape the punishment for his misdeeds, but forgiveness will come after atonement."

"Is punishment great, O Moulvie, for sins of violence?"

"Each soul is weighed in the balance, Monare, but Allah is always compassionate and merciful. What leads one man to sin, may lead another to sainthood. None but Allah and you, know what is in your heart. But rest assured, brother, that the sins of violence, committed when the blood is hot, are not so heavily punished as are the sins of the heart and spirit. But why ask you such things, Monare?"

Then did Monare, with many gestures and much shame, tell the Moulvie Abdul Wahid, all that had happened since first he left Lesotho to go to the City of Gold, sparing himself not at all. He told of Ritual Murder, of Dagga, of his tragic relations with Mary and Libe, and he did not hide from the Moulvie his strange adventures with the handsome youths.

The Moulvie sat a while in meditation, and then said:

"May the Peace of Allah abide with thee, Monare. Do not

grieve overmuch at what you have done—rather must we think of what still has to be encompassed. But before we talk of the direction your footsteps must take, I will tell you something of my own country far across the Great Waters, so that you may take heart and know that you are not the greatest sinner the world has known."

And the Moulvie laughed, as if remembering joyous things. Monare looked up in a puzzled way, but the Moulvie went on:

"Your sins, Monare, are the sins of a man, but you have repented of them. In my country, many have been guilty of such offences, yet by Allah's Grace on the Day of Judgment will they cross the Bridge safely and fall not into the Abyss."

To the wondering Monare did the Moulvie now recount strange tales of India. He spoke of the Pathans and their blood-feuds, of their long-dead ancestor Alexander the Great; he told Monare that because of their admixture of Greek blood, and because of the seclusion of their women, the Pathans on the Border regarded the love of man for man with some tolerance. Also did the Moulvie describe to Monare the effects of the drug opium, or *hafim*, as he called it—not only was this drug esteemed by the *Haqims* for its beneficial qualities, but it had on occasion in the old days even been issued to soldiers as an emergency ration.

Thus passed the afternoon, and when the tea had been served and savoured, Monare asked:

"What now, is your advice?"

4

The Moulvie replied thus:

"There is a port on the coast of the sea, farther to the north, named Lourenco Marques. It lies in the Portuguese territory of Mocambique. There have I a friend, who is also Moulvie at a Mosque. I shall write to him to-day, for I think that a future may be planned for you in that country."

"But how shall I get there, O Moulvie?"

"Monare, you will have to pass through the countries of the Zulus and the Swazis, for Mocambique lies to the north of Zululand and Swaziland. Of course, in these two lands the detectives of the

GRATITUDE OF THE *AMASULEIMAN* 183

white man can follow you and arrest you, but if you reach Lourenco Marques, I think you will be safe. There are certain arrangements which will have to be made about getting you away from this Union of South Africa, and these may take some time."

" Shall I be able to let my wife and son and my old friend Ntoane, know my plans ? "

" Not yet, Monare. As I said, I have a plan for your future which has taken shape as we sat here talking. When perfected you may or may not, accept it. But I am not yet ready to tell you more. For the present I feel you should leave the compound."

" But where, then, shall I stay ? "

" I have a room in my yard—this you may have for a few weeks until my arrangements are complete. Your food will be my concern."

" O Father Moulvie, your heart is very big, I thank you."

" That is no matter, Monare. But I think you should spend these weeks in learning to read and write."

" O my Father ! Am I a child to go to school ? "

" Yet must you learn, Monare."

" But how could these hands grasp a pen ? "

" Nevertheless, Monare, the ability to read and write a little English will be of great help to you in Lourenco Marques—and there you will also have to learn a little of the tongue of the Portuguese."

" O Moulvie! What a fool I shall look walking with slate in hand to school with the *picanins*."

" That need not be ! I—and my son Ghulam Hussain—shall teach you to the best of our ability."

And thus it turned out to be in the event. When Monare returned to the compound at Maydon Wharf, he gave it out that he was returning home, he took leave of his friend Mkize, he drew what pay was due to him, said farewell to the *Makulu Baas*, and on the second night, took his case and rode to the house of the *iSuleiman* Moulvie, Abdul Wahid.

Phase Four

CRESCENT

". . . if there is a Time for Remembering, there is also a Time for Action; to live in the Past, is not-to-live in the Present, and he who is dead in the Present, might as well be buried! . . ."

MONARE OF LOMONTSA

*To
my friend
AZAD KHAN
of
Sajjikot, Pakistan*

this Phase—CRESCENT—
is dedicated

Chapter One

THE FRIEND OF GHULAM

Now was the life of Monare passing through a strange tunnel; for a period of two months he did not stir from the courtyard of the *iSuleiman* family. There he ate, there he took such exercise as was possible; and there, day and night, he struggled with the mysteries of letter-forming and figure-writing. It was a task of much difficulty, and Monare said to himself:

"If ever I learn this marking with the pen, if ever I come to understand what these twists and lines on the paper mean, then it seems to me, that with but little more effort I could learn to become a *ngaka*. How my fingers ache. How my arm tires. Loading sugar at the docks was *umfaan's* work, compared with this.... But wait, soon shall I be able to write home, and to my son, with my own hand."

And Monare persevered, and the time came when he could read and write, and pronounce simple sentences. With some confidence he would say in English:

"How are you, my good sir? Fine, thanks. Don't mention it."

He was helped tremendously by the youth, Ghulam Hussain; the Moulvie, Abdul Wahid assisted too, but he was often absent on his religious duties. Ghulam Hussain, however, spent all his spare time, when he was not himself at school, in the presence of Monare. A great affection sprang up between these two.

It was natural, that living like the two fingers of one hand with an *iSuleiman* family, Monare should learn much about their manners and their customs, for Monare was very observant.

Gradually, too, he came to tolerate their food, which at first, was too rich and highly spiced for his taste. His liking for kaffir beer, however, was in no way lessened.

But something was cooking in the pot, which gave off no odour to warn or tantalise Monare and, when it came to the boil, the Mosotho felt that he had been turned inside out.

2

One evening, Ghulam Hussain spoke thus with Monare, with great gentleness and affection.

"Friend, is there aught which repels you in the customs of the House of my Father, or in our worship of the one God?"

"*Ka Thesele!* ... No."

Monare thought for a spell, and then went on:

"Much do I find to praise in the religion of the *amaSuleiman*. All religions are good. I have seen the blue-crossed African women singing their hymns; I have watched the priests come from that big church of the white men near the Indian market, swinging their wands and carrying in procession their holy fires and calabashes. I have heard the hook-nosed people lamenting in their church near to Albert Park. I have even marched with the big drums behind the red-capped Baruti, singing their songs with them, and beating the tambourin. *Ee!* Cattle of the Chief! I am a much-travelled man."

Monare laughed.

"But much as I admire the ways of the *amaSuleiman*, I was not born one, I am a Mosotho."

"Yes, Brother, you were born a Mosotho, and I was born a Pathan—yet could we both worship Allah."

"*Ee!* What talk is this?"

The Pathan youth now declared:

"A man does not have to be born *iSuleiman*, any more than he has to be born a Christian—he can become one."

Monare now saw where the wind was blowing these words, and after a time he said:

"But I have heard your prayers coming from the mosque. You say them not in Indian, nor yet in the tongue which you use

THE FRIEND OF GHULAM

amongst yourselves. Neither do you use English, nor *sesotho*, nor Zulu. Am I already a *ngaka*, that I should be able to speak with yet another tongue?"

And Monare laughed long.

Ghulam Hussain said:

"Friend, few of us speak the language of the mosque, the language of Allah's Beloved, Mohammed; yet such Arabic words as are needed for your prayers, I can teach you. The point of the assegai rests on this. What is in your heart?"

At length Monare said:

"Friend of my heart, if this becoming a Muslim..." And he stumbled over the new word, and went on: "If I can become *amaSuleiman* like you, my heart is in it."

And he threw his arms around his friend, and pressed him close.

The Pathan freeing himself gently, turned and called in a loud voice:

"*Shuk'r Allah hamdolillah!*" God be praised and thanked! And turning, shouted joyfully:

"O my Father! Come quickly!"

3

Monare gazed at his friend in some amazement.

But quickly, now came the Moulvie, Abdul Wahid, in his eyes a question.

Ghulam Hussain spoke:

"Father, our friend and brother, Monare, wishes to become a Muslim."

"You spoke not of other things, my son?"

"No, Father."

The Moulvie turned to Monare and embraced him, and spoke thus:

"Do you believe, Monare, that there is no God but Allah, and that Mohammed is His prophet?"

"O Moulvie—yes. But what of the Jesus of my Moruti?"

"Fear not, my son. Hasrat Isa is numbered among the blessed.

The Holy Quran states that Jesus, too, is one of the prophets of God."

"And Mary, His mother?"

"Her, too, do we revere for her chastity, her obedience, her faith, and her devotion."

"Then, O my Father, am I ready to learn, and to accept."

Then said the Moulvie, with joy:

"Repeat these words after me."

And in the sonorous Arabic tongue, he recited:

"*La illah il Allah!*"

"*La illah il Allah!*" repeated Monare as best he could.

"*Mohammed rasul Allah!*" chanted the Moulvie.

"*Mohammed rasul Allah!*" echoed Monare, with stumbling tongue.

With happiness, the Moulvie announced:

"Monare, you are now a Muslim. You have repeated the Profession of Faith. 'There is no God but Allah, and Mohammed is His prophet.' This is a very great day."

Now was it the turn of Ghulam Hussain to embrace his Mosotho friend in congratulation.

For a while did the Moulvie Abdul Wahid instruct the new Sheikh in the tenets of Islam, stressing the unity of God, His matchless goodness, mercy and forgiveness. Then did he rise and cry out:

"Ghulam! This calls for celebration. Run to your mother, boy, and ask her to kill two fowls. This night shall we eat chicken *pilau*, in Monare's honour."

He turned again to Monare.

"Now, Monare, there but remains the naming. I have it, we shall call you 'Dost Ghulam,' the Friend of Ghulam."

And the Moulvie and Monare embraced in great happiness.

And so it was that Monare of Lomontsa the Mosotho, became Dost Ghulam the Muslim. But he was still of Mosotho blood and proud of it, and yet he was kin to his *amaSuleiman* friends. What a story he would have to tell, when—if ever—he should see again his beloved wife, his son, and the Moruti Lefa. Here Monare felt a slight doubt. Would the Moruti be as pleased as he, Monare was? But these thoughts Monare quickly dismissed from his mind with the reflection: "All Baruti dislike losing church members."

There was much rejoicing that night as the two men and the boy ate their pilau. Said Abdul Wahid:

"My happiness is the greater, Monare, because your acceptance of Islam is part of my plan for your escape from your troubles. Now, when you reach Lourenco Marques, you will arrive there as Dost Ghulam the Muslim, and not as Monare of Lomontsa. But, as a Moulvie, I could not, of course, hold out any inducements to you to become a Muslim. I left it in the hands of my son, and hoped that through the great love you bear for each other, such a thing might come to pass. May Allah be praised!"

Thus started a new term of learning for Monare, or as he loved to be called, Dost Ghulam, and his talk at that time was most wonder-provoking. His new English and his new Arabic were like the *mafofonyane* which run quickly on parallel lines, head to head and coach to coach, between Germiston and Johannesburg. Could Monare's home-boys have heard him at this time, truly would their sides have split with laughter, and the Moruti Lefa would have suspected Monare of having taken too much home brew.

And now came the last hurdle for Monare to jump. Muslims do not take strong liquor, and poor Monare was a confirmed beer drinker.

The Moulvie used tact and patience, and he warned Monare that no true Muslim drinks wine or the white man's beer or brandy. With great understanding, he left the final weaning to the tender hands of Ghulam Hussain.

Saturday afternoons were Monare's testing times, when it would be proved whether love or habit were the stronger. Before Monare's acceptance of Islam, the Moulvie—out of love and gratitude—had always seen to it that Monare was well supplied with kaffir beer at the week-ends, for Monare could not leave the courtyard. But now that Monare had accepted Islam—well, he had to put up a fight.

Now, when the hunger seized Monare, Ghulam Hussain would bring him draughts of shebert, cool and iced; would make him tea; would be willing to tread strange paths for his friend's sake; would play *morabaraba* with him; would wrestle with the Mosotho in border fashion. Ghulam Hussain, at these difficult moments would embrace Monare, and persuade him to tell of his days in the City of Gold, of his taking of *matekoane*, and of his strange desires. But these two stepped not beyond the bounds of propriety.

With much innocent affection and patience, and kindly cunning, did Ghulam Hussain finally take from Monare the desire for the drinking of kaffir beer.

Now, at Moulvie Abdul Wahid's suggestion, did Monare allow his moustache and beard to grow. What a difference it made to his appearance, especially when Ghulam Hussain placed on his head a red fez.

"Look in the mirror, now, friend of my heart."

Monare looked, and burst into laughter; then he ran to his box to get a copy of the *Natal Mercury*, which had published his photo after the riots.

He looked into the mirror again.

"Not the same Monare," he averred.

Ghulam Hussain replied:

"No, the friend of Ghulam now."

Chapter Two

THE RADIANT STRANGER

TIME LOITERED NOT by the way; the weeks passed.

Monare's health began to suffer to some degree from his close confinement and his earnest studies.

During these days there was much writing of letters between Abdul Wahid and the Moulvie at Lourenco Marques. The arrangements of Monare's departure and transit to Mocambique progressed with dreadful speed.

At last the day dawned, when but one week remained before the arrival of the day set down for farewell. So far the Moulvie had not spoken to Monare of the details of the journey he was to undertake —this exciting discussion was still in the future. Monare spent all his spare time with his great friend Ghulam Hussain, and one night, after parting from the youth, the imminence of another parting soured Monare's heart, and he prayed again to the God of all Baruti, thus :

" O Great Spirit and God ! I have sinned, I know—I have sinned grievously. Yet do I seem already to have died two deaths in payment, and am to die yet again, and still the end is not come ! For it was death to leave my beloved wife, Florinah, and my fields and cattle. A second death it was when I had to bid my son Libe, and my home-boy, Ntoane, farewell. And now again, the grave of love and friendship yawns before me. Soon I must part from those who have been as father, son, brother and friend to me. O God of all Baruti ! Is there no mercy for such as me ? Is there no end to the payment I must make ? Shall I have to wait beyond Death for reunion with all those that I love ? "

PHASE FOUR—CRESCENT

For it may be said in plain and strong language, that there is no comradeship like the comradeship of arms—no greater love can exist between men, than that which dwells in the hearts of those, who —together—have faced great odds and achieved victory.

Bitter and unendurable sadness lay heavy in the heart of Monare, at the thought of being cleaved apart from his heart's friend, Ghulam Hussain. In his loneliness and sorrow, he sobbed painfully into the darkness. As he lay there in despair, with his face pressed into his pillow, and a heartache which seemed like to burst his chest, it appeared that the God of all Baruti listened to his sorrow, and found some compassion in His heart. For though Monare could never say whether he dreamed, or whether—waking—he was granted a vision, he swore until his last day that a Shining Figure at once stood by his bed, and said :

" Take courage, friend. As you feel this night, so, in the years that have been, did I feel. As I am now, so shall you become in the far-distant future. We are all but travellers on a long and wearisome journey—we are far from home. But keep this thought in your heart, friend—nothing that is good shall ever die. Those that there is love between, shall never really be put asunder—not though the flesh divide them. Not though the seas separate them, not though colour and religion segregate them. For they are one in spirit, and at the end, shall be reunited. Nothing—that—is—good —shall—ever—die."

And the vision faded, and the Presence was gone.

But the light lingered in Monare's eyes, and the golden tones of the voice resounded softly in his ears. The Face of the Presence he could not recall. When in aftertimes he thought on this matter, sometimes he imagined that the features had resembled those of the pictured Jesus. Sometimes they seemed to have been rather those of the Prophet Mohammed, as described by the Moulvie.

After a while, he felt a hand on his shoulder, he felt the wetness of tears on his neck. He opened his eyes to find the loving arms of Ghulam Hussain around him.

" Cry not, friend of Ghulam ! unless thy friend weeps with thee. My heart, too, will bleed on the day of separation."

And the friends slept in each other's embrace, and awoke comforted.

2

Now was the closing of a chapter; now came another and more bitter parting of the ways; now came the straining of the eyes to impress upon the heart a loved one's visage; now came the touching of the hands, the linking of the arms, the wistful gaze, the drying of the hot, red eyes. Another blow—deep into the sinews of the heart.

A new country lay ahead; new sights for eyes to see that desired naught else but to remain fixed on friends; new sounds to assail ears that longed only for remembered and well-loved voices —an end, and a beginning.

The days and the nights flew past with the speed of the humming bird. There came a time of sadness which seared the soul. Two nights before the last morning, the Moulvie disclosed his plans, and spoke thus to Monare, who sat with his arm around Ghulam's shoulder.

"Monare—hear your old name for the last time—until, should it be the will of Allah, you shall one day dwell in the village of Lomontsa with your wife and son. Henceforth, speak not that name. You are Dost Ghulam. Remember what I have said, and remember all that my son and I have taught you.

"Hear now the arrangements which I have made. It so happens that I know a white man, who lived for many years in my country; sometimes he comes to sit around the *dastar-khan* with us and eat *pilau*. He is a man of courage and discretion, and can be relied upon. This white man, whose name is Newington, has business in Swaziland, and will be travelling there in his motor car shortly. There is, in his employ, a Swazi, who tends the garden, washes the car, and chops the wood—at present he is away in Swaziland, on leave. The white man is going to Mbabane on business, and when he returns, will bring his servant with him. Newington Sahib is willing that you should accompany him in the motor car as far as Gollel, in Swaziland, if you, in return will give him such help as is necessary on the road with the mending of punctures, the pushing of the car through drifts, or out of mud, or with any task that he may ask of you. Thus will you escape the eyes of police and ticket examiners and other employees of the government, who would see and stare, if you went by train. Now, Dost Ghulam, is it in your heart to do these things?"

"O my Father, I shall do whatsoever you shall command, but be it known that I have no acquaintance with motor cars, nor with the changing of their tyres."

"This knowledge shall be taught to you."

Monare thought for some time, then:

"And from this Gollel, how shall I find my way thence to the city of Lourenco Marques?"

"My son is even now making a map for you, which he will teach you to read. The journey from Gollel to Lourenco Marques will be no lighthearted one. You will have to pass through lion country and through elephant country. You will have to trudge through sand, and wade through rivers. You will have to travel at night, and when you reach the final river, you will be in danger from the police—who watch the drift for such as you. There will be no shops to buy food, no place to rest your head other than the ground beneath some tree. Are you willing, then, that it should turn out thus?"

"Moulvie, I am a Mosotho. I can live off the land. I can kill small game. I am ready to do as you say."

"Good. When you have crossed this final river, you will be out of Swaziland, and in the country of the Portuguese. You will then take train at a station, which will be shown to you on the map when it is ready—and travel in it to Lourenco Marques. I shall write a letter to my friend, the Moulvie, and this, too, shall be given to you, to deliver. Then, if it be Allah's will, your troubles will be over."

"*Ka Thesele!* I thank you, my Moulvie, for all you have done for me, and for all that you are about to do. These things will always remain in this Mosotho's heart—whether in the days to come he shall be called Monare, or Dost Ghulam."

"I have a big debt to pay, Brother. To-morrow shall you be

THE RADIANT STRANGER

taught how to change the wheels of the motor car. In the evening we shall study Ghulam's map. But touching of gratitude—there can be no such talk between you and me. May Allah bless thy journeyings."

And the yawning mouth of sleep ate away most of the remaining hours.

3

The morning of the last-day-but-one dawned, and Dost Ghulam left the courtyard for the first time since his arrival. With his friend Ghulam Hussain, he proceeded to the house of Newington Sahib, on the Berea.

He felt strange in his red fez, and thought that he was the target of all men's gaze; yet to be in the open again was like a good, cool draught of home-brewed kaffir beer. His tongue was alive with questions, and his ears were filled with surprise.

Monare was dressed in his best suit. He felt proud. He had but one regret, and that was that he could not wear the same clothes as the friend of his heart, Ghulam Hussain. The Pathan was dressed in border style—on his feet sandals, or *chaplis*. Covering his legs the Pathan trousers known as *tambi*, made from six and a half yards of linen, which pleated themselves round his waist, to fall to his ankles in graceful folds, tighter round the bottoms even than the trousers of the *tsotsis*. Over his *tambi*, Ghulam wore a long white shirt, called a *kurta*, and on his head the conical cloth cap, the *kulla*, round which was bound his five-and-a-half-yard-long turban, the *lunghi*.

But as Abdul Wahid had pointed out, although Monare was a Muslim, he was still a Mosotho, and not a Pathan. His appearance dressed as a Pathan would really have brought the eyes of the police in his direction, for the Pathans are fairer than many white men.

So, as they walked, the Mosotho had to content himself by admiring the swing of the *tambi* of Ghulam. Soon they reached the large house and garden of Newington Sahib. The Zulu house-servants and the Mosotho looked at each other much as one strange dog regards another.

"*Buka!*" said the Zulus. "A Mosotho wearing a fez."

But Newington Sahib was at hand, and spoke kindly to the Mosotho and the Pathan, and told the cook-boy to give them tea in the garden. "Then," said he, "I will show you how to change the wheels of the motor car, and how to keep it clean."

There were certain things about Monare which, to those knowing about such matters, stamped him as a Mosotho. He was light in colour, as are the Basotho. The way in which he spoke the Zulu tongue was the way in which a Mosotho would speak it. Watching the curiosity of the Zulu servants, Ghulam Hussain decided to warn his friend, that until the Promised Land was reached, he should speak little to any man save Newington Sahib, and that little should be spoken in the English he had learned.

The cook-boy asked:

"Where is your home, and why do you wear the hat of the *amaSuleiman*?"

The Mosotho replied:

"My home is in Maseru. At this time is my master an *iSuleiman*, and it is at his request that I wear the fez."

The cook-boy sniggered, but appeared satisfied.

At last Newington Sahib appeared, and the time for instruction had arrived. Monare's studies at reading and writing had made him observant, and his brains had been sharpened on the stone of attention. Soon he was able to use a jack and a spanner at least as well as he could wield a pen or pencil. He found it difficult to remember that on one wheel the nuts unscrewed to the left, and on the other, to the right, but after some practice, he tumbled to the trick of it. But there were finer points to master, and the teacher had to shout:

"Don't try to loosen the nuts and take them off before you have placed the jack in the right position."

And later, in fear:

"For God's sake put the brake on first."

Then, more quietly:

THE RADIANT STRANGER

"Tighten each nut a little bit first—then go round and tighten them all right up."

Finally, the Mosotho was introduced to the hose-pipe, which he, being unacquainted with its proper manipulation, turned by accident on to the Zulu, and Ghulam, and Newington Sahib, who were watching his efforts. Unfortunately the tap was turned on to full strength. What a dancing and a swearing!

But all ended up in laughter, and the three wet ones retired to dry themselves, whilst the Mosotho learned to use the chamois.

The friends stayed until Newington Sahib expressed himself as satisfied; he also warned Dost Ghulam to be at the house the following morning by six o'clock, not forgetting to bring with him his suitcase.

The Mosotho, with new-found confidence in his disguise of moustache, beard, and fez, persuaded his heart's friend to accompany him on a last walk round the centre of the City of Sugar. At an Indian shop in Queen Street, the Mosotho bought his friend a gold watch, so that Ghulam might remember him when seeking the time of day. A fine carved stick was obtained for the Moulvie, and some silks for the women of the house. Whilst making these purchases, Monare instructed Ghulam to remain outside the shop, in the street.

4

Home, now, for the last evening.

The women of the house had been busy, for chicken *pilau* had been prepared, also dishes of *biriani*. Sweetmeats—made with dates, cream and rice—were on the *dastar-khan*, and long glasses of *lassi* —sour milk—were standing ready. Now the women brought in the flat loaves of unleavened bread—*chapati* and *parata*—and the steaming dishes of rice and meat. Around the *dastar-khan* were dishes of *amb-ki-achar*—whole mango pickles, and plates of *dhall*. The three men—using their right hands—ate with enjoyment, taking fancy bits from any dish, as their taste dictated.

Then came the green, milkless tea of Bokhara, served in small cups. Finally, the cigarette or the pipe, the water-pipe of the East.

Conversation as yet had no place here; first must the inner man be satisfied. When the women had cleared the dishes from the *dastar-khan*, then arrived the time for the exchange of gifts. The Mosotho handed over to Abdul Wahid and Ghulam Hussain the remembrance presents he had bought; these were received with gratifying pleasure. In fact, father and son disappeared to show their treasures to the admiring womenfolk.

Now the moment of surprise approached Monare. On the Moulvie's return he took from a box, a magnificent gold pen; this he handed to the Mosotho, with the words:

"This pen needs no dipping into ink-bottle; within, it bears its own fluid."

"*Ka Thesele!* Is this for me?"

"For my beloved friend, Dost Ghulam. You can now write— see to it that you put pen to paper often, so that we, your friends, may learn through the long years, how you fare."

"O my Father! Never shall I forget you. Nor all you have done for me. This *ngaka's* pen shall remain in my pocket, next to my heart."

Ghulam Hussain interrupted with a smile.

"Leave room for this, friend of my heart."

And he held out to Monare, a thinner replica of the pen.

"This is a pencil for soft writing, for notes, friend. Put it next to the pen, and forget not your friend Ghulam."

Tears of love and joy made Monare's cheeks wet; he found it hard even to breathe or speak. He grasped the hands of Abdul Wahid and Ghulam, and squeezed them tight.

Thus the opportunity for the reading of the map contrived, Ghulam spread the paper on the table, and handing Monare a notebook, said:

"Make such notes as you wish, the tools are in your pocket."

He then started to explain the markings on the paper.

"Here, friend, is Durban. Newington Sahib will drive along this road. You will pass through Stanger, and cross many rivers— the Tugela, then the Pongola, after which you will have arrived in Swaziland. If you will look closely at the map, you will see Gollel. There—that is where you leave the white man's car. From that place on, no human hand can help you—not even these friendly hands—you are under the mercy of Allah. You have to make your way to this drift across the Umbeluzi River—this lonely spot, ninety-six miles from the end of the railway. You must take with you food that will not become stale—for, from Gollel onwards, you must travel by night, and hide by day—of course you'll be able to live off the country, for it abounds with small game as well as large."

Monare pondered.

"That is no difficult task for me."

"But remember always that you are travelling through lion country, even elephants may be met with. You must exercise the greatest care. Most important of all is this place—marked here—see? Look, on the Portuguese border—see?"

"I see it, friend."

"That lonely spot is a police station, set there as a trap for such as you. They are the watchers of the drift and sleep not by day nor by night. During the war, such enemies of the British as succeeded in escaping from their prison camps, tried to cross that border into the country of the Portuguese, but their bones mostly lie bleaching in that river-bed, or in prison burial grounds."

"*Ee!* friend Ghulam, this is the time for the cunning of the jackal."

"*Yar!* Do you remember the night you stood by our side and fought the Zulus?"

"It shall never leave my memory."

"The odds against us that night are naught compared with the odds facing you on this journey."

"What food would you advise me to take?"

"Biscuits and water you must have; these and a water-bottle, we shall supply."

The Moulvie now spoke.

"Here, Dost Ghulam, is something that may prove a very good friend."

And he held out to the Mosotho, a beautifully-chased hunting-knife in a leather sheath.

"Women," he said, "as well as men, bear gratitude, and the women of my house will never forget your bravery. Between them they ask that you will accept this gift."

Monare's heart lurched in his chest; the pain of sorrow laboured his breath. But the memory of his vision came to comfort him, and he recalled the words of the Radiant Stranger that those who loved should be reunited in the end. He sighed deeply.

"Give my heartfelt thanks to the mother and daughters," he said, "and if you will permit, give them this silk in memory of me." And he took from a corner the lengths of silks that he had purchased that morning.

Now said he good night to the Moulvie and Ghulam Hussain.

5

Now was the time for packing arrived. Monare placed on the bed his keepsakes—his golden watch, his golden pen and golden pencil, his hunting-knife. He wondered if, one day, he would display them before the admiring gaze of Florinah, Libe, and Ntoane and the Moruti Lefa. His thoughts dwelt on the past year, and he imagined himself recounting the tale to his loved ones.

Sleep would not bless his eyes, however, and for long hours Monare lay thinking back on his life since first he left Lomontsa. And most of all, he remembered and mourned Koto. He thought too, of all he had observed and of all he had been told about his vast land of Africa—of all the men, white, black, brown and yellow, who had fought and laboured through the long years to make it what it was this night. He wondered if—at any time in the future—understanding would be born between the races of different colours. Too much thinking on this matter only served to increase his sadness, for he reasoned, if the two great tribes of the white man cannot understand each other, how shall they understand us?

Dost Ghulam joined the Moulvie and his son at the Morning Prayer. They then broke their fast, and farewells could no longer be kept in the cupboard.

The Mosotho said good-bye to the Moulvie with the tears shining in his eyes, and set off with Ghulam Hussain for the house of Newington Sahib.

Here the knife turned in the wound of separation for the last time. Monare felt that never again would his shadow fall on his

THE RADIANT STRANGER

heart's friend, nor would any glimpse of the Pathan's face or body fill his eyes with gladness, nor any word or laugh of Ghulam's ever again ring in his ears and pour joy into them—these things did Monare-Dost-Ghulam feel in his deepest heart.

The friends embraced in Pathan fashion, shoulder to shoulder, and cheek to cheek. Then, in tear-choked tones, Ghulam Hussain said:

"For the last time I call you by a hero's name—Monare! *Yar*, this parting hurts me as if you had plunged that hunting-knife deep into my flesh. . . . *Mashuq*. . . . How I mourn! But now you know how to write, write. I can say naught else. May Allah walk beside you all your days, dear friend—and—forget not the name of Ghulam Hussain."

And with a swish of his *tambi*, the Pathan was gone.

Newington Sahib, who had witnessed this parting, had an understanding heart. He knew from his years on the Frontier, how deep the friendship of man for man can be, and how heart-bursting the pain when friend is wrenched from friend. He placed his hand in comradely fashion on the Mosotho's shoulder, and said:

"Come, let us drink tea together, and then shall we load the car."

And thus were heartbreak and regret witnesses to yet another End, and yet another Beginning, in the life of Monare of Lomontsa, henceforth to be known as Dost Ghulam, the friend of Ghulam.

Chapter Three

"ONE MORE RIVER"

NEWINGTON SAHIB proved to be a good driver, and before the sun had risen very high in the sky, the travellers had left the good road, which ends near Stanger, and were riding with many bumps over what the white man calls the National Road to the north.

As the Mosotho looked around, wonder seized him that none of these thousands of Indians he saw working in the cane-fields, had come to their home-boys' help, at the time of the riots. When this wonder found expression through Monare's tongue, Newington Sahib was able to answer the question, thus:

"The Indians who work on these sugar lands, are mostly from the south of India; they are not men of violence. There are few Pathans, or members of the warlike northern tribes, living in Africa. Most of the Muslims in Durban come from near Bombay on the west coast; these, too are traders, not fighters. The Hindus, too, are moneylenders and shopkeepers. Few, indeed, amongst these Indians, would match violence with violence. That is why—in spite of the thousands of their fellow-countrymen on the north and south coasts—the Indians in Durban were quickly eaten up by the Zulus."

Newington Sahib was a man of good heart; he had visited Lourenco Marques, and was able to give the Mosotho much good advice as to his conduct when he should arrive in that city.

In such pleasant fashion did the hours pass. Dost Ghulam watched with interested eyes the bioscope which Nature provided on the windscreen of the motor car. Great rivers were crossed, high hills were climbed, deep descents into valleys were made. Stops occurred for the drinking of tea, and for the eating of food. Here and there, were they again in sight of the Great Waters.

At last, summoning up from within him courage, the Mosotho dared to ask Newington Sahib certain questions which had been gnawing at his brain. Step by step, through the harsh teaching of his life, was cloudily coming to him the conviction that, although Lesotho was ruled by the Chiefs—by the grace of the White King in London—yet would it get more and more mixed up with the affairs of the country which encircled it—that Union of South Africa. Since leaving his homeland, the Mosotho had seen much to distrust and dislike in the manner in which his fellow-Africans were treated by the white men of the Union. He had seen that there were big differences between the three main tribes of the white man. Such differences had raised their heads on occasion, but not so high, amongst the African tribes.

Thinking of himself, he realised that in him, and in many other men, was a warfare being waged within the mind and spirit. He remembered how the teachings of his Moruti Lefa and the orders of his Chief had fought against each other within his own heart.

He had just lived through scenes of blood and terror, brought about by the enmity between the Zulu and the Indian. The Moulvie had told him that in Natal, at festival times, many blows were exchanged between Hindu and Muslim. What, then, did the future hold? He had now, or very soon would have, both son and, he hoped, grandson. What words of wisdom, relating to their conduct and their course through life, could the white man driving the motor car give?

Newington Sahib listened to all this with great attention. Between the English and the Zulu languages, he was at last able to understand what the Mosotho wanted to know. It took time, for the African was diffident and shy, and his English was as yet no better than the white man's Zulu.

As the motor car travelled on, white man and black man exchanged thoughts on the country they both loved. Sometimes the talk twisted this way, and sometimes that, but they came to some accord on this point, namely, that equal labour demanded equal pay, no matter what the colour of the worker's skin might be.

Nevertheless, the observant Monare did not fail to point out that the houses and customs of the white man, brown man, and black man differed greatly, and agreed with Newington Sahib that until the standard of living of the black man and brown man approached the excellence of that of the white man, little could be done to kill the envy and hatred of one race for another.

Monare asked:

"What is the rock upon which rests this division of colour from colour?"

"Prejudice, Monare—that is, lack of knowledge and education."

"But do not all Baruti say that all men were born equal?"

"No man, Monare, even though he be a white man, can expect as a right to be born to a high station. But what the Baruti truly say is that there should be for all men an equality of opportunity."

These words of Newington Sahib's reminded Monare of the Moruti Lefa. He said:

"Thus did my Moruti speak at home. That all men are equal before God. But if all men—no matter what their colour—were skilled at some sort of work of the white man, then surely, there would not be enough jobs for all."

Newington Sahib laughed.

"Friend, that is a mistake made by many men. I think this way. Let me explain it simply. How does a baker know how many loaves to bake? Or, if you prefer it, how does a brewer know how much kaffir beer to brew?"

"*Morena!* Even I can supply the answer to that one. He makes as much of bread or of beer, as he knows may be demanded of him by those who buy."

"And if additional buyers come to live in his neighbourhood?"

"Certainly then, will he make more of the beer or of the bread."

"Then understand this, friend. That if Africans earn more money, surely will they buy more of the white men's goods, and build better houses. Will this not cause more jobs to be offered?"

"*Ka Thesele!* There is the truth. Yes, yes, that is very true. *Ee!*"

Gradually, however, a look of doubt crept over the Mosotho's face.

"ONE MORE RIVER"

"But where is all the extra money to come from?"

"That need be no cause for worry—this is a vast land, it can support many more millions of people. The more gold and coal and iron that is taken from the ground, the more food that is grown, the more articles, which being made in our factories, may be sold to other countries—the more money will there be. Do not worry about money—money has no value of its own, it is but a symbol of wealth, a medium of exchange."

The Mosotho looked puzzled.

Newington Sahib laughed, and went on:

"There I go again. But you know how to write, friend? Then when you write gold, or bread, is what you have written gold or bread in actual fact! No. That is what is meant by a symbol. If you sell a cow to obtain money to buy clothes—has the money itself any real value? could you not take the cow to the store, and exchange it for the suit you desire?"

The Mosotho laughed.

"I think storekeeper would not like a cow in his shop."

"There you speak truth. But you must see that money was invented by man as a convenience, so that he wouldn't have to carry cows around in his pocket."

The Mosotho laughed loudly at this remark, but he had seen what the assegai's point was resting on, and was able to understand when Newington Sahib continued:

"The wealth of this country must lie in what is put into and taken out of the good earth, and in what is done with the products of the earth, and in the hard work performed by the people who live on its surface—and on nothing else."

The two men talked on, and Monare felt the warmth of knowledge in his brain.

Then did Newington Sahib say:

"This hate of race for race, Monare, is also based on fear. Yet do I think that the white man wrongly fears that the educated and well-paid African will wish to come and live next door to him. I think that the African will always prefer to work and live amongst other Africans, even should he at times desire to meet the white man as an equal when matters of import to both races are to be discussed.

If only respect and understanding could be born between the peoples of this country, there would be no more talk of the mixing and penetration which the white man fears, and which is feared equally —if silently—by both brown man and black man."

"*Ee!* Cattle of *Thesele!* My *Baas*, you speak like a Moruti. Much mud have you cleared from my mind, and now I begin to see my thoughts clearly. But still, I do not see how the tribes of the white man can be brought to any agreement on this matter?"

"Well, at this time, of course, there is great hatred between the white men's tribes. One must be just in apportioning the blame. The Afrikaner feels very strongly that were he not to strive to force all people in this land to learn his language, it would speedily be wiped from the tablets of the memory of mankind—and in this he is right, for his language is of little importance outside this country. Yet the Afrikaner rightly thinks that if he were to abandon his language, he would lose his racial identity—he would no longer be an Afrikaner, but just a South African."

"I can understand the Afrikaner wishing to retain his language, but not his forcing of it on others. I am a Mosotho; I love Lesotho; I love my language Sesotho. Yet am I also an African, a black man, and feel kinship with all black men, but I would not wish to force the learning of my language on those who have no wish to speak Sesotho."

"That is a very just attitude. Yet to understand the feelings of the Afrikaner, you must imagine this country to be an African republic, with the white man either departed, or placed as your people are to-day, without the right to vote."

"And then, *Baas*?"

"What language would you say, should be the official language of that African republic? Sesotho, or Zulu, or Swazi, or which one of the many African tongues which are spoken?"

This was an entirely fresh viewpoint to the Mosotho, and he puzzled over it for several miles. At length he replied:

"I would let all tribes keep their own tongues, but for the official language I would chose English."

"Why, friend?"

"It is spoken, they tell me, all over the world, and yet it is not the native tongue of any African tribe."

Newington Sahib laughed, but looked pleased, and murmured:

"A judgment of Solomon!"

After a further period of silence, Monare was moved to ask:

"Can no solution be found to this problem?"

"The Englishman had the solution in his hands many years ago, but he was not ruthless enough to force it. When he ruled this country without help from the Afrikaner, then should he have insisted that there should be only one official language, his own. Not only because it is his native tongue, but because it is a world language. Think of the vast sums of money expended in printing all government papers in two languages instead of one. But would not the Afrikaner have objected to this, you may want to ask? England gave freedom to the Afrikaner, too soon. Another generation should have passed before the Union was formed. By that time would the one language have become established. I do not suggest that Afrikaans should have been suppressed, any more than Sesotho, Zulu, French, German, or any other of the scores of tongues spoken by the people of this country, have been suppressed."

"But what will happen in the future?"

"Well, I am no *ngaka*, but I prophesy thus—that although the Afrikaner is strong at the moment in the *pitso* in Cape Town, in a hundred years from now, there will be no Afrikaans language here, no Sesotho, no Zulu, only—English."

"Is there no other way, which would satisfy all the races?"

"There is, if the people would only take it—a white man has suggested that instead of this country being a Union, in which the rule of the *pitso* in Cape Town holds sway in every province, there should be a Federation, in which each province would rule itself, with a Central Government to deal with the defence of the country as a whole, and with its relations with other lands."

"Something like Lesotho is now."

"Yes, not unlike. In this white man's scheme, the language of Natal, say, would be English, of the Free State, Afrikaans, of Lesotho, Sesotho. Even the Indians would have their own small homeland here in South Africa. Each race would retain its own language and customs, and no race would be able to impose its will on another."

"*Ee!* Cattle of the Chief. But this is a sound plan. Why do not the white men adopt it?"

"Mainly because the Afrikaner will not accept it—they wish their ways and customs and language to be the ways and customs and language of all the people in the land."

"Then, Morena, why do you say that in a hundred years from now, the language of the country will be English?"

"Surely the millions of black men and brown men will have some say in the country's affairs by then?"

"But how will the white man agree to that?"

"I think it will be forced on him. At present the brown men and the black men are like puppies that crawl about with eyes as yet unopened. But when the eyes open, and the puppies see the meat and the bones and the soup, and the garden and the cats and the rabbits—will they not demand the same rights as full-grown dogs?"

The Mosotho replied:

"Would this not lead to much killing?"

Newington Sahib looked sad.

"Such a possibility is in the minds of all men who think. We must pray to Him that gave us life, that the spirits of men may be quickened; that they may realise before it is too late that there is a brotherhood of man, and that man must treat his fellowman as a brother, and not as an enemy."

Some of what was said, was not fully understood by the Mosotho, for neither the white man's Zulu, nor the African's English, were of such fluency that great ideals could be clearly expressed. Yet the black man felt comforted, and not as lonely as he had been before. He now remained silent, and turned over in his mind all that had been spoken.

2

Soon was passed the Tugela River. Late in the morning they left behind Empangeni and its sugar mills. After midday, having

"ONE MORE RIVER"

crossed the waters of the Umfolosi River, the road went away from the sea, and past the Hluhluwe Game Reserve, famous for its white rhinoceros. Now did the main road to the city of Lourenco Marques leave them—on the right—to pass through Obombo, but the road to Gollel wound through the Mkuzi Valley, and the travellers saw orange trees covered in fruit.

Here, for a while, the road passed through a tongue of the Transvaal, thrust out towards the sea. As the motor car approached the land of the Amaswazi, the tobacco lands, the orange groves, the fields of sugar cane, gave way to a country of bush.

Dusk was now falling, for they had travelled over two hundred miles since morning. At this time, they made the passage of the Pongola River, and, as the sun dropped behind the western hills, they reached the borders of the country of the Amaswazi, and passed on to the small town of Gollel. Nothing was there to show them that they had passed into Swaziland—no police post, no customs shed—but Newington Sahib explained to the Mosotho, that from now on would he have to travel by night. Never must the eye of a policeman fall on his face.

"Without a pass, you will be arrested and returned to the Union. Now is the real test of your manhood. For nearly a hundred miles you must make your way north-east until you reach the town of Stegi. At that spot you will be but eighteen miles from the country of the Portuguese, Mocambique. You will have to cross great rivers: the Ingwovuma, the Great Usutu and, lastly, the Umbeluzi. At this crossing must eyes and ears be keen, for on the passage of this river are the eyes of the white man fixed. Beyond this river you have but sixteen miles to travel, and the Portuguese town of Goba shall appear before you. Thence shall you take train to Lourenco Marques."

The motor car now drew up at the hotel at which Newington Sahib intended to spend the night. The Mosotho carried the suitcases from the car into the bedroom, and placed there, too, on the white man's orders, his own possessions.

Newington Sahib took a bath and changed his clothes. Then he said: "Wait here whilst I eat. I shall return and speak more to you about your journey; I shall also see that you get food."

For the space of one hour the Mosotho sat in the white man's bedroom. Sincerely he prayed—not the ritual prayers of the Muslim, but in his own words—to the God of all Baruti:

"O God of all Baruti, it seems that this greatest fight of mine is to be fought against things unseen: these lions and elephants that I have known only in the white man's Zoo in the City of Gold; against the hidden eyes of policemen; against things without bodies with which I could grapple—hunger and thirst and exhaustion. Always before have I had the company of man—if not friend, then enemy. You know what lies in this man's heart—repentance for not going more quickly to Koto's aid; for the wickedness I was guilty of at the house of the *semokolara*; for my intended, and attempted crime against Mary. Forgive these sins, O God of all Baruti, and help me to reach, safely and quickly, this strange new City of Lourenco Marques."

The Mosotho sat and looked at his loneliness: far to the south had he left his home-boy, Mkize; his friend and benefactor, Abdul Wahid; and his heart's friend, Ghulam Hussain. Far to the south-west lay his village of Lomontsa, nestling under the Maluti Mountains; and in the distant west, amid the pale, soft, dusty mine dumps, slept his son, Libe, and his home-boy, Ntoane. From this night on, he was indeed alone, and only the God of all Baruti knew whether at all—at any distant time in the future—he would again delight his eyes on their faces, or enjoy his ears with their voices.

He looked again on all his treasured possessions: the photos of his wife Florinah, and of his son, Libe; the golden pen, and the golden pencil; the golden watch, and the richly-chased hunting-knife. He counted his money and knew himself to be a rich man.

Now Newington Sahib returned, bringing with him packets of food. He said:

"Although you are now a Muslim, and this meat may not be *halal*, you know that whilst you are on such a journey as this you have permission to eat unlawful things—so do not hesitate, but satisfy your hunger. This other packet you will take with you, and your biscuits, and your water-bottle."

The Mosotho ate the food provided, remembering, as he felt his belly warming, that pure Muslims should eat only that meat which has been killed by a Muslim, when, at the letting of blood, the sacred words are spoken.

As the Mosotho's jaws moved, so did those of the white man—in speech:

"It is better, friend, that you should now pack away in your bundle the clothes of the white man, which you are wearing, until you reach Mocambique. Rather on the journey wear such clothes as do the Swazis. Then, should you by chance be seen along the way, interest and suspicion will not be aroused."

The Mosotho found no fault with Newington Sahib's counsel. The white man continued:

"I shall return in half an hour's time. When you have satisfied your hunger, change your clothes and repack your bundle. The moon will soon be setting, and the hour of parting approaches."

The Mosotho now quickly changed his clothes and packed away his red fez and his smart suit. He saw that his water-bottle was filled and that the bread and meat were well wrapped.

Now must black skin bid white skin, farewell. Yet, between two such men are the glasses of colour not worn. For each had respect for the other as a man, and who shall say what is the colour of the spirit?

Newington Sahib promised to acquaint the Moulvie with the progress made, and to pass on the Mosotho's loving messages. The white man also had a proper respect for bravery and, taking a ring of gold from his finger and handing it to the Mosotho, he said:

"Wear this for luck and remembrance. I have heard your whole story from my friend the Moulvie, and I should think that you should now regard yourself as having atoned for your sin. The path of atonement you trod was no easy road to walk. But keep out of the hands of the police, who wish to set you on quite a different way which will lead to the white man's judge—and he may not think as I do."

The Mosotho's throat was dry; he murmured broken words of thanks; he could say but little; his heart was overflowing.

The black hand and the white hand clasped each other, eyes met and fell, a door closed and the light disappeared. And there remained the night and its darkness and its noises and its loneliness, and the black road to the north.

The Mosotho set himself to rights within; he said to himself: "Where such kindness lights the way, only a blind or drunken man could fail to complete the journey. Now must I prove, by my care and by my cunning, that I indeed deserve the respect of the white man—may he be blessed by God!"

3

Thus did the Mosotho set off along the road to Stegi, taking care to remove himself from the bright, golden glance of motor cars and from the notice and salutations of any fellow-travellers who might be afoot.

Through the long night he trudged, and as the day dawned bethought himself of shelter where he might rest his weariness during the hours of daylight, and where he might eat the meat and the bread, and drink of the water in his bottle.

At last he saw, some distance from the road, what in days long past must have been a smart motor car of the white man. Now it lay broken and rusted but ready to serve him as shade from the now-rising sun. As he drew near, he saw that, in truth, naught remained but the metal shape. Wheels, tyres, cushions, lamps, engine—all had been taken by travellers who doubtless had made good use of that which they had removed.

With gratitude the Mosotho made use of what shade the ruined motor car could offer and, lowering his weary body to the ground, he ate and drank, and then made ready to sleep. Many times during the hours of light did the heat of the sun awaken him, and many were the moves he had to make to escape the fierceness of its rays. But at length he opened his refreshed eyes, to see that the sun was setting.

Even although he had eaten but sparingly of the meat and bread, but little remained—and that was not as fresh as was desirable after a day's baking underneath the wrecked motor car. Water, too, would require finding.

Looking at the map which had been given him by Ghulam Hussain, the Mosotho saw that shortly, where the road swept away in a great bend to the west, there must he leave it, and make his way over the mountains—the Umbombo Mountains—to the Abercrombie Pont, where he would make the crossing of the Great Usutu River. But first must he pass over the Ingwovuma River, by the road bridge. The waters of this river he could already see, not too far ahead, gleaming in the light of the rising moon. Here would he fill his water-bottle. Putting the map away, he now counted his biscuits and found them sufficient for the morrow's daybreak food.

"But after that, I pray to my God that I shall meet with a wild rabbit."

He marched off bravely down the road towards the river, and he met with no difficulty in the passage of the Ingwovuma. Once on the far bank, he walked with new strength. By dawn he had reached that place where the road swings to the west, and where he must take the mountain path. Along this rocky way he continued until the sun was rising above the mountains; then he again sought shelter from the light of day. This he found in a small cave leading into the side of the mountain. Looking carefully around him, to make certain that no snakes shared his retreat with him, he ate, drank, and slept.

This time, when he awoke, the sun had set. Water was still in his bottle, and he was able to satisfy his thirst; but of the biscuit, none remained.

His thoughts dwelled on the rock rabbit that he hoped would cross his path. Soon after the middle of the night had passed, and whilst he was yet some five miles from the Great Usutu River, he came off the mountain-side into a small hill-top valley. On the far side, to his great joy, he saw, seated nibbling grass, a family of the tribe of rabbits. Keeping an eye fixed on the fattest member of the family, the Mosotho quickly loosed his bundle of possessions from his stick, and taking stick in hand, silently worked his way to a position farther down the wind.

A clever throw, and the rabbit lay stunned.

"I shall not starve!" cried the Mosotho. "My hand and eye

still work in friendship and have not forgotten the lessons they learned when I was but a small boy."

Thus praising himself, but not forgetting thanks due to Allah, he killed the rabbit and set about lighting a small fire. Later, he cooked the rabbit in the embers and devoured half of the animal with great enjoyment, placing the remainder in his bundle to serve as his next meal. He then continued his journey.

4

Just as the sun rose, he saw before his eyes the road, and but a little distance farther on, the banks of the river which he knew must be the Great Usutu. He found that there was no bridge across the water; but some sort of a square boat, bearing on it a wagon and a motor car, was being moved from one bank to the other. A long rope—hung high above the river—passed from a post on this side to a post on that side and, sliding along this rope, was yet another, which was joined to the square boat.

As the Mosotho watched, he saw that the current of the river tried to force the boat downstream but was stopped in its design by the joining of the boat to the rope that spanned the waters. Making the boat to move by his exertions, was an old Swazi.

"Here must I think what must be done," he mused.

It struck him that should he get into the boat he could by no means avoid conversing with the Swazi; on the other hand, the current was too swift for him to dare to swim across.

"It is no use tasting fowl before it is roasted," he said to himself and, finding a clump of trees which afforded him hiding from the road—yet from which all that happened on the boat could be witnessed—he lay down on his stomach to watch. He noted that the boat, or punt, took over ten minutes to cross the river.

He pondered:

"In ten minutes the old Swazi will either have discovered that I am a stranger, or I shall have to make up a story. He may even be paid by the police to report who travels in his craft."

He kept his eyes on happening events and noticed that motor cars sometimes had to wait twenty minutes on one bank of the river for the punt to complete its journey to the other bank and return.

"Should one come to-night that is open at the back, or one like the lorry I rode on in the City of Sugar, I can climb up and make the crossing secretly."

With this idea held in his mind, he fell asleep.

He wakened in the late afternoon, and ate the remains of the rabbit, and drank water. As it grew dark he descended the path until it joined the road. Then, making certain that no eyes watched, he walked on until he arrived on the river's bank. Here, he found to his dismay that all was not well. Below the edge of the bank, tied to a post, lay the punt. To the right was built a small, yet strong, hut; in front of it sat the old Swazi, cooking his evening meal. As the minutes turned into hours the Mosotho realised that the punt did not make the crossing of the river during the hours of darkness, for soon the old Swazi, relieving himself, looked around the sky, then yawned and stretched himself and entered the hut, locking the door behind him.

What had not yet come to the knowledge of the Mosotho was the fact that animals used this river bank for their drinking place, but he was not to remain ignorant for long.

5

Buck came and went, and the Mosotho, feeling hunger, looked around for smaller game; when he could find none, he lay down under a tree near the hut—but hidden from the road—and fell into an uneasy sleep. He dreamed, and in his dream he and his old home-boy, Ntoane, were sniffing deeply—and with appreciation—at the delicious smell coming from a big tin of kaffir beer.

Suddenly sleep deserted him—he was awake. It was not he, nor was it Ntoane, who was sniffing, nor was the smell delicious. As his eyes opened, he saw, a dozen feet away, the shape of the sniffer and caught in the wind its pungent smell—it was a cheetah!

The animal had scented him but not as yet seen him, for the darkness of the tree hid him. But suddenly its head lifted, its body stretched.

With a wild cry, the Mosotho jumped for the lower branches of the tree, caught hold, slipped, got grip again, and pulled himself out of reach. In the same moment of time did the cheetah leap also, but its teeth snapped on empty air. The Mosotho shivered as the animal raised its head and snarled, and then leapt once more.

The Mosotho's possessions still lay beneath the tree with his strong stick. With his eye, he measured the distance from the tree to the roof of the hut, and from the roof of the hut to the punt. He judged that, with the help of God, thus far could he jump but no farther. But what of his cherished possessions which lay beneath the tree—purse and money, pen and pencil, photos, papers, smart suits?

Only his hunting-knife lay safe to hand. The cheetah now seemed patient and marched slowly round the tree, looking up at every few paces and snarling.

Monare-Dost-Ghulam spoke earnest words to the God of all Baruti:

"Please, Great God, show this man the way out of this trouble."

The cheetah sprang again, this time gnashing its teeth uncomfortably close to the Mosotho, who renewed his prayers urgently. Suddenly, his hand fell to his knife, and his brain cleared. He looked up and saw above him a straight, narrow branch. Quickly he removed his knife from its sheath and, with bold, quick strokes, cut the branch from off the tree. With both arms around the trunk of the tree, he started shaving one end of the branch into a sharp point. God had answered his prayer; it but remained for him to use his eye and arm as twin brothers.

The Mosotho now broke smaller branches within his reach into short lengths and, as the cheetah circled the tree again, he threw one of these short lengths at the animal. The cheetah did not like this at all and leapt in futile rage towards the Mosotho, opening wide its mouth as it jumped, in a snarl of temper. Three times did the Mosotho thus enrage the cheetah, each time judging with greater exactness, the nearness of its approach.

At last, with a silent prayer to his God in his heart, the Mosotho threw the remaining pieces of the branches with all his strength at the cheetah and quickly took firmer hold of his home-made wooden spear with his right hand.

This time, as the cheetah jumped in maddened rage and opened its mouth to swear in wrath, the Mosotho thrust his wooden spear deep into the animal's throat, at the same time letting go of the tree and allowing his falling weight to add power to his spear-stroke.

As the cheetah worried at the stick which stuck in its gullet, and spat out blood and rage, the Mosotho quickly picked himself up from the ground, seized his bundle, and ran with fearful and excited steps towards the river bank. Holding his bundle in front of him, he jumped for the punt and, with God's aid, managed to scramble on to it. The cheetah was now pained and angry, in seemingly equal parts. It had removed from its throat, with its paws, the great splinter of wood, and it was bleeding greatly. As it bellowed after the Mosotho, the noises it made were the most frightening the Mosotho had ever heard. With its mouth full of blood, its swearing sounded like an *impi* gargling.

Monare-Dost-Ghulam, keeping one eye, of necessity, on the cheetah, used his other eye to see if he could by some means increase the distance between them—for if a tired Mosotho could jump from bank to punt, so could an annoyed cheetah.

At last he found the rope which tied the punt to the post; with a quick slice of his knife he cut it, and the current started to swing the boat away from the bank. The cheetah, with an almost human yowl of anger and disappointment, crouched, ready to spring in pursuit of his supper.

The boat was swinging as the cheetah leapt, and its head-quarters flopped into the river. As it tried, with the aid of its front paws, to clamber into the boat, the Mosotho hit it hard and often over the muzzle with his trusty stick. At last the cheetah was forced to abandon its hold, and it slipped off the boat into the river, to the accompaniment of more fearsome gargling. Gradually the punt drifted out into the stream, and Monare-Dost-Ghulam thanked his God with great sincerity. His breathing was so upset that he had difficulty in shaping his mouth to form the words—but doubtless God understood.

No sooner were his thanks expressed than the Mosotho had to quickly offer up fresh petitions, for he knew nothing of moving boats through the water. Was this punt to become an unpraised *Mendi*? His eyes, feverishly searching, fell upon a rope trailing in the water. He seized it, and pulled. . . . Ah! Gradually the punt moved away from the southern bank and out into the wet darkness of the river. Sometimes facing one way, and sometimes facing another, slowly in the faint starlight, the punt crossed the Great Usutu River, aided by the clumsy efforts which the Mosotho made with an oar which lay in the bottom of the boat. After a time, the Mosotho saw a darker mass before his eyes—it was the north bank of the river.

At last, clasping his possessions tightly to him, he climbed out of the punt on to the firm ground and moved quickly, but with great wariness, away from the water's edge. For, thought Monare-Dost-Ghulam to himself:

"If cheetahs drink on the south bank, does water taste any different on the north bank? I am no policeman to desire to intrude on animals' private drinking party."

As for the punt—well, the old Swazi could get it back to his bank of the river as best he could—he wasn't going to waste any sleep over the Swazi's affairs, any more than the Swazi had over his. Doubtless he knew from bitter experience that it was better not to open the hut door when animals knocked.

After a long search, for on this bank there were few trees of any height, the Mosotho at last found a small opening in the cliffs above the river, and there lay down and slept the sleep of utter exhaustion.

Chapter Four

JORDAN CROSSING

When night again fell, the Mosotho was still lying in the cliffs, as if dead. Shortly before the moon rose, he awoke and, drinking from the water that was in his bottle, he searched for any crumbs that might remain of his food. With pains of hunger striking at his belly, he slowly made his way down to the road, and with care—but without speed—continued in the direction of Stegi. At times he staggered under the weight of his possessions, but to leave any of them by the wayside was a thought which did not enter his mind.

Strong as the Mosotho was, it was well after the rising of the sun that he saw, a short distance before him, the small village of Stegi. Here did the white man keep a post for the police, and only with care would he be able to pass safely beyond the village for the crossing of the last river. He was so tired and hungry that he swayed like a young tree as he stood.

He dared not go too close to the village. As he stood there, he said to himself:

"Unless I can find food, I shall be unable to complete my journey; food cannot be looked for until the sun has died in the sky. ... O God of my Moruti, O Allah of my Moulvie, send across my path some small game, while yet I have strength to throw my stick!"

The Mosotho found a resting place near the road and sat down awkwardly and stiffly. Soon he fell into a doze soured with dreams and belly-pains.

What the God of all Baruti thinks of man, cannot be stated with exact knowledge, but it appears true that He hears and understands the prayers of men. When man has done everything that a man can do to remove himself from severe trouble, and can rely now only on God, sometimes will God put His finger in the pot, and stir the porridge. . . . And thus did things fall out on this occasion.

Monare-Dost-Ghulam was roughly awakened by a hard blow on his nose; he opened his eyes to find, lying on his chest, a half-chewed mealie. As his eyes opened wider in surprise, he saw—flying over the bushes which hid him from the road—paper packets, which, as they touched the ground, spilled out meat and bread. His thoughts still on his Moruti, he murmured:

"The heavenly Manna!"

Rising without caution—in his great excitement—he stumbled to the roadside, and saw a motor car moving slowly away in the direction of Stegi. In it was a white man and his family and, as the car moved off, came yet more packets through the windows, which fell on to the roadside. Waiting until the motor car had hidden itself around a bend in the road, the Mosotho—as quickly as he was able—gathered up all the packets he could see and went back to his resting place.

On examining his spoils, he found that, in addition to the half-eaten mealie, he now possessed two packets of meat and bread, and the dead body of a fowl, with still much flesh left on it. Also, did he find one paper bag which contained two apples, one banana, and a broken packet of biscuits.

In spite of the sharpness of his hunger, he remembered to thank God.

"I thank you, God of my Moruti—God of all Baruti!—that it should be through the white man, that the prayer of this Mosotho was answered."

He laughed weakly and then, remembering his new allegiance, he added:

"*Bismillah-er-Rahman-er-Rahim!*—in the Name of Allah, the Compassionate, the Merciful!"

Leaving the fruit and the biscuits for the nightfall meal, the Mosotho soon finished eating the meat and the bread and the fowl. And drinking once more from his water-bottle, he fell into a deep and untroubled sleep.

2

When he awoke that night, the Mosotho was refreshed and strong and, having thanked God, and taken a drink of water, he set off in the direction of Stegi. Praying for the silence of dogs, he slunk like a jackal round the outskirts of the village. He was fortunate in that at the hotel, a dance was taking place for the pleasure of the white people—much noise and laughter did he hear, and the sound of music came to him on the night breeze.

North of Stegi, he rejoined the road and sat down on a grassy bank and ate some fruit and several of the biscuits. Here was the spot at which he must leave the road and set out through the mountains again for the crossing of the last river, the Umbeluzi. According to the map of Ghulam, it was some eighteen miles from where he sat to the Portuguese border, where he must attempt the crossing of the river, and from the river to the railway station at Goba, was a further sixteen miles.

Whether or not he could pass the border before daybreak, depended on two things, he thought.

"First must I find the drift across the river, and then must I discover where the police keep their watch."

Keeping his remaining fruit and biscuits in reserve until he should reach the Umbeluzi, the Mosotho set off on his eighteen-mile walk. By the early hours of the next morning his climbing was done, and he was now descending. Not far below him he saw the gleam of water, and heard its song in his ears. Walking now with great care, he went down to the bank and tried to decide whether the drift should be upstream or downstream. After some thought, he went eastwards and before long saw in front of him a bridge. He halted in dismay—there was no bridge marked on his map. Had he then, lost his way?

Advancing now with special care and caution, he perceived the shape of a man standing near to the entrance of the bridge. As he drew closer, he saw that the shape was that of a Swazi policeman— this, indeed, must be the border! He looked around him in the darkness to see if any marks remained which might identify the drift.

To his joy, he saw—beyond the bridge—a small kraal and a clump of trees, which were shown on Ghulam's map. Also, beyond the bridge, higher up the hill on this bank of the stream, were some dim lights, which he realised must be those of the police post.

The Mosotho sat and ate of his fruit and biscuits, working his brain overtime as he chewed. At last these thoughts came out of his head with some clearness:

"This is the place, beyond doubt, but in the past months the white man has built a bridge. This road is the new road which Newington Sahib spoke of, the new road from the City of Sugar to the City of Lourenco Marques. . . . The drift will still be passable, for the water is not too high—but to reach it, I shall have to pass the policeman."

He also mused that if this were the border, doubtless on the farther bank of the river would be the policemen of the Portuguese. He therefore made up his mind that the river must be crossed through the drift and not over the bridge.

As the night walked towards the sun, the Mosotho felt that if he wished to cross into Mocambique before dawn, then he must move now, for he had no food which might help to sustain him whilst he remained hidden yet another day on this bank of the river.

He noted that at long intervals would motor cars or men come to the bridge's entrance, and be stopped a while by the policeman, and he said to himself:

"The next time that the policeman's attention is held, then shall I pass behind him, and make for the drift."

He therefore set about securing his bundle of possessions upon his back, that his hands might be free. Making certain that all was safe, he awaited the arrival of the next motor car of the white man.

3

Events might have fallen as Monare-Dost-Ghulam had planned them, but as the Mosotho passed behind a motor car which was being examined at the entrance to the bridge, another motor car came quickly round the bend from the south, and its bright eyes fixed themselves on his body and would not release it. The police-

JORDAN CROSSING

man and the travellers in the car which had stopped, turned their heads as the strong lights of the second car blackened their shadows.

The Swazi saw the Mosotho and shouted:

"Halt!"

But so near to freedom, who could blame the fugitive for continuing?

The Swazi was armed with a pistol and, when the Mosotho failed to stand, fired it in his direction. But Monare was running, and when there came a loud bang, he knew then what it was that had whined past his ear a second before, with a noise like the father of all mosquitoes.

By this time the policeman had stopped the second car, so that the light of its lamps lit up the bank along which the Mosotho was running. As his own shadow quickly raced before him, he threw himself to the left and rolled down the river's bank. . . . With a splash, he plopped into the shallow water. Now came sounds of running feet; with cunning, the Mosotho crawled slowly back in the darkness towards the bridge, feeling sure that the eyes and thoughts of the policeman were travelling in the opposite direction. Here was the Swazi's mind rightly read, for the footsteps and shouting voices passed the Mosotho, and continued towards the east.

Moreover, by now had the second white man's car been turned, so that its eyes, too, sent their long gaze in the same direction.

Quickly the Mosotho crawled and slithered over the rocks and mud on the river's edge until he found himself beneath the bridge. For a few moments he crouched there to regain his breath, but as he rested, he heard sounds from up the hill and knew that the firing of the pistol had aroused other policemen, who would soon come down to the bank and join the hunt.

Again was the Mosotho's heart full of prayer, and God could not have been sleeping. Monare noticed that the bridge was protected on either side by a low railing made of iron pipes. Carefully he came out from under the bridge on the upstream side—away from the searching men—and slowly climbed up the arch of the bridge, and reached out one hand for the rail.

Like a lizard he moved, now bringing up his other hand to the rail; and thus—slower than a tortoise—he travelled across the bridge, hand over hand, his body hanging down over the water, borne down by the weight of his bundle. As he progressed—monkey-like—he prayed that his possessions might not have been damaged by the rocks or the water.

Half-way across the bridge, the Mosotho narrowly escaped defeat, for from the Portuguese bank suddenly entered the bridge a motor car with very bright lights. As the Mosotho became aware of the glow and the rumble, his fear nearly caused him to loose his grasp from the rail. But as he uttered an appeal to Allah, he saw, a few inches beyond him, one of the supports of the railing. When his hands reached this spot, he laid his arms one on either side of the iron pillar, his hands grasping the rail on each side. There he remained, still, as if dead.

His upward glance saw the light of the motor car's lamps fall on his hands and his arms; but God was still with him, for the eyes of the passengers—warned by the Portuguese policeman—were fixed downstream. They were doubtless straining to see whether the fugitive was to be found and arrested, or shot dead in his flight.

The lights swept past, and the Mosotho slowly continued with his painful journey. At last beneath him he could see the shallow waters of the northern bank. He waited hopefully until another motor car should arrive at the Portuguese end of the bridge and, with the snarl and chatter of its engine, deaden the sound of his fall into the water. He prayed that it might come soon, for his arms and hands appeared to have no feeling left in them.

But God's finger must still have been stirring the porridge, for in a short time, a motor lorry arrived, panting, on the northern bank. In the resulting din, the Mosotho, with a groan of relief, let go of the bridge-rail and dropped into the muddy water.

There for a while he lay, unable to move; but thinking of his precious remembrance gifts, he gathered sufficient strength to stir and, after the passing of one hour, had quietly crept along the bank away from the bridge into the Promised Land.

Chapter Five

THE PROMISED LAND

WHEN THE MOSOTHO had reached a place of safety, he spread out his belongings to dry and watched with keen eyes the happenings on the other bank of the river. At last the shouting stopped, and the motor cars which had been halted on the southern bank were now straightened, and allowed to cross the bridge. It appeared that the Swaziland Police had now given up their search as hopeless.

The Mosotho was not so foolish as to count his cattle yet, for there was still much to be done. He had no food. He had sixteen long miles to march before he could reach the railway, where might be shops at which he could buy meat or bread or mealies. He was tired; also, he had seen on Ghulam's map that before reaching the railway he would have to cross a small desert of sand, which—he had been warned—was two feet deep in some parts.

The night was walking faster; soon it would be running, put to flight by the sun, but the Mosotho decided to start his journey at once, for he had now reached that plain that lies along the coast by the sea, and the ground would be flat.

Therefore, he started off at once, without resting. True he had no food, yet had not Allah already given him wonderful proofs of His favour? He would arrive at the railway.

The road was dangerous for him to follow, for doubtless would the Portuguese police keep their eyes wide open for any stranger who walked thereon. The sixteen miles seemed never-ending, for the sun was no friend to a tired, hungry man—and one, moreover, who had drained his water-bottle of its last drops. . . . Slowly and yet more slowly did the Mosotho's feet march one before the other, and bitterly he regretted that he had not rested until nightfall. Once he was tempted to leave on the wayside his bundle of possessions, and to return to find it again when he had obtained food, drink and rest. But, thought he:

"I am now in the land of the stranger; these few things of mine —this pen, this pencil, this knife, these photos—may be all that I shall have for comfort and remembrance in all the days that yet remain to me."

And he walked on with ever-slowing steps.

As the sun started to sink, his face grew cooler, yet what was gained by added coolness was lost by increased tiredness, for as the sun set the Mosotho entered the small desert of sand which Ghulam had warned him against.

At last he could move his limbs no longer, and sank, dazed, to the sand.

As he lay there, he seemed to be in a bioscope, and all his life and adventures appeared to pass before his eyes.... He groaned.... His breath hurt him as it came in and went out.... His chest was like a tight band.... He felt his spirit loosening itself from his body. And all the time the picture of his life was passing in front of his glazing eyes.... At last, he saw in imagination himself again walking and walking, and finally sinking into the sand.... Then there came a blackness darker than the darkest night....

While he waited for he knew not what to happen, there appeared —or so he thought—a form he had seen once before—a Radiant Stranger stood beside him and spoke in tones of gold:

"The end is not yet, Brother. The path is still rough and steep before you. Yet shall you see all your loved ones again before the breath leaves your body."

Now it seemed as if the Stranger put forth his hand and raised the Mosotho from the ground and led him a few paces over a slight rise in the earth, and said:

"Look at yonder lights! Always when it is darkest, shall the dawn be nearest! Farewell for this time, but when you shall come to the end of the road, remember me, and I shall stand beside you...."

And the light that was around the Stranger faded, and the figure disappeared as if it had never been, but the Mosotho's eyes widened as they saw, a few hundred yards away from him, the lights of what must be Goba!

He fell to his knees thanking God, and staggered on towards the town.

2

Just as he approached the outskirts of the town, he came across a small dam and, stopping to wash himself, suddenly remembered that now he must become, in truth, Dost Ghulam. With what speed he could, for he was both tired and hungry, he unpacked his bundle and once again changed into his smart suit and placed on his head the red fez.

He took in his hand the few escudos and centavos with which the Moulvie, Abdul Wahid, had provided him, and resumed his pilgrimage. On his ears fell the noise of clankings and puffings, coming apparently from a spot not far away and, guided by these sounds and by the red and green lights of the signals, he came at length to the railway station, where the last train of the day stood at the platform in readiness to depart. There, too, he found a man, selling meat and bread and tea, of whom he bought sufficient to stay his hunger and thirst; then he walked to the ticket-seller's window and said, with correct pronunciation, taught to him by Newington Sahib:

" Lourenco Marques! "

The engine eagerly whistled, so the Mosotho took his seat in a carriage and felt at last, indeed, he was in the Promised Land.

Listening to the voices upraised in strange tongues on all sides, the time passed easily and quickly, for it was only a journey of two hours to the capital city. To prevent any of his fellow-passengers from asking him any questions, the Mosotho pretended to be asleep; the pretence was not of long duration, for his great exhaustion soon turned the trick to reality. At last he was awakened by flashing lights before his eyes, and his gaze fell on the platform of the station of Lourenco Marques.

He was too tired to appreciate the beauties of the building then, but during his life in the city he was to return often to the station, and to the square outside, for there, indeed, were sights to please the eyes.

The Mosotho knew where to go—to the mosque in the Rua Salazar—but he did not know how to reach this place. It was now late at night, and there were many people walking about the station and the square on their way to their homes.... Suddenly, from out of this bustle, a voice sounded in his ears:

"*Asalaam aleikum!*"

Although it seemed like years since he had heard the musical Arabic words, he quickly pulled himself together and returned the greeting:

"*Aleikum, asalaam!*"

As he turned, he saw standing beside him and smiling, a pleasant-faced, bearded man, who said:

"You are Dost Ghulam?"

Summoning his best English to his aid, Dost Ghulam replied:
"Yes, Moulvie, sir! I am that man."

"I have been meeting the trains for two days," said the stranger. "I believe you have a letter for me from my old friend, Abdul Wahid, who wrote to me telling me to expect you...."

Dost Ghulam sighed with relief.

The Moulvie went on:

"But let us not waste time here; it is better that you should not be seen until you are more acquainted with the city and its customs. Come, then, with me in my motor car to my house, and we will eat and drink and talk and sleep."

And thus Dost Ghulam, the Mosotho, arrived at the house of his new friend—friend of the Moulvie Abdul Wahid—and found with him in the city of Lourenco Marques, rest and companionship.

3

The Moulvie's name was Mazaffar Khan; he, too, was a Pathan; he was married with two sons and a daughter: this much was told as they travelled in the car to the mosque in the Rua Salazar.

THE PROMISED LAND

This *Jamma Masjid*, or Cathedral Church of the Muslims, was a large building, and leading off one end of the courtyard was Mazaffar Khan's house, wherein had a room been allotted to Dost Ghulam. It was not long before food was set before them. The Mosotho's appetite was good, and he ate largely of the chicken and rice, washing it down afterwards with glasses of sour milk. When the *dastar-khan* had been removed, the two men sat talking.

When the Mosotho had handed over Moulvie Abdul Wahid's letter and sundry messages of goodwill from Durban, Mazaffar Khan set out in fair words the plans he had made for Dost Ghulam's future. He said:

"My eldest son, Mohammed Khan, runs a store in the Avenida Paiva Manso, and many travellers from the ships that sit for a while in the waters of the Bay of Espirito Sante, come to his shop. My younger son, Fazal Khan, who still attends the school, helps him in the afternoons. It is my wish that you should help Mohammed Khan in the mornings and evenings; in the afternoons it has been arranged for you to take lessons in simple Portuguese, and for you to improve your English. . . . Do these plans please your heart?"

"Moulvie, I am very grateful; I have already done some little work as a merchant in the City of Gold."

"Your story is known to me; but this shop work is somewhat different from the selling of trousers to Africans. Nevertheless, I am confident that you will readily learn. The people who buy will be mostly South Africans, Rhodesians, Englishmen, and tourists from America; there will also be Portuguese—although not so many—and Chinese and Indians."

"*Ee!* But I have travelled far from Lomontsa. I shall try my hardest, Moulvie, to do the work you require of me."

"You will do that, I know. . . . Also, you shall be my house-guest for the time being. I will pay you the equivalent of ten South African pounds per month for your services, until such time as you have become really competent."

"*Ka Thesele!* I want not money as well as friendship."

"Friend, you have earned the gratitude as well as the friendship of all Muslims who know of your brave deed in Durban. Should you desire aught else in the way of, say, clothes, it shall be my pleasure to supply them. Now tell me, have you not money which you are desirous of changing into escudos and centavos?"

"Of money I have plenty—more than three hundred pounds. You who know my story will understand that I have had to send my money home to my wife in small amounts only, and by stealth. What other cattle I have bought, are in my son's name. But on my way here, there were times in plenty when I thought my money would be parted from me."

Now Dost Ghulam told the Moulvie of his adventures along the way from Durban to Lourenco Marques; Mazaffar Khan listened with great interest and at the end, commented:

"Mosotho you are, and will always remain. But in order to escape attention, now you should swear by Allah, rather than by your Chiefs."

Dost Ghulam looked puzzled; so the Moulvie explained:

"By this, I mean that instead of your *Ka Thesele!* and your 'Cattle of the Chief!' now must you say rather, *Mashallah!* or *Alhamdolillah!* or *In'shallah!*—lest Muslims wonder at your strange oaths."

Dost Ghulam could see the force of this warning, and promised to guard his speech.

Mazaffar Khan yawned.

"Let us rest now, and we will meet at early morning *na'maz*? Is this agreeable?"

"So be it—we shall meet at prayer."

And the men retired to rest.

4

Ghulam Hussain and Abdul Wahid had taught well, for when Dost Ghulam appeared at the early morning prayer in the mosque he acquitted himself well; he made no mistakes, he took up his position on the left of the worshipper who entered the mosque just ahead of him, and spread his prayer mat. He made his prostrations in the ordained manner and all was well.

When *na'maz* was finished, and Dost Ghulam returned to the Moulvie's house, he found there, waiting to meet him, the two sons

THE PROMISED LAND

of Mazaffar Khan. Both were strong and manly, but the younger, having recently returned from a trip to his homeland, wore his hair Pathan fashion—long at the back and sides, something in the style of some white women. This made Dost Ghulam smile.

"I should have thought this one a girl."

But he was to learn later, that with fashions as with food, it did not pay to make up his mind too quickly. Even as he sniggered within his mind, he recalled how strange the *tsotsi* trousers had appeared to him when first he left Monontsa.

After they had broken their fast, Fazal Khan went off to school, and Mohammed Khan took the Mosotho to the shop in the Avenida Paiva Manso. To the eyes of Dost Ghulam this store appeared a cave of glittering wonder, filled with curios of silver and gold, jewels, beautiful coats of brocaded silk, perfumes, figures carved from ivory and wood, and leather purses and bags with cunning designs worked into their surfaces.

For some days he did little but dust the shop and its contents with great care, handing to Mohammed Khan such articles as were desired by customers. He first had to overcome his shyness at direct speech with all races of white men, and learn properly how to add and subtract in escudos and centavos.

He found Mohammed Khan somewhat careless in the matter of mid-morning *na'maz*; but in the afternoons, at the mosque, he always attended the early evening prayers. Sometimes, instead of returning to the mosque for the midday meal, he would go with Mohammed Khan to eat at the Hotel Mahommedeno, which was situated in the same street; he found that his self-confidence was gradually increasing.

He found strange—yet pleasant, too—the custom of the siesta: the closing of all shops, and the stopping of most types of work during the hottest hours of the day. On Sunday nights, usually with young Fazal Khan, he visited the Cinema Varieta, where a special entertainment was produced for the Indian community.

He was in touch, now, through his home-boy, Ntoane, with his beloved wife, Florinah, and with his son Libe, who now had a better job than that which he had held at Nouroe Mines—he was now a *Baas boy* at the South Rand Mine. Often letters arrived with the Durban postmark from Ghulam Hussain. When Fazal Khan spotted these letters, there was always a lot of fun and horse-play, but under all the joking Monare felt that Fazal was a little jealous of his love for Ghulam.

At week-ends the menfolk bathed near the famous Polana Beach; often they took a small boat and rowed up the Incomati River. Dost Ghulam was fond of going to the Native Market at Xipamanine to buy fruit and vegetables and live fowls for the Moulvie's wife.

These days and nights were pleasant, indeed; and were to be remembered by the Mosotho to the end of the way.

Phase Five

NEW MOON

". . . living on borrowed time—time lent by God! . . ."

THE NOBLE JUDGE

Chapter One

AT THE RUA SALAZAR

Now was Monare-Dost-Ghulam able to compare the lot of the African in the Union of South Africa, with that of the African in Mocambique. He learned that in the country of the Portuguese, there was much freedom for the brown, yellow and black peoples. He found that his Indian friends could enter any shop or hotel or train that was open to the white man; the people of mixed race, known in Mocambique as the " mulattos," were also allowed the same privilege. To his even greater amazement, he was told that Africans, too, could rise to enjoy this same equality, provided that they were judged to be—after examination by the Portuguese—ready for " assimilation." As far as the Mosotho could judge, the qualifications required for assimilation were that an African must read, write and speak simple Portuguese, that he must possess steady work, that he must live in a respectable quarter, and that he must have adopted the more hygienic habits and customs of the white man in respect of living and dressing.

Monare-Dost-Ghulam questioned his friend the Moulvie continually regarding these matters; and after answering the Mosotho's questions as best he could, the Moulvie turned the talk in the direction of South Africa.

" What of the English in South Africa? "

Monare replied :

" They are not so cruel and hard in their dealings with us as are the Afrikaners but they often treat us with contempt and speak roughly to us."

The Moulvie sighed.

"In my country, before it gained its independence, there was great friendship between my people and the British. I have often wondered why the same fellowship does not obtain in Natal, but since staying in the City of Sugar with Abdul Wahid, I can put my finger on the reason. The English who used to come to my country as officers in the Indian Army, or in the Indian Police, or in the Indian Civil Service, were men of good family, sons of the Chiefs. Such men were not actuated by any desire for gain. Yes, they desired promotion and *izzat*—honour—but their whole lives were devoted to the service of the people."

"Such a man was Newington Sahib."

"I did not meet him in Durban, but there I saw other sorts of Englishmen—men of lesser education and of inferior breeding.... Tell me, Dost Ghulam, did you not find that it was from the Englishman with few good manners and with little learning, that you Africans received the harshest treatment?"

"My Moulvie, I know but little English even now, but I have noted that amongst the English who speak clearly and pleasantly, and in softer tones, were to be found those who treated us with courtesy.... Yes, Moulvie, you are right—it was the rougher ones, those who were not so clean in their dress or person, who tried to bear down roughly on us."

Now for a while did the two men smoke the hubble-bubble, the silver-stemmed *huqa*, whilst the Moulvie pointed out to the Mosotho, that it was those members of a white race who were closest in their living conditions to the coloured people surrounding them, who feared most their darker-skinned brethren, and—fearing them—hated them. The Moulvie spoke, too, about the Communists who had visited his country and warned Monare that by listening to their counsel he would be but exchanging one slavery for another yet more unendurable.

Again the men sat in quietness, and tea was set before them by the women of the house.

2

After a while the conversation came back again to the subject of Mocambique. The Mosotho asked:

"What of the white man's *pitso* in this country—who had a vote in the election of the members? Does the Indian, or the mulatto, or the assimilated African have the right to vote?"

"All people living in the country—other than the Africans who are as yet unassimilated—have the right to vote."

"*Helele!* What, my Moulvie? Indians, mulattos, Africans—with the same vote as the white man? Surely you make mock of me?"

"My son, on such a matter I would not joke with you. I have told you but the truth. . . ."

"Then great must the effort of the Africans be to become assimilated!"

"That is true—yet must any African in Lourenco Marques desiring to become assimilated, be proficient in the Portuguese language. . . ."

The Mosotho was quiet for some time, then he said:

"Soon will I speak the language of the Portuguese well enough to appear before their Tribunal. Then will I send for my wife Florinah—and she shall arrive to find me living like a white man. Will she be allowed to live like a white woman?"

The Moulvie laughed, and replied:

"Even those *mafofonyane* you told me about must have a speed limit. Would they not otherwise fall off the rails?"

"Yes, yes. But what has that got to do with Florinah?"

"Only that you must not try to travel too fast, or you, too, will come off the rails."

"What talk is this, my Father?"

"First, Brother, before we can send you in front of the Tribunal, must we find a story for you to tell of who you are, and how you came here."

Now did Monare-Dost-Ghulam's face take on such a pathetic

look, so like to that of a naughty child's, that the Moulvie smiled broadly, then said :

"In this journey from Gollel, friend, you crossed three rivers?"

"That is true, my Father."

"How many times did you cross them?"

"Once only, Moulvie."

"And when was that?"

Dejection was now wiped from the Mosotho's face by puzzlement.

"I crossed them when I came to their banks, O my Father!"

"Then thus must it be with this question of your right to be in this country—when we reach the bank of the river of the Tribunal, then only shall we attempt to cross it. But do not worry overmuch, I have a plan for the crossing, but not until we arrive nearer the bank! But you also spoke of the woman of your house. Understand, that to pass the test of this Tribunal, not only must you speak the language of the Portuguese, but you must prove to the Tribunal that you have given up African ways of living, and adopted those of the white man."

"I can smoke, I can drink, and I can make love to the lovely girls, whether they be Africans, mulattos, or Indians!"

This time the Moulvie made no attempt to hide his laughter.

"Have you not heard the white man's saying, 'Do as I say, not as I do?' No, friend, these are not the requirements of the Tribunal. To pass its test you must live in a clean, neat house, wear good clothes—such as you wear even now—you must also possess a good job, and be ready to prove to the Tribunal that you earn enough money each month to maintain yourself and your family in such a state."

"And my wife?"

"If you pass the Tribunal's test, no trouble will be made about your wife—but from what I have heard and seen of your people, she will have to wear different clothes."

"There will be no trouble about that—I have gold in plenty."

The stone beneath the mattress now reminded the Mosotho of its existence. He asked :

"But what of passes? Should I have to carry one?"

AT THE RUA SALAZAR

"No, no, no! Only unassimilated Africans carry passes—none others."

"Then shall I become a real gentleman."

Both men chuckled over this; then did the Moulvie say:

"If after a while, we can arrange for you to appear before the Tribunal, and if you are successful in passing its tests, then will there be no bar to your rise—you may become a police officer, or even a magistrate."

"*Ka Thesele!* Cattle of the Chief! . . ."

Here the Mosotho broke off in some confusion, and remembered the Moulvie's advice.

"*Ma'shallah!*" he continued. "But this seems like *ngaka's* business!"

Indeed, it did seem that some powerful medicine was working for the Mosotho's good.

3

Letters continued to arrive from Ntoane and from Libe, giving, second-hand, news from the village of Lomontsa in the Maluti Mountains. Soon would the child of Libe and Makopoi be born, and Dost Ghulam hoped that his grandchild would be a boy. His wife was in good health, though sorrowing for her husband's absence; but both crops and cattle were blessed by God, and the Mosotho's heart was glad. Not so good, was the news received about the Cities of Gold and Sugar; for in letters from Ntoane and from Ghulam Hussain, Dost Ghulam learned that the Great Detectives had not sat in idleness. For it was, apparently, common talk in the compounds of the Golden City, that the Ritual Murder of Koto had been committed by men of the Chief of Lomontsa, although, so far, no arrest had been made.

Ghulam Hussain's letter brought the Mosotho's heart into his throat, for the Great Detectives had been making inquiries at Maydon Wharf for one, Monare of Lomontsa. The police had even visited the Mosque at Cato Manor, for they knew that the Mosotho had saved the life of the Moulvie, Abdul Wahid—although they did not know, fortunately, that he had lived there for several months.

But there was one sentence in Ghulam Hussain's letter which brought much happiness to the Mosotho's heart—" Next month I may be coming on a visit to Moulvie Mazaffar Khan, and we shall be together again ! " This news was already known to Mazaffar Khan, who had heard by the same post from Abdul Wahid.

Dost Ghulam grew daily more excited ; he studied the Portuguese language with great attention, and he performed his duties at the shop with increasing skill and decreasing shyness. His heart was full of love and good will towards all men ; he even refrained from talking too much in front of Fazal Khan about the approaching visit of Ghulam Hussain, for he could tell that the boy was jealous, and he wished to spare him pain.

He had written to Ntoane and to Libe about his plans for assimilation, and also to Abdul Wahid. The two Basotho in the City of Gold were very interested to hear about Mocambique, and hoped, one day, to be able to arrange to pay it a visit. But nothing, so far, had been told to Florinah concerning her future life as a white woman ! Knowing well the wagging tongues of women, the three Basotho decided to say nothing to Ma-Libe about her new status, until she had left Lomontsa.

At this time, too, did Moulvie Mazaffar Khan have good news for the Mosotho.

One night, when the Moulvie and his sons and Dost Ghulam were talking after the evening meal, the Moulvie said :

" I have known one of the Portuguese members of the Tribunal for many years—he is a man of good heart and great learning. Without dealing in names, I have recounted much of your story to him, and he holds a high opinion of your courage. It has been arranged that one night soon, he will join us here at our evening meal. When that night comes, you must show him the watch presented to you by the Mayor of Durban, and also the pen and pencil of gold given to you by the Moulvie Wahid and his son. I think, too, that the story and the photographs as published in the *Natal Mercury* should be produced. But tell him naught else of your story, just say that you came to Mocambique because of the good tidings you had heard of the treatment of Africans here."

But this talk frightened the Mosotho ; he asked :

AT THE RUA SALAZAR

"May he not say to the police, 'There is an unassimilated African without a pass, living at the mosque?'"

"No, my son, that will he never do. He is my friend, and if you find favour in his eyes, he will use his influence with other members of the Tribunal. But should aught miscarry, I have my friend's word that he will forget that he has ever seen you. Should that happen, you will naturally not be able to appear before the Tribunal while he is a member, for he is a man of great honesty."

"But how shall the Tribunal grant me such a privilege, even if I pass its tests, seeing that I have no birthright here?"

"It is allowed by the Portuguese Government, that a man living here without rights may yet obtain such rights on certain conditions, provided that he is not a convicted criminal, and provided that he satisfies the Tribunal in other matters."

"I have been to jail——"

"The facts about that are known to me—I do not consider you a criminal—but beyond that provision there is but one door to unlock, and you have its key in your possession."

"What door is this?"

"Such applicant for birthright must be either one running from injustice in his own land——"

The Mosotho laughed.

"I have no key to open that door."

Mazaffar Khan smiled.

"Neither is that the door through which you must enter. But to continue—or such applicant must have rendered great service to mankind! And that, my friend, in the opinion of this Portuguese, you have already done by your act of bravery in the City of Sugar!"

Monare-Dost-Ghulam's hopes were high in his breast. Soon would he see the beloved face of his heart's friend, Ghulam Hussain, and why! by that time, he might even be living as a white man! Then would he send for Ma-Libe, and later for his home-boy, Ntoane, too, and for his son, Libe, and his wife and child.

Indeed did his roots seem to be of the highest quality, and his *ngaka's* blessing must be upon him.

That night he wept in gratitude and thankfulness, and prayed long to the God of all Baruti!

Chapter Two

THE MILLS OF GOD

MONARE'S FUTURE appeared to be painted in vivid colours on the canvas of his life. Not only had he the interview with the Moulvie's Portuguese friend, and the visit of Ghulam Hussain, to look forward to, but he learned now that next year would that Muslim Potentate, Prince Ali Khan, son of the Aga Khan, be staying for a while in the land of Mocambique....

Discussions on this subject taught Dost Ghulam that although the countless Muslims of the world all worshipped Allah and His Prophet Mohammed, there were certain differences between them. he found that the two great divisions of Islam were the Sunni and the Shiah sects; the Moulvie explained the matter thus:

"We Sunnis believe that the rightful successors of Mohammed —on Whom be Peace!—were his Four Companions; whereas the Shiahs maintain that Hazrat Ali, the Fourth Companion, should have succeeded to the *Khilafat*, when Mohammed the Blessed was taken to Allah. The Aga Khan—Sultan Sir Mohammed Shah—is a direct descendant of the Prophet's daughter, Fatima, and a great and renowned leader of the Shiah sect; he is an Ismaili, and thus the spiritual head of the wealthy Khoja class——"

"But," added Mazaffar Khan, "no matter how we may differ on the question of the *Khilafat*, we are all Muslims!"

The Moulvie's colourful stories of the ceremonies connected with the Aga Khan's visits to his East African followers, intrigued the simple-minded Mosotho—the weighings of the Sultan against gold and diamonds were to him as a legend come true.

Dost Ghulam of course, by this time, had some knowledge of the finer points of dogma of Islam—he knew the Six Points of *Iman*—Faith : belief in the Unity of God, the Angels, the Inspired Books, the Prophets of God, the Day of Judgment, and the Decrees of God. He was aware, too, of the *Amal*—the duties enjoined on all Muslims : the Recital of the *Kalimah*, the Creed ; the bowing in prayer at the five stated times, daily ; the observance of the thirty days' Fast of *Ramazan* ; the giving of *Zakat*, alms ; and the performance of the Holy Pilgrimage, the *Hajj*.

Monare-Dost-Ghulam was never to forget his first observance of the Fast of *Ramazan*. He had heard his Moruti speak of Lent, but *Ramazan* was a penance altogether more severe. For thirty days, from sunrise to sunset, he was forbidden to eat, drink, smoke—or even to swallow his own spit ! During the hours of daylight, however, he still had to work and pray ; but never, in all his life, had his ears been enchanted by such a joyful sound as that of the *Azan* chanted by the *Muezzin* at sunset. For this call to prayer marked the end of the day's fasting, and was followed by delicious draughts of iced sherbet or sour milk, by the first most-satisfying pull on a cigarette, and by the unforgettable pleasure of gratifying hunger.

Yes, life was full of interest, and the Mosotho's brain was filled with strange knowledge—which, he thought, would add to his fame as a praiser in Lesotho, should he live to see his homeland again.

2

The day of days came and went—the visit of the Portuguese member of the Tribunal celebrated itself in the Moulvie's house in the mosque courtyard. All that day was the Mosotho like a pony new to the saddle ; he could neither sit nor stand ; at times he laughed with no reason that any could see ; at other times, the tears ran down his cheeks.

His friend, Fazal Khan, coming to the store in the Avenida Paiva Manso from school, found Dost Ghulam with his eyes wet. With some amusement, he asked :

"Is your friend from the City of Sugar not coming, then? Is that why you weep?"

This cheeky remark changed the Mosotho's mood—with a huge laugh he rushed at Fazal Khan and started wrestling with him, to the great danger of many carved tables, and other goods of value, standing nearby. Now did the Mosotho discover that the girlish curls of Fazal Khan told no true story of his body: although the Pathan was slim, his grasp was of steel, and his strength equal to that of Dost Ghulam!

With a tricky hold, he pressed down the Mosotho's shoulders to the floor and, laughing at him with impudence, lowered his head and brushed the surprised face of the Mosotho with his long curls.

Roaring with injured pride, Dost Ghulam threw off the amused boy and chased him round the shop—only the coming of customers preventing him from seizing Fazal Khan. But it was surprise that had been born, and not dislike, and when the shop was again empty, Dost Ghulam placed his arm round Fazal's shoulder, and said:

"Fazal, you are very strong—you must teach me to wrestle in the Pathan fashion. Ghulam Hussain started to show me in the City of Sugar, but I left before he had finished."

But mention of Ghulam Hussain was to Fazal, like a tree is to a dog; and so—in a manner—he lifted his leg and said, with petulance:

"I will throw you, and him too!"

Dost Ghulam laughed loudly at this boast and, seizing the boy again, tickled him until he cried for mercy—but now was all ill-feeling gone, and the three Pathans went off together for a special meal at the Hotel Mohamedeno.

With nightfall came the Portuguese, and with modesty—after the evening meal—the Mosotho showed to him his gifts of remembrance. As it chanced to happen, the Portuguese liked even better what he saw and heard of the Mosotho than what he had already been told by the Moulvie. On parting, he said quietly to Mazaffar Khan:

"We shall be pleased to receive Dost Ghulam at the Tribunal as soon as you judge him ready."

Words giving such great joy to those who hear them, are not

THE MILLS OF GOD

often uttered; and the Mosotho, in his excitement—and somewhat to the alarm of the Pathans—burst into the singing of the *Mokorotlo*:

> "*Likhoma helele banna*
> *Hona koana re tsoang*
> *Helele banna kea tsaba!*"

That night there was much happiness and laughter in the house in the courtyard of the Mosque in the Rua Salazar.

3

Does the fowl or the pig know—when it is fattened—that it is being fed for the pot? Dost Ghulam had no warning in his bones that dark shadows were fast gathering around him; for often when the cup of joy is filled to the brim, and on its way to kiss the lips, does some clumsy hand knock it from the grasp. The Great God of us all doubtless has His reasons for sending hail-storms when the crops are ripening, and it is useless to rebel against His hand.

Thuswise did events now follow each other in the life of the Mosotho.

A week before the arrival of his heart's friend Ghulam Hussain, the Mosotho visited his favourite spot in the city—the great square before the station. There he stood, watching the passing pageant and dreaming dreams of the day—not too far distant—when he and his beloved wife Florinah should come from that station proud and secure in their privileges as assimilated Africans, no longer to be beaten by the police, no longer to be pushed off the pavements by the white man, no longer to be called "Bloody Kaffir!"

He thought, too, of meeting his home-boy, Ntoane, and his son, Libe, at the same station, and of the joy he would experience in showing them round the city which he had come to love so well. In his heart he offered up thanks to Allah.

He remembered, too, his journey across the Land of the Swazis, and of how Allah had helped him; he considered his life in the City of Sugar, and recalled the Night of Terror, when he had found, and taken, the Path of Atonement.

His heart was so full of love for all who had helped him, that his chest felt as if it would burst.

As he stood and strolled thus, the morning newspaper, which is written in both English and Portuguese, came on to the square for sale. With but little interest he studied the posters carried by the newsvendors; it was more for practice in reading the two foreign tongues than for any active interest in the world's news—his own concerns were too important to him to leave room for aught else.

"Great Mining Disaster on Reef."

Thus read the poster.

Dost Ghulam mused:

"I am happy not to be in the City of Gold . . . I wonder how the Orlando Moruti is these days . . . and that lovely girl, Mary, his daughter—she is probably married by now. I wonder if she ever thinks of me . . . and those days at the house of the *semokolara* at Benoni! *Ee!* what a sinner I was! I thank God for my friend, Ntoane, and my wonderful son, Libe—who did not turn from me in hate but helped me to stop taking the *matekoane*. I wonder how the selling of trousers proceeds in the City of Gold. How far have I not progressed since those days! My son will soon be returning to Lomontsa for the birth of my grandson!"

This last thought marched proudly!

He continued with his reflections:

"Libe . . . I wonder if he is still *Baas Boy* underground at the South Rand Mine . . . Mines? Mines? Great MINE disaster on the Reef——"

Suddenly he shouted:

"Guardian! Guardian!"

And ran across the square after the newsboy selling the Lourenco Marques newspaper. Roughly pulling a paper from the boy's grasp, he read:

"Fall of rock at South Rand!"

Throwing a handful of small coins at the paper-boy, he moved

THE MILLS OF GOD

blindly yet quickly away from the station, crying brokenly as he went:

"Libe! Libe! My son, my son Libe!"

4

He burst into the house in the Rua Salazar just as the Moulvie was leaving it for the Mosque. At first he could not speak; but at length, waving the newspaper, he gasped:

"My son Libe!—there has been a fall of rock on his mine!"

"Allah forbid!"

The Moulvie seized the paper and read out:

"'Twenty Africans and one white man buried alive!' . . . but how shall we know that your son is amongst those buried? Might he not be off duty?"

The Mosotho, with tears running down his face, shouted the reply:

"Still must I take the train now—at once!"

"Wait! The train for Johannesburg does not leave until a quarter to three this afternoon—Ah! I see now! I will go quickly to the house of my friend the Portuguese who is a member of the Tribunal; he can speak on the telephone to the Portuguese Consul in Johannesburg, and thus, maybe, we shall get definite word. I can't leave you here—come, let us go together!"

The two men ran from the courtyard as if bewitched, and quickly calling a taxicab, rode with speed to the house of the Portuguese. By the Grace of Allah, he was sitting on his veranda, and listening to their hurried story, said with great kindness:

"Will you wait here a while? I can do better than you suggested. I will go to a member of the Government who knows our Consul in Johannesburg personally, and through his influence will I get the telephone call put through like lightning."

Thus saying, he left the house.

The Moulvie and the Mosotho sat together in the shade, Dost Ghulam murmuring to himself over and over again:

"O God, have mercy. O God, have mercy . . ."

The Moulvie comforted him, then said:

"Rather than mourn before it is time, let us plan. Should it turn out that your son is indeed one of those buried alive, let us arrange, here and now, the details of your journey to Johannesburg —if only you had passed the Tribunal! Then could you have gone disguised with your beard and moustache and wearing your fine suit and red fez, as Dost Ghulam, a Muslim subject of the Portuguese. But now, should the chance be evil, and you have to leave by this afternoon's train, then must you shave off both beard and moustache, and enter the train as a Mosotho . . . As you have no papers or Pass, you will have to leave the train at Ressano Garcia, cross the river at the Border, and get on the train again at Komatipoort on the South African side . . ."

While thus they talked, the Portuguese friend of Mazaffar Khan had wasted not his time; even as the two visitors drank the coffee brought to them on the veranda by the women of the house, he returned to them with the sad news that Libe, son of Monare, was among those trapped like rats in the depths of the South Rand Mine.

5

Now came a time of difficulty; there were four hours yet to tick-tock by, before the train should be ready to depart. The Mosotho was weighed down heavily with fear; his brain did not work with its usual sharpness; he felt dazed, as if with too much smoking of *matekoane*; yet within his head—like a lion pacing round and around a cage in the zoo of the white man—was the restless thought:

"If I were there, I would be pulling away the rocks from my son's body! To those who work, he is but another man—these hands and arms would work with the strength of ten, for to me it is my son!"

The shop in the Avenida Paiva Manso was closed; Mohammed Khan and Fazal Khan stood near the Mosotho with love and kindness and sympathy in their hearts—but no word of theirs could enter that hard cage of thoughts. Like a child, the Mosotho allowed Fazal Khan to do all that was necessary—to shave off his care-

THE MILLS OF GOD

fully-trimmed beard and moustache; to help him change his clothes and pack his cases; to exchange escudos and centavos for pounds and shillings; to place within his pockets his gifts of remembrance . . . Then was food brought, but the Mosotho refused to eat—only coffee would he drink.

At last, when it became apparent that the hour of departure was running fast towards them, Dost Ghulam aroused himself from his despair and spoke:

"O my Father, and my dear friends, once again must I leave those whom I love . . . This heart knows that there will be no return . . . some enemy has buried a medicine horn of ill-omen in an unseen corner of my *kraal*, and its work of bewitchment continues with none to stop it . . ."

The three Pathans tried to comfort him; and to restore hope to the heart from which it had fled, the Moulvie spoke thus:

"My dear son and friend, put your trust in Allah—the Compassionate, the Merciful—Who has power over all witch-doctors, and to Whom the Future is as the Palm of His Hand! Who shall say—other than Allah—that the tree shall fall this way, or that? Rather than despair, think of your dangerous and difficult journey. Think of the chance—which is in the Mind of Allah—that you may arrive there to find your son safe! Think of your plans for the return journey. For should it be the Will of Allah that your son is saved, then will you have to make plans with great care and cunning for your return journey to the land of Mocambique!"

The Mosotho smiled in such a sad way that tears came into the eyes of the Pathans.

He said, "I do not think my roots are strong enough to bring me back to this Promised Land. I pray with all my heart and soul that it may indeed be so, but I feel that this is a time of farewell. Still, my Father, I can see the sense and truth in what you say. How do you then advise that I shall cross the Border from Mocambique into the Union?"

"The station of Ressano Garcia is not far from Lourenco Marques; this is the last station in the land of Mocambique; across the river, on the other side of the Border, is the South African station of Komatipoort. Between these two stations are

PHASE FIVE—NEW MOON

Police and Custom Guards. A Mosotho without papers of any sort would find it hard to remain undiscovered. To be discovered means to be questioned, and to be questioned—in your case—means to be arrested!"

With some of his old spirit, the Mosotho replied:

"It seems that I shall have to do some more travelling on boats, or climbing with hands like the monkeys, if I am to cross that river!"

But travel sharpens the eyes, and the much-journeyed Fazal Khan now threaded the needle of dilemma at his first attempt; he said,

"I have noticed, my Father, that the mail trains which arrive here from South Africa carry with them their own attendants—those who serve the food, those who attend to the luggage, and those who make the beds. These last-named are yellow-faced men, something like Dost Ghulam to look at——"

The Mosotho smiled for the first time, but rather tightly:

"They are known as Cape Coloureds."

Mohammed Khan now said:

"There must be some arrangement by which they are admitted to Mocambique—wait, I will go to the station now, and make enquiries from the Parcels Clerk, who is a friend of mine . . ."

And without further delay, Mohammed Khan departed on his mission.

The Mosotho did not altogether agree with this new plan; if he were to pretend to be a Bedding Boy, he would have to wear cap, coat, and trousers; moreover, the language of the Cape Coloureds was largely Afrikaans, of which he knew little. Rather, he felt, would his success be more likely if he crossed the river as he had done in Swaziland. These thoughts he made known to Mazaffar Khan. The Moulvie rightly pointed out that in this case the most important factor was time—should the Mosotho be delayed even a day by the crossing of the river, this would eternally weigh on his heart, should it transpire that his son had been in danger.

At this moment Mohammed Khan returned with a glad, excited face.

THE MILLS OF GOD

"The two Governments have agreed that all those who serve on the mail trains, shall be allowed in and out of Mocambique without let or hindrance. It is laid down that should any unlawful advantage be taken of this, the Union Government will accept responsibility——"

The Moulvie cried impatiently:

"Go, Fazal!—buy a khaki coat and hat and trousers of the right size and pattern!"

As Fazal Khan went quickly to do his father's bidding, the Mosotho said:

"But those who have come down in the train from the City of Gold, and who return again this afternoon—will not these Guards and Bedding Boys say to one another, 'Who is this man we know not, and who cannot even *praat die Taal*?'"

"My son, your anxiety and sorrow has dulled the keenness of your brain! Pull yourself together, and put your trust in Allah! If you take care, these men of the mail train shall not even see you! When we arrive at the Booking Office this afternoon, we will purchase for you a first-class ticket—there are but few Africans who travel in such state, and we have friends who will see that you shall travel alone, at any rate as far as Ressano Garcia . . . Now listen to me with care—when the train is about to enter the station at Ressano Garcia, place these khaki clothes—which Fazal is now buying—over your suit, and the cap put on your head——"

"And when the train shall stop?"

"Then must you obey your house-snake, and do what it shall whisper in your ear—maybe it will counsel you to descend from the train and run to the tea-room, as if buying an article for some white man; maybe you will be urged to jump down on to the track and stand between two coaches, as if looking for something which has been dropped. Your task is not to remain hidden from the Portuguese, but from the men of the mail train!—there lies your danger!"

"I shall try to obey your commands, O my Father. But when the train moves between Ressano Garcia and Komatipoort? How do I then hide from the real Bedding Boys?"

"The distance is but short—there is but little more than the river to cross; doubtless will there be a lavatory for the use of the Bedding Boys—if necessary, lock yourself in there for a time. Remember, the days are getting short, and it is now dark by five o'clock—at that hour will the Mail be crossing the river and the Border! Should the Police, or the Customs Guards come knocking on the lavatory door, call out with confidence, 'Coming, my *Baasie*,' and when you come out, greet them with respect, and walk as if busy, down the corridor. Then, as the train pulls out of Komatipoort, go back to your compartment, change into your own clothes, and throw the uniform out of the window."

This plan was discussed by the four men in great detail, for by now Fazal Khan had returned with the purchased clothes, which were tried on and found to fit. Many times did the Moulvie force the Mosotho to repeat the Afrikaans words which he must say, should he be greeted by any of the mail train staff.

Now was a meal served, and the Moulvie told the women of his house to prepare a basket of food for the Mosotho to take with him on his journey. As they ate, this time for once, they talked; usually was the meal taken in silence, and conversation reserved until the food had been appreciated. But to-day Time was an uninvited but important guest at the *dastar-khan*.

6

Around the *dastar-khan* many things were decided. It was arranged that the Moulvie should send a telegram to Ntoane, asking him to meet the mail train at Germiston at nine o'clock the next morning. The Moulvie also promised to give the Mosotho's loving messages to Ghulam Hussain, and to delay—should it be possible—his return to the City of Sugar until the Mosotho should arrive in Lourenco Marques again—although there was little confidence in the Mosotho's heart that any return to Mocambique would be allowed. Still, to give himself courage, and to comfort the hearts of his friends, he promised that he would send them a telegram as soon as the matter of Libe's safety were decided for good or for ill, and promised furthermore to let them know the time and date of his return.

THE MILLS OF GOD

As the return would in no way be as urgent as the departure, the Moulvie agreed that a crossing of the Border by the river should be attempted; and promised that upon receipt of the news of the Mosotho's departure from the City of Gold, he would set out in his motor car for the bank of the river, and make arrangements for the Mosotho to be ferried across in a boat. This would undoubtedly be a costly and a risky business, but what had been done before, could be done again, with Allah's Blessing.

Should he be able to return, and events as planned be set in train, then should the Mosotho descend from the mail train at Komatipoort, and walk along the west bank of the river—after sunset—towards the road bridge. Somewhere on that bank would the Moulvie and his sons be waiting with a boat.

At last came the moment dreaded by all—the time for gathering together of suitcase and food-basket; the time for the altogether too short drive to the railway station.

Monare-Dost-Ghulam cast his eyes for the last time on the comfortable room in which he had lived and studied and slept; he looked with love on the graceful arches and pillars of the *Jamma' Masjid*, where he had bowed his head in prayer—the equal of all Muslims, whether black, brown, yellow, or white. With a heart tightened by the pain of separation, he followed Mazaffar Khan to the motor car.

At the railway station, a first-class coupé had been set aside for his use; a ticket was bought; the Pathans placed on the seat fruit and chocolate, and they rested a while for the final thoughts to be expressed.

While they sat thus, the Moulvie opened his shirt, and taking from round his neck a small, flat gold case on a fine chain—the case being the size of a matchbox, but very thin—he spoke thus:

"This case, or *tavis*, as we call it, contains within it a paper on which are written Words of Power—some of the Ninety and Nine Names of Allah. I have worn this since I returned from Holy Mecca, many years ago. Now Dost Ghulam, accept this with my blessing, and with my love and that of my sons. May Allah the Compassionate, the Merciful, walk with you on your journey, and may He help you to endure whatsoever may befall, and may He comfort you should the worst happen. Let me remind you, this last time, you have set your foot to a path of extreme danger, which may well lead to your death! To us, this snatching away of the Cup of Joy, and replacing it with the Draught of Sorrow, must appear cruel. Yet how shall man read the Mind of Allah? Though your body may be subjected to vile indignities—though you be killed and fall to dust—yet remember, Dost Ghulam, that you shall live on in the Spirit, and maybe in another Place shall we all meet again, and much that now appears dark, shall be made light! Surrender yourself to the Will of Allah, my son, and the path, wheresoever it may lead, shall be made easier for you to tread!"

Farewells now had to be made, for the engine was hissing out its steam with great importance; red lights at the platform's end had changed to green; the cold, sad winds of sorrow which help to blow departing trains from stations, had started to murmur—soon would the wailing voice of the engine, bring a time of hope to its end!

Good-bye to the dear friends; good-bye to the foolish dreams of long years of safety and happiness; good-bye to the proud plans for the acquiring of white man's privileges; good-bye to the pleasant land of Mocambique, that paradise for the African with both will and desire to rise!

The dear friends called "Return!" But somehow that heart knew that there was no way back; the circle must be completed.

Suddenly there were no more friendly faces; the carriage swung round, and there was no Past or Present, only the Dreaded Future!

7

Never did train move so slowly; Monare-Dost-Ghulam wished with all his heart that the Mail would leap forward like a *mafofonyane*. Glad he would be when the Border was passed—his body and heart desired action, for thought was more painful than the beating of policemen!

Monare felt dazed—as on the night of Koto's murder—and doubtless his dulled feelings helped him much between Ressano Garcia and Komatipoort. He knew what had to be done, and did it, although it seemed but a dream to him. He put on the clothes of the Bedding Boy; he hid himself from the eyes of the men of the mail train . . . It seemed that he hid in the corridor, walked there, jumped down here, stood between coaches, and said, twice, " Good evening, *Baasie*," without consciously having willed himself to do any of these things! Some mind-behind-the-mind made him act as he had been instructed to act . . . His own mind was filled with but one thought and vision—to pull at the rocks which he could see lying on the body of his son . . .

Later, memory could show him no picture of that short journey from Ressano Garcia to Komatipoort; later, he noticed that the khaki clothing was gone—therefore must he have thrown it from the window!

He slept.

As the train was leaving Middelberg, Monare awoke and ate of the food and fruit supplied by the Moulvie's wife. His mind, though sad, was clearer and brighter; he looked forward to the meeting with Ntoane on the station at Germiston. During the long night, might not those buried have been rescued? He prayed long to the God of all Baruti . . .

But when he saw Ntoane's tired, sad face on the platform, he knew that this time might the porridge have been burned. God's finger was doubtless busy elsewhere! But now he called to mind the parting words of Mazaffar Khan: " Surrender yourself to the Will of Allah, and the path will be made easier . . ." Therefore he drew all his courage into his voice and said to Ntoane:

" Greetings, old friend and home-boy! Is Libe then dead? "

A small smile lit up Ntoane's face.

" Not dead, Monare—but they have been buried now for a day and two nights, and there is but little hope! "

Monare got down from the train and embraced Ntoane. Ntoane said:

" I have a taxi waiting, home-boy. Let us get quickly to the South Rand Mine; I myself have been underground all night, and am very weary. Yet would I still have been labouring, were it not that I felt that I should meet you at the station."

Monare answered:

"I thank you, friend . . . Will they let me descend and help with the rescue?"

"Yes, you are the father of one of those buried—I have already spoken to the *Makulu Baas*!"

As the taxi drove towards the mine, Ntoane explained to Monare what he would have to do beneath the surface, for he had not worked underground. He spoke of the dangers of sparks from the tools of the workers trying to shift the fallen rocks; he told Monare that there might be a gas down below which could suddenly explode from one of the sparks, and kill the buried men—if indeed they were yet alive—and those trying to rescue them.

Outside the window of the taxi there now appeared a crowd of men and women, Africans all; many were weeping, and there were others comforting them. Behind the crowd, rose into the air the chimney of the engine-house, and the huge, spinning wheels of the winding-engine itself. The taxi stopped, and the two Basotho got down from the cab and pushed their way through the crowd to a spot near the engine-room where stood a group of white men. The faces of these white men were sad and worried.

Ntoane spoke a few words to one who appeared to be the *Makulu Baas*; this man turned, and to Monare's great surprise, put out his hand and took within it that of the Mosotho. Speaking in Sesotho, he said:

"You are the father of Libe? I am glad to see you, but sad that it should be such an occasion. Libe is one of my best men—all that can be done to save them all, is being done."

He looked long at Monare, then said:

"You seem a strong man; and you are a father . . . Soon will those who have been working underground to move the rocks, come to the surface. Is it your will that you should go down into the earth with these others who have rested, and help in the work of rescue? Wait! Remember, you may well be going to your death—Ntoane has told you? Do you still wish to go?"

The Mosotho replied:

"My *Baas*, if it is but to die with my son, I wish to go!"
The white man replied:
"So be it!"
And turning to another white man, shouted:
"Johnson! . . . Here is another volunteer for you!"

Chapter Three

FALSE DAWN

BRAVE THOUGH THE MOSOTHO had proved himself to be, it was with a feeling of great fear, even terror, that he at last felt the cage dropping down into the depths of the earth. He himself was a figure that would have made his wife Florinah run in fright—on his head he wore the miner's steel hat with safety lamp, by his side was his gas mask, and in his hand a pick!

"Now shall I never dread the Hell of my Moruti, for this surely must be its courtyard!"

Thus thought Monare as the cage slowed down to a jerking stop. The Mosotho and his dozen or more companions stepped out into a large tunnel, where waited other men with tired faces, who staggered as if drunk, as they walked to the cage. These, said Mr. Johnson, were the men who had been working since dawn, and who were now going to the surface for rest and food.

Mr. Johnson now went ahead, and before the amazed eyes of Monare stood a baby *mafofonyane* with some trucks attached to it. Mr. Johnson signed to the men to sit in the trucks and, himself mounting the driver's seat, set the *mafofonyane* in motion. Away clanked the train with many groanings and screechings into the middle of the earth. After a few minutes of rattling and roaring, the *mafofonyane* squeaked to a halt, and the men set foot to ground once more. Mr. Johnson led them through a smaller tunnel until at last they came to what was but a hole in the ground, through which they must crawl. This small tunnel sometimes widened and sometimes narrowed, and here and there lay pieces of rock, and broken wooden mine props.

Mr. Johnson spoke:

"Now men, are we nearing the place where our brothers lie buried; walk with care, and do not let your picks catch in the rocks. First will we work with our hands, until the rocks will no longer move—then only shall picks be used, and not at all should there be smell of gas!"

The electric lights which had defeated the darkness of the big tunnel, here shone not at all; the place was lit but by the dim flames of the safety lamps. In this light Monare saw before him two men with jugs of liquid, from which came hunger-making smells; Monare's lips were wet—he could drink happily of soup or coffee. But as he drew nearer to the men, he saw that the liquid was being poured slowly into pipes which ran away into the rock.

Mr. Johnson, seeing the direction of Monare's gaze, said:

"Your son and the others lie beyond that rock; twenty feet of it lie between them and us; yet by back-breaking work have we managed to push through the rock these pipes, and are now able to give those buried, soup and coffee, for they have not eaten for forty-eight hours! Later, when they have fed, if you will place your mouth close to this end of the pipe and speak—your son shall hear your voice. And if you will then place your ear against the pipe, you shall hear his reply!"

Now was Monare's heart lightened somewhat, and was filled with thanksgiving to Allah—soon would he hear the voice of his beloved son. . . .

At length was the feeding of the prisoners at an end, and Mr. Johnson signed to Monare to approach the end of the pipe. With fast-beating heart, Monare obeyed, and placing lips to the pipe-end, called:

"Libe! Libe! My son! It is your father Monare who calls!"

Quickly he placed his ear against the end of the pipe, and waited, with the blood beating in his temples. Faintly, in a strange hollow manner, sounding as if each time the words were spoken, they were repeated, came the beloved and well-remembered voice of his son:

"O my Father! I thank God for this! Now can I die happy, if that is to be my fate! When Ntoane called through the pipe last night that you were coming, I prayed that you would not be too late!"

The ghost of a laugh floated through the pipe.

"We meet in strange places, O my Father!"

Monare sobbed with relief, then, hearing no more, placed his lips to the pipe again.

"How are you, and the others, and the white man?"

"The white man is badly hurt, my Father, and so are two of the Africans—if we are not released soon, I fear that we may die. The rest of us are tired, and find breath hard to draw in and blow out—but we have suffered no injury. We are pressed so hard by the rock, that we can move our bodies but an inch or two."

Monare raised his head and told Mr. Johnson what his son had said, and then, putting his lips to the pipe for the last time, called:

"Courage, my son Libe!—now is the work of shifting this mountain of rock about to be started afresh."

2

The two hours which followed this talk between father and son, were the most filled with agony of all those that Monare had lived—harder to bear even than those of his passage across the Umbeluzi River; harder than those of his fight against the Zulus. Slowly, with great care, were rocks loosened from the heap that lay before them; slowly, too, were the loosened rocks passed back behind them. As the minutes passed, the workers found it increasingly difficult to breathe; their movements grew languid and heavy . . . At last came a tapping on the pipe, and Mr. Johnson signed to Monare to answer.

Libe's voice came along the pipe faintly:

"My Father, we cannot breathe . . ."

When he was told of this, Mr. Johnson ordered two of the men to carry to the pipe-end, a large iron cylinder which had been lying to one side of the spot they were working in.

The white man said to Monare:

"Now must we give them this oxygen, instead of food and

drink, otherwise will they die! This medicine will make their breathing easier."

And the oxygen was pumped along the pipe-line.

Sounds now came from behind them, and they saw the light of lamps approaching. Mr. Johnson said:

"Now is the time for rest; two hours of this work is as much as a man's strength can stand; moreover the air is getting foul; therefore shall we all go to the surface for food and drink and rest, whilst these who now approach, shall take our place."

Monare replied quietly:

"Shall I leave my son while yet he lives? Shall I go while the breath is yet in me? No!"

The white man's eyes showed understanding, but his voice said:

"To stay here longer without rest, food, drink, and fresh air, is to die by one's own will! This oxygen would help you to breathe more easily, but it is needed for those imprisoned beyond the rock."

Monare sighed, and repeated:

"How can I leave Libe? *Morena*, I feel that my life is done—let me use the little that remains, as I will."

The white man placed his hand on Monare's shoulder, and spoke thus:

"The men who come are rested; they are fresh, they will work even as we worked, in the beginning; more quickly will those imprisoned, be released!"

Monare's voice grew hoarse:

"My *Baas*, if within were your own son—could six men drag you away?"

"Monare, waste not the precious air in vain talk! Rest you must have, if you would live to see your son again. Come with me now, and after eating and drinking you and I shall descend again. We shall stay but one hour up there under the sky whilst these others shall have their full four hours' rest."

Monare agreed to this, and by this time the new shift had arrived at the rock-face; words and instructions were exchanged, and the tired men of the old shift slowly crawled and crept back to the trucks hauled by the baby *mafofonyane*, and were carried back to the cage in the shaft. As they shot into the light of day their eyes burned with a fierce pain, and their hard-worked lungs drew in deep breaths of fresh air.

As they got down from the cage, many crowded around them for news; Ntoane brought Monare food and drink, and spoke with him awhile. He promised that if Monare would sleep, he would awaken him within the passing of an hour.

Monare slept.

3

When the friendly hands of Ntoane dragged Monare from the depths of sleep, it seemed that but a few minutes had passed. Looking down at Monare with a smile was Mr. Johnson, who said :

" I have kept my promise."

Monare sat up suddenly.

" What is the news, my *Baas* ? "

" They are still alive—there is but ten feet now between them and us ! "

" Let us then descend ! "

Again they entered the cage and dropped deep into the stomach of the earth; again they rode behind the baby *mafofonyane*; again they crawled through the narrow tunnel; and again they stood by the fallen rocks, where men worked, sweating and groaning.

Monare said to himself :

" Indeed do we look like devils from Moruti's Hell ! "

And indeed they did, with their sweat-lined faces coated with dust, and the lights flickering on their foreheads. Now came through the pipe-line a terrible wailing and a shrieking, and a babble of talk . . .

Mr. Johnson said :

" To be buried alive is too much like Death itself ! Who can blame that poor fellow if his brain is turned ! "

He looked around him and murmured :

" Safety is leaking from the pot—if we do not break through

FALSE DAWN

quickly now, those beyond the rocks will be dead! . . . Now is the hour of desperation!"

By this time was the space behind the workers filled with the rocks which they had removed; beyond that lay the hole which was narrowed by broken props and pieces of the roof. Therefore did Mr. Johnson obtain further workers to clear the space behind them by loading on to the trucks of the baby *mafofonyane* the rocks which had been cleared. This done, he arranged the workers so that rocks could now be passed directly back from the rock-face, from one hand to another along the line of men, until the last hands of all placed the rocks on the trucks. Each time the trucks were filled, the baby *mafofonyane* drew them away and returned with empty ones.

Monare did the work of five men. Though his breathing was like the puffing of an engine, and his legs and arms ached as they had never done before—yet did he continue to lift and pass the heavy pieces of rock. When again the time arrived for his shift to return to the surface for rest and food, Monare refused to accompany them. Two other Africans also expressed their determination to remain and aid the fresh workers who were then arriving from the earth above.

Monare said to Mr. Johnson, quietly and painfully:

"Death is not far distant from us all; yet the more hands that help, the more chance is there that Death will grow tired of waiting, and—for this time—depart."

Mr. Johnson replied:

"The more that work, the quicker will the air become foul and weak; yet to those who volunteer, I will not withhold permission to remain."

Now did all those in Monare's shift—excepting four men who were themselves at grips with Death—agree to remain. The volunteers were sent back to the trucks, where the air was fresher, and the new shift took their places at the rock-face. Monare, however, refused to obey this order of the white man, and remained at the obstructing rock-wall, and continued to tear down with bleeding hands huge pieces of the barrier.

Now was oxygen pumped along the pipe-line once more;

when this had been done, coffee and soup were fed to the imprisoned men by the same means. Then was the remaining food shared out amongst the workers, for as Mr. Johnson remarked, the next time the feeding-time of those imprisoned arrived, they would be either released or dead! It was indeed the hour of desperation!

Mr. Johnson now ordered that shovels should be brought up to clear away the smaller rocks and the dust; and at last, as Monare staggered back from the barrier, with a huge rock clasped in his arms, a man behind him croaked joyfully:

"'There is a hole!'"

Mr. Johnson and the other white man came close to the rock-face, and saw that in truth had the door to the prison at last been forced. It was not yet fully open—there was not yet room for a man to emerge—yet could they now hope!

Now must all work with great care, lest the remaining portion of the prison wall fall inwards and crush those trapped within.

4

This joyful news gave added strength to the arms and legs of the workers, and soon were the bodies of their friends exposed to the lights of their safety lamps.

Little speech remained in their mouths, yet was there sufficient breath in all of them to cheat Death. With the tenderness of women the Africans lifted out from their prison the rescued men, and passed them back to be taken to the surface; but apart from a quick embrace, Monare saw little of Libe, and spoke with him not at all.

Right at the back of the prison could be seen the body of the injured white man, with a large rock resting on it.

Death doubtless looked over his shoulder and tarried, thinking, "Perhaps I shall not altogether be cheated!"—for the white man lay in a position of very great danger. Should the rock pressing on him be removed, then might the roof, which it appeared to support, descend in its place and crush him. Here was a task for fresh, strong men; not for those tired with much toil, and almost unable to breathe in the foul air—yet must the attempt be made.

FALSE DAWN

At this time might Monare have ascended to the daylight with the others with the praise and warm gratitude of all, for he had done much more towards the rescue of those imprisoned than could have been expected from one man. Moreover his heart was full of longing to see his son, Libe, and to speak with him. Yet the spirit within him would not release him from the earth's belly: there was still work for a strong man to do.

Turning to Mr. Johnson—who still waited—he said:

"*Ka Thesele!*—that was good work you did, my *Baas*, and never shall I forget you, and I shall always pray for you. I think that for once we may praise ourselves without earning rebuke from God! I am very tired, yet is there strength left in my shoulders. I think that if these others—these fresh men—could lift up this rock which imprisons the white man, even if it is but an inch, I could then bear on my shoulders the weight of the rock for those seconds required for the white man to be removed."

Mr. Johnson looked round the circle of men.

"No, Monare, you have done enough! There are others here only too willing to undertake that task."

Monare also took a quick glance round: then he smiled, and said: "Are not mine the broadest shoulders?"

Mr. Johnson knew the worth of Monare—of the others, he knew not how they might stand or crumble under the weight of the rock. He knew only that they were brave men all! Therefore said he:

"Right, Monare! Sit down and rest, and we others shall examine the rock and see if, and how, it may be raised."

By careful searching the two white men found that the large rock which imprisoned the injured miner rested its weight on the rock on which the body lay. Had it been otherwise, the white man would have been crushed like an egg. Nevertheless, the positions of the two rocks and their shapes, prevented the imprisoned man from moving as much as a finger or toe. It seemed also that there was a space of some six inches between the top of the rock which had tried to flatten the white man, and the roof of the tunnel. Farther on, some mine-props remained in place, but it was doubtful whether the roof would stay like a black sky over their heads, or fall in and crush them. Then, too, they could not see whether or not their lifting of the prison-rock might not shift other, unseen rocks which might touch it on the far side, and thus start a fresh and more dangerous rumbling and tumbling of the roof.

Yet must the attempt be made; therefore all that could take hold placed their hands beneath the rock; the others standing ready to lift out the white man and carry him tenderly to the waiting *mafofonyane* and its trucks. Monare stood with shoulders bent, waiting to take on to them with his great strength, the weight of the rock. Mr. Johnson told them all, that none must lift or pull, save at his order.

When all were in place, Mr. Johnson gave the command to lift. Slowly the rock rose until it touched the roof. Then, quickly, Monare bent and placed his shoulders beneath the rock, and pressed himself upwards, until he felt it move a little. He gasped out one word:

" Right."

Mr. Johnson called:

" Let go of the rock very slowly, and then pull out the *Baas*! "

Watching Monare with fearful eyes, the workers slowly took away from the rock their hands, and with great gentleness moved them towards the body of the injured white man. As the rock settled itself on the shoulders of Monare, he staggered a little, and the sweat poured down his face; but clever hands were slowly —inch by inch—moving the white man from underneath the rock. The injured man groaned, for some of his ribs had been crushed; yet did he progress towards Life—although with the slowness of the tortoise—and leave Death behind him.

Monare felt that his legs were going to collapse like dry sticks; his chest seemed about to burst; and his shoulders felt as if they had been pierced by assegais: yet he endured.

Now called Mr. Johnson:

" The white man has reached the truck of *mafofonyane*! "

This was the agreed signal for Monare to free himself; but Monare now felt added weight come on to his back, and he knew that the roof must have loosened—now when he got from under the rock, might the roof fall in! Therefore with what breath remained to him, he cried:

"Run for the trucks! The roof falls!"

And as the men obeyed the note of danger in his voice, he allowed himself to collapse like a pricked balloon; and, as he fell, he rolled his body outwards, in the direction of the *mafofonyane*, so that he might not become the filling of a rock sandwich!

As the rock dropped down, so did the roof above it fall too; and with a roar and a rumble, the tunnel filled with rocks small and large, and with dust. Those lifting the white man to the truck, hurried, with the fear of death snarling at their heels; but Mr. Johnson stood, and looking back, saw Monare rise, only to be knocked down again by a piece of rock which hit his head. He did not rise again.

Back, into the dark hell of dust, staggered Mr. Johnson, until his feet tripped over the body of Monare. Stooping like a drunken man, he caught up Monare and stumbled towards the trucks. Willing hands came to help him, and soon all were packed in the cage, and rose swiftly towards the upper earth.

5

Monare opened his eyes to see the face of Ntoane floating above him like a smiling moon; he tried to raise his head, but it was as if a hammer had struck him; he lay still, and looked around with his eyes—he was lying in a hospital bed. The well-known head of Ntoane disappeared, and in its place came that of a white woman nurse, who gave him a bitter draught to drink. Soon was his head clearer, and the pain drew back from his temples. Some time passed.

Then said Ntoane:

"Try turning your head to the left."

Monare obeyed, and there—in the next bed—lay his beloved son, Libe. His gaze moved again and picked up the face of Mr. Johnson. Monare tried to speak, but his voice sounded in his ears cracked and strange:

"*Morena!* My mind clears—I am deeply grateful to you for saving my life!"

Mr. Johnson laughed, and replied:

"What I did, any man could do—but what you did, could have been done by few, and will not quickly be forgotten by African or white man!"

They talked awhile, and Monare was told that the injured white man would recover, and that all the others who had been rescued were feeling better. Then said Ntoane:

"The white doctor says that we may go, as soon as your head is clear."

Then did full memory return to Monare, and he knew that he must go, and that speedily!

But before he could answer, Mr. Johnson broke in:

"First are there photographs to be taken!"

And before Monare could protest, all around came the plops and flashes of the picture-takers!

Now did Mr. Johnson touch on the matter of rewards, saying to Ntoane and Monare that not only did the Mine Manager wish to speak with them, but that the *Makulu Baas* at the Chamber of Mines wished to reward them for their bravery.

Mr. Johnson continued:

"The people of the newspaper also wish you to visit them in the morning; maybe there will be more making of pictures."

"I want no reward, my *Baas!* What I did was but to save my son! Moreover, the little help I was able to give you was more than repaid—for did you not save my life when the rocks struck me down? If the *Baas* will excuse us, my friend, my son, and I all wish to leave the city to-night for Lesotho. I have not yet looked on the face of my wife. And soon is expected—a grandson!"

With many fair words did the brave white man seek to persuade Monare to stay in the City of Gold and receive that which his strength and courage entitled him to; but the taking of the pictures had given fresh strength to Monare's ancient fear of the Police, and he turned a deaf ear to the eloquence of Mr. Johnson.

"*Baas*," he said, "whatever may be due to me, let it be placed

FALSE DAWN

in the deserving hands of my friend Ntoane, who, with my son Libe, will return and wait on you in a few days' time. As for me, I will return one day to thank you for saving my body from being buried in the earth's middle. Think not that I am lacking in courtesy, but I must leave this City to-day."

Mr. Johnson now shook hands with the three Basotho, and said again:

"Thank you, Monare, for your great help!"

The Basotho were now left alone. Monare, trying with care to see if his head could now be lifted, found success; next he tried the strength of his legs, and was joyed that they would carry him. Now quickly he walked to the bed of Libe, who seeing him approach, rose up, and father and son embraced. Ntoane looked on with happy, smiling eyes.

Monare said:

"Here is no place for talk; again will my picture appear in the newspapers. Soon will the Police know that I am once more in the City of Gold! Let us quickly gather our clothes and our possessions and get away to some secret place, where we can talk and plan for the future."

Ntoane thought for a few minutes, then said:

"A friend of mine is cook-boy to a white man at Houghton; the *Baas* and his family have gone to Cape Town for a holiday, but my friend is still living in the servants' quarters—there let us go, and no one shall find us!"

The three Basotho thanked the nurse and the doctor, collected their cases and clothes, and went out through the front door of the hospital—but here was gathered a great crowd of Africans. There were even white men in motor cars, with cameras in their hands.

As the Basotho came out, a great cheer resounded and the people closed in on them. It took some time for the Basotho to push their way through the friendly people. Once they were stopped by a white woman, who cried:

"Where is the brave African who saved my husband? I wish to thank him!" This woman—with eyes red from weeping—was the wife of the injured miner, and she pressed into Monare's hands a bundle of notes, saying:

"Money cannot talk the language of gratitude, yet accept this for now, until my husband shall recover. Then shall we talk again, and decide how best we can reward you!"

The tears came into Monare's eyes, and he passed on—having thanked her—thinking:

"How strange is the path chosen by Allah for me to follow! Maybe the end is not yet, as I had thought. Maybe I shall again walk in the pleasant land of Mocambique!"

At last the three Basotho finished passing through the people, and securing a taxicab, drove off towards the house of the white man at Houghton.

6

In the taxi, Monare thought of his friends in the Cities of Sugar and Lourenco Marques; as they passed a post-office, he stopped the car and sent telegrams to the Moulvie Abdul Wahid and to the Moulvie Mazaffar Khan, giving them the good news about his son's safety. To the latter telegram he added the words, "leaving by to-morrow night's train," and signed both messages with the name of Dost Ghulam.

Arrived at the white man's house at Houghton, they found Ntoane's friend busy cutting the grass. He welcomed the three Basotho, and as the day was now dying, put the kettle on for some tea, and started to prepare food. Ntoane's friend was not a Mosotho —his name was Alfred, and he had been born in Johannesburg; but Ntoane had known Alfred and his father for many years, and as he said to Monare:

"Here need not words be twisted—say what is in your heart, tell us with your tongue what you have already written with your hand; tell us all that has happened since you left this place for the City of Sugar in 1948. Alfred you may trust as you would trust me!"

Now did Monare tell his companions of his days in the City of Sugar, of his friend Mkize, and of the Time of Terror which came after the white man's Christmas. He told of his meeting with the Moulvie Abdul Wahid, and of how he had come to fight at his side against the Zulus. With pride he displayed the golden watch which the Mayor of Durban had given him, and nothing that was to happen to Monare could ever take from him the joy and satisfaction that came to him when he saw the love and admiration in the eyes of his son, Libe.

He spoke to his companions of the taking of the photographs in Durban—which they said they had seen in the newspapers on the Rand—and of his decision to leave the City of Sugar. He explained how he had come to stay with the Moulvie Abdul Wahid, and told of his friendship with Ghulam Hussain. With pride he displayed his remembrance gifts of golden pen and pencil.

But of greatest interest to the listening Basotho, was Monare's acceptance of Islam. He had to explain to them at great length that there were many tribes among the Indians; how some were *amaSuleiman*, some were Hindus, and others Christians. He told how the tribe of the Moulvie, the Pathan tribe, was one of the proudest in all India.

What had first attracted Monare to the religion of the *amaSuleiman*, was, of course, his regard for the Moulvie Abdul Wahid, and for his son, Ghulam Hussain—but what had kept his interest and deepened it, was, without doubt, the fact that amongst these followers of Islam was there real and true equality.

Libe said eagerly :

" Not like the Christians, O my Father, where the white men stay in one church, and make coloured Christians worship in another ! "

" Not like the Christians, my son ! Amongst the Muslims there is nothing of that sort. In the Mosque, if the rich man comes late, there is no place reserved for him—should the one to arrive before him be a beggar, then must he stand on the beggar's left ! "

Alfred said :

" *Ee!* Monare—that is the religion for us Africans ! "

Monare went on to tell them about his long talk in the motor car with the white man, Newington Sahib, and how his thoughts had been broadened and made clear through the discussion which started on the subject of equal pay for equal work. He repeated to them the warning of the Moulvie Mazaffar Khan, that they should close their ears to the speeches of the Communists, who strove to use the misery and poverty of the African people to secure their own ends.

Libe now questioned:

"And what of these Indians, my Father?—other than these Pathans you love so much! Are they our friends or our enemies?"

"My son, like us, are the Indians oppressed! They have no say in the *Pitso* in Cape Town; they, too, must put up with much ill-treatment from the white man. Doubtless some amongst them like to bear down harshly on the Africans, even as the white man bears down harshly on them. But so many of them have sympathy and charity in their hearts, that I could not say that they are our enemies. I think that we Africans must put out of our minds that the Indians and coloured people are not of our own blood and descent—rather must we look upon them, and claim, as brothers-in-misfortune. As in this country the white man places all who do not possess white skins in one *kraal*, and calls them "non-Europeans," let us behave as if indeed we all did belong to the same *kraal*, and stand together against the harshness of the white man. I would like to see every African a Muslim."

Ntoane said, at length:

"Little time have I had, home-boy, for speech with you since you got down from that train! But if it were not for your face, I would never say that you were the same man who greeted me all those long years ago, when you first walked into my room at Msilikazi!"

Libe quickly interjected:

"I am proud of my father!—if there is any change in him, it is a wonderful change!"

"Nay, Libe—think not that I wish to belittle your father, who is my old and true friend. I but say that he talks now more like some Moruti, but of a kind I have never met before!"

Alfred gave voice to his thoughts:

"This knowledge doubtless comes from great travel; although Monare will doubtless enjoy our *mahleu*, and—in spite of his Moulvies!—drink a scale of fine home-brewed kaffir beer with us, he speaks and acts without fear, freely—not as if he were, like us, a poor African who may at any moment be called upon by the Police to produce his Pass!"

Monare laughed.

"I am not only a Muslim, member of a religion of freedom and equality, but I have come now from the land of Mocambique, where this freedom is in the air, and can be breathed by such as have the desire and will to do so."

Now were many questions thrown at Monare, and he spent a long time answering them to the best of his ability. He explained to his companions what an assimilated African was, and what privileges he commanded, and the tests an African had to undergo to become one.

The story of his journey across Swaziland was received with many expressions of wonder and praise; he showed to them the ring of gold given to him by the white man, Newington Sahib; he displayed, too, the golden *tavis* presented to him by the Moulvie Mazaffar Khan, and spoke of its origin and of its power.

Now that the two Basotho and Alfred had emptied their bag-of-questions, Monare asked of Makopoi and of the expected birth of his grandchild.

Libe answered:

"Any day now, my Father . . . I am sure it will be a boy!"

The time for eating had now arrived, and the four men ate long and well. But too much food after too much hard work means too much desire for sleep—therefore did Alfred quickly obtain extra blankets from the house, and set them out on the two beds in the *ntlo*. Alfred and Ntoane lay on one bed, and Monare and Libe on the other.

Soon the peace of the night was broken by the snoring of the exhausted men.

7

Early in the morning, as was his habit, Alfred rose from his bed and prepared tea; he then shook the sleeping men until they opened their eyes. When they had finished drinking, they went to the shower room and cleaned themselves. Whilst Alfred prepared porridge for their breakfast, the other three discussed Monare's plans.

Monare said :

" In two days' time I shall be back home at the Mosque in the Rua Salazar at Lourenco Marques ! Soon will come my friend Ghulam Hussain, and whilst he is staying with me, I shall appear before the Tribunal of the Portuguese, and—Allah willing—I shall become an assimilated African. Then Ntoane, must you and Libe visit the Portuguese Consul here, and obtain a permit to visit Lourenco Marques—what a time we shall enjoy ! As for your mother, Libe, I think she will need some strong speech before she will be agreeable to leaving Lomontsa. But as you all realise, I dare not go to Lesotho to fetch her—the necessary persuasion will have to come from you, my son, and from you, Ntoane ! After you have visited me, you will be able to tell her how I am living in Lourenco Marques like a white man ! "

Thus boasted Monare, forgetting the Arabic words so often on the lips of Muslims—" *Insh'allah !* "—if God wills !

Monare remained deep in thought for a while, then quietly he said to Ntoane :

" Home-boy, what of the matter of the killing of Koto ? "

" Monare, I think the Great Detectives search for you in Durban ; yet doubtless has the Chief of the Lesotho Police asked the Chiefs of the Police here too, to keep open their eyes and their ears. We cannot read the minds of these Great Detectives, yet this can we say with certainty : that had they used cunning, then would they have kept close watch on your son Libe. They would have discovered that he was one of the buried miners, and knowing how great is a father's love for his son——"

Monare interrupted.

" They would know that I would come back even from across the Great Waters if I knew that my son was in danger ! "

Libe said eagerly :

" If they had thought thus, O my Father, then would they have been waiting at the mine ! "

Monare laughed, but it was not a happy laugh.

FALSE DAWN

"Well, with this taking of pictures for the newspapers, the detectives will know soon enough!"

Alfred said:

"Let us put this matter to the test—I will go and buy last night's *Star* and this morning's *Rand Daily Mail*, and we shall see if the photos have been published."

Whilst Alfred was away, the three Basotho talked of their beloved homeland.

Alfred returned quickly, but dolefully, saying:

"Look!"

The four men examined the newspapers eagerly.... Much space had been given to the rescue of the buried miners, and right in the middle of the principal page of each newspaper appeared the faces of Mr. Johnson, Ntoane, Monare, and Libe.

Worse still—for the pictures were not as clear as the takers would have chosen them to be—the names of the three Basotho appeared in heavy, black lettering.

Libe spoke urgently.

"When we have finished eating, let us go quickly into the city and buy such gifts as you, O my Father, would wish to take back with you to Mocambique, or to send by my hand to my mother. Then let us ride quickly.... Perhaps it is better that you do not take train from here—or even from Pretoria! We all have money in plenty—why not let us take a taxi from here to Middelburg, or even to Belfast? You can join the train there, where the Police will never suspect your presence!"

Ntoane brought down his hand hard on the table on which the food was spread and, amid a great rattling of cups, said:

"*There* is more cunning than is in a housesnake! Libe, you would make a good *ngaka*, or even a great detective! This is excellent advice! As soon as we have finished eating we will go to the city and make our purchases, then maybe have a good meal at the Mayibuye Restaurant, and then leave the City of Gold with the speed of *mafofonyane*!"

And so it was arranged; and the four men set to and ate up all the food and drink that the generous Alfred had provided.

8

Later that morning, their arms full of gifts for loved ones and friends in Monontsa and Lourenco Marques, the three Basotho sat at a table in the Mayibuye Restaurant and discussed their future plans.

All African men in the Union of South Africa must carry with them night and day, Passes and Tax Receipts. A Mosotho from Lesotho must be in possession of a Permit to seek work or, should he have lived in the Union for more than one year, a receipt for the payment of his tax. Should Africans desire to use the streets of the city late at night, then must they obtain Special Passes from their white men employers—otherwise will the Police arrest them. Little freedom is there for the wretched African ... Such matters did the three Basotho talk about as they ate, for Monare's stories of life in Mocambique uncovered differences between his looked-forward-to privileges as an assimilated African and Ntoane's and Libe's lack of privileges, as great as that between night and day!

Ntoane said:

"In Natal, but a few weeks past, a Moruti and his son were unable to open the door of the coach reserved for Africans, and as the train was about to depart, the Ticket Examiner pushed them into a white man's carriage, and told them to walk along the train until they arrived at the coach intended for them. As it happened, the white man's coach they passed through was filled with children going home from school. These ill-mannered children kicked and abused the Moruti and his son as they walked through the coach, and brought on them much shame and sorrow and hurt—even the newspapers of the white man could find no excuse for such evil behaviour."

Monare suggested:

"It was the fault of the white children's parents."

Now Libe joined in:

"Now are Africans not always allowed to gather for weddings or funerals; twice in this last month have the white man's Police broken up such gatherings and beaten the people with sticks!"

FALSE DAWN

Filled with love as was Monare's heart for Florinah and Libe, he now greatly desired to leave the Union, where he was at the mercy of such white men as were influenced by hate or anger. In strong words he spoke again to his son and Ntoane of the pleasure of life in Mocambique; and at last did they agree that as soon as Monare had passed the Tribunal's tests, they would pay him a visit and see for themselves.

When they had finished their food, they left the Mayibuye Restaurant, and went to the house of a taxi-driver known to Ntoane, who would, for a reasonable sum, take them to Belfast.

As they left the City of Gold, on the road to Springs, there stepped out from the pavement to bar their way, a policeman. Monare's heart seemed to stop beating.

Ntoane reassured him:

"It is but to examine the licence of the taxi-driver."

The motor car stopped, and the policeman asked the driver for his driving licence, and for his exemption for the carrying of passengers. These were produced, examined, and returned to the taxi-driver. The policeman appeared satisfied, and was about to wave permission for the Basotho to continue their journey—who had buried an evil medicine horn in that motor car, Monare was never to know, but suddenly with no reason that could be seen, the policeman said:

"Where are you going?"

Before anything could be done, the African taxi-driver replied:

"To Belfast, my *Baas* . . ."

The policeman opened wide his eyes.

"You black bastards must have plenty of money!"

Now was the chance missed, and the path lost. Had but one of them spoken up and told the policeman that they were the Africans from the South Rand Mine, and that one of them was the Mosotho who had saved the life of the injured white man, even then, might all have been well; for the policeman would probably have believed them, as the story of the rescue was common talk in the city.

The policeman might easily have said, "Lucky bastards!" and allowed them to proceed.

But when they said nothing, the policeman straightened up and sneered:

"Too bloody well-dressed for decent kaffirs! Show me your Passes, quick!"

Thus were the words of Fate spoken!

Chapter Four

JUDGMENT DAY

THERE WAS SMALL CHANCE OF ESCAPE; a tight band of despair encircled Monare's chest—the way had been long but he had come to the end! Yes, he could jump out of the taxi, but how far would he get? It was strange to sit there, free, and yet to know that within the next few seconds arrest must come.

The policeman was satisfied with the papers of Ntoane and Libe, and seemed no longer interested or annoyed when he held out his hand for Monare's Pass and Tax Receipts. Now, when it was too late, did Ntoane try to explain to the policeman who they were; Monare sat dumb with hopelessness and despair. Ntoane explained thus:

"*Baas*, this man Monare is he who saved the white man from death at the South Rand Mine; this Mosotho next to me is his son, whom he also dug out from the rock-fall. When he heard of his son's danger, he came quickly from where he was working, forgetting to bring Passes or Receipts with him . . ."

The policeman looked at Monare, then asked him this question:

"Where were you when you heard of this fall of rock?"

Ntoane spoke quickly, before Monare could answer.

"In Durban, my *Baas*."

The policeman smiled harshly, and continued:

"Why then, do you travel to Belfast? Is that some new short road to Natal?"

And he laughed, but in an offensive manner.

Ntoane's brain was quick, and he answered:

"We go to find a girl for his son's marriage."

But the policeman, wise to the ways of Africans, said sarcastically:

"Since when does Masotho mate with Shangaan! Rather than that you should choke yourselves with further lies, let us go to Marshall Square, where doubtless the truth shall be forced from you!"

Turning to Monare, who sat next to the driver, the policeman ordered:

"Get into the back!"

And to Ntoane, who sat behind, he commanded:

"Sit next to the driver!"

Then, getting into the back of the taxi, between Monare and Libe, he said, roughly, to the driver:

"Proceed to Marshall Square!"

On arrival at Marshall Square, sanity to some extent returned; at Ntoane's request, Mr. Johnson was spoken to on the telephone, and did not delay in coming to the Police Station.

Ntoane, Libe, and the driver of the taxi-cab were immediately released with grudging apologies; the case of Monare, however, was somewhat different. Monare knew that his only hope was to keep his mouth closed, and to leave any speech to Ntoane and Mr. Johnson. Mr. Johnson spoke to the sergeant who was in command of the Charge Office:

"This Mosotho, Monare, is a very brave man; yesterday he saved a white miner from death; his own son—that man there, Libe—was also imprisoned by this fall of rock. Can you blame him, if—in his hurry to reach the mine where his son was buried—he forgot to bring with him his Passes and Receipts? Have you not heard of this man, who displayed his bravery in Durban at the time of the Riots, and who was rewarded by the Mayor for his courage?"

Under this fountain of words, the sergeant lost some of his official harshness, and his expression changed; and he listened with interest when Mr. Johnson continued:

"I don't know why they were going to Belfast—but surely the roads are free to all? I myself will be responsible for producing

JUDGMENT DAY

this man's papers within a week! Do you not know that his face will to-morrow appear on the front page of all the newspapers of the land? He is to receive a medal from the King! Do you wish that the story of police foolishness shall be printed next to his photo?"

The sergeant was now quite convinced; and he said:

"Very good, sir! I shall release this Monare to your charge, to report here with his papers, one week from to-day—I will just confirm that with the captain. . . ."

A door opened and closed, and a chance came and went; for when the door reopened, and the sergeant emerged, behind him strode a captain of the white man's police who said in excited tones:

"Monare of Monontsa? Oh no! He cannot be released to anyone! He has an urgent appointment in Maseru! There he is eagerly awaited by the Basutoland Police to answer a charge of murder!"

The faces of the three Basotho went white; Libe made as if to run to his father, but by now, other policemen had placed the handcuffs on Monare's wrists!

Mr. Johnson looked as if he had been hit on the head by a rock! The captain saw the puzzled look in Mr. Johnson's eyes, and explained:

"This is a very strange case. Nearly two years ago was a man called Koto killed in a Ritual Murder in Basutoland. Now have the Police of Basutoland completed their investigations—they are waiting to arrest the Chief of Lomontsa who ordered the killing, and all those concerned in the murder. But first they wanted this man, Monare, who was in charge of the band of men who murdered Koto. Since this Monare won fame at the time of the Durban Riots, the police have lost trace of him. . . . I am sorry, Mr. Johnson, if he is a friend of yours—he is certainly a brave man!"

The captain now produced a warrant and read it out to Monare, who made no reply. Then the captain turned to Libe and said:

"I am sorry for you, my boy—your father will probably be taken to Maseru the day after to-morrow I advise you to proceed there, for in that place will the matter be decided!"

Now in a stunned silence, were Monare's precious remembrance gifts taken from him—his watch, his pen and pencil of gold, his handsome hunting knife, his chain and *tavis* of gold, his well-filled purse, his photographs of Florinah and of Libe. A receipt was passed to him, which slipped through his slack fingers to the floor. Libe picked this up.

Said the sergeant :

" These articles will be given to the escort when it arrives, and will be taken to Maseru. For this time, make your farewells ! For now must Monare go to his cell ! "

Father and son embraced to the clinking clatter of the steel handcuffs ; friend and friend clasped each other, and the tears made wet their cheeks ; white man and black man shook hands, and even the white man's eyes were not dry.

As Monare was taken away to his cell, the last friendly voices called :

" Do not lose heart ! What can be done, shall be done ! "

There remained but the dark, damp closeness of the cell, and Monare's sobs to mourn the death of Hope.

2

The writers of the news in the *Rand Daily Mail* and the *Star* had a story such as they had never expected—their fingers tired from the typing they performed. What a story ! What talk and argument there was amongst those who read ! What tears and sorrow came to the hearts of Africans ! All Lesotho mourned when the tale was told.

Ntoane and Libe sat with Mr. Johnson and recounted to him the story of Monare's life. When at length they had finished, Mr. Johnson sighed and said :

" You misjudged the mind of the Police, Ntoane. But even though Monare was concerned in this inhuman and horrible Ritual Murder, still would I be happier had he escaped to the Land of Mocambique ! I feel that he has more than paid for his misdeeds, yet, I fear, will it go ill with him. With your consent, I will tell his story to the Chiefs at the Chamber of Mines, and although they

JUDGMENT DAY

will not be able to effect Monare's release, yet can they speak words of influence to those high in the Government of Basutoland; and also I am certain that they will pay for a lawyer to defend him. My advice to you, Libe, is that you should return to Lomontsa, where your mother will need the comfort of your presence. But rest assured, on the day of the trial I shall stand by your side!"

In far Lomontsa, too, was there wailing anguish as men were torn from their homes by the Police; even in the *kraal* of the Chief was there weeping, although no rude hands were laid upon his person. He was invited with great politeness to proceed to Maseru and there to report to the Chief of the Police. But was his end the same as that of the others—the loneliness of the dark cell!

All along the Reef did the policemen pounce like hawks, as those who had hunted that dark night with Monare, and who were now working on the Mines, were seized and arrested.

Down by the Great Waters in the City of Sugar, the work of loading and unloading the ships that sit in the sea stopped, while Basotho discussed eagerly what had happened. On the hills behind the city, the Moulvie Abdul Wahid and his son, Ghulam Hussain, wept and uttered prayers to Allah the Compassionate, the Merciful. In his house on the Berea, Newington Sahib's face grew sad as he read the news of Monare's arrest. "Poor fellow," he said to himself, "he was a brave man and a good sort." In the land of Mocambique, the Moulvie Mazaffar Khan and his two sons mourned the tragedy of a friend.

At Orlando, the Moruti sorrowed at the eternal fight in men's souls between good and evil; and eastwards, at Springs, a beautiful Mosotho girl wept, for a reason which she could not tell her husband.

Doubtless, in his cold grave the sad ghost of Koto grieved, too —and if, as the Baruti say, Koto yet lived on unseen, then would he knowing all, understand, forgive, and feel regret. For he had loved Monare well.

Saltest and most bitter were the tears shed in Lomontsa, at the house of Monare. It was the Moruti Lefa's sad task to tell Florinah of her husband's arrest. Florinah had no knowledge of her husband's wonderful plans for her, yet for some time had she possessed the feeling that soon would she look upon his face again—what terrible fulfilment of a dream!

Soon the policemen of the escort arrived in the City of Gold, in their smart, clean uniforms and riding breeches and spurs, wearing their red-edged helmets. But gloom on their faces, too, for they liked not this arresting of a hero!

3

What were the thoughts of Monare, as he sat chained to his companions in a darkened and curtained compartment of the Kaffir Mail, returning from his adventures to his homeland, Lesotho?

His mind was dazed and blank; he did not feel even his fetters. As yet, the Mercy of God's shock protected him from the thoughts and memories that beat against the closed door of his mind. The three members of his *impi*, who—working on the Rand—had been arrested and were returning to Maseru with him, spoke among themselves sullenly. They blamed Monare for their misfortune, but if Monare heard their muttered reproaches, he answered them not. Slowly the effects of the shock wore off, and thoughts crowded into Monare's mind; the first to gain admittance was:

" At last I shall see Florinah! "

But soon the dam of feeling broke, and Monare cried forlornly, with the hard, painful sobbing of a man.

" O God, cannot the sack of Mercy be pierced? So close was I to all that I desired! "

And Monare mourned the past most bitterly. Yet with even greater heartbreak did he think of the wonderful future for which he had struggled so hard and so long, and which had now closed and barred its door in his face. The passing stations were known only to Monare's ears, not to his eyes; but at last the train came to Ladybrand, and soon was the carriage of the prisoners joined to the Maseru train. At length the engine puffed its way towards the River Mohokare, the Border, and crossed it; then came the train to the white gates stretched across the line, and the engine whistled proudly as if to say, " Now I enter Lesotho! "

The white gates opened, and the train entered the enclosure

where all are searched by the Basutoland Police. . . . Then onwards and upwards puffed the engine, and the carriages followed it, until at last it paused, sighing, at the station of the capital city, Maseru.

Now at last did Monare see the light of the sun and the blue of the sky, and feel the soft air of the home-country on his face. Silent crowds stood on the platform, and in the front—supported by the Moruti Lefa and his wife—Monare saw his beloved wife, Florinah. He moved towards her, but his fetters forbade the steps of love to be taken; yet quickly, as the police moved the prisoners to a lorry, looks were exchanged, and hope and faith made fresh again.

4

Joy and delight were absent from the courtyard of the jail when the prisoners met at exercise the next morning. Monare greeted his Chief thus:

" May the Chief live long for us!"

Having said this, he laughed roughly and continued:

" How did this buried matter come above ground, my Chief?"

The Chief looked at Monare sadly, and yet in a puzzled way, as if he were gazing at a stranger.

" First, Monare, I must tell you that not for many long days did I know that Koto was your friend; and as far as sorrow can be expressed in such a case, I proffer it! As for the arrests, you must have heard that Koto's body was discovered by a herd-boy?"

" Yes, Chief, so I heard before I went to the City of Sugar. I heard, too, that when the police found that the body was mutilated, then did they enquire where new villages had been set up."

" That is right, Monare—the death of Koto was widely spoken of throughout Lesotho. . . . First went the old woman to the Police—the old woman with whom you drank beer—and whispered in their ears the name of my village——"

" But were there not other Medicine Horns being prepared at that time?"

"Yes, but others, too, had seen Koto at the place of drinking and recognised men from my village present there at that time—these men also went to the Police."

"My Chief—but how did they learn our names?"

"Present that night at the place of drinking was one, Phomane, and there he saw, and knew, Phafa. Before the body of Koto was unearthed, Phomane went to the mines at Middelberg to work; but a short time since he returned home, and whilst here in Lesotho, he fought with Phafa about some cattle. At the District Court he lost his case and in anger went to the Police, and told them that Phafa was with Koto on the night of the killing."

"And Phafa?"

"Phafa, thinking that he could already feel the rope around his neck, said that he was but working under the orders of the *Letona* appointed by the Chief—and he gave the Police your name!"

"And now the rope is around the necks of us all! This was most unlucky, my Chief. Yet I cannot blame Phafa too much—at times, courage deserts the strongest."

And Monare mourned awhile those few moments wasted in speech, which had cost Koto his life, maybe. He then asked the Chief:

"Phafa took my place at the *khotla* when I ran away to the City of Gold?"

"Yes, Monare—but never could I rely on him as I relied on you!"

"Still, by rising to the position of *Letona*, he has received part of the Devil's wages for what he did! I, too, received pay for my service to the Devil! Did I not become a man of fame—owner of many cattle and of much gold"

"Monare—you are a changed man! Never, in the old days would you have spoken thus!"

But at this moment a warder stilled their voices, for it was time to return to the cells.

There was but little delay in setting up the Court and in appointing the day of the trial; the next morning they were informed that their fate would be decided on the seventh day; furthermore, now would they be allowed to see at certain times such relatives and friends as desired to visit them and also the clever lawyers who had been engaged to defend them.

Thus was one of Monare's prayers granted; he was again able to look on the face of his beloved Ma-Libe—not alone, true, yet to see his wife in the presence of others was better than not to see her at all.

When Ma-Libe came, she embraced Monare and spoke thus:

"O Father of Libe, these eyes wept for you! This heart ached, and these ears longed for the sound of your voice, even if that voice were only raised to curse me! Far better those days of walking late in the night, and of the drinking of kaffir-beer, than these latter days when you rose high in the councils of the Chief! Is it not the duty of every Mosotho to obey the orders of his Chief? Is that not what you did? How then can they place you in this cage of iron?—and speak of Death!"

Ma-Libe cried hopelessly.

Monare comforted her, then replied:

"I know not the answer to this riddle; but I know this much now—that a man cannot serve two Chiefs! We, the people of Lesotho, are trying to do that very thing—to obey the Law of the White man, and at the same time, to obey the Law of the Chiefs! Perhaps it was wrong of the Chief Paulus Mopeli to have signed a treaty with the white man—better might it have been for our fathers to have fallen on the soldiers of the white man and killed them, or themselves been killed! Had events thus fallen out, to-day we should have been enslaved by white man, or enslaved by the Chiefs—but not by both!"

This was cold comfort for his sorrowing wife; further, Ma-Libe did not understand too much of what Monare had said. She felt, however, that this new Monare was a man far removed in outlook from the husband she had known. She dared to suggest:

"Your words and your manner seem strange, O Father of Libe!"

Monare smiled tightly:

"Much has happened to me since last we were together; yet in one respect I have not changed at all—for you must know,

Florinah, that I love you with all my heart; you have been a good wife and a good mother!"

Ma-Libe opened wide her ears and eyes to hear her husband call her by her given name, Florinah; from this she knew how moved he was. When she heard him speak of their life together, as past, she wept again.

When Monare had spoken softly to her in love, he continued, as if speaking to himself:

"The Witch Doctors we must get rid of, or the Chiefs, or the White man—then only shall we know how to conduct ourselves!"

Ma-Libe held her hands over her ears in terror at these frightening and blasphemous words.

Monare continued:

"Why is Ritual Murder ordered? Do the Chiefs really believe in the benefits of the Medicine Horn? Are they themselves frightened of the Witch Doctors? Most Baruti talk much of blood —they are like the *Ngaka* in this respect.... The Christian Moruti talks of the Blood of Jesus, and says there is merit in It—and the *Ngaka* says that there is power and virtue in human blood! In the Cities of Gold and Sugar, I have seen one white man give his blood to another, to save his life. There must be virtue in blood!"

They were silent for a while, Ma-Libe looking up at Monare in wonder at his words; then continued Monare:

"I think that the good or evil of this matter lies not in the blood itself, but in the shedding of it!"

Behind them, the Moruti Lefa and his wife stood, unseen and unheard. In the eyes of the Moruti was such a look as Monare might have seen on the face of the Radiant Stranger. Softly the Moruti spoke:

"Continue, my son Monare, and say, where does the good lie, and where does the evil lie?"

Monare seemed unaware that a strange voice had interrupted him; he continued, as if alone:

"Where the blood is shed willingly, there is it full of power and virtue! Like that of your Jesus, Moruti, like that of the white man who gives his blood to save others! But when blood is shed with violence, and is taken without consent, then does it act as Devil's blood towards those that steal it!"

Then was the Moruti's voice raised in thanksgiving so loud that all in the courtyard turned to listen.

"O God, I thank Thee for the words I have just heard spoken by a real home-born Mosotho!"

And turning to Monare, he continued:

"My son—I care not if what they tell me is true, that you are now an *iSuleiman*! You have taken your stand at last, as a man, on the side of God!"

The Chief Gaoler came running to see what was happening, for there was an uproar in the courtyard; some—those who feared the Witch Doctors—raising their voices against Monare; and others—being glad that the secret thoughts of their hearts had at last been spoken openly—praising him.

The voice of the Chief Gaoler cut across their arguments.

"Silence! I shall remove all visitors if this disturbance continues!"

But the Moruti Lefa spoke apart with the Chief Gaoler, and promised him that there should be no more unseemly conduct.

5

When all was quiet again—the prisoners and their friends doubtless busy with their urgent, private business, the Moruti called the Chief to his side.

"May the Chief live long! You can answer this question of Monare's—why does *Liretlo* continue in the land?"

"This is not a matter for discussion between Moruti and Chief!"

"Do you fear then, O Chief, that Monare should learn the truth?"

"You would not speak to me thus, outside these walls!"

"Take not offence, my Chief! Think not that I take advantage because you are a prisoner! Many men have come to their meeting with Death through the killing of Koto and, in the past, of others like him! Especially have these murders increased during the past five years!"

"Why say you that, Moruti?"

"When, Chief, was the National Treasury of Lesotho started?"

"Four or five years ago."

"How did this National Treasury come into being?"

"The matter was put to the Chiefs by the Resident Commissioner."

"Will you tell us what was proposed?"

"It is common knowledge. From that day was it arranged that all taxes and fines, which had in the past been collected by the Chiefs, would in future be gathered by and paid into the Basutoland National Treasury——"

"How then would the Chiefs obtain money?"

"The Chiefs are now paid fixed sums of money yearly by the National Treasury—as are the sub-Chiefs——"

"Can the Chiefs now fine tribesmen for their misdeeds?"

"No longer are tribesmen fined by the *Pitso* of the Chief; the Treasury set up District Courts to try men for offences and crimes, and to fine them, or award such punishment as is necessary."

The Moruti Lefa laughed. He said to Monare:

"You see, my son, that the Chiefs—in their folly—agreed to the setting up of that which was to destroy them, the National Treasury of Lesotho! They thought that a regular income was to be preferred to an income drawn from a share of the taxes, and of the fines which they themselves used to impose—am I not right, Chief?"

"Such was the opinion of the Chiefs, Moruti."

The Moruti continued, addressing himself to Monare:

"Since the Chiefs have surrendered their powers to the Basotho people, they have found that much more respect is given to the District Courts, than is given to the Chiefs themselves! This is but natural, for it is the Court—and no longer the Chief—that has the power to punish, and to collect the fines and the taxes!"

Monare was still puzzled; he asked:

"I heard talk of such courts whilst I was still selling trousers

JUDGMENT DAY

in the City of Gold—but what have they to do with the continuance of *Liretlo* ? "

The Moruti laughed bitterly.

" The Chiefs surrendered for a regular income, rights and privileges which have come down to them from their forefathers—they exchanged their birthright for a mess of pottage ! They cannot now fine tribesmen, and few indeed are the orders and commands that they may give ! How then shall their pride and dignity be protected, preserved, and upheld ? Only through the remaining customs of Lesotho, chief among which is *Liretlo* ! Thus may they assert themselves, and feel again Chiefs indeed—instead of pensioners of the Treasury ! This ordering of a killing for Ritual Murder is one of the few commands that are left to them—only thus can they make their power felt ! Never in Lesotho's history have so many Ritual Murders been ordered, as in the past five years—since the Chiefs have been made as oxen ! "

The Chief said angrily :

" You go too far, Moruti—nor will such talk help in the saving of the necks of those in this jail ! Yet, will I admit, that the Chiefs were wrong in their agreement to the setting up of this National Treasury ! By their assent, did they sign away the independence of Lesotho ! "

The Moruti's attack grew stronger.

" Furthermore, was it not the Chiefs who agreed to the hanging of two of their number who fought always for Lesotho's independence from the white man ? "

" Which two Chiefs do you speak of ? "

" O Chief—where there are no names and no villages mentioned, there can be no talk of Medicine Horns ! But you know the two of whom I speak—the two convicted of a Ritual Murder for which they were not responsible ! I say that they were innocent, and that the evidence against them was false ! Yet in their trial, did not Chiefs sit as Assessors next to the white Judge ? Could they not have used their influence to secure an acquittal ? Since their hanging, who now sits as Regent ? A woman ! How can the Paramount Chieftainess withstand the cunning of the white man ? I say that the end of Lesotho is in sight and that it is the foolishness of the

Chiefs that has brought the end so near! But I have no wish to offend you in your person—what I speak of will soon be a matter to be read in history books! After all, my work here is to comfort and help—I ask your pardon."

Those who had been listening to the words of the Moruti Lefa, sat by with big eyes and puzzled ears; much of it was beyond the understanding of the simple tribesmen. Ma-Libe listened not at all, but was content to hold her husband's hand. But Ntoane listened with a crooked smile, and Libe drank in the Moruti's words with eagerness.

The Moruti was now calmer; he smiled and said:

"I seem to have preached a sermon, and it is not even Sunday! But the news from Bechuanaland disturbs me—there, to-day, the white man rules. Had not Seretse Khama brothers, or uncles—other than the Old Regent? Could not a Bechuana have ruled in his place? But no, they must put in a white man Commissioner to rule! *Ee!* whoever heard of a white Chief for Africans! I do not think that ever again will an African rule in Bechuanaland. And if *Liretlo* continues here, and in Swaziland, then will the doom descend on us too! The white man's government of the English—it is not as in the *khotlas* of other days. I am afraid that in London they bargain with the Afrikaner over our dying homelands!"

For a while there was silence and sadness in the jail courtyard.

6

During the days which still remained before the trial, Monare and his fellow-prisoners spoke much with their friends and relatives, and discussed what should happen to their wives and children in the coming years, when they themselves might not be in this world to care for them. This was a period during which pain often stabbed at their hearts—yet some hoped to escape the gallows, notably Phafa. But the Chief and Monare were prepared to meet the worst that God might send them; though these, too, prayed for a miracle.

The afternoon following the visit of the Moruti Lefa, Mr. Johnson came to see Monare; after greeting him, he said:

"There is no escape from the trial, my friend. Only after a

JUDGMENT DAY

verdict of 'Guilty' has been brought in can anything be done to help you. Then can representations be made to the Judge on your behalf, that he should sentence you to imprisonment rather than to death. Your bravery has brought you powerful friends in Durban, Johannesburg, and Lourenco Marques. Should the worst befall, know that a fund has been started by the Chamber of Mines, for the education of your son, and his children, and for the upkeep of your wife. A brave man like you, Monare, will face with courage the quick mercy of the rope, as you did those slower and more terrible forms of death, which you confronted and conquered in the middle of the earth!"

Monare expressed his gratitude to the white man, and asked if news had been conveyed to the Moulvies at the City of Sugar and the City of Lourenco Marques. Mr. Johnson laughed as he replied:

"No one could fail to know of your arrest! Your name and face, and a record of your deeds—both good and bad—appear each day on the front pages of all the newspapers in the land! On the day of your trial, there will be more people here in Maseru, than ever there have been before! Among those thousands will be your friends Abdul Wahid, Ghulam Hussain, Mazaffar, Mohammed Khan, and Fazal Khan. You shall certainly see all your friends before all is finished."

Now was the time of punishment, of which the Moruti Lefa had warned Monare; death could he face with some calmness, but the sight of his mourning and beloved wife, Florinah, and the sad eyes of his son, Libe, squeezed his heart in a grip of iron, and brought him to despair. Like all men in such a case, he tried to bargain with God; but God appears to make no bargains in these latter days, no matter what He may have done in the time of the Scriptures: help will He give, where the Path of His Will is followed. This was the lesson that Moulvie Mazaffar Khan had sought to teach Monare; but realisation of this truth was a hard and bitter lesson for the Mosotho to master. Yet one morning he awoke with this thought in his heart:

"Since I arrived in the City of Sugar, no grave sins have I committed; I have done my best to atone for the past; I have true and loyal friends who are labouring to soften the stony hearts of those in high places to save me, much as I worked to shift the rocks that imprisoned my son! Only by the Will of God did I succeed, and only by His Will can my friends win or lose their fight. When man has done all in his power, then must the issue be left to God! Rather than show misery and despair to those I love, should I try to make their last days with me, happy! If I am to die, then will the shock to them be great; yet will my loved ones have the memory of these well-spent days to remember me by, and will not think of me as a coward! Now will I force back my tears and cause the smile of hope to appear on my face!"

And Florinah and Libe were much comforted by the manner and speech of Monare during these last days, and drew some measure of content from his calmness. But the darkness of night hid from all but his fellow-prisoners the terrible anguish of approaching separation which Monare felt within him, and which would not be denied in the still, quiet hours before the dawn. Then was the relief of tears granted to him, and then, too, did the Hand of God touch him and renew his courage for the daylight visits of his loved ones which were such a poignant delight.

It was thought among the prisoners that the trial might not last too long. The verdict was expected on the second day; and the clever lawyers, paid for by the Chief, and by Monare's friends, discussed with the prisoners how their defence should be built.

The Chief spoke, and nothing could alter his mind, which he had made up with determination:

"I shall plead 'Guilty,' and you men must plead 'Not Guilty,'"
and thereby proved the nobility of his forefathers and his fitness for his rank.

He continued:

"You, Phafa, I cannot hold much hope towards—nor to you others who aided Phafa to strike down Koto at my command—but Monare may escape the worst."

The lawyers pleaded with the Chief for permission to pull down some of the evidence erected by the Great Detectives; they thought that thus might doubt be born in the minds of the Judge and the Assessors; but the Chief replied that Phafa had confessed and, confessing, had involved Monare. He said further:

JUDGMENT DAY

"The days I have spent here in converse with the Moruti Lefa and with Monare, have made me know that here, in Lesotho, has the End of a Time arrived. I am Chief by right of descent from the Great Moshoeshoe, yet do I understand that I am Chief only whilst the God of all Baruti wills! What I have done, what I have commanded, in this matter of Ritual Murder, have I commanded and done without evil in my heart! I have done but as those before me did. Yet am I now convinced that I did not act with the Will of God. What was good in the days of the Great Moshoeshoe, is, maybe, not good to-day! It looks as if God intends to make use of me in some manner at present hidden from me, and that is why things have come to this unhappy end. Nevertheless, I shall defend myself before the Judge, for whatsoever I have done was done without wrong intent; Ritual Murder was sanctified by the custom of the years! Also, shall I do my utmost to save the lives of these, my tribesmen. I have spoken!"

And the Chief remained silent.

And all the clever, wise talk of the lawyers moved him not to speech again.

Now dawned the morning of the trial.

7

Never, since the coming of the White King and the White Queen and their Royal Daughters, had Maseru seen such crowds as waited outside the Court on the morning of the trial.

By kindness of the Police and Officers of the Court, were Monare's son and wife given a special place to sit; also present were Ntoane, Monare's Pathan friends from Durban and Lourenco Marques, and Mr. Johnson.

The people stood as the noble Judge accompanied by the two Basotho Chiefs, the Assessors, entered the Court and sat on their thrones; a groan of anguish sounded as the prisoners were brought in to answer to the charge of Ritual Murder.

The Judge spoke, kindly but firmly:

"There will be no demonstrations, otherwise will the Court be cleared!"

As had been ordained by the Chief, so were the charges pleaded to—the Chief, " Guilty," and all the others, " Not Guilty."

Another murmur arose as the Chief pleaded, this time one of amazement. The Judge made no move to quieten the buzzing of voices—he, too, was struck with wonder!

All he did, was to say to the Chief:

" Chief, in a trial for murder, a plea of " Guilty " may not be entered, for there is but one sentence for murder, and that is death. Do you understand ? "

The Chief bowed.

" My Lord, I understand; nevertheless is the guilt mine ! "

The Judge said to his Clerk:

" Enter the plea as ' Not Guilty.' "

Now did the trial proceed, and the Great Detectives brought their witnesses, who gave their evidence without lying; the clever lawyers tried their best to trip the feet of the witnesses, but as they spoke but truth, who could succeed ?

Next came the turn of the accused to give evidence; they denied not that they had struck down Koto. Yet did Phafa maintain that what he had done, had been done only at the command of Monare. The others spoke not thus; rather did they say that they had acted in accordance with ancient custom, as had their fathers and their grandfathers; they agreed that Monare had spoken against the killing, and had at the end, fought beside Koto.

Now did the noble Judge put to Monare that same question which the Moruti Lefa had asked him long ago:

" Did you not leave Monontsa with the intent to murder some as yet unchosen person for the purpose of filling the Medicine Horn ? "

And Monare answered in a clear voice:

" Yes, Lord ! "

At these words, Ma-Libe threw herself to the floor, and cried in a heart-breaking way:

" O God who is so great, please help the father of Libe to overcome the trouble that has come upon him ! He allowed them to kill !—to kill !—to kill ! O God !—to kill ! "

The poor woman was taken outside by the wife of the Moruti

JUDGMENT DAY

Lefa, and comforted; but all noticed that the face of Monare grew grim and white.

And so the day passed, and at last when the sun was sinking, came the end of the evidence; the lawyers spoke at length great words of wisdom in defence of the accused, until even they—well-paid and used to much speaking—were tired, and sat down. Then did the noble Judge say:

"The Court will now adjourn to consider its verdict. See that you are all here present in this place at ten o'clock to-morrow morning!"

And everybody rose in respect as the mighty Judge and the powerful Chiefs left the Court. Now arose an uproar, some saying this and some saying that; and during this noise the prisoners were removed to the Jail, where they were allowed private speech with the men of the law, and with such relatives and friends as desired to see them.

That night was Monare's gloom lightened somewhat by the presence of his Pathan friends, whose faces he had seen in Court that day.

When all had departed, there commenced a time of great difficulty for the prisoners; they knew not yet their fate, yet had they to live through the long hours of the night in patience.

Who can blame them if they prayed to this god and that for a miracle to take place? That they might be released on the morrow to enjoy the simple pleasures of home? Who can blame them if they longed with sad, tired eyes for the sight of loved faces, and the touch of hands dear to them? Who can blame strong men for weeping on such a night?

Yet was it but a test, for the worst was to come!

On the morrow, when they were led into Court, the Judge spoke the words of doom:

"We find all the accused 'Guilty'!"

Chapter Five

THE UNKNOWN MERCY OF GOD

THOSE PRESENT IN COURT might have been struck dead—so silent were they when the fateful words were spoken.

Then, such a cry of horror arose, that all the Sergeants of the Court could not quell it; beneath the high shrieking of the condemned men's womenfolk, sounded the grief-filled groans of the male relatives and friends.

Throughout this scene of anguish the pencils of the newspapermen worked busily, and the makers of photographs popped their flashlights and pressed their bulbs.

Libe moved to his mother's side; Ntoane and the five Pathans wept unashamedly; Mr. Johnson buried his face in his hands; and the Moruti Lefa prayed earnestly.

At length was order restored, and the mighty Judge coughed, and drank from the glass of water on the table before him. Then he spoke these words:

" First must I say that this is the verdict of us all! "

The Judge looked towards the two Basotho Assessors, who bowed their heads in agreement. Then continued the Judge:

" Yet before passing sentence, I have some comments to make; also shall the accused have the chance to plead what extenuating circumstances there may be. But the Government is determined to stamp out this cruel and terrible crime of Ritual Murder! "

The noble Lord looked round the Court, and proceeded thus:

" There are several unusual factors about this case. First there is the plea of ' Guilty ' offered by the Chief—rarely is such a plea made in a case of murder! Then must I note the frank, manly

THE UNKNOWN MERCY OF GOD

manner in which the Chief admitted his guilt. There is also the strange chain of circumstances which culminated in the chance, but tragic encounter, between the two friends, Koto the murdered man and Monare the second accused. Had Monare acted sooner, although Koto might have been left unmolested, doubtless would the Chief's *Letona* and his *impi* have found another victim, and still might they have stood before me this day! But had some of the other accused men have supported Monare in his attempts to save the life of Koto, a general fight might have ensued, as a result of which, had some members of the *impi* been killed, still might the survivors have appeared in this Court, but on a less grave charge!"

The Judge looked round the crowded Court, which listened avidly to his every word. Then he said, with great solemnity:

"Be that as it may, it should be clearly understood that whosoever takes any part in a murder—whether in the actual committing of the deed, or in the planning of it, or in the disposal of the body, or the suppression of the evidence—is equally guilty with him who strikes the fatal blow!"

The Judge's voice was now hoarse, and he drank of the water again. Now did the words of doom come.

"It is now my sad duty to ask of you, who stand in the dock, whether you have anything to say in mitigation of the crime of which you have been adjudged 'Guilty,' before sentence is passed upon you."

At these dread, foreboding words, the crowd released a loud, long sigh, and a buzz of talk started, which was quickly silenced by the Officers of the Court.

The Judge inclined his head towards the Chief.

The Chief, stricken though he was, rose and said:

"My Lord! I shed the tears of despair for these my tribesmen, who stand with me this day, awaiting sentence of Death! It must be known to you, that a Mosotho will always obey the commands of his Chief! Now—according to your white man's Law—are these men, who did but obey my commands, thrust into the same pot upon the fire, as me, their Chief! I am not an elected Chief, my Lord, but a direct descendant of the Great Chief Moshoeshoe, who created the Basotho Nation! I know the history of my people, and this day I wonder whether my noble grandfather was right when he asked for protection and friendship from the white man —is it then protection, to destroy his sons?"

A moan, like the noise of the wind rushing through a cave, rose from the Court; then was there a shuffling of feet, as if those listening were hard put to it to contain their feelings; then again the stern call to order. The Chief resumed:

"The white man has had customs which were as inhuman as he judges Ritual Murder to be. I have studied at the Chief's College, and would like to ask my Lord, whether the burning of people at the stake because of their religious beliefs, was not as wrong and evil as you consider *Liretlo* to be?"

Here again the crowd of Basotho stood up from their seats in excitement, only to be quietened by the rough voices of the Sergeants. The Chief then said:

"What the white man did in those days of old, perhaps the Basotho people are guilty of to-day—but is it not the duty of the bigger and elder brother to warn his smaller and younger brother of his mistakes, rather than to kill him for making them?"

A voice shouted:

"Our Chief, you have spoken the truth!"

The hoarse voice of the Court Orderly silenced him. The Chief went on:

"When the Great Moshoeshoe and his small tribe left Butha Buthe, on their journey to Thaba Bosiu, there was, at that time, a great famine in the land, which turned many people into cannibals and man-eaters. Some days' march behind the band of my ancestor, travelled that of his grandfather Peete; on the way, Peete was killed and eaten by members of the Nthatisi and Rakotsoane Clans, in order to save themselves from starvation and death. These men had been cut off from the rest of the tribe during the Lifaqane battles—because they were starving, and could find no game to kill, they became eaters-of-man! These same people, having eaten Peete, followed Moshoeshoe to Thaba Bosiu, where my ancestor defeated the Dutch under Wepener. Now when Moshoeshoe was told of the eating of his grandfather by these tribesmen, he said,

'The people of the Nthatisi and Rakotsoane Clans have chosen themselves to become the grave of my grandfather—leave them! Let them be! For if I order them to be killed, then shall I also be ordering the destruction of my grandfather's grave!' Thus did the elder brother, Moshoeshoe, show mercy and understanding to his younger brothers of the Nthatisi and Rakotsoane Clans! Since those days have the tribes learned not to eat the flesh of man—no matter if they die of hunger—and, no doubt, since the days long gone by, has the white man also learned that it is wrong to burn people alive for their religious beliefs!"

In spite of the sadness of the hour, yet did this last sentence of the Chief's cause laughter, even from the white men in the Court; the Judge put his hand to his face, perhaps to smile. The Chief waited until there was silence, and then spoke again:

"This belief in the power of human blood has—at different times—lived in the hearts of all races. Here, in my country of Lesotho, Ritual Murder has come down as a custom from the days of my grandfather's grandfather! The Medicine Horn has been held to provide protection for a new village, and to give power and strength to warriors when setting out to give battle! Yet, should it be judged a bad and evil custom—well, then—since I claim descent from the Great Moshoeshoe therefore must I accept the responsibilities and penalties of rank, as well as its privileges! Therefore, my Lord, sentence me to death if you will, but spare these men who feared to disobey me!"

The Chief looked round at his fellow-countrymen and at the noble Judge and the two Assessors, then said:

"If a man, possessing three sons, feels the desire to eat mutton, and sends them to steal and kill a sheep from another man's *kraal*— who then, is to blame? The sons who obeyed the father, or the father who ordered his sons? Must not the sons obey the father's bidding? Is this not written in your Scriptures, my Lord?"

The Chief's eyes watered, and his voice grew thick. Turning to the Judge's Clerk, he asked:

"May I have water to drink?"

The Judge leaned forward and instructed the Clerk to fetch from outside a glass of cool water. When the water had been handed to the Chief, and he had drunk of it, he said to the Judge:

"My Lord, you ordered your servant, the Clerk, to fetch me water to drink—he obeyed you! But had he refused to obey, would he not have been guilty of Contempt of Court? And would you not have punished him?"

Shouts of "*Ka Thesele!*" were quickly suppressed.

The Chief spoke again:

"So would these men here have been liable to severe punishment, had they disobeyed my orders! When I commanded them to find one of the Bafokeng Clan, and to kill him for the Medicine Horn, they carried out my orders because of their respect for me. And you, my Lord, and your Assessors, the Chiefs, should know that the respect of a Mosotho for his Chief, is greater even than that which he has for his father!"

Somewhat of an uproar occurred now; for what the Chief had said was in the minds and hearts of the people; yet quickly did the stern voices of the Sergeants bring silence again. Then the Chief concluded:

"Therefore, my Lord, do I ask that the punishment be mine! Whether or not *Liretlo* is right and lawful, still was it these men's duty to obey me, and I pray, my Lord, that you will allow them to go free!"

And the Chief sat down and hid his eyes from all.

Quiet as the dead of night was the Courtroom; then suddenly came a clapping of hands from some of the white men present, and then came the cheering of the Basotho people, whose admiration could not be restrained.

Again the noble Judge made no motion with his hammer to end the noise—perhaps his secret feelings were the same as those openly displayed!

2

When order had been restored somewhat, then did the harsh voices of the Sergeants begin to command silence, and the Judge, tapping with his hammer, said:

"I do not allow such demonstrations in my Court, yet must

THE UNKNOWN MERCY OF GOD

I add my tribute to yours, and salute your Chief as a brave man and one worthy of his ancestors! But what has been so nobly said cannot affect the sentence. I do not believe that there is one Mosotho present here who does not know that the Law of Basutoland forbids Ritual Murder! This crime is far worse in the eyes of the Law than ordinary murder—for what is done in a moment of anger is an act that can be understood by all, for are we not all at times angry? But this murder of a man, who but for chance, would have remained unknown to his killers, is an act of cold, calculated cruelty!"

For a time, all were silent; then the Judge asked the other prisoners if they had aught to say in their defence before sentence was passed—leaving Monare to the last. All but Phafa simply asked for mercy for the sake of their families, but Phafa, regaining something of his courage, asked:

"*Morena*, does not the Scripture say, 'an eye for an eye, and a tooth for a tooth'? Why then should seven die for the killing of one?"

Again did the Judge explain—hiding his impatience—that all concerned in the killing of another were equally guilty, no matter should they number seventy times seven! Phafa sat back, discouraged.

When Monare's name was called, he had it in mind to reply that he had naught to say; but before he could speak, one of the lawyers arose, and said that if his Lordship would allow, several witnesses wished to testify to Monare's courage and character.

Now was the story of that dark Night of Terror in the City of Sugar, retold by the Moulvie Abdul Wahid. An educated man, and one used to speaking in public, he made the events of those hours of fire and bloodshed live in the ears of those who listened. When all was done, no one moved, nor spoke. The eyes of all followed the figure of the Moulvie as he returned to his seat, and then swung as one eye towards the dock, where Monare stood with the tears running down his cheeks. Only then, did a great release of breath rise from them like a giant's sigh.

Then came Mr. Johnson with his tale of horrors in the bowels of the earth. Again those present listened as if under the spell of *ngaka*; at length this evidence was finished, too; the lawyer in his turn had spoken from his stored wisdom and brought tears to their eyes with his praising of their hero.

The eyes of the noble Judge, too, seemed to glisten, but at last he cleared his throat and said:

"I have listened to this evidence with great interest; yet if sorrow is felt at the tragic situation in which this brave man finds himself, yet must tears be shed for the poor victim, Koto, and for those who mourn him. This must we not forget: a man has been killed deliberately—no matter if since that day, twenty have been saved from death!"

The Judge appeared to think for a time, then he addressed Monare:

"Monare, you know what would have happened had the body of Koto been discovered whilst you were yet within the country of Lesotho?"

Monare raised heavy eyes to the Judge.

"I should have been taken by the Police, Lord!"

"And then?"

"Brought before you, Lord, and tried, and sentenced."

"And this would have happened nearly two years ago?"

"Yes, Lord."

"Therefore, had punishment overtaken you at once, your body would by this time have been lying cold in its grave, and your spirit would be elsewhere! But God, in His Wisdom, has given to you these two years of added life, doubtless to see what you would do with them—think not that I belittle the bravery of your deeds—although it will be my sad duty soon to sentence you to the punishment which the Law has decreed, that fact does not lessen my great admiration for the courage and endurance you have displayed! Yet—think on my words!—this bravery, this courage, these deeds of kindness and protection that you have performed, have all taken place since the Police started looking for you! Were it not for your determination, and your will, which led you to the City of Sugar, and then, as a result of your actions during the Time of Terror, afforded you the chance to go yet farther, to the city of Lourenco Marques—if it were not for these things, then a year

THE UNKNOWN MERCY OF GOD

ago, would punishment have caught up with you! Monare, you have been living on borrowed time—time lent by God! And, as far as human beings can judge, you have used that time well! Yet must you look for reward or punishment for your actions during that time, to Him that lent it! I can but judge of your acts to the time of the murder. I know your feelings; I know you have a wife and a son; but the Law, though sometimes without mercy, is never without justice! Do you not agree?"

"I admit my guilt, Lord."

"Then what I have to say may seem cold comfort to those dear to you, yet I believe that through the honesty and courage of your Chief, and through the brave deeds you have performed during this past year, much good will come to your country, Lesotho, and its people, the Basotho nation! The eyes and the ears of the world are this day fixed on us here in Maseru, and as a result of this trial, I believe that everywhere, men who think, will start searching to find a means of preventing the recurrence of such tragedies as this."

The Judge bowed his head for a few moments, and all the relatives and friends of the prisoners, and the lawyers, and the newspapermen and the takers of photographs, and even the harsh-voiced Sergeants, held their breath—for they knew what must now come.

Solemnly the Judge took from beside him the square of black silk, and placing it on his head, said the dread words of the death sentence, to each and every one of the prisoners. As he concluded:

"... to be taken back whence you came, and thence on the appointed day, be taken to the place of execution, there to be hanged by the neck until dead ..." There was such deep silence that a hundred separate breaths could be distinguished. Then said the Judge slowly and sadly:

"And may God have mercy upon your souls!"

Now only was the silence stabbed with sobbing.

The Judge and the Assessors rose and departed, and the prisoners were taken back "whence they came."

3

Now did a nation mourn; the day fixed for the execution of Monare would be remembered in the years to come as another *Mendi* Memorial Day, and Basotho yet unborn would rise on those days to praise him. But if the people of Lesotho were saddened, what of those nearest and dearest to the prisoners!

The days before the Last Day of All were few indeed, and the hours sped by with the rush of the *mafofonyane*; to Libe, Ma-Libe, and Ntoane, each minute was sodden with anguish; their minds worked madly, yet without hope, in desperate endeavours to think out a scheme to save him. The Pathans, with the inborn courtesy of their race, returned to the City of Sugar and Lourenco Marques soon after the end of the trial, for they felt that the last hours of Monare should be sacred to those of his own blood. Yet before they left, had the two younger Pathans, Ghulam Hussain and Fazal Khan, worked out a plan in detail, whereby they would capture the jail by cunning, and set out for the Mocambique Border with Monare in a fast car. As one necessity to the success of the plan was the possession of revolvers, and such weapons had the boys never handled, much less owned, saner counsels prevailed. These two boys became great friends of Libe's, and Libe made a firm promise to visit both of them when his child should be of a suitable age.

Monare's parting with his *amaSuleiman* friends cracked Monare's heart, for it was his meeting with the *iSuleiman* Moulvie, which had set his feet not only on the path of atonement, but on the road which appeared to lead to a happy future. Monare could but think to himself: "One day my wife, and my son and his wife, and my grandson-to-be, may yet profit by the road I have travelled, and live respected and happy, in the pleasant land of Mocambique."

The Moulvie Abdul Wahid said, on parting from Monare:

"Dost Ghulam, I had but small chance to do all I did desire to do in gratitude, yet know, and believe, that never shall one of your family want for anything whilst I and my son live!"

Mazaffar Khan was struck with wonder at the calm manner of

THE UNKNOWN MERCY OF GOD

Monare, and asked him whether perhaps he had found that peace lay in surrender to the Will of Allah?

Monare said:

"My friend and teacher, the words you spoke to me on the station at Lourenco Marques, have never been far from my thoughts; often have they given me the courage to endure; and now, at the end, but for the sickening, dreadful thrusts of the spear of separation, I could go to what awaits me without too many tears. Love breeds like rabbits, and some of its children are joys, and some sorrows. Now have I to die eight deaths instead of one! Farewells must be said, and last sight taken of eight loved ones! A little shall I die when you and Ghulam Hussain and the others depart; less life will remain after my farewell to Ntoane; and when I have seen for the last time my beloved wife and son, but little will be present to greet the Moruti Lefa on the day of execution!"

Monare wept, and the Pathans one by one embraced him, and gazed upon him for the last time. At the end came Monare's heart-friend, Ghulam Hussain, and when this farewell was said, indeed it seemed that some part of him had gone, and left him incomplete. The Pathans waved for the last time, and were but a memory, those five strangers from afar, who had brought to the Mosotho, friendship, generosity, learning, confidence, self-respect, and wonderful plans that would now stay for ever unfulfilled.

Meanwhile did the clever lawyers argue before the noble Judge on points of law; yet did Monare know within his heart that there could be no appeal; each farewell as it was said, even though each handshake or embrace bled his heart anew, seemed yet to act as a white man's *sehlari* might act, and numbed his feelings for a while.

Mr. Johnson, at parting with Monare, said:

"I shall think of you at the moment of doom—and remember, your family shall be amply provided for. God bless you, Monare."

Now came an event which, had the conditions differed, would have been the occasion of great feasting—the birth of a man-child to Makopoi! Monare's cold heart was warmed when Libe came with Makopoi's child to show his father, and spake these words:

"O my Father, may this child one day be proud of me, as I am proud of you!"

4

The morning before the Last Day, came Ntoane to say good-bye. He said:

"Old home-boy and friend, always were you too simple for this world! I shall never forget your fear of the *tsotsis*—in those days were you ready to listen to anyone. To-day you are changed, and I am proud to be known as the home-boy and friend of Monare. *Ee!* had you never met the Orlando Moruti's daughter, much trouble might you have been spared. Then might you not have been tempted by Koto's fashionable trousers, and wanted to parade yourself in a white man's suit before Mary, like a peacock!"

And Ntoane laughed in a most friendly manner at which Monare could not take offence.

"Much have I been impressed by your Pathan friends. If the real *amaSuleiman* are like them, it seems a great pity that their missionaries did not come to Lesotho rather than the Christians. For I see that in their religion is the dignity of man upheld, no matter how lowly may be his task in life. Amongst them seems to exist a freedom and a unity which Lesotho badly needs. Instead, here amongst us Africans we have the witch doctors and their followers, then the Catholics and the Methodists, also the Salvation Army and the Apostolics, the Blue Cross people and Jehovah's Witnesses—and each calls the other liars, and fights with them!"

Monare is silent, for he is thinking of the past two years, and his many and wonderful experiences. At length he replies:

"The Black People of Africa need unity; if they were but united, the little that they now demand would be given to them willingly with both hands by the white man. From all I have seen and learned, I have in my heart the fear that a time of great oppression is coming for the African; the white man wants to keep us in our place, and to him, that means at the bottom! I think that through oppression may come unity. I cannot even imagine what lies beyond the death I meet to-morrow, but I pray that somehow I may know what happens to my beloved country."

Ntoane rose, but Monare stopped him, saying:

THE UNKNOWN MERCY OF GOD

"Thank you, home-boy, for what you did at the time of my taking the *matekoane*. But for your friendship then, I would never have lived the life of the past two years; yet would I have come to the same end, maybe earlier, but as a drugged coward! Take this ring of gold, the white man, Newington, gave me and wear it in remembrance." And taking the ring from his finger, he placed it in Ntoane's hand.

The two old friends, home-boys and sharers of many joys and sorrows, now came to the time of the last farewell. Ah! the suddenness of parting from a friend who has been part of life! The brutal cutting of the last ties! The heart that gets lonelier and lonelier! Yet without, beyond the walls of the prison, life goes on; the dead are soon forgotten; their bones fall to dust, and their flesh is eaten! But what of the Spirit? What thought must I cling to—or shall I go mad in these last hours? Now comes my son, Libe, with downcast eyes and pale face. Ah, Libe! I remember the night your small thin body lay ill, so many years ago, and I promised my Moruti's God that I would give up the drinking of the kaffir beer and the beating of my wife, if He would make you well! I kept my promise, and the God of my Moruti kept his promise. Now what bargain can I make with God? Perhaps Koto said those very words when he felt Phafa's knife cut his flesh that night so long ago. That night could I have been Koto's God, and answered his prayer! And as he was that night, so shall I be to-morrow. These strong arms, lifeless, buried in the earth; these eyes blank and unseeing; these ears dead to the sounds of my grandson's first words; maybe this is all a dream; perhaps I shall wake up at the *semokolara's* house at Benoni, and find that the past two years were but a sleep between a night and a morning, a long sleep, heavy with *matekoane*: now is God's mercy shown, for he sleeps indeed, a deep, long sleep.

Libe sits by his father's side and curses the wasted moments as they pass. At length Monare wakes with a mind cleared of fear; for a time these mad thoughts have retreated far within him; he looks at Libe and smiles.

"My son, of whom I am so proud, and whom I love so much! Libe, when all is over, you will be the comfort of your dear mother;

she who was a 'mine-widow' for so long, will now be a widow in truth. She will not miss me as much as she now fears; I have been but little at home since you were a very small boy. Also will she have some pride in my memory; she will forgive me the crime for which I die, for it was done at the command of my Chief; also I die in good company!"

"No, my Father, speak not so bitterly! You know how my mother loves you!"

"Yes, my son, forgive me. Before I slept I seemed to dream strange dreams. But let our last talk in this world be happy, let us talk of the future in which, through you and your son, I have some share."

"That which must happen to-morrow might never have come to pass had you seen not that newspaper in Lourenco Marques. O my Father, that it should be I that have brought you to this end. It was my foolish suggestion to take a taxi, that brought us into the hands of the police!"

"No, Libe, do not reproach yourself—it is the Hand of God that has led me every step of the way. Had you not stayed by my side when I was a slave to *matekoane*, I should still have eaten my chicken dinner, still would the rope have wound itself round my neck, but I would not have found the path of atonement! When the time of mourning is over, Ntoane and the Moruti Lefa will speak to you of certain matters; should it be your desire, you will have the means to travel and see the countries of this earth, for money is plentiful. I shall indeed be happy if one day your mind holds the same thoughts as mine about this Lesotho, this Africa! Travel will show you what life could be for the Black Peoples. But two years ago I was what the white man calls a 'bloody ignorant Kaffir'—and that, too, will you be called, my son, in spite of your money! It is only unity and determination amongst the Africans that will earn them the respect of the white man. I am still too ignorant to know how our people must be aroused and led, but I would die happier if I thought my son, Libe, would carry on my thoughts from the point the rope will stop them to-morrow!"

"I know but little, my Father, yet have I listened with eagerness to your talk since you returned. I admire greatly your *amaSu-*

THE UNKNOWN MERCY OF GOD 313

leiman friends, and I promise to listen well to all Ntoane and the Moruti wish to instruct me in."

Now talked they for a while with love and affection of the days which were past; and embraced each other. Monare wishes to draw the assegai of parting from his wounded heart, so he rises and says to his son:

"Farewell, my son, Libe, I love you much. Wait outside for your mother, for when I have said my last words to her, she will need your comfort!"

And father and son looked upon each other for the last time, and Monare's heart cracked yet a little more.

5

The Last Evening cast its shadows before it; now, has it arrived. Monare is to see his wife, Ma-Libe, to say his final farewell. What can he do, other than to show his great love, and his regret? What comfort can man give to woman about to be bereaved? From all the talks Monare had had with Baruti and Moulvies, nothing had he learned that could be of use at his last meeting with his simple, loving wife. What should this woman—who had never been more than ten miles away from Lomontsa—understand of the Will of Allah? Here could comfort only come from within; if Florinah had any belief or faith in her husband's continued existence—somewhere, in some form—after the morrow's ceremony, now was the time to cherish it!

The mother of Libe did not weep when she entered in; she had the set, sad, uncomplaining face of the dog or horse, about to be shot. Monare reproached himself for his earlier, long absences from home, for his lack of real understanding of the mother of his son . . .

"Here is one who has indeed surrendered herself to the Will of God, and in so doing, has found some measure of peace."

Husband and wife embraced, and Monare put his thoughts into words:

"Florinah, my beloved wife, much do I regret the wasted years, yet has it been the custom of the Basotho people for many years, to leave home to work on the mines of the white man. And few indeed are the white men who provide accommodation for the families of Africans. Yet did I once or twice speak with Ntoane in the City of Gold on this matter, for it was in my mind to bring you to that city, to live in a location. But these locations are mostly places of evil—given over to the brewing of illicit kaffir beer, and to the prostitution of women—and I feared for your safety."

Tears came into Florinah's eyes; she said:

"Do not reproach yourself, dear husband, and father of Libe; I am happy and grateful for the times when we were together; I am very proud to be your wife. I know that my son and I have always been protected; I know, too, that it was your love for us that brought you quickly from this place Lourenco Marques. Your life there, as I have now heard you and your friends speak of it, sounds too high and mighty for a Basotho woman; yet doubtless would I have been happy there with you, and I thank you for your loving thoughts which sought to plan a place for me by your side. Even though we meet for the last time, still am I glad and proud that you came to Libe's aid. Your Chief and you both showed great bravery in the Court before the white Judge. There, this woman failed you with her tears, but now am I determined to gather together what courage there is in this woman's body and spirit, and to appear before all as should the wife of Lesotho's hero, but—Oh, Monare!—never to hear your voice again . . ."

And now Florinah wept hopelessly, and the tears ran down the cheeks of Monare.

"Beloved wife, I wish you to wear in my remembrance, the golden charm and chain given to me by my friend Mazaffar Khan, and also the watch of gold, with which rewarded me the Chief of the Council of the City of Sugar at the time of the Terror. My son, Libe, will keep the pen and pencil of gold, and the hunting knife—remembrance presents from the Moulvie Abdul Wahid and his family. Of money there is plenty, and this shall my son give to you as you need it. All these things will be handed to Libe, to-morrow."

This dreaded word caused tears to flow again, until at length Monare said:

THE UNKNOWN MERCY OF GOD

"For this time, Florinah, beloved wife, it is farewell—yet have I been told in a dream or vision, that those that there is love between, shall never be put asunder; they shall be reunited in the end. That end may be far distant, Florinah, still, can you believe in the truth of my words? There is comfort in them. And now, in this body of Monare, in this life of Lesotho, I take leave of you, and pass you to God's mercy, and to the strong arms of Libe, my son."

The final embrace, how shall the breaking heart know when to drop the arms, turn away the face? To continue is but to make the parting harder, yet how shall a man, of his own choice, break the clutch of loving arms, draw back from the touch of clinging lips, turn the eyes from a beloved face when he knows that never again shall they stand together? Yet must the knife descend, and the flesh part!

Monare now lies alone; all pretence assumed for others' benefit has gone. He lies, weeping the scalding, bitter tears of absolute despair; torn from the arms of friends, son, and wife; nothing now stands between him and the terrible, unknown Mercy of God.

How shall this night be endured?

6

One friend has Monare failed to remember, one who has not forgotten Monare—the Moruti Lefa.

Monare does not hear him enter the cell; he opens his eyes to find him seated on the bed. The Moruti speaks somewhat shyly:

"I knew not whether you wished for what comfort I can give you, for you are now *iSuleiman*—yet will I spend these last hours with you, if it should be your wish."

The Mosotho seized the hands of the Moruti, and wept again with rough, deep sobs; when he had quietened, he said:

"When one stands so near to God, it seems to matter not whether one be Christian, *iSuleiman*, Jew, or Hindu. All Baruti doubtless have knowledge to give out to the different races, laws of living. I can see now, that here and there must these laws vary, even as the colour, customs, and the lands of the people vary.

But unless the souls of men are coloured like the skins of their bodies, I think there can be but one law for the spirit."

The Moruti pressed the hands of Monare.

"This indeed, must be true!"

"Then comfort me if it is in your power! For I have called on the God of all Baruti in vain!"

"If you will but see it, Monare, much mercy has been shown to you. You have had a fine wife, and a wonderful son, and strong and loving friends. You found, too, that which you prayed for after Koto's death—a path of atonement!"

"Yes! But to-morrow, and all the days to come! Never more shall I see the cattle grazing on the slopes of the Maluti Mountains! Never again shall I come to my hut, tired in the evening from tending the crops, to eat and drink the good food prepared by my wife! Never shall my grandson sit upon my knee! Why has God chosen me for all this grief?"

"You chose it yourself, my son."

"I chose it? I?"

"When you allowed Koto to die."

"But why me? Why was *I* faced with such a choice?"

"I think, Monare, the earth is but a school—here come spirits to learn. You, perhaps, Monare, had to learn to become free, to make up your mind about life, and take up your stand on the side of good, and never to waver as you did the night that Koto died. And you have learned your lesson well! All Lesotho is proud of you, and doubtless those Who Sent you here are satisfied."

"But what good is all this to me—here and now? To my wife and son? To Lesotho itself?"

"You have made the Basotho nation famous, as did Moshoeshoe in days long past, and if the whole story of your life could be told, and the manner of your coming to your death explained in full, doubtless even the white man would take notice, and seek to find a better foundation on which to build a country and a nation, from these tribes of different colours!"

"Could such a thing be done, Moruti?"

"Why not? I have pen and paper, and can get more from the warder. Come, tell me your secret story during these long dark

THE UNKNOWN MERCY OF GOD

hours of the night; and what is missed, shall I ask Libe, and Ghulam Hussain, and the others, to recount! Yes, Monare, here is the hand of God again—by His Mercy, shall your death be not in vain! We shall write your story, and shall all men read it, and learn therefrom! Hasten! Let us not delay! Moreover, may there be much money in the sale of this book, for Ma-Libe and your family!"

A strange end to a strange life. Who could say that a Mosotho, condemned to be hanged for a Ritual Murder, would spend his last living night in the making of a book! Yet so did it happen, and Monare told to the Moruti through the ebbing hours of his life, the story of his many adventures and of what he had learned from his own eyes and ears—soon to be closed for ever—and from the eyes and ears of others. His most secret thoughts did he disclose, and he held back nothing. And so passed the Last Night, and when the Warder brought the chicken dinner of custom, he must have wondered, but he said naught.

7

The last sun rose, and as the tired, despairing prisoners stretched themselves, all through the lands of Southern Africa did they live in the thoughts of many people. Basotho stood by the head-gear of mines in the City of Gold with sad faces; quietly, too, waited their home-boys far away on the docks in the City of Sugar; in the home-land, Basotho stood in the fields and in their homes, waiting for the hour to strike.

In Mosques at Cato Manor, and in the city of Lourenco Marques, the *amaSuleiman* prayed for their friend and hero.

In a room in the City Hall, at Durban, a Mayor took off his spectacles and wiped them; then sighing, went on with his day's work. At the South Rand Mine, Mr. Johnson thought of the man whose life he had saved for the hangman, and sorrowed.

Outside the Central Jail at Maseru stood the loved ones of those about to die; here stood Ntoane, Libe, and Ma-Libe, with the Moruti Lefa's wife ready to comfort.

PHASE FIVE—NEW MOON

Within the Jail the Governor asked the condemned men if they had aught to say.

The Chief said:

"Tell my fellow-chiefs, that *Liretlo* must end, otherwise shall the pride and independence of Lesotho die!"

Said Phafa and the others:

"We do not wish to die; yet as the rope is ready, tell our loved ones that our last thoughts were for them!"

Now came the turn of Monare.

"I forgive you Chief, for the orders you gave; you are greater in your doom than ever you were in your pride, and I salute you for the last time! I forgive you, Phafa, and forgive any who may have done me injury. Tell the white man if he will listen, that too many laws and too many policemen make for too little understanding. Tell my friends and my family that they were in my heart until its last beat!"

Now was the time for the sad procession; by God's Mercy was the Moruti Lefa at Monare's side when his hour came. As the hangman's noose sat loosely round Monare's neck, his eyes opened wide as he saw before him the golden glow and the face of kindness of the Radiant Stranger.

The Voice spoke:

"Endure, Monare—it will soon be over! Behind me stands your father, hero of the *Mendi*, waiting to greet his son!"

The amazed ears of the Moruti Lefa could never afterwards believe that they had heard correctly the last, quietly-spoken words of Monare of Lomontsa; for as the noose tightened, and the signal for the opening of the trap-door was being made, Monare said, almost under his breath:

"So it is true! There is no Death!"

The signal passed, the trap-door opened, and down, down dropped the body of Monare of Lomontsa, the Mosotho. But as his neck broke, and the last breath was loosed from his body, the Radiant Stranger took him by the hand, and together they passed over to the Other Side.

And all Lesotho mourned, AS MONARE DIED.

GLOSSARY

AFRIKAANS	Language of the Afrikaner.
AFRIKANER	White South African of Dutch descent.
AMASULEIMAN	African name for Muslims.
BAAS	Master, Sir.
BARUTI	Plural of Moruti—Priests (plural).
BASOTHO	Basuto—plural of Mosotho; is used as Noun or Adjective in this text; members of the Basuto race.
BOHALI	Marriage dowry paid by bridegroom to bride's father; usually cattle.
BUKA!	Look! (*Zulu*).
COOLIE	Labourer; used in a derogatory sense by many South Africans when referring to Indians.
EE!	Exclamatory remark.
GOU! GOU!	Quickly! Quickly! (*Afrikaans*).
IMPI	Regiment (*Zulu*).
KAFFIR	Arabic word meaning unbeliever; borrowed from Arabs by South Africans and used to mean "native" in a derogatory sense. Resented by Africans.
KESELE	One of the "praise" names of Moshoeshoe.
KHOKHOBISA-TSOENE	Literally "hiding-of-the-monkey"; the rite of circumcision as applied to women.
KHOTLA	Meeting place of Chief's Council in a village.
KHOTSO	Peace.
KHUBELU	Red.
LESOTHO	Basutoland
LETONA	Headman.
LETSOMA	Harvest-time.
LIRETLO	Ritual Murder.

GLOSSARY

MA	Mother-of, as in Ma-Libe.
MAFOFONYANE	Electric train.
MAHLEU	Sour Porridge, slightly intoxicating.
MAKULU	Big, important.
MARALLO	The "secret night" at the women's circumcisional school.
MASHUQ	Loved one (*Punjabi*).
MATEKOANE	Dagga.
MOHATLA	Derisive cry of "Tail!" called after the uncircumcised.
MOKOROTLO	War- or Praise-song.
MOLIMO	God.
MOPHATO	Women's Circumcisional school.
MOQEKOA	Youngest wife.
MORENA!	Title of respect accorded to Chiefs.
MORUTI	African Priest.
MOSOTHO	A Basuto, inhabitant of Basutoland.
MOULVIE	A Muslim priest.
MUSHLA	Good (*Zulu*).
NA'MAZ	Prayer (*Arabic*).
NGAKA	Witch Doctor.
PITSO	The Chief's Council.
PULA	Rain.
PUTU	A very stiff porridge made from mealie-meal.
RA	Father-of, as in Ra-Libe.
SEHLARE	Medicine.
SEMOKOLARA	Drug-pedlar.
SESOTHO	Language of Lesotho.
SETSOEJANE	Young circumcised girl.
SJAMBOK	Whip.
STERTREIM	Worn after circumcision to hide male genitals; a short fringed leather curtain, not unlike jockstrap.
TSOTSI	A rascal, vagabond, spiv.
YAR!	Dear Friend! (*Punjabi*).